D0306081

Louise Fennell lives in London. *Fame Game*
is her second novel.


*Also by Louise Fennell*


Dead Rich

# FAME GAME

## *Louise* FENNELL

**SIMON &
SCHUSTER**

London · New York · Sydney · Toronto · New Delhi

A CBS COMPANY

First published in Great Britain by Simon & Schuster UK Ltd, 2013
A CBS COMPANY

1 3 5 7 9 10 8 6 4 2

Simon & Schuster UK Ltd
1st Floor
222 Gray's Inn Road
London WC1X 8HB

www.simonandschuster.co.uk

Simon & Schuster Australia, Sydney
Simon & Schuster India, New Delhi

A CIP catalogue record for this book is available
from the British Library

ISBN: 978-1-47111-336-9
eBook ISBN: 978-1-47111-337-6

This book is a work of fiction. Names, characters,
places and incidents are either a product of the author's imagination
or are used fictitiously. Any resemblance to actual people living
or dead, events or locales is entirely coincidental.

Typeset by M Rules
Printed and bound by CPI Group (UK) Ltd, Croydon, CRO 4YY

For my beloved family
Theo, Emerald, Coco, Mum, Julia, Duncan,
and, of course, for Susan

Anybody can be good in the country. There are
no temptations there.

OSCAR WILDE

The toughest thing about success is that you've
got to keep on being a success.

IRVING BERLIN

# The SPENDER Family Tree

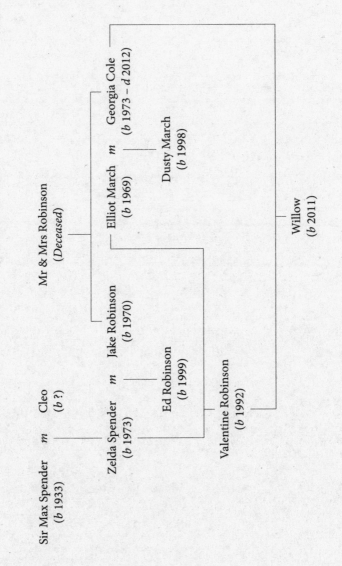

Sir Max Spender (b 1933) *m* Cleo (b ?)

Mr & Mrs Robinson (*Deceased*)

Zelda Spender (b 1973) *m* Jake Robinson (b 1970)

Elliot March (b 1969) *m* Georgia Cole (b 1973 – d 2012)

Ed Robinson (b 1999)

Valentine Robinson (b 1992)

Dusty March (b 1998)

Willow (b 2011)

# CHAPTER ONE

Boy Banbury woke to the sound of a telephone ringing somewhere in the distance. He groaned, struggled out of bed and
stumbled onto the wide landing of his huge and decrepit
house, Banbury Court.

His bare feet slapped softly on the worn tread of the
sweeping stone staircase. The old house-phone sounded
calamitous on that dark morning. It hardly ever rang and the
sound of it now filled Boy with trepidation. Reaching the hall,
the cool flagstones felt slightly damp underfoot and he shuddered. Clutching his pyjama bottoms with one hand, he
rubbed his naked torso with the other, in a vague attempt to
get warm.

'Hello, hello.' His voice sounded bleary with sleep.

As Boy put the telephone down a few minutes later, he
heard a rustle above him. Two of his teenaged daughters had
emerged from their rooms and were listening expectantly.

Flora spoke, her voice husky. 'Is Mum coming home?'

Boy looked up. 'No, darling, I'm sorry. That was my old pal,

Jake Robinson. He's coming down to stay, with his family – the Spenders.'

'In the middle of the fucking night! Why?' exclaimed Doone, his eldest and undeniably feistiest daughter.

'Come down, we'll get some breakfast and I'll tell you why. Oh and, Doone, a word of advice. If you are going to do a balcony scene; put some pants on. Lucien Freud might have got away with ogling his daughter's bush, but I'd really rather not have to, if you don't mind.'

Doone stepped back. 'Oh, for God's sake!' She pulled her tattered red kimono tightly around her, hastily covering her short silk slip and long legs. 'The other Freud might have had something to say about *that*. Honestly, Boy, you are disgusting!'

Doone Banbury was nineteen, beautiful and generally annoyed by almost everything and everyone. Her short dark hair had been ruffled by the night and her silver eyes glittered with indignation as she flounced downstairs after her father.

Kitty, the youngest, emerged. 'Why is everyone up? It's not even morning yet.' Her pretty face was screwed up and her pink cheeks looked hot. 'Was that Mum?'

'No, of course it wasn't! It was the bloody Spenders!' Doone huffed tactlessly.

Flora put her arm around her little sister and hugged her. She knew that Kitty would be feeling more disappointment than her sisters. She was the one who missed their mother the most. Kitty was only eleven and although Flora did her best to make her feel loved, she knew it wasn't enough. She felt a familiar twist of anger towards their errant mother.

Flora's dark hair tumbled in a dishevelled mess down her Rolling Stones 'lips' T-shirt. She watched quietly as her family trailed despondently after each other, towards the only really lived-in room in the house, the kitchen. She was left alone on the landing for a moment, and as she stood there, she felt a small stab of excitement.

The Spenders, Britain's ex-favourite family, were coming to stay with them! The most infamous family in England, if the press were to be believed, and they were coming to stay with *her*.

Flora was delighted, although, to look at her, no one could ever have guessed.

With her pierced nostrils, tattooed shoulder and skinny frame, Flora's fierce look belied her sweet nature. She was sixteen and desperate for her grown-up life to begin. The Spenders' arrival was more than she could ever have hoped for in her wildest dreams.

At last, she thought, something was happening to relieve the tedium of her existence in this mouldering mausoleum.

She wanted to whoop with excitement as she scampered downstairs to join the rest of her family. But she couldn't because, whatever happened, she had to remain cool.

# CHAPTER TWO

Jake Robinson swung the Mercedes sharply through the old stone gates of Banbury Court. The turning had come up more suddenly than he remembered and he'd almost over-shot it.

The car juddered across a cattle grid and Zelda Spender stirred. She opened her legendary violet eyes to be greeted by the tranquil rural scene of ancient landscaped parkland. Some horses drifted by gracefully, through a low-lying mist.

Jake felt a surge of hope. Perhaps everything would be alright, now that they were here. Hidden away, safe from all the madness they had left behind in London.

Zelda wriggled uncomfortably in her seat and closed her eyes again. 'Fucking hell!'

Jake's heart sank as he realised that not all the madness had been left behind in London. Most of it was still sitting right next to him. His fabulous, famous wife might not have been entirely responsible for their fall from grace but ...

Jake glanced at his sleeping nieces in the rear-view mirror.

The baby, Willow, stirred in the back of the car. Her teenaged sister, Dusty, smiled softly and patted her, saying, 'Good girl', without opening her eyes. Then Ed, his son, woke up, looked out of the car window and said simply, 'Wow!'

Banbury Court rose majestically out of the mist. Dusty slowly opened her eyes and was instantly captivated. It was the most romantic house she had ever seen, a huge Georgian mansion of quite spectacular beauty. From a distance, it belied its true state of dilapidation.

Jake turned right abruptly, following a sign marked 'The Dower House'. He swung through ivy-clad gates and stopped outside a long, low house, which was almost entirely covered with roses. Dusty squealed with delight.

The front door opened and a young man emerged. He was wearing combats and a battered grandpa shirt. He greeted Jake as he got out of his car.

'Morning, Mr Robinson! I'm Frank. Boy asked me to open up the house for you. Feels a bit damp, I'm afraid. No one's been in there much since the old lady . . .' He hesitated as he saw the children pouring out of the car.

'My girlfriend, Karen, will be in later with some basic supplies for you. I've left my mobile number on the kitchen table.' Frank seemed totally oblivious to the fact that one of the world's most famous actresses had just emerged in front of him. He merely nodded at Zelda and said, 'Morning.'

Zelda ignored him and stomped into the house.

Jake looked apologetic. 'Difficult day, thanks so much, sorry, bloody early and everything . . .'

Frank smiled. 'No problem. I'm always up before dawn, I look after the estate for Boy. It'll be good to have someone in the Dower House again.'

Jake could see that Frank was a warm and impressively handsome young man. He was surprised Zelda hadn't noticed; she really must be in a spectacularly bad mood, he thought to himself despondently.

Frank helped unload the suitcases from the boot of Jake's beloved old Mercedes. Then he tactfully left them to it.

Carrying her baby sister Willow on her hip, Dusty appeared slight, but she was stronger than she looked, emotionally as well as physically. She'd had to be; having lost her mother so recently, she found herself in almost sole charge of her baby sister which, at fourteen, was a huge responsibility.

Since they had moved in with their Uncle Jake and his wife Zelda Spender, Dusty had received more help and support from her young cousin Ed than the older members of the family. But she understood. Things had been very complicated for everyone lately; the Spenders were having a very rough time. She had been brought up in the chaotic world of her famous mother, the singer Georgia Cole, Jake's sister, and that had prepared her for almost anything.

Dusty and Ed dashed off to explore the house and choose their bedrooms. Zelda sprinted upstairs after them, just in time to find her son hurling himself across the bed in what was, quite obviously, the master bedroom. He shouted, 'Mine!'

Zelda followed him in. 'Not so fast, buster, I'll think you'll find this is mine.'

Ed jumped up again and grinned at his mother. He was the most agreeable teenaged boy in the world.

The children disappeared and Zelda surveyed her surroundings glumly. The old-fashioned bedroom was large with low ceilings and was overstuffed with what she considered to be very dreary 'brown' furniture. The curtains and bed were draped in reams of Colefax and Fowler chintz. It was about as far from the modern minimalist chic that Zelda favoured as it was possible to imagine. Standing there, Zelda suddenly had a terrifying premonition of being old.

She sat down on the bed in despair. How had this happened to them? Everything she loved had been taken; gone, lost, ruined. She could hardly bring herself to think of the architects of the family's downfall.

Her ex-PA, Kate, 'Don't mention that fucking girl's name!', and her scandalous revelations. Thinking of that double-crossing bitch and her tell-all book made Zelda so enraged she felt that she could almost commit murder.

Then there were all the other losses, not least her ex-agent Lucien Dark's destruction of her entire fortune, which she had worked so bloody hard for all her life, and then, worst of all ... but she just couldn't bear to think about *that*. Somehow she had to keep herself together. To think, plan, sort things out.

Get herself back; back to London, back to life. They might have been hounded out of the city by the paparazzi for now but one thing was certain, she wasn't going to be staying in this dreary dump for long.

She noticed a tattered satin dressing gown draped over a

chair. It suddenly occurred to her that the old lady, Boy Banbury's mother, must have died here; in this bed probably. She shuddered and jumped up, thinking she might just have a quick look around the rest of the house, in case there was another room she could sleep in.

Zelda had finished recceing all the bedrooms when she ran into Jake on the landing. She looked awkward. Everything was so uncomfortable between them since Kate's book. Now the whole world was aware of her bad behaviour, things that she had never wanted anyone to know.

In the furore that surrounded its publication, she was surprised Jake had stayed. But here he was, asking her where she'd like her suitcases? She waved towards the master bedroom. It was the only one that was even vaguely habitable after all, and frankly she was getting used to sleeping with ghosts, so one more wouldn't matter.

One thing was certain: Jake wouldn't be sleeping with her. Kate had put paid to that.

Jake had barely spoken to Zelda since the first devastating extract of the book was serialised in the *Mail*, and he had moved into the spare room at the London mews house. Although he had deliberately avoided reading Kate's book, he wasn't a fool and his wife's indiscretions were hard to ignore when they were being discussed at length, in every sector of the media. Jake was good at denial but even he was struggling with this crisis in their marriage.

The revelations had brought the familiar, bloodthirsty pack of paparazzi back to torment them again, on an almost unprecedented scale. There was no way that any member of the family could leave their home. They found themselves under siege, in a very small house. Tensions ran high.

Zelda had spent her time harassing her new agent, Helen Baldwin, who finally suggested in desperation that Zelda should try to get her family out of sight, out of London, 'to allow the media to move on ... and to put a little space between the scandal and your future projects.'

Which Zelda translated, not inaccurately, as, 'Get the fuck out, you washed-up has-been, and stop bothering me!'

The final straw was when a particularly reckless journalist was discovered trying to take photographs through the baby's bedroom window, in the middle of the night. The police were called, but by the time they arrived the culprit had disappeared.

The family had all had enough; they were frightened and frayed. One thing was clear: their mews house was no longer a viable place to live in the maelstrom of a media feeding-frenzy. The family needed to get away, without being followed. In a brilliant stroke of ingenuity Jake had managed to orchestrate a moonlight flit through a somewhat surprised neighbour's flat.

And so, here they were at what felt like the end of the road.

The end of this particular road had turned out to be Boy Banbury's estate in Oxfordshire. It could be described as quite a lovely road; but not to Zelda, not today.

She glanced out at the garden. The lawn was overgrown, the borders wild with flowers and shrubs. If the mist had lifted, to reveal a sunny morning, things might have seemed different. But the sky was a dull grey, and, as she stood there, dejected, looking out onto that chaotic, neglected place, the dreadful reality of her situation finally dawned on her.

Everything she loved was lost.

# CHAPTER THREE

The Banbury family had been sitting around in the kitchen for ages. It was everyone's favourite place to congregate at the Court.

It was a vast room, with four sets of French windows leading out onto a walled vegetable garden. The Aga kept it warm all year round and, on this particularly chilly summer morning, it was alive with excited chatter about the spectacular fall from grace of their new neighbours and guests.

In fact, the Spenders were the topic of choice at practically every breakfast table in the land, and the Banbury girls were pretty thrilled to find themselves in a somewhat exclusive position at the very heart of the drama, amongst all the main protagonists.

That is, except for Doone, who thought the whole thing, 'Absolutely dire. Typical of our disgusting celebrity-obsessed society.' She declared herself mortified that they should be sheltering such 'low-life scum' and she threatened darkly that, 'Everyone better make fucking sure no one finds out they're here,' because, apparently, her Leeds Uni friends would not understand at all.

Boy responded brusquely to her derogatory remarks. 'It isn't in anyone's interest to find out where the Spenders are hiding, except the press obviously! That's the whole point of them coming here.' He felt this might be an appropriate moment for some sage fatherly guidance. 'You should know better than to judge them until you've met them anyway.'

He proceeded to clatter about looking for a clean saucepan. The old butler sinks were piled high with unwashed pots and pans.

Boy had been quite surprised to hear from Jake. They had seen very little of each other in the past twenty years. When they'd run into each other by chance, in the street, a couple of days previously Boy had thrown out a casual, 'If things get too tough come and hide out with us. My mother's house is empty now so . . .' The sort of glib throwaway line he often uttered. He was a generous man, despite the fact that he had little left to be generous with. He never seriously imagined that Jake would ever need to take him up on it; certainly not so soon.

But Jake Robinson was the kind of friend you could just pick up with any time, he was funny and clever. They had been inseparable at Cambridge. Having him around again might be fun.

Since Jake had married Zelda Spender, they only got the chance to see each other occasionally, when Zelda was away filming. Then they would go off, on riotous nights out, get completely wrecked and Boy would have to spend days recovering. Jake had always been able to drink him under the table.

He hadn't actually laid eyes on Zelda for years. He was pretty sure she had always disapproved of him and he certainly disapproved of her. She struck him as a dreadfully spoilt woman and he could never work out what Jake saw in her. Nor could he understand how they were still together, particularly after this recent humiliating debacle.

But then Jake was a very loyal person. Boy was feeling rather cheerful at the prospect of having him around. He had been quite overwhelmed by all his daughters' demands since Frances, their mother, had . . .

There was a clatter. Flora had found a saucepan, which she handed to her father. Boy got back to thinking about breakfast. He took some eggs from a basket by the Aga and as he broke them into the pan he thought longingly, 'If only there was some bacon too.'

Doone and Flora sat quietly at the kitchen table ignoring their little sister, Kitty, as she gaily performed a song from *Les Misérables*.

Boy had an old tweed jacket draped over his shoulders, his chest was bare and with his pyjama bottoms slung low he looked much younger than forty-two, almost like a brother to his daughters. He began humming along to Kitty's song, a cigarette clamped between his teeth, as he expertly proceeded to scramble some eggs.

'Less of the Glums, someone get the fucking toast!' he mumbled.

Doone got up to pop up the toaster, which was beginning to smoke a bit. Flora surreptitiously helped herself to a cigarette from the packet on the table.

Doone spun round. 'Get your own cigarettes! I'm fed up with you cadging mine.'

'Can't afford any. I haven't got a student loan like some people.'

Doone looked daggers at her sister.

Boy took the saucepan off the Aga and took another drag before asking, casually, 'Student loan! Doone, darling, how crafty of you. How did you get that?'

'It's not rocket science, I just applied. *Everybody* has one.'

'Really, do they? Maybe I should apply for one. How much is it? Could be bloody handy; things are pretty tight at the moment.'

'Things are always pretty tight! And you have to be a student to get one, *obviously*.'

'That sounds perfect. I could study again. I'd like that. Maybe something useful this time, like estate management or something.'

'Bit late for that, I'd say, Boy-oh!' Doone sparred. 'If that's all you can come up with then we really are buggered!'

Kitty stopped singing. 'Maybe the Spenders can lend us some money. They are very, very, very rich.'

Flora jumped up to sit on the Aga and casually lit the ciga-rette she'd stashed. 'Not any more, Kitty. That's why they're hiding here, because they can't afford to go anywhere else. Most people would have just disappeared to hide in another country. But disappearing is expensive when you are as famous as them. We are the cheap and easy option.'

'Nothing new there then.' Doone took the lit cigarette away from Flora and defiantly put it into her own sultry mouth, gently blowing the smoke into her sister's face.

Boy was surprised at how well-informed his sixteen-year-old daughter was about the Spenders' situation. He was mystified by the endless fascination people seemed to have for the details of celebrities' lives and he was vaguely disapproving of his young daughter's expertise in that area.

Flora had got down from the Aga; it was too hot to sit on. She buttered the toast, Boy doled out the scrambled eggs and they tucked in. All except for Doone, who pushed hers away dismissively and said, 'I bet they are all ghastly, and I hope you don't expect us to hang out with them.'

'I think they look lovely, they can hang out with meee!' said Kitty.

'Me too,' Flora agreed. She certainly intended to hang out with them, as much as humanly possible.

Boy looked at his eldest daughter warily. 'There, everyone else is on board. They are our guests, they have had an absolutely horrific time . . . so I'd appreciate a little compassion from you.'

'Oh, yes, because we are all so lucky and nothing horrible has ever happened to *us*. Jesus, Dad!' Doone stood up and stormed out of the kitchen.

Boy knew she very was cross, because she never, ever called him Dad.

At the other end of the room something stirred on one of the enormous battered sofas. An old wolfhound slowly got down, shook itself, yawned loudly and followed Doone out.

Boy considered going after her. But he thought perhaps he'd better leave it for a bit. Yes, he'd let her calm down first.

*

Doone felt very annoyed. She had kept her loan a secret from her father for a reason and now her bloody sister had gone and mentioned it. Her family really was the limit. She couldn't believe she had the whole summer stretching ahead of her with them and some new lunatics to add to the mix. It was going to be hell. She wondered how she might get away.

Maybe I'll get a job, she thought. God, what a nightmare. She opened the library door and let the dog out onto the lawn.

'There you are, Oscar, I'd make a run for it if I were you.'

The dog looked up at her adoringly, then he loped out into the garden.

# CHAPTER FOUR

Zelda had had a little lie down. Then she had pulled herself together again, and made a plan. Zelda adored making plans; she prided herself on her resourcefulness and resilience.

This plan had a way to go, but it went roughly along the lines of: tell the new agent, Helen, to push for a job that could redeem her client, Zelda, in the eyes of the public ... OK, she wasn't quite sure what that job might be yet, but that's what her bloody agent was for!

In the meantime she intended to get herself back into shape. Locked up in the mews house in London, hemmed in and stressed, she had been guzzling all sorts of forbidden things and she was feeling distinctly out of control. Get the body back into tip-top nick and the mind would follow. That's how it always worked for her and she didn't see why it wouldn't do so now. She just needed to get on with it.

She had rummaged through her luggage and was dismayed by the lack of warm clothes; Jake had made them pack in such a rush. She wasn't used to packing her own cases anyway and she certainly wasn't expecting to be hiding out in a damp bloody fridge of a house, in the vilest summer on record. She eventually found a tracksuit and some trainers.

So now she was up and ready to go.

Headphones on, cap on; not that a disguise was really necessary in the middle of nowhere, she realised, but old habits die hard.

Zelda set off at a steady jog up the drive, which was full of cracks and pot-holes in the tarmac, not a running surface she was used to. She saw a grass track to her left and swung onto it, running steadily up a gradual slope through a wood.

Watery sunlight had begun to filter through the old beech trees and even Zelda had to acknowledge that it looked rather charming. Perhaps this would be a nice place to run after all. She pushed on, up the hill, and was amazed to find that the path opened up to reveal a wide, dark lake, which disappeared around a bend further along the treeline.

Zelda stopped for a moment, her hands resting on her slender hips, panting gently, before turning up her iPod and continuing her run. Listening to one of her favourite songs, she felt her spirits lift.

As she ran, a pair of ducks took off, startled, flying low across the water.

For a while she found herself running in sunlight, and she began to smile. Then she disappeared back into the shadows again as she moved lithely along the far side of the lake. She was wondering whether to do a second lap, she was enjoying herself so much, when she suddenly felt something knock her from behind.

She was falling and the 'something' dragged her tracksuit bottoms down with it.

Something? Someone!

Zelda realised to her horror that she was being attacked, brought down on the hard ground, by a maniac! She kicked out wildly, which wasn't easy, with her trousers at half-mast. She kicked again and felt her foot hit its mark – hard. Her attacker swore and relaxed his grip. She struggled to her feet, clumsily pulling her trousers back up, and ran off blindly screaming, 'Help . . . *help*!'

But she knew no one could hear her. She was in the horrible, frightening, desolate countryside; being pursued by a monster. She didn't dare look back. She could feel him coming after her.

She ran on wildly until she arrived back at the Dower House, where she burst through the front door, screaming hysterically, 'Jake, *Jake*! Call the police!'

Jake emerged from the study. 'What's the matter?'

'Someone tried to rape me!' Zelda felt like bursting into tears. 'I was running, and he attacked me; knocked me over from behind. Call the police!'

'By the time they get here he'll be gone. Where were you?'

'By . . . by the lake.'

'OK, I know where that is. Sit tight, I will go and see if I can catch the bastard. Are you alright? Apart from knocking you over did he . . .?' Jake looked concerned.

'No, I kicked him off. But he was very strong. Don't leave me, Jake . . . don't go after him. Call the police.'

But Jake was up and at the door, shouting, 'Ed, get down here, look after your mother, now!'

Ed appeared. 'What's up?'

'Just hang on with Mum for a minute, OK?'

Jake rushed out, slamming the front door behind him, then darted back in again to grab a golf club from a dusty old bag in the hall.

Ed asked his mother what was wrong.

'Someone attacked me in the woods. I knew we shouldn't have come here.' She sniffed and hugged Ed.

Filled with fury that someone should have tried to hurt his lovely mother, Ed immediately grabbed another golf club and flew out after Jake, shouting at his cousin Dusty, 'Call the police!'

He was running along the drive when he heard something from the woods. To his surprise he saw his father, calmly walking next to a tall, fair-haired man and they were laughing. As they drew nearer Ed could see a huge amount of blood running down the man's face.

*

'I seem to have located your attacker,' Jake announced as they entered the kitchen. 'May I reintroduce you to my old friend Boy!'

'What the hell are you talking about! Have you lost your mind? He attacked me, tried to rape me!'

'I didn't, actually.'

Jake handed Boy a drying-up cloth, which he held to his face and mumbled, 'Thanks.'

Boy stepped towards Zelda and she pulled back dramatically, shrieking, 'Stay away from me!'

Boy retreated, embarrassed and a little annoyed. 'Frank and I were doing a bit of tree-felling up by the lake. You appeared out of nowhere, we yelled "Timber!", but you just kept on coming! So I had to tackle you, or the tree would have, and that could have been quite nasty.' He held out her headphones. 'These came off when you kicked me. I'm sorry I frightened you.'

'Well, I'm sure Zelda's very sorry she kicked you!' Jake offered.

'I am not! He attacked me. Whose side are you on?' Zelda glared furiously at her husband.

Dusty appeared, still carrying the baby. 'The police are on their way.'

Zelda looked panicked. 'Well, stop them! The last people we need snooping around us now are the local coppers. We know how watertight they are! They'll be onto the press with our whereabouts within seconds. You didn't tell them who we were, did you?' Zelda's voice rose again.

Dusty looked confused. 'Sorry, I thought you said . . .'

Boy interjected, 'Don't worry, I'll sort them out. We're not in London now. Nobody is interested in *that* sort of thing here.' His implication was clear.

Zelda knew he meant no one was interested in *her*. God! He really was bloody rude. She'd known coming to this place would be a disaster. Collecting up what was left of her dignity, she swept out of the room.

'Sorry about that,' Jake said. 'Let's have a look at what she's done to you. A nasty kick in the face, that's familiar – ouch!'

'My mother kept first-aid stuff up there.' Boy pointed to a cupboard. Dusty handed the baby to Jake and went to get the things she needed to patch up their host's face.

She came over with a bowl of Dettol and some cotton wool. 'Hi, I'm Dusty.'

Boy smiled a bloody smile and said, 'Hello, Dusty,' as if he really didn't know who she was.

Which was kind, because, as Dusty was only too well aware, everyone always knew exactly who she was: the daughter of the late, great, tragic Georgia Cole, famous singer and even more famous fuck-up. Yes, that was Georgia's legacy to her daughters, to be known as 'those poor little girls' for evermore.

Dusty gently bathed away the blood from Boy's handsome features. He was tanned from a life spent mostly outdoors, and she could see small white lines when he creased and uncreased his eyes as he tried not to flinch while she cleaned him up.

In turn, Boy studied Dusty's sweet face. Fair-haired and with flawless skin, she was much prettier in the flesh than in her pictures. A child-woman. He supposed she must be a bit younger than Flora, with the same caring nature, he could tell. Flora's Goth exterior concealed her soft heart from most of the world, but not from her father. Boy knew that the motherless girls had much in common, both caring for younger siblings.

Dusty stepped back and put the bloodied cotton wool back into the bowl.

'I think it's OK now, the cut's not too bad. But you might get a black eye.' Dusty wrinkled her nose. 'Bad luck!'

Boy thanked her. 'You must come up and meet my girls. They are very excited that you're here. They're pretty sick of me as a companion. Bring Ed too, all of you, in fact!' He looked at Jake. 'Come for supper tomorrow night, after you've settled in?' He started to head towards the door.

Jake stood up too. 'Love to. Thanks so much. God, I'm sorry about all this, hurling ourselves on your mercy, then attacking you!'

'No, no. It's fine, a mistake, understandable, and she's obviously quite highly strung.'

'You're not kidding.' Jake continued out onto the drive with Boy.

'Highly strung, but a very nice arse!' Boy laughed.

'Sadly, you are not the only bloke to have noticed that.' Jake grimaced. 'Hey ho!'

Boy turned to his friend, a little embarrassed by his faux pas, and gave him a manly pat on the shoulder. 'It's really nice to see you, Jake. Glad you're here; could do with a friend. Surrounded by too many women. No idea what's going on most of the time.'

Jake studied his friend's face. 'Sorry, so caught up in my own stuff, forgot to ask about Frances. Any news?'

'Not really. I'll tell you about it tomorrow. Come about eight?'

'Lovely, thanks, Boy. This is beyond the call.'

A police car pulled into the drive.

Boy approached it at once. 'Sorry, Peter, I was just about to call you; false alarm. Just a bit of a misunderstanding.'

Sergeant Peter Powell nodded to him then looked across at Jake. 'Morning, Mr Robinson. We heard you were here.'

Jake was taken aback. 'Oh, right, thanks. We were hoping to be under the, you know, radar.'

'Don't you worry, your secret's safe with us. Most discreet force in England, the Thames Valley Constabulary.' He touched his nose. 'We're not like them in London, no, no, no. A lot of important people live around here. Happy valley and all that.'

'Very grateful, Peter, sorry to get you out here ... sure you've got a lot of important things to do?' Boy patted the top of the police car.

Sergeant Powell put the car into reverse.

Before pulling away again he glanced up at Boy and said, 'I should have that cut looked at if I were you, Lord Banbury. Might need a stitch and a bit of witch hazel on it. Witch hazel works a treat when someone's been beaten up.' His face was impassive as he drove off, narrowly missing a battered green van, as it swung into the drive.

A young woman jumped out and went to open the back doors. Boy gave her a silent wave as he strode off, and she waved back gaily.

She grinned at Jake before disappearing into the back of the van. He heard a muffled, 'I'm Karen ... look after the house ... got you a few supplies here. I'll make up the beds and then, if

you give me a list, I'll get whatever else you . . . for tomorrow.'
She re-emerged, pushed back her unruly auburn curls, smiled
and said, 'Told you're keeping yourselves out of the limelight?'
Without waiting for an answer she picked up the box of groceries and walked into the house.

Before Jake could respond, she was gone. So that was
Karen, Jake thought; Frank, the estate guy, was clearly a very
lucky man.

Maybe this was what he needed, a simple country life.

'Jake!' Zelda shrieked from the house.

'What?' he hissed, as he went back inside.

He found his wife in the hall.

'Dusty tells me we are going up to that idiot's place for
supper tomorrow! Have you forgotten there is a baby in the
house? Who is going to look after it?'

'Oh, I expect we can take her with us, or maybe you can stay
behind and look after her!' Jake teased.

Zelda was flummoxed. The last person on earth she wanted
to spend an evening with was bloody Boy Banbury. But being
left here, looking after the baby, wasn't something she relished
the prospect of either.

Karen appeared from the kitchen. 'I can babysit tomorrow
if you like.'

Zelda looked up sharply. 'Who the hell are you?'

'Oh, sorry, hi, I'm Karen, I look after the house.' She held
out her hand to Zelda. 'Pleased to meet you.'

Jake was impressed; she didn't seem in the least bit
intimidated by his fractious, famous wife.

Zelda didn't take the proffered hand, but just said, 'Oh, good. Can you do something to sort out my room? It smells like someone died in it.'

With that she turned on her heel and stomped off to investigate the Internet connection, or at least to find Ed and get him to fix it for her.

Jake noticed that Karen raised an eyebrow slightly as she went past him to 'sort out Zelda's room'. He felt embarrassed on his wife's behalf; her tactlessness knew no bounds. But he was trying to make allowances for her behaviour. He understood that she was on the verge of a breakdown because of everything that had happened. She was still, understandably, in a terrible state about Valentine, her beloved son.

He knew he'd lost a lot himself too. But it was different for him. He and Zelda were miles apart now. Kate's 'tell-all' book had gone off like a bomb, ripping through the family, revealing some very compromising secrets. Jake wasn't sure if they could ever get back to where they were when they'd moved back into the Mews. A golden time, that brief renaissance in their marriage.

But at least he hadn't relapsed. He was proud of that and grateful for it. He knew that taking to the bottle would be the last thing he and his family needed, when they were in a full-blown crisis already.

Although he wouldn't be able to get to meetings for a while, his sponsor in AA had assured him that he could call any time, day or night, if he felt he was in danger of a slip. He had managed so far, and having weathered a raging media storm, he felt pretty confident he'd be OK. When they had settled in a bit he intended to get back to writing his novel. The study at the Dower House was very peaceful and he felt he would be happy, locking himself away to work there.

There were reasons to be cheerful. You just had to look for the positives; he was trying to take that advice to heart, but it wasn't always easy.

# CHAPTER FIVE

Cleo Spender put down the telephone to her agent, turned to her husband Max and said brightly, 'Well, that all seems to be fine. Apparently the television company is still delighted to go with my *Against All Odds* show. It will be signed and sealed later today.' She jumped to her feet with the agility of a thirty-year-old. Which was impressive for a woman in her mid-seventies.

She smoothed down the skirt of her slim, chic Chanel day dress and said, 'Ha! So that little bitch, Kate, may have dragged us all through the mud. But apparently there is . . . how did my agent put it? Plenty of appetite for a show featuring the magnificent Cleo Spender, pitched against the elements.' She threw her magnificently toned arms in the air. 'Ta-da!'

Max smiled at his wife and said, between gritted teeth, 'Appetite for seeing you suffer, more likely, my sweet!'

Cleo shot back, 'Maybe you should come with me on this trip. They'd certainly like to see *you* suffer!' Thinking vengefully: so would I! 'After all,' she continued, 'it's only going to be a jaunt in a little boat, through the Northwest Passage, in the chilly old Arctic, so it won't be like Everest. I know you couldn't have climbed *that* with me, obviously! But a boat? After all the time you've spent cruising? It would be a doddle for you.'

Max ignored the double-entendre. 'No, no, darling. I wouldn't want to cramp your style. It's you they want, you are the star, always have been, always will be.' He wandered away.

He did feel a little twinge of guilt. The success of his long and happy marriage to Cleo had always been conditional on his playing the loving, generous husband. Now most of their money was gone; bloody bankers and hedge-fund mis-managing people! And Kate, that sly little PA, had not pulled any punches with her revelations about Max's predilection for dalliances with young men. She even had the temerity to suggest that some of the boys might have been slightly under the age of consent. Which would have been libellous, if it hadn't been true.

Max had assured Cleo that he would be pursuing a prosecution. But in reality he wouldn't, since stirring up any more dirt than was stirred up already would be extremely unwise. Their daughter Zelda felt the same way. What was it she'd said? 'We are just going to have to suck it up!'

He was relieved that Cleo was going to be away filming. A sabbatical would do them both good. He accepted that he would have to take things a bit easy for a while. He was beginning to feel his age; he would be seventy-nine in a few months. Maybe this would be a sensible moment for a bit of a break from what he called his extra-curricular treats . . .

There was always Jamie, loyal, lovely Jamie; their butler

and his friend. Jamie, who'd stood by them, through thick and thin. When he'd heard of their financial difficulties, he had even offered to work for no pay.

Max had insisted that would not be necessary, but Cleo was tempted to accept. Which frankly gave Max a bit of a fright. She could be quite tight-fisted, it seemed, not something that had been in evidence when she was spending his money like water, during the long, extravagant years of their marriage.

But when it was *her* money – money earned from her *Cleo Climbs Everest* show; almost a million! – she was as tight as hell. This did not bode well for the future and was another reason for Max keeping his head down and his dick clean. An expression that Max had never heard until his wife hurled it at him threateningly when the revelations in the book, and sub-sequently in the press, ran slightly amok.

'Ah, well,' he sighed to himself. At least they weren't in as much of a pickle as Zelda.

Max had lost a considerable chunk of his inheritance because of the mismanagement of his estate by his trustees, and many other financial vagabonds and thieves. But he hadn't lost anything like as much as Zelda and Jake, who had been stripped of everything by Zelda's ex-agent and nemesis, Lucien Dark.

Max had never liked that man, hadn't trusted him from the moment he first set eyes on him. Lucien might have once been the most powerful agent-manager on the planet, but he had lost some members of Max's family their entire fortunes.

Not only Zelda and Jake were affected, but poor little Dusty and Willow too. Their mother Georgia had been 'looked after' by Lucien Dark, up until her untimely death. So her fortune, from her astonishingly successful singing career, was lost along with the assets of many of the most famous entertainment-industry people in the world. There were a lot of very poor, furious actors, singers, directors and writers out in the cold, because of Dark.

Oh, yes, Max thought, there will be a great day of reckoning for that bastard, sometime soon. He was still on remand awaiting trial. There were the other charges too, some of them very unsavoury indeed. Yes, Lucien Dark would be going to prison for a very long time but, unfortunately, that didn't mean anyone would be getting any of their money back.

This was beginning to be a bit of a problem.

Max Spender was always happy to chuck his money about, that was the point of having it as far as he was concerned. His father had earned it, not him, and he had never been terribly interested in his money, until it was almost gone.

Now that he didn't have the wherewithal to be so profligate, he was finding his family's financial demands rather awkward. He had already handed over quite a few thousand to Zelda, to tide her over, just until her new deals were signed, she had assured him.

But since Kate's book, there were no deals for Zelda, her next big film role had been re-cast and her lucrative contract with the cosmetics company Fabulous was well and truly over, cancelled due to her 'tarnishing the brand and its fabulous reputation'.

Now Zelda was muttering about boarding-school fees for Ed and Dusty and round-the-clock nannies for Willow; these were all things that were going to cost a lot more that Max could presently afford, and a lot more than Cleo would be interested in shelling out for.

Times were hard indeed, and Max was pretty sure they were going to get harder.

His mobile rang. 'Zelda' flashed up on the screen; his darling girl!

He pressed 'ignore'. He really wasn't feeling up to that now and he was slightly worried that she might have found out that Cleo had been commissioned to do another show.

That would cause a lot of resentment between the two most competitive women on earth: his wife and his daughter.

He thought he might just go down to see Jamie in the kitchen, have a glass or two of Bollinger. Cheer himself up a bit.

# CHAPTER SIX

When Boy had returned from the Dower House that morning, he found his eldest daughter alone in the kitchen.

'What's happened to your face?'

Boy toyed with the idea of telling her that a tree had fallen on him, but he realised that the truth would come out soon enough. So he'd better just be straight with her. Annoyingly, it did rather confirm her worst suspicions about Zelda Spender.

He tried to play it down, unsuccessfully.

'So she kicked you in the face, before she'd even said hello, or thanks? Nice!'

'I think I gave her a bit of a fright.'

'I can't imagine why. I thought falling underneath every man she met was her speciality.'

'Oh, don't believe everything you read. I'm sure she's a very nice woman once you get to know her.' He tried to sound convincing; for his friend Jake's sake, he wanted to keep the peace. Being on the wrong side of Doone was a scary place to be.

He wasn't sure how to break his other news, so he just dived in. 'Well, I've asked them all to supper tomorrow night. So you can judge for yourself.'

Doone said, 'Pity I won't be here. I'm going to see Charlie, some of the band are down and he's asked me over.'

Disquietingly for Boy, Doone had recently made friends with the lead singer of the Giant Spiders, Charlie, who had moved nearby to start a llama farm. His reputation as a very wild man was well-known, even to Boy, and he had already had words with Doone about their friendship.

Boy said, 'Oh shit! But I will need you here. I can't cook for them!'

'You should have thought of that before you asked them!' But then she had a flash of inspiration, a way of diluting an evening with the Spenders. 'Maybe I should get Charlie to bring his chums over here for supper?'

Not what Boy had anticipated. 'But we are trying to keep the fact that they're here a secret!' he protested weakly.

'Charlie's band are so famous, they certainly wouldn't be "grassing up" the Spenders,' Doone reassured him, slightly patronisingly. 'The Celebrity Code of Honour and all that.'

Boy was perplexed, having not a clue what a Celebrity Code of Honour might be.

Doone patiently explained what her pals had told her. 'Never share the famous person's whereabouts, phone number, address or email with anyone, ever. If you are famous and talking about someone else who is famous too, they are always "fabulously kind, down-to-earth, lovely people", no matter how vile or deranged.'

People only broke the code at their peril. Everyone knew that.

Everyone except Boy, apparently.

'Anyway,' Doone said, 'I can't see what you're worried about. No one need know that the Spenders are staying with us. They aren't, technically anyway, they are in the Dower House.'

Boy admitted that she had a point. And before he knew quite what had happened he found he had somehow agreed to his daughter's plan.

Now Doone had gone off for a long walk with her beloved dog, Oscar.

She felt much happier at the idea of having some of her friends over with the Spenders. Charlie hadn't been to Banbury Court before and Doone knew that, despite its shabby state, it was hard for anyone not to be seduced by its grand, romantic charm. She also knew she'd end up being the one having to cook the dinner; she might as well do it for people she liked.

She started to make plans: lots of pasta, cheap and delicious, no 'showing-off' food, not that they could afford any, anyway.

She didn't think Zelda Spender would eat pasta, but what the hell.

*

Flora and Kitty pushed open the door to the cellar and were immediately hit by the familiar smell of dry plaster and stale wine. Neither of them had been down there since the night their mother left.

Flora flicked the light switch and the old cellar sprang back into somewhat dusty life. This place, part vault, part nightclub, had always been almost sacred to Flora. The impending dinner party seemed like a good reason to get it all going again; there hadn't been any parties at Banbury Court for such a long time.

A lot of happy, and some embarrassing, memories had been formed within the crumbly old walls and under the nightclub's starlit sky; the ceiling was papered in midnight blue, printed with huge silver stars. The walls were covered with old posters from the '60s and '70s: Jimi Hendrix, Rod Stewart, Elton John, the Byrds.

She and Doone used to love dancing around on the old sprung dance floor, pretending to serve each other drinks at the bar, smoking their first cigarettes, snogging their first boyfriends or, in Flora's case, boyfriend, singular – if a snog with your best friend's brother, once, counted as a boyfriend?

Procol Harum's 'A Whiter Shade of Pale' and anything by the Rolling Stones were their favourite old records. They used to play them over and over on the jukebox, dancing wildly for hours, until their mother or father came and told them to 'Go to bed!' Flora flicked a switch to see if the jukebox was still working. Pressing some buttons, 'Satisfaction' suddenly boomed out.

The girls grinned at each other and started to dance. By the end of the song they were both quite puffed. They threw themselves onto the wide velvet banquettes; clouds of dust flew out of the cushions.

Flora said, 'I think we need to clean it up a bit, before

tomorrow night. The bar is filthy and we should get some more glasses.'

Kitty asked, 'Can I do sweeping and mopping?'

'You sure can,' Flora said, 'but don't get it too wet, we don't want it to be like Glastonbury.'

Flora went off to find a light bulb for the lamp on the bar. She was going to search for candles too, as she liked the way they looked in the old wine bottles, which were caked in wax from the '60's – way back when her grandfather had had the cellar converted into a nightclub.

*

Their grandfather, Guy Banbury, was a famously wild and profligate man. His family home was once one of the finest small estates in the country. But he had managed to go through the family's considerable fortune in one generation, which was a tragedy for Boy and his mother.

Guy loved speed. Everything had to be fast. Racing cars were his passion for a while, a very expensive passion. Then he moved on to racehorses for a few years, but they didn't prove to be fast enough either. Latterly, he spent considerable amounts of time at the gaming tables with the Aspinalls and Goldsmiths, but with less success than his chums.

He lost his fortune very fast indeed.

Amongst Guy Banbury's many and various claims to fame were an Olympic gold medal for fencing and a brief dalliance with Audrey Hepburn.

In fact, it was Audrey's idea to call Guy's baby 'Boy'. When she heard that Guy had become a father she said, 'How positively charming, my darling, now you are a Guy with a Boy.' So they both started referring to the baby as Boy. It stuck, and Boy's mother's desire to call him Titus was overruled; one thing Boy was eternally grateful to Audrey for.

'So he wasn't all bad,' Boy would say of him kindly, 'just a bit reckless.'

This was the man who had left Boy with debts up to his ears.

People assumed that Boy was hopeless with money, but he'd never actually had any money to be hopeless with. When his father died in 1990, he left an almost bankrupt estate. Boy had no choice but to sell off the only good land he had left, to pay death duties and to disperse his father's staggering debts. A wiser man would have sold up.

But Boy soldiered on, always believing that somehow, some-day, he would manage to pull off some marvellous wheeze so that the family fortunes, and Banbury Court, could be restored to their former glory.

Thus far, no such wheeze had presented itself and Boy oper-ated a make-do-and-mend approach to estate management. His only member of staff was Frank, with a bit of part-time help from Karen. Despite Frank's Herculean efforts, he and Boy were not doing much more than skimming the very sur-face of what needed to be done to keep the estate afloat.

Things had been pretty desperate for a while. Then the Frances thing happened . . .

\*

Flora preferred not to think about her mother at all. She had blocked her out, just as she felt her mother had blocked them out. Ferociously, she punched the dusty cushions on the banquettes, coughing as the dust filled her throat.

Kitty reappeared lugging a huge bucket of water, slopping it everywhere.

Flora watched her. 'Be careful, Kitty. Look, squeeze the mop out like this or it will be too wet.'

'I know, I know, I can do it. Let me!'

Kitty mopped away gaily for a while, halting only to point out something to Flora. 'Look, someone has spilt wine everywhere on this bit.' The floor was stained darkly under a low table. Kitty pushed it back so that her sister could take a look. 'I've tried to clean it but it won't come off.'

'It doesn't matter, no one will care or see, it's so dark. That's why it stinks of old wine down here,' Flora said.

A couple of hours later they were standing admiring their handiwork, when Doone appeared.

They were a bit nervous about what she would say. You never really knew with Doone. But she seemed pleased.

'This looks great. I'm just going to the village to get some things for tomorrow's supper, I've asked some friends over,' she said mildly, as she ducked back upstairs.

'You're not supposed to! Who have you asked? Dad said no one must know they're here!' Flora sounded livid.

Doone turned and looked down at her sister, 'It's OK, they'll be cool, they're just as famous as the fucking Spenders anyway!'

'Who? Who are they?' Flora was panicking, running after her.

'Charlie and the rest of the Giant Spiders.' Doone looked pleased with herself. 'And some other friends who are staying with him.'

Flora was amazed. She knew Doone was friends with Charlie, but she had never, ever asked him over before. He was bringing friends; didn't she say that? He was bringing friends! OMG! Who? What did she have to wear? Nothing! She ran back down into the cellar, needing to tell Kitty.

Kitty just said, 'I hate spiders!'

Not the reaction Flora was hoping for at all. She went off to her room, to try on everything she owned. She wouldn't let it show, but this was the most exciting news: a band!

The Spenders coming to stay was only, like, the best thing ever.

# CHAPTER SEVEN

Zelda was alone in the kitchen. She poked around in the groceries that Karen had left in a box on the table: coffee, some bread, butter and pasta. Only the coffee was useful as far as Zelda was concerned. She never ate bread or pasta; wheat allergy! But even she knew she couldn't live on coffee alone. At the bottom of the box were some apples, she could eat those, and peas, but they were in their shells, so far too much of a hassle.

She crunched an apple as she waited for the kettle to boil. Surveying her surroundings she was horrified to see how tired and beaten-up the kitchen looked – not exactly dirty, but somehow old and unhygienic. She glanced down at the floor; she could see that the worn flagstones were cleanish, but then she noticed something. Were those mouse droppings?

She shrieked, 'Jake!'

Karen appeared. 'Hello?'

Zelda glared at her accusingly. 'There's mouse shit on this floor!'

Karen looked down to the spot where Zelda was gesticulating furiously.

'Oh, yes. So there is,' she responded mildly. 'There are always lots of mice around at this time of year. Old Lady Banbury used to feed them; thought of them as pets. They probably think she's back.' She smiled at Zelda. 'Hey ho! I'll get a brush.' And she disappeared.

Pets! Zelda couldn't believe it; how disgusting. The kitchen really was filthy. She needed to get a proper cleaner; Karen was obviously useless. In fact some proper staff were needed a.s.a.p. Not to mention a nanny or two, particularly when the holidays were over and Dusty was back at school.

The funds Max had given her had already run out. When they were under siege at the mews house in London, she had found it necessary to bring in all sorts of vital people: masseurs, personal trainers, make-up artists, the diet doc, her favourite beautician, the Botox guy, homeopaths, a tutor for the teenagers, cleaners, two nannies . . . They had cost a small fortune and they had made the place very claustrophobic.

But old habits die-hard and, when she wasn't working, Zelda had no idea what else to do with her time. She had spent quite a lot of her father's money on Net-A-Porter; standards had to be maintained after all. She needed clothes, needed to look her best, so that when the storm clouds had passed she would be ready for any amount of close-ups; ready for her film career to re-energise, ready for anything.

Unfortunately, that meant she was totally out of cash. She

was surprised by how much things cost. She never used to have anything to do with her own finances.

It pained her to think of it now; she'd left Lucien Dark in charge of everything, which had left her with nothing. That bastard! Why was it taking the stupid CPS so long to take him to court? Or was it the SFO or both? What a lot of useless people, initials galore, but not a successful outcome in sight.

She tried her father again. No reply.

Well, she would just have to ring her mother, desperate times and all that. Perhaps she should ask them down to stay? That might make it easier to get her father alone and persuade him to do her bidding. Yes, she would do that.

She picked up her phone. The signal was weak and so she walked around and eventually went outside to call her mother. Cleo answered straight away, because she had some news that she couldn't wait to share with Zelda.

'Mummy, it's me.'

'Hello, darling, how are you getting on? Your father told me you'd bolted to the country.'

'That's why I'm ringing. It's lovely and quiet down here. Not a pap in sight. So I wondered if you and Dad would like to come and stay? It's really nice and sunny.' She had always lied easily to her mother.

'Oh, darling, I wish we could, it's just that I am going to be frightfully busy . . .'

Zelda interrupted her. 'I think you'd love it. We're on Boy Banbury's estate. It's not far from London.'

'Oh, I love Banbury Court! I knew Boy's father, really quite well. A fabulously handsome man.'

I bet you did! thought Zelda.

'Maybe we *should* come down and see you before I go. After all it will be terribly dangerous, and who knows I might never . . .'

'What will be terribly dangerous?' Zelda snapped.

'Oh, darling! I haven't had a chance to tell you yet, have I? My new show has been green-lit. It's called "Against All Odds" and my agent says it will be huge!'

There was a silence. Zelda was trying to get herself under control. Her mother had another show and *she* couldn't get arrested. She was wild with envy.

Cleo understood. Zelda's reaction was nothing new.

'We could come down at the weekend, perhaps? I'll speak to your father. Yes, it would be lovely to see you before I go. I can tell you all about it then. You are going to be so excited for me.' She couldn't help rubbing it in. ''Bye, darling.'

Cleo could just hear a slightly strangled ''Bye' from Zelda, as they both hung up.

'Jake!' Zelda yelled again.

Karen reappeared with a dustpan and brush.

Zelda watched her for a moment, then said, 'My parents will be coming to stay this weekend. Can you make one of the spare rooms habitable? My mother has rather high standards. So if you could keep the vermin at bay we'd all appreciate it.'

As Zelda swept through the house, she heard the roar of a motor starting up outside. From the drawing-room window, the pleasing sight of Frank mowing the lawns caught her eye. The sun had suddenly come out and he had taken his shirt off, revealing a tanned, toned torso. Zelda watched him for a few moments and she began to feel a tiny bit better.

So, her mother had another show. Annoying, but it occurred to Zelda that it would leave her father alone and, therefore, hopefully more vulnerable to his daughter's charms? She really needed money and she was pretty sure her mother wouldn't be parting with any of hers. Maybe it was a good thing that Cleo was off again. Didn't she say something about it being dangerous?

She jumped slightly when Dusty came in. Zelda was still frequently surprised by the fact that, since Georgia's death, she and Jake had his sister's children living with them and, although Dusty was a great companion to their son Ed, the baby was far more than Zelda had bargained for.

'Ed and I are just doing a picnic. We thought we'd take Willow up for lunch by the lake. Do you want to come?' Dusty asked.

'Lunch? Oh no, darling, thanks. No lunch for me.' Zelda really was quite hungry. She wondered what she'd done with that half-eaten apple.

It had not escaped Dusty's notice that Zelda never seemed to eat anything. No wonder she was in such a bad mood all the time. She was obviously starving.

*

Karen helped Ed and Dusty get everything together. She had found an old Fortnum's picnic basket in the back kitchen and was wiping it down. Ed made sandwiches and Dusty was mushing up some banana for Willow. Karen could see that both of them were used to looking after themselves, and looking after the baby too.

She hadn't seen Zelda Spender touch Willow at all.

She had read a bit about the family, like everyone, but she couldn't quite remember what the baby's history was. Celebrity gossip wasn't really her thing.

Karen couldn't help being intrigued by Zelda. Even though she knew the actress had been humiliated in the press just lately – *that* couldn't have escaped anyone's notice – she had expected someone more resilient. The woman she saw today seemed to be in some sort of emotional meltdown.

Karen felt she could overlook Zelda's rudeness, as she assumed it was brought on by stress; she'd heard that celebrities were always stressed out, checking into expensive clinics suffering from 'exhaustion'. She thought they could do with a spell of duty during the lambing season, that would show them what exhaustion was.

Then she recalled that Zelda had another son, a very beautiful young man; she couldn't quite remember ... was he a model? Something terrible had happened to him. Hit by a car? A car crash? She couldn't recall the details.

No wonder Zelda Spender was a mess. Yes, Karen was prepared to make allowances. She was a reasonable and compassionate woman. Which was why she and Frank got along so well.

\*

Jake was happily ensconced in the study. It had a huge green-baize door, which was remarkably soundproof. So Jake was pleasantly oblivious to Zelda intermittently shrieking his name. He was keeping his head down, particularly since he'd overheard a massive Zelda meltdown when she discovered that there was no Internet at the Dower House. He had let Ed deal with it, but he chuckled when he heard his fractious wife calling it 'the fucking Dire House'.

He had his computer open on the desk in front of him. The lack of Internet connection didn't bother him at all; in fact it was probably a godsend, no distractions. He didn't need it for research on his book, as it was a novel that required no research. It was set in a world he knew only too well: the lives of the rich and famous, a sort of contemporary *Brideshead Revisited* with *Vile Bodies*, or that was what he was aiming for anyway. He was a big Waugh fan, which he was finding far more of a hindrance than a help.

He suddenly remembered one of the AA teachings: no comparing, 'neither inferior nor superior'. Comparing was *a very bad idea*, so he must forget about comparing his writing to Waugh's. Which he had to admit did seem sensible.

His attention was drawn to a random photograph of a mouse, in an ornate silver picture frame, on the desk. Next to it was a picture of Boy at Cambridge. The younger Boy smiled out at him, all twinkling eyes and floppy blonde hair. When he scrutinised the photograph more closely, he noticed a familiar dark-haired figure in the background, in cricket whites. It was ... him! He picked up the photograph to take a better look.

Jake found himself hurtling back through time, back to their happy years at Trinity. To that cricket pitch, sunny days, Pimms and punts and those lovely, pretty, clever girls . . .

So, rather than working on his novel as he'd intended, Jake found himself on a cheerful trip down memory lane, back to those carefree years before his meteoric early rise as a hugely successful TV scriptwriter, before his marriage to Zelda. Long, long ago.

All of which had, somehow, brought him back to Banbury Court and his old pal, Boy.

He found that his happy reminiscences about his beloved university had opened a tiny crack in his imagination and given him a way into his novel. He felt something shift within himself, and a rushing flood of ideas tumbled from his fingers. He began to write like a man possessed.

If he had looked up from his work he might have noticed that his wife had put on a tiny bikini and was out on the lawn, sunbathing, apparently oblivious to the fabulously fit man with a mower, who was noisily spinning around on the grass.

It was turning into rather a beautiful day after all.

\*

Dusty and Ed lay on the picnic rug, giggling. The remains of their feast was scattered about, sandwich crusts, apple cores and ginger beer. Karen had given them an old copy of one of the Famous Five stories and Ed was reading them out loud in a faux '60's voice. They thought they were hilarious, which could probably be attributed to the joint they had smoked rather than the comedic skills of Enid Blyton. They were both enjoying this brief respite after such a frenetic morning. The soft summer afternoon made them feel very mellow and child-like.

Dusty was suddenly serious. 'Have you noticed your parents aren't sleeping in the same room? What do you think will happen to them, to us? Everything has gone wrong since Mum died.'

Ed closed his eyes. 'They'll be alright. They have gone through like tons of shit before and they're always OK, really pissed with each other, then fine again. It's the way they work.'

He leant over and poked Dusty in the ribs in rhythm as he said, 'We – will – all – be – fine.'

Dusty poked him back. 'I – hope – you – are – right – or – we – are – fucked!'

Willow was slowly crawling towards the lake, where she could see a duckling swimming just offshore. A murky orange shape had caught her eye; a vast golden carp loomed just beneath the surface. As she reached towards it she began to topple, slowly, silently into the water.

Dusty leapt across the path and grabbed her ankle.

A shadow fell across them, just as Dusty pulled her baby sister out of danger and into her arms.

'Oops, that was close,' the shadow said.

Dusty squinted up at the detached husky voice as it said, 'Hi.'

Dusty felt at a disadvantage, realising that the owner of the voice must have witnessed her lousy child-minding skills. 'Hi! Er, she's a fast crawler. Phew!' She giggled nervously.

Ed was staring, mesmerised. He had never seen a more beautiful girl. She looked like a Goth Lady of Shalott. Her pale, pierced skin and long dark hair made her an impressive but incongruous sight in the midst of such a bucolic landscape. With her tall, slight frame silhouetted against the bulrushes and the dark rippling lake behind, she reminded him of a twisted version of a princess from a childhood storybook, a book that Ed had loved when he was a little boy.

As Ed sat up, he mumbled, 'Do you live here?'

'Yep, I'm Flora.' She smiled warmly despite trying to seem cool. 'You're coming up to our house for supper tomorrow night, aren't you?'

Ed, a bit stoned and totally smitten, found himself unable to answer her.

Dusty spoke for him. 'We are, thanks. I'm Dusty and this is Willow.' She took Willow's arm and made her do a little wave, as she smiled up at Flora. 'Is your dad OK?'

Flora shrugged. 'I think he'll live. He's used to being kicked in the teeth by women.' Suddenly feeling shy, she turned to walk off, calling blithely, 'See you guys later.'

Ed wanted to make her stop, to turn around. So he called out, too loud, 'I'm Ed!' His voice trailed off with embarrassment.

'I know.' Flora answered as she strode away along the bank. 'See you!' and she gave a little wave.

*

Zelda woke early and alone in Lady Banbury's chintzy old bed. She hadn't slept well. She felt a bit spooked but she hadn't dared call out to Jake.

He had spent the previous evening locked away in the study so they hadn't had a chance to speak at all since they'd arrived.

She spent most of her sleepless night going over all the mistakes she had made, tormenting herself, and now she felt wrecked again. She decided to go downstairs and make herself a cup of tea.

As she walked through the hall she saw that a handwritten letter had been posted through the front door, and bent to pick it up. It was marked: *For the personal attention of Ms Zelda Spender*.

The script was italic, smart, on good paper. She opened it, vaguely wondering if it was an apology from Boy for attacking her. But it wasn't; it simply said:

*I know where you live.*

Not particularly original, and certainly not the worst thing anyone had written to her, but chilling nonetheless. Cold in its brevity.

Zelda felt slightly anxious. Nobody was meant to know where she lived.

She hadn't seen any of her weird fan mail for years. Her ex-agent Lucien's office would always make sure that it was intercepted. In fact she hadn't opened any letters at all. There had always been someone else standing between Zelda and the world. She suddenly felt exposed, unprotected. She missed her team: her security guys, her staff, her friends. She might text Shona, her best friend and stylist. Ask her to come down to stay, get her to bring some new clothes. Yes, it would be lovely to see Shona.

She wondered if there were enough rooms at the Dower House, as with Max and Cleo coming for the weekend, it might be a bit of a squash. She'd have to ask that girl, the redhead, when she came in later.

There must be somewhere for Shona to sleep; she wasn't fussy and had often slept on sofas when Zelda needed her, on film sets and so on. She'd be fine. Zelda knew she could always rely on Shona.

She made herself a calming chamomile tea and wandered out into the garden. The pigeons were coo-ing and the freshly cut grass smelt heavenly; she breathed deeply as the early-morning sun warmed her face. She sipped her tea and looked across the lawn, to a densely overgrown thicket in the distance. A light breeze picked up, and the birch trees rustled gently as something caught her eye, a branch bouncing as if released by someone. Zelda turned and rushed back into the house. Slamming the kitchen door behind her, she ran through the hall calling out, 'Jake, Jake! There's someone outside. Jake!'

Jake emerged from the study, still in yesterday's clothes. He looked perplexed. 'Were you calling me?'

'I've been shouting for ages, I could have been killed! There is someone out there in the garden. I just saw him! And there's a letter. Call the police.'

'OK, hang on a minute, slow down. Before we get the police here again, let's just go over what has happened. Who did you see? It wasn't Boy again, was it?'

'No, no, no! You're not listening. I got this letter.' Zelda went into the kitchen. She looked on the kitchen table where she'd dropped it. 'I left it here, it was on really nice paper.' She began looking frantically under the table, in the cupboards. 'Where is it, somebody's taken it!'

'What did it say, this letter, on really nice paper?' Jake mocked.

'It said, *I know where you live*,' Zelda hissed indignantly. 'Obviously they know where I fucking live. They posted it through my door!'

Despite her bravado Jake could see that his wife was shaken, so he put his arm around her. They were both aware that it was the first physical contact they had had for quite some time. Zelda leant into Jake's shoulder.

'Well, it's probably a pap who is just trying to have some fun with us.'

'It was addressed to me!'

'Fun with you, then.'

'He's outside, in the bushes, on the other side of the lawn! I think we should get him arrested,' Zelda persisted.

'Exactly the kind of place a pap would be. It'll just be one of those buggers who's found out where we are. With luck he'll want to keep us to himself, so we won't be overrun. Let's hope so anyway. I'll go out and have a look around. OK?' Jake gave her a strong, bracing squeeze. Which, she had to admit, was better than nothing.

Zelda felt a little easier. Maybe Jake was right; perhaps it could be a photographer. Some of them really liked to persecute people; to persecute her.

'Why don't you go and run a soothing bath? I'll report back.'

Jake unlocked the front door and set off purposefully across the garden.

Zelda went upstairs, turned on the taps, and the water splashed loudly into the old claw-foot bath. She felt safer in Lady Banbury's rather charming and, Zelda had to admit it now, very comforting bathroom.

Sometimes she forgot how wise and kind Jake could be. Good in a crisis. Their life was one long crisis these days and, after all that had come out in Kate's book, it was a miracle he was still prepared to come anywhere near her.

He had insisted that he didn't ever want to read what Kate had written, but inevitably some stuff had found its way to him; the extensive press coverage was hard for anyone to ignore and 'well-meaning friends' seemed only too happy to filter information through to him. Of course she had denied some of it, but she knew that he had already been forced to accept that some of the worst things were true.

He had stood by her and, the way things were at the moment, she couldn't imagine what she would do without him. She began to feel anxious for him; what if there was a maniac outside?

No, she told herself firmly. Calm down. It's a pap. That's all, just another bloody pap. She pulled off her silk nightdress and slipped into the massive bath, filled with lovely Czech & Speake bubbles. They were the old lady's, but Zelda didn't think she'd mind now.

She lay back and closed her eyes.

*

Jake heard her yelling from the end of the garden. He sprinted back, across the lawn and upstairs, just as Ed and Dusty were converging on the bathroom.

'Hang on, you two, let me just see what's up.' Jake rushed in. Zelda was standing in the bath, her perfect body covered with bubbles. She was pointing at the shelf above the bath, where there was a letter propped up. It said:

*I know where you live.*

Jake tried to think.

'OK, OK, darling, let's get you out of the bath.' He wrapped her in a towel.

Ed came in. 'What's going on?'

'Mum's just had a bit of a shock.' Jake was trying to buy time, but he wondered what the fuck *was* going on. The country was supposed to be quiet. A haven! So far it had been non-stop trauma, for Zelda anyway.

'You see, I told you! He was in the house, in here! He moved the letter, he must have been up here while we were looking for it in the kitchen.' Zelda was shaking slightly.

'Let's just try to think about this calmly for a minute. This could still be the sort of thing a pap would do.' But he didn't sound convinced. Zelda certainly wasn't.

Ed said, 'It's probably a maniac.'

'Oh, thanks for that, Ed.' Jake wrapped Zelda more tightly in the towel and led her into the bedroom, where Dusty was waiting anxiously.

'Dusty, can you stay with Zelda while she gets dressed. I'll go and call that nice policeman. I'll ring Boy too, just in case they

have had problems with a phantom letter-writer in the past.'
Jake was thinking out loud. 'OK, darling? I'll just be a minute
or two. Dusty is going to stay with you.' Jake touched her
shoulder kindly and left the room with Ed in hot pursuit.

Zelda sat on the edge of the bed, quietly taking a few deep
breaths.

Dusty perched tentatively next to her aunt. She was quite
nervous around Zelda, who had always made it clear that she
only had Willow and Dusty living with them under sufferance,
because they had nowhere else to go.

But she did look rather vulnerable, semi-naked and
alarmed. Dusty felt a little pang of pity for her. She wasn't quite
sure what had happened but whatever it was must be serious
because Zelda did not scare easily.

Dusty reached out and rubbed her back, asking gently,
'Shall I find you some clothes to wear?'

'I don't know. Yes, clothes.' She closed her eyes. 'Something
black, something so that I won't look like me.'

Dusty stood up. 'A burka perhaps?'

Zelda laughed weakly. 'Not such a bad idea! But I think it's
been done.' She was rallying. 'Don't worry, I'll find something.
Could you just look in the cupboards with me, to make sure the
bastard isn't hiding in there.'

When they were satisfied that there was no one hiding
anywhere in the bedroom Zelda got dressed and went downstairs.

Jake had rung the police. 'Just to keep them up to speed,'
he'd said.

He didn't want to alarm anyone but paps didn't usually pull that sort of stunt. Both he and Zelda knew that; they just didn't want to admit it.

# CHAPTER EIGHT

Sergeant Peter Powell was sympathetic and kindly towards Zelda when he arrived at the scene later that morning.

'I can see that you have had a most upsetting and frightening time, Miss Spender,' he said.

Although he didn't think for a moment she had anything to worry about; he could see that she was a 'hysterical female'. In his experience he found that most famous people were prone to hysteria. He had once been called out to Arnold Schwarzenegger's hotel, about a wasp.

So he knew that he would need to humour her, make her feel like he was taking her seriously. He had his own ideas about the poltergeist-type letter that had, allegedly, 'moved around' the house. There were teenagers at home, he noted, and although he certainly didn't subscribe to the popular theory that teenagers made paranormal activity more prevalent, he did know that they loved a prank.

Zelda Spender, teenagers and the moving note had 'prank'

written all over it, as far as Sergeant Powell was concerned. He placed the letter in with his paperwork.

'I intend to find the perpetrator of this misdemeanour and I shall make sure that you are not bothered by anyone else from now on,' he told them.

Zelda asked, reasonably, 'But what are you going to do, Officer?'

Sergeant Powell touched his nose in a gesture familiar to Jake, who had seen him do it when he was teasing Boy Banbury about being beaten up. Jake wasn't altogether sure that the police officer was taking this seriously enough.

'I shall put you under twenty-four-hour surveillance with immediate effect,' the policeman replied.

Jake was surprised. 'Are you sure you can spare the man-power?'

'Don't you worry about that, that will be my problem. As I say, we are the experts on this and we shall make sure you are properly protected while in our area.' The sergeant looked pleased with himself.

Jake was sceptical but he didn't think he could argue with the policeman at this point. He'd said he would put them under twenty-four-hour surveillance, so they couldn't ask for more.

Sergeant Powell made for the door, saying over his shoulder, 'You won't notice us of course, totally undercover, but anything out of the ordinary at all and I will report back to you. You can relax safe in the knowledge that we have everything under control.'

As the policeman drove away, he passed one of the Banbury daughters on the drive. She was throwing sticks for a huge dog. A pretty girl, if she didn't have that spiky hair, he thought. He waved, but she didn't wave back. Perhaps she hadn't seen him.

He would have one of the tech guys come out later and rig a surveillance camera on the gates to the Dower House. He knew that he might have given the Spenders the impression that the surveillance would consist of police officers on round-the-clock watch. But he hadn't actually said as much. He knew that was what they needed to think, but what *he* needed was: a) a way of giving them peace of mind; b) to keep the peace; and c) – most importantly – to keep the costs to the force as negligible as possible.

He congratulated himself on his skilful handling of a para-noid celebrity. He was pleased with his cunning plan.

*

Zelda had rallied quite quickly, since she was used to being pursued and persecuted; one way or another it had been happening to her all her life. She had developed coping mech-anisms, through necessity, from an early age. Her mother's mantra was 'Spender women do not scare easily', which was almost true.

So Zelda's thoughts turned to the familiar, and comfortingly distracting, subject of clothes. She had begun to think about what to wear to Banbury Court for supper that evening.

Even though she knew it was probably going to be a grim ordeal, it didn't mean that she had to look awful too. She had been through her bags more thoroughly and couldn't find anything that would remotely fit the bill. She was reminded that their hasty departure from London had seriously limited her wardrobe choices. She knew she needed Shona, and she needed her fast. She wondered if the woman had managed to get her some freebies? She always could.

She texted her pal again. 'Could you be an angel and get some samples for me from Dolce and Roberto and get to Oxfordshire with them by this evening? I've got nothing to wear! Are you coming to stay?'

Zelda vaguely wondered why Shona hadn't responded to her previous text. In fact, she realised, she hadn't heard from her for a few days, which was odd. Shona had been her most reliable friend for ten years. She thought perhaps the text had gone astray? Since discovering there was no Internet connection at the Dower House she had serious doubts about all telecommunications. To get a phone signal she often had to walk halfway up the garden; nightmare!

She went outside to put in another call to her new agent's office, only to be told by Helen's PA, when she eventually got through, 'Miss Baldwin is in LA at the moment, can anyone else help?'

Zelda was impatient. 'No, I'll try her mobile.'

'She may not be available yet, the time dif—'

'I am aware of the LA time difference, thank you. I have spent half my life working over there!' She hung up. God, those people could be annoying and patronising. She couldn't believe how quickly people had gone from deferential to dismissive.

She tried Helen's mobile anyway, but it went straight to voicemail. She didn't leave a message.

She stomped back into the kitchen. She had no one to talk to and nothing to do. Karen had delivered the papers, so she made herself a cup of coffee and went through them apprehensively. She was surprised to find there wasn't anything about her at all. Perhaps Helen was right, moving out of sight might really prove to be out of mind to the press.

She came across a piece about her mother in the *Mail*. The headline said: CLEO TO TAKE ON THE NORTHWEST PASSAGE!

The article went on:

*Anyone might think that conquering Everest in her senior years would satisfy Cleo Spender's thirst for adventure. But it was announced today, by the production company responsible for the Everest show, that Cleo Spender and a small crew would be attempting to cross miles of deadly ice-strewn waters, through the Northwest Passage, the only route to the North Pole from Canada, in a small inflatable boat.*

*In a statement, Cleo Spender said she was 'determined to undertake this challenge in order to draw attention to the dramatically declining glaciers, due to global warming, a subject that is very close to my heart'.*

Zelda was gobsmacked. So this was what her mother was talking about. Dangerous! It sounded like suicide. Her mother really would do anything for publicity. Global warming? Close to her heart? Ha bloody ha! Zelda knew her mother didn't have a heart, just a huge, massive ego that was endlessly voracious in its desire for attention and accolades. Zelda had to hand it to her mother, this would certainly feed the beast.

It also triggered the uncomfortable question of why *she* couldn't get an offer of work. Not that she would ever do anything so mindlessly stupid and obviously attention-seeking as her mother's foolhardy shows. But there must be something out there. She felt devastated by the unfairness of everything. After all, she had only blotted her copybook a bit; she didn't think she had behaved any worse than anyone else she knew.

Her only mistake was to get caught. Hiring that vindictive little bitch of a PA had been one of the worst mistakes of her life.

She tried to calm down, telling herself that she only had to stay out of the limelight while the dust settled. Helen Baldwin was bound to come up with something soon, as she was meant to be the best agent in the world. Zelda knew she just had to be patient.

She tore the article about her mother out of the paper, furiously shredded it and threw it into the rubbish bin, slamming the lid with a 'Huh!'

Her phone pinged. It was so unexpected that she gave a little jump. It was a text from her mother. 'Dad and I would love to come down. We'll be there tomorrow evening. Send the postcode for me to give to our driver. Don't read today's *Mail*, I want to tell you my news myself!'

Zelda groaned and slumped into a kitchen chair. There was a knock on the front door. Forgetting her fright for a moment she went to open it, to be greeted by Frank.

'Just thought I'd pop in and check that everything was alright? Boy mentioned you'd had a problem with an intruder.'

Zelda opened the door wide. 'Oh, hi, yes. Come in.'

She followed Frank into the kitchen. He was wearing a checked cowboy shirt and combats, belted with a plaited thong. His worn leather boots, with various buckles, rattled as he walked. His hair was cropped short, accentuating his strong brown neck. He was slim and obviously very fit. Zelda guessed he must be about thirty.

She also noted that he was quite at ease with women, even one as famous as her. Usually, when she met someone new, they were weird for ages, unable to see her at all, as her fame always stood in the way; it blinded them and turned most people into grovelling, obsequious nincompoops or monosyllabic fools.

This one was different. He behaved quite normally in fact, even looked her directly in the eye when he spoke, which she wasn't used to at all. It somehow made her feel wrong-footed.

She offered him a cup of coffee.

'Thanks. Just black.' He leant against the worktop and watched Zelda as she faffed about filling the kettle and trying to find things in the unfamiliar kitchen.

He reached across her to open an overhead cupboard. 'I think you'll find the cups are here' he said, and his chest briefly touched her shoulder. She could feel his firm, warm body though his soft shirt.

She felt him hesitate, before he stepped away.

There was a beat, before he continued, 'I've been checking

the boundaries of the estate, to see where the weaknesses are, the obvious entry spots. If we do have a problem with trespassers, it's as well to know where they are getting through. Sadly the fencing and walls aren't what they were. I found a few places where I think someone could have got in. I've told Boy, and he says he'll let Sergeant Powell know, so that he can keep an eye out. I understand he is planning put the Dower House under surveillance?'

Zelda handed him a cup of very strong instant coffee, without catching his eye. She shivered at the thought of the intruder. Rubbing her bare, lightly tanned arms, she said uncertainly, 'I hope so.'

Frank took the cup and sniffed it. Trying not to grimace he said, 'Thanks. Can't say I noticed any evidence of officers out there yet, but perhaps they were disguised as trees!' He smirked and Zelda knew he was referring to the tree-felling, trousers-down debacle.

So she also knew that he had seen her bottom. She couldn't help being relieved that she had been wearing her favourite Agent Provocateur pants that day. She was mortified to find herself blushing slightly, not something she had experienced since she was about twelve.

Jake wandered in. 'Hi, Frank, coffee? Oh, good, you've already got one. Zelda make it for you? Bad luck!' He smiled cheerfully and pushed the button on the kettle, to make his own.

# CHAPTER NINE

Dusty and Ed crept along the edge of the drive, keeping low under the trees. They scampered out of the gate and turned right, racing off up the fields, towards the Court.

They didn't notice the unmarked van, parked up to the left, or the engineer who had just finished fitting the small surveillance device on the Dower House gatepost.

*

When the engineer reported back to Sergeant Powell, he told his boss that he had seen a couple of teenagers, a boy and girl, behaving suspiciously, sneaking about. Which confirmed the sergeant's earlier conclusion that the culprits were indeed the family's children.

Terrorising grown-ups was often the only thing kids had to do in the country. He certainly knew all about that. Another mystery solved by Sergeant Peter Powell. He gave a satisfied sigh as he sat at his desk and tucked into a couple of Jammie Dodgers. He was glad he hadn't put the force out too much for the fantasy fear of a feeble-minded actress.

He felt that he had already exceeded his duty by fitting the surveillance camera. He didn't think the Spenders would be having any more trouble and if they did, he knew exactly how to nip it in the bud. The local youths knew better than to cross him. He had an old-fashioned, hands-on approach to his police work, and it had always served him well.

*

Dusty and Ed were both panting hard when they got to the final cattle grid, which led from the park into the main entrance of Banbury Court. They tiptoed over the metal bars that kept the sheep and cattle from the extensive gardens, and proceeded to walk up the drive.

They weren't sure about going closer to the house or indeed sure of what they were doing. But they wanted to have a quick snoop, to see what the house was like. That was what Dusty wanted to do anyway. Ed was hoping to run into Flora again, but he didn't want to admit that to his cousin.

Just as they began to lose their nerve and turned round to go back, there was a sudden roar from an engine and a crunch of gears. Then a muddy old Land Rover thundered over the cattle grid.

It scrunched to a halt and a young woman stormed out. 'What the hell do you think you're doing? I almost hit you!' Her spiky short dark hair and kohl-smudged eyes made a dramatic first impression on Dusty and Ed. Her clothes were extremely eccentric: a sequinned chainmail vest over a torn chiffon shirt, skinny jeans and strange embroidered leather boots. She appeared quite intimidating and terrifying as she strode towards them. 'Well?'

'Sorry! Um, I'm Dusty and this is Ed, my cousin,' Dusty jabbered, mortified, and very pink-cheeked. 'We just came up to say hello. We are staying at the Dower House.'

'Hmph! Might've guessed! You're a bit early for supper.'

'Oh no, we were just coming to see if anyone wanted ... any help!' Ed was good at thinking on his feet, particularly when confronted by fearsome, angry women. He had been brought up by one and had learnt to improvise and appease in times of crisis.

Doone was sceptical but decided to call his bluff. 'OK, that would be great. Jump in, you can help me unload the supplies.'

They all piled into the front seat of the Land Rover. Ed was pleased; they were in.

Doone sped off and moments later the battered old vehicle pulled up with a jolt outside the imposing back entrance to the house. Dusty and Ed grabbed some stuff and followed Doone into Banbury Court. Huge heavy doors opened onto a dark hall, with long passages running from it in every direction. The walls were covered in old hunting prints, some photographs of men in vintage racing cars and, Dusty was curious to note, one enormous picture of Audrey Hepburn, signed 'to my favourite Guy x Audrey'.

Muddy wellingtons and trainers were scattered all over the floor.

With arms weighed down with bags, Doone shot off down

one of the passages, while Ed struggled under the bulk of a huge box of wine.

She looked back over her shoulder and her silvery eyes flashed eerily in the gloom. 'Follow me and don't drop those bottles or it will be a *very* dry night.'

'Shall I get the others from the car?' Ed puffed.

'Let me show you where it goes, then you can bring in the rest,' She disappeared round a corner, with a mumbled after-thought: 'Thanks.'

They soon found themselves in the vast kitchen. It reminded Ed of their old house, or a very shabby version of the Great Hall there, the room that had everything: the huge fireplace, sofas and chairs everywhere. He felt a stab of homesickness. Putting the box down on the table he rushed off to get more things from the car and to gather himself together.

As he walked swiftly back down the passage he almost bumped into Flora, who said, 'Oops! Oh! Hi! Is Doone back?'

'Is she the scary one with spiky hair?' Ed asked.

'Yep, that's her. Sorry, was she rude?' Flora wrinkled her studded nose charmingly.

'Not really, she was just generally scary, the clothes and everything.'

'Oh, yeah, I know. She's going through her warrior phase, or that's what Dad says. I think she just misses our mum, but then we all do.'

'So, like, where is your mum?'

'She's ...' she began.

Then Kitty appeared suddenly. 'Doone says we have to bring everything in now or it will melt.'

'No! Not ice cream again? I thought she said she was cooking? She wouldn't let me!' Flora was indignant.

'No one would let you cook, Flora. You know what happened last time.' Kitty laughed.

Flora glanced at Ed and said, 'Nothing happened, I'm a good cook. They just have no taste.'

'We wished we hadn't any tastebuds when you cooked that spicy chicken – whoa!' was Kitty's parting shot.

When Ed finally got back to the kitchen with the last box, Flora asked him if he'd like a drink. He was surprised when she waved a bottle of vodka at him. But before she could pour him anything, Boy arrived, followed by Dusty. They were carrying the last of the bags.

'Hi, Ed. Thanks for helping.' Boy spied the vodka in Flora's hand. 'Great, vodka! Well done Doone and her student loan.'

'You have to bloody well pay me back,' Doone said, as she emerged from the old walk-in larder. 'Entertaining *your* friends has cost me a fortune.'

She didn't appear to be remotely fazed that some of those 'friends' were standing in front of her.

'Your friends are coming too, aren't they?' A tiny note of panic sounded in Flora's voice. Doone gave her sister a cautionary don't-say-who stare.

'Of course I'll pay you back, darling, just can't find my wallet or any of my cards, has anyone noticed it lying around anywhere? A reward is on offer to the person who recovers it!' Boy said cheerfully.

'And what reward would that be?' asked Doone.

'No washing up for a week.'

'No one does any washing up anyway.'

'OK. No washing up for a year.'

Doone rolled her eyes. 'You are a ridiculous man.'

'We'd better get going,' Dusty laughed. 'Come on, Ed. Willow will be awake and we can't leave her for long with you-know-who in charge.'

Doone raised a knowing eyebrow at her father.

As they set off to walk back down to The Dower House, Ed found himself wondering whether he had any black clothes. He really needed to make an impression on Flora and black was obviously her thing. But he glumly remembered that he didn't possess a single article of clothing in black. A feeling of hopelessness suddenly, uncharacteristically, overwhelmed him. Why didn't he own any fucking black stuff? All he had was a bagful of slightly grubby Abercrombie & Fitch, in sludgy colours. He knew his chances with Flora were doomed unless he could find something to wear that night. He had never, ever given a moment's thought to his clothes before, and now he was in a panic.

\*

Flora had been trying on things endlessly and still had nothing to wear. She felt so much pressure. She needed to impress the band. There was nothing for it, she would have to raid her mother's dressing room. It was out of bounds, she knew that, but desperate times . . .

When Boy found his daughter rummaging amongst his wife's clothes he found it hard to be cross. She was wearing a vintage Thea Porter dress, black chiffon embroidered with silver, which had belonged to her grandmother originally. Boy remembered Frances wearing it often. He had a sudden memory of her drifting across the lawn towards him, slightly stoned . . .

Flora looked contrite. 'Sorry, Dad, Mum won't mind, will she? I just can't find anything for tonight and . . .'

Boy looked at his daughter lovingly. 'I think she would love you to wear her things, darling, and you look wonderful in that dress. Just right, I'd say. Gorgeous, in fact, so let's get ourselves together and get this *parday started*!'

Flora rolled her eyes.

# CHAPTER TEN

When Karen arrived at the Dower House to babysit, the atmosphere was fraught.

Jake was yelling, 'Everybody, hurry the fuck up!' up the stairs, but to no avail.

Dusty was the only person downstairs with Jake, who said kindly, 'Dusty, darling, you look absolutely beautiful.'

Karen agreed, although she found it hard to believe that Georgia Cole's daughter really was only fourteen. She was small and slight, but now that she was wearing very high platforms, with her blonde hair loosely tied and interwoven with beads and flowers, she looked like a model of at least eighteen, very different from the young girls Karen knew from the village, who were mostly a bit plump, though not dissimilar to Dusty with their responsibilities for looking after young babies. Although the girls she knew were at least a couple of years older than Dusty and the babies were their own.

She wondered where, or indeed who, Willow's father was.

Ed arrived downstairs, wearing a black T-shirt of Zelda's.

Jake noticed that his son was wearing mascara. But he tactfully decided not to embarrass him by asking him about it in front of Karen and Dusty.

'Ed, mate, got a minute?' he asked, drawing his son out of earshot.

'What?'

'Are you wearing make-up?'

'No!'

'Well, someone must have thumped you then, because you've got two black eyes.'

'Fuck off, Dad!'

Dusty turned to Karen and said, like a proud parent, 'Willow is asleep and she never wakes at night.'

'Don't worry, she'll be fine with me,' Karen replied. 'If she does wake, I'll tell her some jokes, that usually sends people off!'

Dusty grinned. 'Aw!'

'You'll have a good time up at the big house tonight,' Karen said. 'I haven't seen the family buzzing around like that for a long time. Frank is up there helping. Everyone's excited, even Doone! So you go and enjoy yourself. Willow will be safe with me.'

Be your age for once and have some fun, she thought, while you still can.

*

Boy carried a tray of drinks outside. Placing them on a mossy, chipped marble table, he surveyed the scene.

James Wyatt had designed the grand and graceful terrace to

catch the last of the evening's sun, on the west lawn. A vista of ancient trees bordered a mown path, which ran through long summer grass down to the lake. It was Boy's favourite view. He'd always felt that it was one of the most romantic aspects at Banbury.

Flora had taken cushions from the drawing room and placed them, after much consideration, on a vast stone bench. Then she had scattered some more on all the old Lloyd-Loom chairs, which Frank had brought outside for the party. Monumental stone pots were overflowing with white roses, which wafted their evocative scent across the warm summer evening.

Boy sighed and helped himself to a drink.

When Flora came down she found him sitting, gazing pensively out towards to the lake. She knew her father was a very handsome man, but tonight he was wearing one of his father's old Deborah&Clare flowery shirts, which he always wore for special occasions. He loved them, but Flora thought they made him look a bit of a hippy, which she didn't think was cool at all.

'What do you think, Dad?' She indicated her decorative contribution to the evening with a sweep of her hand.

'Perfect! Divine decadence, darling.' He smiled at Flora. They often liked to speak to each other in movie sound bites. He could see that she was wearing a lot more eye shadow and mascara than usual; divine decadence indeed. He was still mystified about the age girls were supposed to be before they wore make-up, or got piercings or tattoos for that matter. Flora had returned from school after her GCSEs with her Goth additions and, although they suited her, he knew he should have somehow stopped her having them done. That was mother territory he felt, sadly, only too aware that it was too late for many things to be undone now.

Kitty appeared. She was wearing dungarees, a gold cardigan, a feather boa . . . and lipstick.

'Darling, you look fabulous. But lose the lipstick.' He certainly knew *she* was far too young at eleven for make-up.

Kitty huffed off again.

Doone emerged and stood next to Flora for a moment. Both looked spectacular. Doone wore a fitted red Coco dress, slit high to reveal her long, tanned legs, and Flora was sensational in the black dress studded with silver. Her hair was swept up in an abandoned fashion, and it appeared to be held together by one huge nail.

Boy raised his glass. 'Here's looking at you, kids.' Flora smiled.

When Kitty re-emerged, with slightly smudgy orange lips, he found himself wondering how his girls had managed to survive, let alone keep themselves together, to the extent that they had. As they began helping themselves to drinks, he could hear they were excitedly arguing over who should sit next to Charlie and the other members of his band.

Boy felt quite moved by the sight of his beautiful family, done up in such finery. He was struck by the extraordinary contrast in his daughter's looks and characters. Their personalities mirrored their colouring in some strange way; Flora, his pale-skinned, dreamy Goth-girl and Kitty, so fair and easy-going. Doone most resembled her mother Frances, dark and furious but also . . .

His reverie was interrupted; the band had arrived. Frank showed them out onto the terrace with their entourage. Suddenly, there seemed to be a large crowd of people milling about, introducing themselves to each other.

Charlie appeared to be very relaxed and unselfconscious, for someone quite so newly, madly famous. He helped Doone hand round some drinks, then settled down to talk to Boy, much to Doone's annoyance, so she went and chatted to one of Charlie's guests, a trendy old man with a mass of spiked dark hair, who was wearing black skinny jeans while his hands were covered in diamond-encrusted skull rings.

Flora had noticed him arrive, but she'd had no idea *he* was coming. She couldn't believe bloody Doone hadn't mentioned it.

Johnny Toogood, a.k.a. the Bastard, was only the lead singer in her favourite band of *all time*. She could hardly breathe. Particularly when, a few minutes after they had arrived, his supermodel girlfriend had emerged from the house. Flora listened as he introduced her to Doone: 'Oh, hey, this is Lily, Lily – Doone.'

Lily smiled in an absent, fey way and wafted off across the terrace. She looked even more beautiful in the flesh, in a see-through golden gossamer dress, than in any of her pictures, which was saying something.

Flora thought she might just die of excitement. She turned to her father and said, 'Here's Johnny!' Boy wasn't sure if they were still doing the movie sound bites thing.

He tried, 'You talkin' to me?'

As Flora moved off, she answered, vaguely, 'I'll be back.'

She wanted to slip away to check how she looked but as she sidled across the terrace Johnny suddenly stepped in front of her. 'Hey, I like the nail! Where'd you get it?'

Flora paled visibly, which was quite remarkable, as she was the palest girl in the world already. She mumbled, 'Oh, um. I got it from the old workshop here, actually.' She couldn't believe she had said 'actually', ugh! So embarrassingly uncool and Sloaney.

'Wow, do you think there are any more of them? I fuckin' love that – mental!'

Which Flora took as the praise it was intended to be. She smiled happily and before she knew it, she was animatedly talking to Johnny the Bastard as if they were old friends.

Doone was trying not to panic. Charlie had told her that his group would be about ten people, but she had already counted fifteen and more seemed to be arriving. She scampered into the kitchen to raid the larder for extra packets of pasta. Much to her relief she found Frank calmly making more salad.

'Don't worry. I've laid more places in the dining room. No more than thirty-two people and you will fit round the table. I'll do a final count when the Spenders arrive. You go on outside. I'll do this.' He smiled at Doone. 'Go on, out!'

Doone ran her hands through her hair, ruffling it nervously. Then she grinned at Frank, and said, uncharacteristically, 'Frank, you are the *best* person in the world!'

'Ah, yes. That I am! Now go!'

Doone strode back through the house, heading off the quick way, via the marble hall. She heard Zelda Spender's voice before she saw her, those instantly recognisable, clear-cut tones echoing through that vast empty space. 'Fuck, it's freezing in this mausoleum!'

Doone greeted their little group. 'Hi, come outside, it's warmer out there.' She turned to Zelda politely. 'I'm Doone, by the way. We haven't met, hello.'

'Really, is it warmer outside? I haven't brought a coat and I don't want to freeze to death.'

Much as Doone suspected, she was a rude woman. 'Don't worry, we can always lend you an old Barbour or something.'

Zelda had no clue what a Barbour might be. She knew it wouldn't be a hairdresser though, sadly, because that was something she needed even more than a coat.

Doone had to concede that Zelda looked magnificent, done up and glittering in all her superstar glory. She was wearing a tight black McQueen dress with very high red heels. Her make-up was flawless and she had donned a massive diamond cross. The effect was more devilish than devout. Doone speculated that the Spender family couldn't be *that* broke if Zelda was still dripping in diamonds.

She led them outside, onto the terrace. The sun was slipping down low behind the trees and, in the warm glow of that golden summer light, the party looked like parties at Banbury always had, for generations: glamorous, relaxed and still somehow rather grand. No one could have guessed how truly frayed around the edges the whole place was.

The light was in Dusty's eyes and so it took her a moment or two to adjust before she took in the group that was scattered about on the terrace that evening. She knew of the band but they'd never met, which was unusual because she had met most contemporary bands with her mother, who had always taken a particular interest in any 'new boys'.

Flora said, 'Hello', and was just asking her what she wanted to drink, when Dusty suddenly saw Johnny, her ex-almost-stepfather! She rushed across the terrace and flung her arms around his neck, exclaiming, 'What are *you* doing here?'

'Might say the same about you! We're staying with Charlie.'

Dusty's heart sank at the ominous 'we', and she looked around until she found who she was looking for; it didn't take long for her to pick out the trademark tousled-blonde head of Britain's most beloved supermodel, Lily.

Lily: the girl who had taken Johnny from her mother, Georgia, and, in Dusty's eyes, had broken her mother's heart.

She turned back to Johnny. 'Really! Still with *her*?'

'Don't be like that, Dust. We're OK, aren't we?'

Dusty refused to reply. Her lips were pursed with disapproval.

He asked gently, 'Where are you staying?'

'It's a secret, we're in hiding,' she snapped.

'Country bumpkins? That'll suit Zelda!' he smiled, but to no avail, so he changed tack. 'Seriously, Dusty, you OK? Sorry I haven't been in touch much since ... but the tour and everything ...' He trailed off as he saw Zelda approaching.

'Johnny! Still following us around, I see ... and still with *that* girl. I'm surprised. Thought Kate's book might have put you off her a bit, seeing what a little slag it showed her to be.'

Johnny, famously one of the nicest men in the music business, wasn't having that. 'Like you can talk,' he retaliated.

Boy overheard their exchange and intervened diplomatically, insinuating himself between them and saying casually, 'Zelda, hi! I just want to introduce you to someone if you wouldn't mind ... he is dying to meet you, a *massive* fan apparently.' He somehow managed to make this sound unlikely.

He felt Zelda hesitate, glancing antagonistically at Johnny the Bastard.

Things had been going so well, the last thing they needed was a row before dinner had even begun. Boy grasped her gently by her slim upper arm and when she resisted, his grip became a little firmer. 'Come on, you'll like him – he's young, and quite hot, so I'm told.'

Doone overheard her father and was incandescent. What the hell did he think he was doing?

She watched beadily as Zelda was introduced to Charlie. The Charlie she knew was very, very cool indeed, so she couldn't help being alarmed to see that when confronted with Zelda Spender he became a bit of a jibbering idiot. What the hell did men see in that awful woman?

Jake came up to her. 'Hi, we haven't really met properly. I'm Jake. You must be Doone? Last time I saw you we played tag on the lawn, but you were only about six, so you probably don't remember.'

'No, I don't,' Doone responded, more harshly than she'd intended. Which she instantly regretted. Zelda's husband had a nice face, very good-looking for an old guy. She thought he must be at least forty; but he was slim, with kind eyes. Stubble on his chin, but not designer stubble, she thought, more 'I don't really give a shit' stubble. She liked the look of him. Poor man, married to that creature.

She watched as Charlie giggled with Zelda, his long curly hair bouncing with delight. She couldn't stand it another minute; she'd have to go inside.

'Will you excuse me? I need to check on dinner. I think we are all here now so ...' She looked apologetically at Jake.

'Let me know if you need any help.' He had seen how the land lay; Doone was clearly smitten by Charlie the pop star. Jake thought he should move Zelda on a bit or the poor girl might spontaneously combust. He wandered over to introduce himself to Charlie just as Boy was offering him another drink.

'And you haven't got anything. What can I get you, Jake?'

'Oh, don't worry, I'm fine.'

'Moscow Mule? Wine?'

'No. No thanks, Boy. I'm not drinking.'

'Why not, it's a party, you are always drinking!'

'Not any more.'

'Really? Shit!'

Zelda had overheard them, and turned away from her new admirer. 'Yes, he has stopped drinking. So no leading him astray please, Boy.'

'Of course not.' He was affronted. 'I just didn't know.'

'Well, you know now.' Zelda stalked off to chat to a particularly handsome member of Charlie's group, who was animatedly talking to Lily.

'Hi, I'm Zelda.' She held out her hand, while giving a hostile coldshoulder to the supermodel. Lily stood her ground. Despite her fragile beauty, she was tougher than she looked.

'Oh, right,' he said. 'Yeah, course. Hi, Zelda. How are you? I'm Aaron. This is, um, Lily.'

'Yes, yes, we know each other.' Zelda didn't even glance in her direction. 'Aaron, I loved your last album. I know you write all the good stuff, really brilliant. I was listening to it only yesterday, when I was attacked by a maniac, as I ran around that lake down there!' She waved her elegant arm across Lily's face, so that the girl had to duck out of the way, to avoid getting her teeth knocked out.

Lily gave up and wandered off to talk to Ed.

Zelda was triumphant. She had got rid of Lily and captured the lovely Aaron's attention. She usually found that a compliment and a dramatic anecdote, all in one sentence, would do it.

Unfortunately for her, Boy had overheard her. 'Well you weren't actually attacked though, were you? In fact, you were saved. If anyone was attacked, it was me.'

Aaron could instantly see that there might be truth in this, as Boy had a cut on his cheek and the beginnings of a black eye.

Zelda looked livid. 'I'm covered in bruises too. You just can't see mine!'

With a hint of a supercilious smile on his face, Boy said,

evenly, 'Well, I've seen plenty of you. Remind me, which bit is it that's bruised? I just have an image of you in my head that I can't quite shift, and that bit of your anatomy isn't bruised at all. Though I can't help feeling your manners might be improved if it were –' Boy looked her directly in the eye – 'only slightly, of course.'

Boy turned and walked away before Zelda could respond. She couldn't believe he had just implied that she needed to be spanked, what a bastard! But she shouldn't be surprised; he was obviously very violent towards women. She turned to Aaron and lifted her dress to show him a tiny bruise on her perfect thigh.

Kitty came out, rang an unnecessarily loud bell and yelled, 'Dinner!'

They all trooped inside.

*

The dining room looked spectacular in the dusk. The huge table was decorated with roses from the garden, their pale pinks, lilacs and creams were scattered across the acres of white linen cloth, cunningly disguising the cigarette burns and stains that liberally marked it, after fifty years of practical service. Flora had spent most of the afternoon arranging the flowers 'just so' and she was pleased with the effect. Vast candelabra (silver plate – the real ones had been sold long ago) dripped with dozens of candles and the warm light made everyone look their best.

It wasn't really the kitchen supper Doone had had in mind, but even she had to admit everything looked wonderful.

Frank helped her to carry in the huge bowls of pasta. Spaghetti, fusilli and penne had all been called upon to stretch rations to the max. Frank produced a vat of bolognese sauce and another of pesto. 'Is this for the veggies?' Boy had asked Doone earlier, slightly mystified as to why they had to have choices.

Everyone was having a great time enjoying the simplicity, and unpretentiousness of the evening. They were all happy with 'nursery food' and, as the evening wore on, they began to behave more and more like out-of-control children.

Jake had read somewhere that the age people are when they first become famous is the emotional age that they stay at forever; which meant that Zelda would be seventeen and Johnny the Bastard about eighteen, which figured. He looked around the table; that must make Lily, what, fourteen? He couldn't quite remember how old was she when she did that infamous and iconic shoot. Could that be ten years ago or twelve? It was an interesting theory, he thought he might share it . . . until he realised that his own first little brush with fame was when he was twenty-two. He sighed. Was he still that age emotionally? Probably!

He certainly wished that he could be quaffing wine, like Doone and Charlie on the other side of the table. Having placed herself next to her new friend, Doone was earnestly discussing Leonard Cohen with him.

This dinner was the first proper social thing Jake had done since swearing off the booze and as people got progressively merrier he found himself feeling more and more isolated. It didn't help that Zelda was flirting with anything with a pulse. She was also telling anyone who would listen that she had a stalker, exaggerating the story ever more wildly the drunker she got.

A genial host, Boy dashed backwards and forwards, filling people's glasses with what he had taken to describing as Uni-wine.

Seated between Lily and Zelda, Aaron soon realised he was in the hot seat. He tried gamely to share his attention as equally as possible between the two women. It hadn't gone well and now neither of them was speaking to him, so he had to talk across the table, at a girl whose name he had forgotten, because she didn't interest him at all. She was the girlfriend of the band's tour manager and Aaron couldn't help feeling the dude could do better for himself – particularly given the excess pickings amongst the beautiful girls that always hung around the musicians.

He couldn't have known that their manager chose his girl-friends precisely because they were a bit plain, as that way they weren't nicked off him by members of the band. He had learnt that lesson the hard way, a long time ago, when the lead singer of his most successful act pinched his first wife. He swore then that he'd never make that mistake again.

The people who had smoked spliffs began to demolish the ice cream and, as the party started to get more out of hand, one of the models from Charlie's party was trying to demonstrate her catwalk strut down the middle of the dining-room table, and a few glasses were getting broken. Flora couldn't help noticing that the girl ought to have followed her father's advice about pants.

Seeing the damage that was being done, Doone stood up and asked everyone to follow her. 'We are withdrawing!' she called out gaily.

Boy really hadn't seen his girls having such a great time for ages, and so he was thrilled, until he discovered where they were withdrawing to.

The Banbury girls led the way down to the nightclub.

'Whoa, man this is crazy, where are we going?' Johnny said. 'I really hate cellars. I got locked in my wine cellar in LA for like two days, it was fucking scary.'

Dusty held her ex-almost-stepfather's hand. 'It's OK, just stick with me.'

There were gasps and wows from everyone when they entered the bar. It had been completely transformed. The walls were hung about with fairy lights, there were tea lights in glasses all around the dance floor and scented candles masked the worst of the damp smell.

When Kitty hit the 'play' button on the jukebox the room went wild. Everyone was dancing. Frank enthusiastically dished out drinks from behind the bar.

Boy intercepted his eldest girl as she leant over the bar to grab a bottle of vodka. 'Doone darling, I didn't know we were coming down here tonight. When did you do all this?'

'We've been clearing it up since yesterday. We wanted it to be a surprise. You used to love it so much.' She smiled slightly blearily at her father.

He tried to look enthusiastic. 'Great, well done, you. Terrific, yes, everyone seems to be enjoying it anyway.' He could see that he was talking to himself because Doone had stopped listening; she was watching with naked hatred as Zelda was trying to drag Charlie off for a dance. Boy knew he had to intervene for his daughter's sake. He stepped between them, took Zelda's hand and niftily steered her onto the dance floor.

She pulled her hand away. 'Get off, stop manhandling me!' She twisted away from him and stomped back to the bar, perching herself precariously on an old bar stool, and proceeded to chat to Frank.

That problem averted, Boy then noticed Johnny the Bastard getting cosy with Flora on the banquettes. *That* needed to be intercepted forthwith, since the old goat was ancient enough to be Flora's grandfather and he had his girlfriend, Lily, with him. This rock-and-roll stuff was a nightmare, particularly when combined with the tender hearts of his precious girls.

Kitty turned the music up full blast while Frank disappeared upstairs with a tray full of dirty glasses. Zelda followed him, attempting to say, 'Wait for me, I want to help.' She knew she was quite drunk, but she couldn't stop now that she had started. She had had such a frightening time since she arrived in the country; in fact not just that, everything had been hideous for ages. She needed to let off steam, or that was how she justified her reckless drinking to herself anyway. She needed to talk to Frank, a sensible down-to-earth person, a real man.

Having followed him into the kitchen she was uncertain

how to proceed. He was perfectly nice to her and everything, but she wasn't getting the vibe. She couldn't feel any spark of interest from him, which was very unusual and frustrating. Perhaps she should try a different tack.

'Frank, that was the nicest evening I've had for so long. I'm sure you don't know but my life has been really, really sad lately and . . .' She put her hand to her forehead and squeezed out a tear, but then she found herself crying, for real, because her life actually was really, really sad.

Frank pulled out a kitchen chair and sat her down on it, which wasn't quite the 'hug' situation she was hoping to instigate. Moments later, Ed rushed in and was promptly sick in the log basket.

'Whoa there, fella.' Frank gently took Ed's arm and led him across to the sink, which fortunately had been cleared of pans for the first time in ages.

Ed continued to throw up, somehow managing to say, 'Shorry, shorry.'

Zelda got to her feet. 'Ed, darling, come and have a little lie down over here. Look, here's a lovely sofa.' She led her son across the room, at arm's length. 'There you are, that's better. My poor baby.'

Then she turned to Frank. 'We're all a bit of a mess, you see. Everything is ruined.' And she flung herself onto the sofa next to her son.

Frank gave her a large glass of water and left them to it. After a while Zelda began to feel better and went back down to the party.

Lily was dancing on a table with abandon, and Kitty was copying her every move, which was unnerving to watch. Boy went and grabbed his youngest child, sitting down on the banquettes and pulling her onto his knee. He wanted to send her up to bed but he didn't think she'd go, unless he took her, and he didn't want to leave Flora alone with Johnny.

Aaron was snogging his manager's girlfriend. He was very drunk and decided that he was experimenting with the theory that 'all cats look grey in the dark'. In this particular dark, this cat felt pretty hot. He wondered if they should go upstairs and find a bedroom. He decided that a quick knee-trembler outside against a wall might be safer. After all, it would be rude to get caught in the act, particularly as he liked his manager.

But the girl wasn't going to play ball. In fact, she laughed in his face when he suggested it, saying, 'I'm not one of your sad-arsed little groupies, you'll have to try a lot harder than that to interest me!' Normally he would have just dropped the girl after that, but there was something about this one that really made him want to persist.

She was talking to her boyfriend now, and he could tell the guy wanted to go home. He approached his manager. 'Hey, man. If you want to go, don't worry, we'll look after ...' He couldn't remember her name. 'Yeah, she can come back with us. No bother.' But she just laughed at him again and took her boyfriend's arm, leaving without a backward glance. Aaron was hooked.

Another record struck a chord with the drunken, stoned crowd and they all started jumping about on the dance floor, when suddenly all the lights went out. A loud groan went up as the sound died on the old jukebox. There was hardly any light, just a few little candles.

A voice called out, 'It's OK, don't panic! Just a fuse, it will be fixed in a minute . . . carry on!'

They were all squashed into the bar, sweaty and puffed from all the dancing, when a voice that the Banbury girls didn't recognise echoed down the stairs. It said, 'Fuck, it's dark!' Then there was a loud bumping noise followed by a louder, 'Fuck!'

At that moment the lights abruptly went on again and, just as the music cranked itself back up, England's most beautiful and beloved bad boy shouted out, 'Hi, everybody, I'm *back*!', raising both arms above his head in a victory salute.

Everyone turned to see a dazzling blond man of about twenty; he was even taller and more handsome than anyone remembered. In fact, Kitty thought, he looked just like an angel.

They all shouted, 'Yeay! Valentine, Valentine, yeay!' and jumped about wildly.

Valentine was laughing as his mother and Ed hugged him drunkenly, and Zelda started to cry again. 'My darling, you're here. You're here!' Jake gave him a hug too and said, 'Great to see you, dude. What the fuck are you doing out of hospital? I was going to collect you!'

'I was sick of it, checked myself out this evening, thought I'd surprise you all.' He took a drink from Frank, raising his glass in a small gesture of thanks.

He tapped the cast, which went up his whole leg. 'This

needed to get out! So I sprung myself and got a cab down.' Apart from the leg and a small scar on his left cheek no one could have guessed that Valentine had broken twenty-five bones, in the car crash that had almost killed him. He'd been kept in an enforced coma for the first three weeks after the accident, so that he missed the most painful part of his recuperation. Valentine was a very lucky young man.

He had to speak loudly to be heard above the noise. 'We satnav'd to the Dower House but you weren't home. Luckily, the lovely Karen greeted me and she sent me up here. So how's it going?' He glanced around the room. 'Looking good, fresh country folk, whoo whoo!'

He turned awkwardly on his crutch, to find Lily standing in front of him, rendering him uncharacteristically lost for words. He hadn't expected to see her, least of all here. He'd thought she was still on tour with Johnny.

His heart leapt as she leant forward, without a word, and kissed him full on the lips, for an embarrassing amount of time. Then she took his hand and led him onto the dance floor by the crutch. Once there, she pushed him onto one of the banquettes, where she proceeded to give him a not-very-private lap dance.

Johnny was propping up the bar seemingly impervious to his girlfriend's provocative behaviour.

\*

Jake decided it was time to take Zelda home when he overheard her slurring at Frank, 'I love you, Shfrank – you are a lovely man.' She looked blearily at Jake. 'Isn't Frank a lovely man, Jake? Don't you jusht love him too?'

Jake could see that she had moved on a bit from alcohol. Whatever she had taken, it wasn't pretty. He gave Frank an apologetic look and Frank smiled back sympathetically. No words required.

'Come on, darling, let's go upstairs for a little air, shall we?' He knew from past experience that getting her out would be a slow process, so he took her home in stages. 'It's lovely out here, look at the stars!' Then, 'Shall we go and sit in the car?' Then, 'Oh, look, here we are home again. Isn't that nice.' Ignoring her drunken pleas, 'I wanna go back to the pardy', 'I'm not leaving . . . gonna dance . . . night.' And, 'Why do you always spoil my fun?'

He was glad that he had resisted the urge to have that drink now.

Having poured Zelda into bed and paid Karen his last twenty, which she assured him was 'more than enough', he nipped upstairs to check on Willow. She was fast asleep in her cot, a picture of serenity and innocence, a welcome sight after all the madness up at the Court.

He thought he had better nip back and fetch Ed and possibly Dusty too. Frank had kindly said he'd bring them down later, but whatever Zelda had taken was strong and it occurred to him it might be doing the rounds. Karen had already left, but he knew he could get there and back in no time.

*

Zelda woke with a jolt. The room had stopped spinning, but she could hear something: a weird knocking. She sat up, confused and disoriented. She couldn't think where she was. There it was again, a soft, slow thump, thump, thump against the bedroom door.

She wanted to call out to Jake, but she was too afraid to make a sound. She could see a tiny glimmer of light under the door and a shadow? Was that a shadow? The door was suddenly rattled loudly and Zelda found her voice. 'Jake?'

No response. The shadow was gone.

Zelda crept out of bed and stumbled towards the door. Her eyes were adjusting to the darkness, she looked down at the bolt; it wasn't fastened! She fumbled and finally managed to get it closed.

Then she started calling for Jake again. But he didn't come.

*

It took Jake a while to prise Dusty and Ed away from the nightclub.

Firstly, Boy asked him to keep an eye on Flora while he made sure that Kitty went to bed. Jake could see that his old pal was beginning to look a bit stressed from his efforts at teen damage limitation.

Ed was uncharacteristically intransigent, insisting he wanted to stay until Dusty left. 'She's only a bit older than me, Dad, it's not fair if I have to go and she doesn't.' He felt a bit better having been sick and was now determined to persuade his father to let him stay on.

In the end Dusty saw what was going on and agreed to go home too.

She told Jake she'd 'had enough anyway' because she had. The proximity of Johnny the Bastard and Lily brought up a lot of sad memories of her mother's final months. Then, since Valentine had arrived, she couldn't help noticing that his relationship with Lily was clearly far from over. She suddenly felt very low, as thoughts of her mother crowded in and tumultuous feelings about her dysfunctional family life began to swamp her.

She was relieved to be bundled up by Jake and taken home, like a child. It felt good to be looked after and a novelty for her. Ed hiccupped all the way. His father opened the car windows, 'Just in case.'

The cool, soft summer air blew in and Dusty gazed out at the moonlit parkland. The car's headlamps swept down the drive, picking out the shiny chestnut coat of a horse, which stood majestically in their path. Jake swerved to avoid it and the car bumped across the close-cropped grass. The jiggling motion triggered the first retch from Ed. Jake pulled up sharply and, leaning across his son, he pushed the car door open. Ed was very sick into the field.

Jake was relieved that he had decided to go and fetch them; it was clearly in the nick of time.

When they opened the front door to the Dower House, all was silent and serene. They tiptoed upstairs as quietly as they could, which was not very quietly, because Ed was protesting, 'I'm fine. Don't you worry 'bout me. I'm going back. Because I feel *great* now . . .'

They all heard a loud whimpering sound.

Ed said, 'Whoa, what is that scary noise?' His eyes focused briefly on Dusty. 'Did you hear that? Whoa!'

It was coming from the master bedroom. Not so much whimpering now, more a very loud yell; it was Zelda. 'Jake! Is that you?'

Jake left Ed leaning on Dusty and sprinted up the final few steps.

He tried the door to Zelda's room. It was locked.

'Zelda, open the door.' He knocked. 'It's me, Jake, open the door.'

He heard a shuffling, sniffing noise then the bolt was drawn back. Zelda opened the door. She was naked, her face was ravaged with mascara and tears and her hair was, literally, standing on end. She threw her arms around Jake.

Ed said, 'Ehew, get a room, you sickos.'

Jake held her up. 'OK, let's get you into bed, what's wrong?' He tried to sound sympathetic but she was so pissed he felt a sharp stab of annoyance.

He turned to Dusty. 'Can you help Ed to bed? I'll just see what's been going on here and I'll be along.' Then he gently manoeuvred his deranged wife back into the bedroom.

Zelda tried to compose herself. 'He was here!'

'Who was here?'

'The letter man!'

Jake wrapped a dressing gown around her and sat down next to her on the bed. 'Where?'

'He was rattling my door.'

'Did he say anything? Did you see him?'

'A shadow,' she murmured, then looked at her husband accusingly and demanded, 'Where are the police? They are doing a fucking useless job! Where the hell were you? Didn't you hear me? I was calling to you. Oh, God, he could have killed me! The door wasn't even locked . . .' She started to rant, drunkenly.

Jake put his arm around his wife. 'Tell me exactly what happened?'

'I woke up. There was this horrible banging, sort of thumping on the door. I saw a shadow under, under. He was there.' She gesticulated wildly. 'I had to lock the door. I was so scared. Then I listened and listened until I heard you. Oh, Jake, where were you?'

'I just nipped back to get the kids. So tell me again – you woke up to a horrible noise and you locked the door.'

'The shadow, the shadow!'

'Yes, and you saw a shadow.' He gave her a squeeze. 'Do you think you might have been having a nightmare?'

'No! He was *here* and he wanted to kill me, I know he did! You don't care, do you? You'd be glad, after all I've done. You think I deserve it!' Her voice was rising and in her black-eyed, hair-raised state she looked as deranged as she felt.

Jake tried to placate her. 'Don't be mad, of course I don't want anyone to kill you. Calm down for God's sake, Zelda. You are really pissed and not thinking straight . . .'

'Oh, fuck off, you teetotal twit. I will look after myself if you won't help me. I will call the Sergeant Wassisname myself.' She sniffed indignantly and reached for her mobile. It said 'no signal'. She threw it across the floor and stood up, walking the overly cautious walk of the inebriated.

'Where are you going?' Jake demanded. 'Wait! I will go out and have a look round. You come and get back into bed.'

She straightened her back. 'Don't you bother yourself. I'm going to use the house-phone.'

'There isn't a house-phone. It was disconnected when Lady . . .'

Zelda collapsed against the wall. 'This fucking horrible house! We have to go back to London, now!' She looked pleadingly at her husband.

'We can sort everything out in the morning.' He pulled her up onto her feet and led her back to bed.

She lay back and began shivering. Jake pulled the bedclothes over her and, thinking she did look rather vulnerable, his heart softened.

'Will you sleep in here tonight?' she asked, her voice tiny and terrified.

She seemed to have forgotten about ringing the police and Jake couldn't help thinking that Sergeant Powell would be sceptical about Zelda's intruder. After all, if someone had been in the house and banging on her door, why wouldn't he have opened it? She'd said it wasn't locked. No, he was sure she had just had a nightmare; the drunken terrors – he knew them well.

He checked on Ed. Dusty had already arranged him on his side, in the recovery position, in case he was sick again. There was no sound from Willow.

Jake left a brief note in the hall telling Valentine where he could sleep.

Then he grabbed some pyjama bottoms and slipped quietly into bed next to his comatose wife.

It was the first time they had shared a bed in a while and it felt strangely comforting.

# CHAPTER ELEVEN

Jake could see light through the curtains, which revealed Zelda was still sleeping soundly. There was a loud thump downstairs. He got up, grabbed the golf club he had brought upstairs the night before, just in case Zelda hadn't been drunk-dreaming, and carefully opened the bedroom door.

As he crept downstairs; he could hear a slight knocking sound. He crossed the hall on tiptoes and burst into the kitchen.

Valentine turned to Jake and grinned. 'Oops, sorry! Didn't mean to wake you.'

Jake wasn't particularly surprised to see that Lily was perched on the edge of the kitchen table and that Valentine's plastered hips were clasped firmly between her thighs.

Jake raised the golf club, in a gesture that was something between a salute and a way of shielding his eyes, then he turned on his heel and went back up to bed. Zelda stirred and gently wrapped herself around him. She muttered 'Hello!' as she reached down and stroked him through the cloth of his pyjamas bottoms, which he had worn to try to avoid this inevitable outcome. But to no avail. No matter how furious he was with Zelda, in close enough proximity, he always found her impossible to resist.

So that sunny summer day began in the spirit of reconciliation.

*

Valentine and Lily had not seen each other since she had gone off on the US tour with Johnny and the Bastards, in the tumultuous time before Valentine's accident.

They had spoken briefly when Kate's book had caused a media storm by revealing their affair. Apparently, Johnny was cool with it. Which proved that Lily really was the kind of person who could get away with anything; the press and public adored her, and no matter how badly she behaved, she was always forgiven. She never, ever commented on any of the scandalous stories about her and also, wisely, she never gave interviews. She was the most famous supermodel in the world and she maintained a silent, enigmatic public persona. Perversely, after each scandal her value seemed to skyrocket and all the big brands vied to pay her ever more eye-watering fees for her endorsement of their products.

Valentine seemed to be cut from the same enchanted cloth. His cred was much higher since his accident and Kate's book had done nothing to dispel his glamorous bad-boy image. His agency had been overwhelmed with clients competing to have him front their worldwide advertising campaigns. He had just been booked for a shoot with Lily, for an enormous buyout fee.

He had even been offered a supporting role in a massive new movie, despite his agent informing the producers that they would have to wait until his plaster-cast was off before he could meet them. The press had somehow twisted his image from woeful to wonderful and everyone revered him.

This was something that annoyed his mother more than somewhat. Zelda's own career was on the skids because of Kate's book but Valentine's career had gone stratospheric, despite his truly appalling treatment of women. But what Zelda failed to take into account was that Valentine had garnered a certain amount of sympathy, from the press and public, when Kate's book revealed the scandalous news that Jake was not Valentine's father, as Zelda had always led everyone to believe. In fact, his father was the war correspondent Elliot March, who also happened to be Georgia Cole's ex and Dusty's father too.

This news had provoked a tabloid feeding-frenzy and Zelda was pilloried for her deception. Jake, Valentine and, to some extent, Elliot were pitied despite some pretty dodgy revelations about their own behaviour. But the media liked their heroes and villains to be clear-cut, no bleary edges; you were either bad or good and Zelda had been tagged as 'very bad indeed'.

Zelda felt that she had been judged harshly. After all she hadn't known herself, until just before the story broke, that Valentine wasn't actually Jake's son. She had suspected as much, but until the DNA test she hadn't known for sure. Jake had been remarkably understanding under the circumstances.

Early on in her marriage, Zelda had had a very brief affair with Elliot, during one of the many tricky stages in her relationship with Jake. Nobody had been any the wiser at the time. Now the repercussions had proved rather a nightmare. The moral outrage in the media and amongst the public was huge. Zelda had suffered so much abuse on Twitter she had been forced to quit it.

As far as she was concerned it was just another example of the unfair double standard that had always existed; licentious men were studs, libidinous women were slags. Lily had somehow got away with being an exception to that rule. Zelda was still smarting from the injustice of it all.

It turned out that the film that Valentine had been offered was being directed by an old friend of Zelda's, a friend who had failed to return her calls when she'd rung to ask if there might also be 'a little something in it, for me?'

So, now her son had become another rival to contend with. She was very peeved indeed; the sun seemed to be shining out of her golden boy's arse. He could do no wrong.

He could probably get away with bloody murder, she thought to herself, bitterly.

*

Later that morning, Zelda was looking for something to sort out a dreadful hangover. She wandered into the kitchen wearing her dark glasses and an old satin Agent Provocateur nightdress, looking as fragile as she felt.

Ed was sitting at the kitchen table animatedly talking to Lily.

'Hey, Mum, nice to see you with some clothes on! Look who's here?'

Zelda didn't know what he was talking about ... clothes on?

She muttered, 'I can see, I'm not fucking blind.' Although she did feel almost blind, her head was splitting. She wondered what the hell Lily was doing in her kitchen? Then she remembered that Valentine was home again.

She faux-smiled and said, disingenuously, 'Oh, Lily, I didn't know you and Johnny were staying? How ... *nice*.'

Dusty shuffled in, still in her pyjamas, her hair all tangled. 'Is Johnny here? I want to talk to him.' She leant down to rummage in a cupboard. 'Where are the Raisin Wheats?'

'No, course Johnny's not here, you idiot! And you ate them all yesterday.' Ed was munching handfuls of cornflakes straight from the box. Zelda thought her young son looked rather peaky.

Karen whizzed through the kitchen. 'Or the mice might have had 'em,' she remarked as she disappeared into the utility room.

Lily spoke in a breathy whisper. 'Johnny is at Charlie's. He sends the car to pick me up.' She lit a Gauloise, took a deep drag then handed it to Ed. He looked chuffed, as he adored Lily, and her broken English and beauty captivated him; Ed and every other boy on the planet. He took a puff and immediately started to go green.

Zelda snatched the cigarette out of Ed's hand and chucked it into the sink. 'Johnny really is a very *understanding* boyfriend, isn't he? Has anyone seen Valentine this morning, *apart* from you?' She took off her sunglasses and glared at Lily.

Everyone ignored her, so she slammed around in the medicine cupboard for a while, found some Nurofen, took six and swept out of the room.

She was not happy to see Lily back in Valentine's life. The girl had an effect on him that Zelda felt was unhealthy, in a way that she couldn't quite put her finger on. He was in love with Lily, she could certainly see that, but it was an obsessive, crazy love that sometimes made her son seem like a stranger to her.

She had always been particularly close to Valentine and she resented the presence of the girl who threatened that bond.

*

Karen followed Zelda out into the hall. 'Miss Spender, I wanted to ask about the bedrooms. I think your son has moved into the one I'd prepared for your parents, so I wondered what you would like me to do?'

'Find another?'

'Well, that's the thing. There aren't any others, unless I re-do the blue room?'

The blue room was where Jake had been sleeping until last night. Despite the very promising start to the day Zelda couldn't be sure that her husband would want to continue to share her bed. Perhaps she should ask him? Then again . . .

'Yes, make that one up for them. Jake was only in there because I had a cold,' she lied. 'He can move back in with me, now that I'm better.'

Karen didn't think she looked better. She thought she looked very hung over.

*

112

Zelda flung herself onto her bed, carelessly bouncing Jake awake.

'God, you won't believe who's downstairs.'

'Lily?'

'How did you know?'

'I ran into her with Valentine early this morning.'

'You might've said!'

'We'd found better things to say and do!'

Zelda laughed. 'Will you move in here with me now?'

Jake noticed that she hadn't mentioned her fright in the night. Could she have forgotten so easily? Had she been that drunk?

'Of course I'll stay in here, I missed you.' He reached for her and she rolled into his arms.

'That's lucky because my parents are arriving this afternoon and there's nowhere to put them except your room!'

'Well, I'm very grateful to them ... after all I owe them a lot. Not least because they made such a bloody sexy daughter for me to fuck!'

Making love again that morning to Zelda with her sunglasses on reminded him of the wild times they had had at their house in Saint-Tropez. He had a vision of her emerging from the pool, light from the water flashing around her as it flowed off her perfect, honey-coloured body. She'd lifted her shades and, fixing her eyes on his, she'd pushed him backwards onto the vast sunbed and thrown her cool, wet body on top of him ...

They lay contentedly in each other's arms for a while. Jake

leant over and took off Zelda's sunglasses. 'I don't think you'll be needing those now.' Yes, he thought sadly, they would miss that beautiful house in the South of France. Another lovely part of their lives destroyed by Lucien Dark.

In fact, Zelda certainly hadn't forgotten the terror of the night, not at all. She knew the intruder wasn't a dream, although she acknowledged that her memory and the order of events was a little confused. She could see why Jake might not believe her and, although she felt safer knowing he would be sleeping with her for the foreseeable future, she still felt threatened and anxious.

She had decided to take some action of her own.

*

Jake couldn't get any signal on his phone so he decided to go out for a quick walk to try to find a quiet spot where he could ring the police. He wanted to make doubly sure that there hadn't been anyone suspicious around. He couldn't help feeling some of the officers on duty would have made themselves known if they had seen anything. But he thought it sensible to check.

Sergeant Powell assured him that he would get back to him straight away with a report from the front line. Which Jake found comforting.

He carried on walking up though the park, towards Banbury Court. It was a warm summer morning and he soon began to feel hot, so he shrugged off his old blue linen coat and rolled up his shirt-sleeves. Taking a deep breath he felt the fresh, clean air fill his lungs, and found he could breathe again, really breathe.

He realised that his whole family had been operating in such a fraught, breathless, suffocating atmosphere for so long that they had almost failed to make it through. The relentlessness of the disasters that had befallen them was astonishing.

His sister Georgia's tragic death, followed by the collapse of Lucien Dark's company, Dark Artists, and the decimation of the family's wealth. Then his own personal shock at the devastating discovery that the son he had always thought was his was, in fact, someone else's; Valentine, his golden boy, was not his at all.

No wonder Kate had been able to have such a field day with her book.

Apparently, she had left out one pertinent piece of information. For whatever reason, Kate had not detonated the bombshell news that Valentine had slept with Georgia Cole, and that the result was a beautiful baby girl: Willow. Perhaps she didn't know.

Fortunately, that particular aberration remained a secret, and it was in everyone's best interests to keep it that way. No one came out of the situation looking good, not Georgia and certainly not Valentine. It was a seriously tricky one. Protecting Willow and Dusty from more scandal was not the least of the family's concerns.

So Jake's feelings towards Valentine, his ex-son, were mixed. He loved him still, of course; you couldn't just un-love someone who you thought had been yours all your life. But he did feel some sort of connection between them had been irretrievably broken. He wondered if Valentine felt the same.

LOUISE FENNELL

He heard the sound of galloping hooves behind him and a girl's voice called out, 'Look out!' Flora pulled up next to him. Her long dark hair trailed in the light breeze and flowed down the back of an oversized tweed coat. Her slim legs were bare and studded biker boots seemed to weigh down her feet. She rode bareback and hatless and was obviously very much at ease on her restless white horse.

'Morning! How are things at the Court today?' Jake smiled up at her.

'Poor Dad! He is in shock . . . it went mental after you left.' Her horse pulled the reins from her hands as it lunged for a lush clump of grass.

'Really? It seemed pretty mental when we were there!'

'Well . . . Oh! Here he comes, he can tell you himself.'

The old Land Rover came roaring up the drive and came to a halt next to them as Boy grinned out at his friend. 'Morning, Jake, do you want to get in? Come back for a drink? Uh, no, sorry – keep forgetting! A cup of something anyway.'

Flora leant over her horse's neck to speak to her father. 'I have done some of the clearing up. But I didn't do the log basket.' She turned to Jake. 'Somebody was sick in it! Isn't that disgusting?' She gathered up her reins and pulled her horse's head towards home. 'See you!' And she galloped off.

Jake jumped into the Land Rover.

Boy gazed after his daughter as she raced away. 'Flora has developed a bit of a dark look lately, but it hides a very soft heart. She's a good girl.'

'I am going to have to get used to looking after girls too, now we've got Dusty and Willow, might need some tips! Never having had daughters, or none that I know of anyway!' Jake laughed. 'Then again after all the revelations of late ... who knows?'

'Bloody hell! Are you alright about all that?'

'Well, as you can tell, Zelda is a complicated person. Full of surprises! I think I've got my head around the most recent stuff. She has had a terrible time herself so ...'

Boy couldn't believe his friend was really OK with what had gone on. Frances had been a bloody nightmare but Zelda made his wife look like Mother Teresa.

'Tell me what happened after we left the party. Flora said it went mental!'

'Oh, God. More people kept appearing. Christ knows where they were coming from. When I came down this morning I found strangers scattered all over the house. There were a few sleeping on the kitchen sofas and there was one girl in the dog basket, in a state of undress, in a very undignified pose!' Boy looked at Jake and raised his eyebrows. They both laughed uproariously.

'Ah, nothing really changes, does it?' Jake looked out of the window and they began to reminisce about all the parties they had held at Banbury Court whenever they came down from Cambridge.

They were still laughing when Doone found them in the kitchen, trying to empty the log basket without getting sick on their hands, and failing.

'Jesus, eugh!' Boy was giggling in a carefree way that Doone hadn't heard for a long time. She ignored Jake. She didn't intend to have anything to do with a person, no matter how nice, who was connected, in any way, to that vile woman, Zelda.

She poured herself a cup of coffee. Hugging her old dressing gown around her slim frame, she slumped onto a kitchen chair, trying to attract her father's attention without actually asking for it.

Jake was watching her, thinking how much like her mother she was. Dark, sharp and very beautiful, she was also slightly intimidating. Frances had been just the same when they were all up at university together. Boy was the only one man enough to take her on. The rest of their friends had all been terrified of her, Jake himself included. He realised that Boy still hadn't told him where she was.

He knew that now wouldn't be a good moment to ask though.

So he simply said, 'Thanks for looking after everyone last night. My lot all had a blast.'

Doone wanted to respond with something rude about his wife, but as she looked at him now, smiling warmly at her in his dishevelled, disarming way, she decided against it and went with, 'Pleasure. Was Ed alright?'

'He was a bit sick.' Jake looked down at the sick-splattered log in his hand. 'Ah!'

Boy held out a rubbish bag. 'Just chuck that in here. I'll put them back in the log pile, rain'll wash them off.'

'God, you are disgusting, why don't you just throw them away?' Doone exclaimed.

'Waste not, want not; you know me.'

'I certainly bloody do. Have you found your wallet yet?'

'I don't think anyone has looked properly.'

'You mean you haven't looked properly. It's *your* wallet. Just don't forget that its contents are mine.'

Boy made an I-don't-know-what-she-means face at Jake.

But Jake knew exactly what she meant. It was an all too familiar conversation, the sort of conversation that he'd had with Zelda a million times. Not so much recently, now that she was in the same financial sinking ship, but familiar nonetheless.

So Boy really was on his uppers. Jake felt a surge of gratitude towards his old friend. To have taken on the added burden of non-rent-paying thirsty, party-loving Spenders in such straightened times was kindness personified. They owed him; that much was certain. But Jake had no idea how, when or indeed with what he would ever be able to repay him.

# CHAPTER TWELVE

Valentine lay on a sofa in the Dower House kitchen, with his cast propped up on an old beanbag. Ed was perched on a stool next to him. They were playing cards. Having no access to the Internet meant they had to think of new ways to pass their time.

Although, Valentine had said, 'I can always find something to do.'

'Or someone!' Ed said. Dusty certainly knew *that* was true. Kate's revelations meant that no one in the family, or indeed the wider world, was left in any doubt about how Valentine made use of his time.

Even his plaster-cast had failed to slow him down; Valentine had been very well looked after while in hospital. Two young Australian nurses were particular favourites. They had hoped to keep in touch, but he'd given them a fake phone number. There was a limit to the amount of girl-power a boy could stand and Valentine already had an army of willing little troopers' mobile numbers filling his phone.

He was desperate to get his cast removed, so that he could get back to work again. In the past, he had always relied on his mother's inexhaustible supply of money to fund his wayward lifestyle but since that had been so inconveniently destroyed he knew he needed to start earning a lot more from his modelling and acting career. Up until recently, he had treated it as a massive joke, a bit of fun while he finished his PPE degree at Oxford. He was looking forward to his shoot with Lily; it would be a great excuse to spend more time with her.

Valentine had been surprised and thrilled to find her, the girl who was never far from his thoughts, when he arrived at the Banbury Court nightclub. It was a massively unexpected bonus to the bother of the family's country exile. In a way, he was relieved that he hadn't known Lily was going to be there. It meant he hadn't had time to anticipate their meeting and so it was more spontaneous. Their furtive fuck in the old wine cellar, behind a dusty door, was certainly spontaneous.

He had thought about her such a lot as he lay in his hospital bed. He frequently found himself tormented by thoughts of the past; at least until the plentiful, blissful supply of morphine kicked in.

When Lily had left him to go off with Johnny on his world tour with the Bastards, Valentine had been hurt and furious. No one had ever played as hard to get as her. Now here she was, back in his life, back where he planned to keep her. He just had to prise her away from that grizzled old boyfriend of hers. Then life would be sweet.

Valentine had a feeling he was going to enjoy his little spell of R&R in the country. The house was a bit old and shit, but his room was OK. Nice bed anyway.

He found himself thinking about something that Lily had said to him earlier that morning. 'Johnny likes to stay at Charlie's so much, he thinks of renting a country house for us nearby. Then I could be your neighbour.'

Valentine had replied, 'Then I would have to love my neighbour, wouldn't I?' He'd pulled her roughly towards him. 'I'd have to love my neighbour over and over again.' He had kissed her hard, so that she couldn't reply.

Eventually she managed to gasp through his kisses, 'Yes!'

So he was confident that was sorted.

\*

Cleo and Max Spender arrived at the Dower House after lunch.

Cleo stepped out onto the gravel drive, looked up at the house and said, 'What a dear little cottage, so quaint. I do adore the country.'

'By most people's standards this is a very large house, Cleo. A cottage is something else entirely.' Max wandered inside, leaving Cleo to boss their driver about.

The man was patiently unloading a number of huge suitcases, under his boss's gimlet gaze, when Zelda appeared.

She had made an effort to disguise her hangover: full make-up, a twisted ponytail and a crisp white shirt over her favourite pair of J Brand jeans. She wanted to look fantastic to greet her mother, showing her that she might be down but she certainly wasn't out. 'Here you are, at last! I thought you were coming for lunch?'

'Sorry, darling, we ran a bit late. I had so much to do,' Cleo accepted Zelda's embrace with a slight turn of her cheek, 'with plans for the show and so on.'

Zelda was about to respond, when she noticed some other things being unloaded from the boot of the Daimler. Her parents had brought supplies, including a couple of cases of champagne, some white and red wine, and Daylesford bags that turned out to contain, amongst other things, a large ham, a dozen sides of smoked salmon and a massive brick of foie gras.

'Alms for the poor!' Cleo cried gaily.

Zelda bit her tongue. She felt that her mother's uncharacteristic generosity might bode well and she was reminded of her mission to extract funds from her parents, whatever the cost to her pride.

She would begin her charm offensive immediately. Linking arms with her mother, she led her into the house, crying out, 'Granny's here!'

She felt Cleo stiffen slightly.

Zelda corrected herself. 'Cleo's here!'

*

Everyone had gathered to greet the intrepid septuagenarians, Cleo and Max Spender.

Cleo was in her element, regaling the family with her audacious plans for her reality-TV show, *Against All Odds*.

Dusty asked, 'Where *is* the Northwest Passage?'

'Up north!' Cleo replied with a vague wave of her hand.

'It's in the Arctic. A lot of icebergs,' said Jake.

'Cold then? That'll suit you, Ma.' Zelda bit her lip, too late.

Cleo ignored her daughter. She felt she could be magnanimous, since she was the one with the new gazillion-pound TV show and Zelda was stuck in this damp, godforsaken hole, with nothing.

She knew Zelda would be eaten up with envy. This was satisfaction enough for Cleo. Before the bottom had dropped out of Zelda's world Cleo had put up with a lot of patronising talk from her daughter, so she was revelling in her reversal of fortune.

'It's a tiny little boat, sort of like a Riva, I think,' she said.

'I thought it was a RIB, Granny, which is an inflatable boat. Nothing like a Riva, which is only like the flashest motorboat on earth!' Ed snorted.

'I can't pretend it will be comfortable, but after Everest . . .'

'Won't it be dangerous *and* boring?' asked Zelda.

'You forget that I once spent two weeks on holiday in a house next to Charles Manson. Just before . . .'

'That could hardly be described as boring.'

'I was staying with Ronald Reagan.'

'Who's Ronald Reagan?' Dusty asked.

Everyone groaned.

Cleo suddenly remembered something. 'Darling, where's the baby?'

Dusty was pleased. 'She's been having a nap. I'm just going to get her. Valentine, do you want to come?'

Valentine kept his eyes on the cards in his hand. 'Nope.'

Dusty was peeved by his indifference. Although she had

always had Willow all to herself, even when their mother was alive, and she quite liked it that way, she still felt that Valentine should feign some interest in his daughter. Embarrassing and twisted though the situation was, he could make an effort to be kind.

The discovery that Valentine had fathered Willow had come as a massive shock to everyone in the family, but it had hit Dusty the hardest. It was one of their dirtiest little secrets and she was very relieved that it was one of the few things that the press had failed to get wind of. She felt she would have died of shame if people knew that her mother had slept with Valentine, a family member and still a teenager at the time.

The Spenders had all agreed to continue with the 'father unknown' story, so wisely put about by Willow's mother, Georgia.

Dusty couldn't believe that she had ever admired Valentine so much. He really is a heartless bastard, she thought bitterly.

Valentine could feel her disapproval and changed the subject. 'What's happened to that little boyfriend of yours ... Alan?'

'Alex.'

'Right, yes, Alex.'

'He's in London. That's where he lives.'

'You must be missing him. Poor Dusty, young love, eh!' Valentine knew how to be cruel. He always knew where the weak points were.

Dusty left the room without a reply. She had much to be upset about. She missed her mother dreadfully and she also missed her home, school and everything else that was familiar. She missed Alex, who was the kindest, sanest, funniest person she had ever met and she wished she was with him rather than stuck away, in the middle of nowhere.

Her family all really had a lot to answer for.

# CHAPTER THIRTEEN

Zelda left the house and set off up the garden to find a spot where she could get some phone signal. It was driving her mad that she couldn't tell whether she was receiving any replies to her increasingly desperate texts.

Still nothing from Shona. She had sent three more texts and left a phone message for her stylist and best friend. She was almost anxious that something might have happened to her. Shona was always so dependable. In desperation she had sent a text to another absent pal, Rocco, asking if Shona was OK.

She sat down tentatively on a lichen-encrusted bench, not wanting green muck all over her favourite jeans.

She glanced up and noticed how very beautiful the garden was. Ancient brick walls seemed crumpled by the weight of wildly tangled climbing roses. Lavender borders, like purple hedgehogs, were lively with butterflies and bees. The freshly mown grass still gave off its heady summer scent. Zelda took a deep breath and wondered where Frank had got to? She had a small flashback of the nightclub . . . had she tried to seduce Frank? Had he turned her down? She felt a stab of annoyance, which might have been shame, and went back to examining her phone.

There was a text from Rocco: 'Miss you! Come back all is forgiven! Heard S is working for R. Love ya. X'.

Since the hacking debacle nobody ever used names in their messages, but Zelda knew exactly who 'R' was. She felt Shona's disloyalty like a stab to her gut. That bloody bitch, she thought, and she'd always said she loathed that diva 'R'!

But beneath her anger was a deep hurt. Zelda had shared all her most intimate confidences with her stylist, over the years. Now it seemed she didn't know her best girlfriend at all.

In a way she didn't. Although Zelda had incessantly dumped all her problems on Shona, it had never worked the other way around. It began to occur to Zelda that Shona had been there for her because she worked for her, not because she loved her. This was a sobering realisation.

She was so upset that she could barely focus on her other messages. There was something from her agent Helen, but that was just to say, 'Don't worry, I'm on the case.'

Zelda thought, bitterly, 'Yeah, sure.'

There were a couple from the lawyers and accountants with a status update on the Lucien Dark trial date; still not set! She couldn't face thinking about that now.

She felt overwhelmingly lonely, like she didn't have a friend in the world. She had her family, that was all, her mad family, and she knew that wasn't enough. After all, they hadn't *chosen* her, not like friends chose you. Not like her best friend, bloody Shona, who had chosen to drop her, the moment a bit of shit hit the fan!

She stood up and set off back towards the house. Dusting off her perfect bottom with one hand she saw that it was covered with green mould from the bench. Her best jeans! The final straw. She made a small growling noise.

She looked at her phone once more before going back into the house. There was a new text from an unknown number

It simply said, 'I CAN SEE YOU.'

She screeched, dropped the phone as if it had scalded her, and darted into the house.

\*

When Sergeant Powell arrived he was unimpressed by what he found, or, more to the point, what he didn't find. He had been called out to the Dower House just as he was about to go off duty, so he was not best pleased. A clamouring multitude of people filled the kitchen. They were all contributing their own theories and making a terrible din. He could see that he would need to assert himself.

He raised his voice. 'If I might have everyone's attention for a moment? I need to speak to Miss Spender and her husband alone. We need to get the *facts* straight before we can take this matter any further.'

He could tell this lot were as divorced from reality as it was possible to be.

Jake took Zelda by the hand and said to the policeman, 'Let's go into the study. Follow me.'

Jake closed the study door and began to explain what had happened. 'Zelda was outside, in the garden, when she received a text from an unknown number. Didn't you, darling?'

Zelda nodded.

'What did the text say? May I see it?'

'It said, "I CAN SEE YOU." Didn't it, Zelda?'

Zelda nodded again.

'May I see your phone, Miss Spender?'

'Well, that's the thing, Officer, Zelda was so frightened she dropped her phone and when I went to retrieve it, um, the text had gone.'

'So you had deleted it?' The sergeant directed his question to Zelda.

'No, no! She says not.'

'I see.'

From the tone of his voice it was clear to both Jake and Zelda that the policeman did not see.

'So the text has disappeared?'

'It might have been deleted when the phone was bumped as it hit the grass?' Jake suggested loyally.

'Of course there is no possibility that you could have mis-read what you saw, Miss Spender? It couldn't have said, for instance, "CAN I SEE YOU?", as in someone wanting to arrange a meeting?' He was rather pleased with himself. If there was a text, she could easily have misread it.

'I'm not fucking blind – or mad!'

'Of course you're not.' Jake patted her leg. She caught his eye and saw the doubt there.

It was look she knew well. Her husband didn't believe what she said because she had lied to him consistently throughout their marriage. How could she expect him to believe her now?

Peter Powell took a deep breath. 'I have checked the security footage for last night. There was quite a bit of activity here, throughout the night; a Mercedes came and went a couple of times, yours, I believe, sir. A limousine came and went too. Not the sort of cars driven by any intruders I've ever apprehended.' The sergeant sighed. 'So we haven't found anything to shed any light on last night's alleged incident either.'

'So, what are you going to do to stop this maniac from trying to fucking kill me?' Zelda squeaked.

Sergeant Powell did not like foul language, particularly from women. He tried to remain calm. 'Well, firstly, there is no evidence that any person is trying to kill you. We shall continue to be vigilant and wait to see if this *person* reveals himself. Then, perhaps we will find out his intentions.'

'I don't see how his intentions can be misconstrued! You didn't hear him banging on my bedroom door last night!'

'Nor did anyone else, Miss Spender. So, until this person shows himself, as I say, we can only be vigilant.'

In the furore that followed the policeman's remarks, a few things began to worry Jake.

The first was that Zelda was losing her mind.

*

When Sergeant Powell was seeing himself out, he ran into Cleo.

She didn't bother to introduce herself, since she could see by his expression of awe and wonder that he knew exactly who she was.

Cleo held his hand a fraction longer than was absolutely necessary. 'Oh, you are wonderful to have come all the way out here for *this*. My daughter does seem rather overwrought. She hasn't been getting much of the right sort of attention lately and I think she is beginning to get a little ... desperate. You are very kind to humour her with your precious time. We are all very grateful.'

Sergeant Powell was chuffed. He adored Cleo Spender, 'a proper star' as far as he was concerned. No foul-mouthed harpy she. He and his wife had watched her Everest show. She was an amazingly brave, beautiful lady, and nobody's fool.

She had obviously drawn the same conclusion as him about her daughter's imaginary stalker. They were of the same mind, Peter Powell and Cleo Spender. He couldn't wait to get home and tell his wife all about his extraordinary day.

\*

Jake took Zelda upstairs and gave her a sedative. She was completely exhausted and, like a child, he knew she needed some sleep. He stayed with her until she drifted off. Then he went downstairs to see his in-laws, to get everyone a drink and generally get things back together.

He found Boy in the kitchen, talking to Max and Cleo.

They greeted each other and Boy looked concerned. 'I just saw Peter Powell on his way out, is everything alright?'

'Yes, yes, fine. Zelda has just had a couple of shocks and she's not coping too well.'

'I wouldn't be coping too well with a hangover like that.' Boy laughed.

Cleo raised an eyebrow. 'It is so lovely to see you, Boy. I can't remember when I was last at Banbury Court. But it was so much fun . . . the nightclub!'

'It's still there,' Boy said.

'That's where my lovely mother got her hangover,' Valentine interjected.

'The girls decided to re-open it; turned into quite a night. No one's feeling one hundred per cent today,' Boy said.

'Oh, how fabulous, I long to see it again.' Cleo put on her nostalgic look, shamelessly angling for an invitation.

'Granny loves a trip down memory lane,' Valentine added.

Cleo looked annoyed by the 'G' word.

Max felt Boy had already shown his family rather a lot of hospitality; they owed him, big time. So he said, enthusiastically, 'Why don't you bring your girls down here tonight? We've brought a few supplies. We could have a sort of picnic supper!'

Max loved a party.

Boy knew the cupboard had been stripped absolutely bare at home so, having glanced at Jake and been given an affirmative nod, he accepted the invitation gratefully.

# CHAPTER FOURTEEN

When Zelda woke she felt very disoriented. The curtains were closed but there was enough light for her to see the dial on the bedside clock. It said 8.15. Was that morning or night? She listened; she could hear voices downstairs, laughter. It sounded like a party. Bloody hell! Had they forgotten all about her, forgotten that someone was trying to scare her to fucking death? Did they even care? She didn't think they did – no, they didn't care at all.

She stumbled out of bed and into the bathroom. She turned on the taps and stomped about trying to find something to wear, something to make them sit up and bloody notice her.

By the time she emerged from Lady Banbury's calming bath, fifteen minutes later, she had made a plan.

To her surprise her phone had some signal, so she made a call. To someone who did care about her, who knew how to protect her too. Someone she had almost forgotten existed, until the blinding flash of inspiration that made her feel that everything might just be OK after all.

Now all she needed to do was get through the night without any more frights. From the sound of things there were plenty of people around to keep trouble at bay. She would go downstairs and show her sceptical, cynical family that she was abso-bloody-lutely fine. No thanks to them.

Not mad at all, in fact she felt she was the sanest person amongst them.

*

Valentine had been too preoccupied with Lily to notice the Banbury girls much the previous night, in their subterranean nightclub lair.

But, since he had arrived downstairs for dinner at the Dower House, Doone had piqued his interest. She was a beautiful girl. When he gave her the benefit of his most dazzling 'Hi' smile, she had turned away without a word and drifted off to get a drink.

Ah, aloof? There was nothing Valentine enjoyed more than a challenge.

For the time being he would play it cool, turn his attention to her sister Flora, which would not be a hardship. She was very cute and it hadn't escaped his notice that Lily's boyfriend, Johnny the Bastard, had been all over her like a rash the previous night. So flirting with her a bit would be fun.

He asked Flora what she'd like to drink and hopped across the room to get it for her.

To the cheerful sound of corks popping, Max was doling out glasses of champagne and Cleo was reminiscing in a corner with Boy when Zelda made her entrance. No one had expected her to come down, so she had the advantage of surprise. She wore a bright red Roksanda Ilincic dress, which fitted her fabulous curves perfectly. Her dark hair was curled and fell in thick soft waves down her bare back. She smiled her best smile and everyone broke into spontaneous applause.

Even Boy was impressed. She looked sensational.

He and Jake had had a brief chat earlier about the intruder-stalker situation and he wondered, looking at her now, whether her family were right to jump to the conclusion that it was all in her mind. He found himself thinking that, even if she was a bit of headcase, she certainly looked stunning enough to attract an army of stalkers.

Handing his daughter a glass, Max gave her a squeeze. 'Glad to see you've rallied, darling. Don't let the blighters get you down.'

She smiled at her father and said, 'Thanks, Dad, I'm fine.'

In the dining room, the foie gras, smoked salmon and the ham were all laid out on a sideboard, lit by candelabra. Various salads, which Karen had thrown together earlier, made it all look very tempting. The table had been laid informally and everyone helped themselves to food. Most of them were hung-over hungry. As the effects of the wine and food kicked in, the atmosphere began to buzz.

Boy had politely waited until last to get something to eat, so there was nowhere left at the table for him to sit, except between Zelda and Cleo. As he took his place he felt a small frisson from Zelda. What was that?

He ran his hand through his thick blonde hair and smiled

warmly at her. 'Are you alright? Sorry about the . . .' Zelda took an unladylike swig of her wine, which made Boy smile. 'Steady!'

'I'll be fine, all under control. Thanks for last night by the way. Lovely party. What I can remember of it.'

They both laughed and surprised themselves when they began to talk to each other normally. Their animosity seemed to have dissolved. Zelda noticed that the cut on his cheek looked better but there was still a hint of a black eye.

'Are you wearing make-up?' she teased.

'Fuck, no! Are you?' Boy replied.

'Nope!' Zelda teased. 'What you see before you is all absolutely au naturel!'

Boy found himself looking into her fabulous violet eyes and thinking, as sensational as she looked all done up, she would look pretty damn good au naturel too.

'Hmm!' He raised his eyebrows and grinned at her but, as he reached for his wine, he looked up to find Jake watching him from across the table. He raised his glass and smiled, but he felt odd; guilty? He wondered where that came from. He realised he hadn't flirted with anyone for a long time. It felt good, but entirely innocent? Maybe not if he felt uncomfortable about it.

He could still feel Jake's eyes on him, so he turned to Cleo and said, 'Yum, yum – real food! We haven't seen this in a while!'

Cleo looked bemused.

Zelda was hurt. Boy had turned away from her just when

there was a bit of a thaw. What a tricky bastard he was. She decided to turn her back on him, as she had Valentine on her other side and they had a lot of catching up to do.

Max was happily ensconced next to Doone, who was just the sort of young woman he adored. Clever, tricky and very beautiful, she reminded him of some of the other women in his life and they got along famously.

Flora was sitting quietly, next to Valentine. She was happy that Zelda was commandeering the conversation, because she felt shy and tongue-tied in his presence. She liked to be cool, and sitting next to Valentine she felt anything but. The scar on his cheek, his post-hospital pallor and his plaster and crutch did nothing to dim his staggeringly powerful presence; he was a very beautiful boy. She was embarrassed but flattered by his attention, charmed by his easy intimacy and teasing humour.

He turned to her. 'I think my mother would look great with a nose stud, don't you?'

She glanced at Zelda, and panicked. 'I'm not sure.'

'You're right, she is a bit old for one,' he said.

'Oh, honestly, Val, you are vile.' But Zelda laughed as she said it. 'Piercings are hideous.'

Flora looked hurt.

'Oh, they look alright on you, because you're quite pretty,' Zelda went on, 'but you'd be a lot prettier without them.'

Valentine smiled and said, 'Ah, damned with faint praise. Well, I think you look great and your little bits of ironmongery are magnetic.'

Flora blushed. Zelda prodded her son hard, on his good leg.

141

As Zelda turned away from Valentine she couldn't help thinking how incorrigible her son was. She wondered where he got his seemingly endless desire to seduce everyone he met. Then she remembered; he got it from her.

She turned back to Boy, who looked surprised. 'Ah, there you are. Hello again. Thought I'd lost you.'

'You're not a bit careless with women by any chance, are you? Haven't you lost your wife?' She cringed, inwardly. She hadn't meant to sound quite so harsh. She'd meant it as a joke.

Boy was shocked. His first instincts had been right; Zelda Spender was not a nice woman.

'I might have lost my wife, but I'm told that you have lost your mind. Which is worse, do you think?'

Zelda was livid. She pushed her chair back and flounced off, into the kitchen.

Cleo put her hand on Boy's thigh and said, 'Take no notice of my batty daughter. Tell me more about your darling father. I didn't see Guy much after the late '70s – did he have a good life?'

'He certainly had a good time. Not sure that his could be described as a good life though. My mother certainly wouldn't have described it that way.'

'No, I don't suppose she would. He was very attractive. You resemble him, same lovely eyes.' She smiled her most winning smile.

Boy tried to smile back. 'I know I do look a bit like him, but I'm not like him at all. Or I hope not anyway.'

As Cleo began to regale him with a story about a trip she had taken to Marrakesh with Guy, Boy could feel Jake watching him again. But this time he didn't acknowledge that he had noticed. They were such old friends, but what did they know of each other now, of each other's lives? Not much, it seemed. He began to wonder what he had let himself in for. The Spenders were a bundle of trouble and his old chum's wife made him feel the most troubled of all.

Doone helped Max bring in a couple of trays of coffee. Max cried, 'Stimulants!'

Valentine watched Doone covertly, taking in her slender, slightly boyish frame. He could see that her legs were long and slim despite the bagginess of her strange harem pants. She was wearing a man's shirt too, half-tucked into the mad trousers. Her wrists were loaded with cords and bangles. She really was stunning. She felt him watching her, so she looked right back at him, defiantly. Her cool silver-grey eyes were hard, like chips of ice.

He looked away. He was a master in the art of getting a woman's attention. He knew precisely when to look, and when to look away. He knew when to be strong, and when to be vulnerable.

He took Flora's hand and said, 'Come with me, I need you.' She looked uncertain. He laughed. 'I just need some help to get to the loo!'

She was embarrassed. 'Oh, yes, sure.' She stood up and tentatively helped him to stand. He hobbled along, using her as a crutch.

When they got back, his mother raised an eyebrow, but he just grinned at her as he manoeuvred himself back into his chair.

Valentine knew that Doone had watched them leave and registered their return. He was going to enjoy getting to her, by using her little sister as bait. Although he had previously used it as a technique on girls who were friends, sisters were a new development. Yes, Valentine could tell he was going to love his break in the country. Things were going unexpectedly well again.

He had made a plan to go house hunting with Lily. She was going to recce houses for Johnny to rent and she told him she was, 'Coming in Johnny's limo', so that Valentine could 'lie in the back in comfort'. He'd replied, 'Then we'll both be coming in Johnny's limo!' which made him flinch, so crass; but then Lily always made him feel a bit like a fourteen-year-old boy. Johnny would be in the recording studio all week, apparently.

Flora had observed that Ed spent a lot of time watching his brother at dinner. Although she could see why everyone was so enamoured of Valentine, as the evening wore on, he had made her feel slightly uncomfortable and she began to sense that there was something false about him.

Ed was much more straightforward and he was very fit too, tall, with tousled dark hair and soft grey eyes. Flora liked him and, although he was younger than her, he didn't seem so. He was very funny and self-assured. So she was happy to follow him and Dusty, when he suggested they escape upstairs for a smoke.

He offered her a cigarette and lit it for her, which was cute and charmingly old-fashioned. Emboldened by booze he decided to tell her his most embarrassing story, which luckily went down a storm. Flora had a beautiful husky laugh and Ed was determined to make her laugh a lot from now on.

*

The front door creaked as Dusty closed it. She was going outside, to try to get some signal and text or, better still, speak to her boyfriend, Alex. She stood for a moment, looking out into the dark, before stepping tentatively onto the drive. Gravel scrunched underfoot; the air was cool on her face. She took a deep breath and set off towards the walled garden.

She glanced nervously back at the house. The light from the windows threw squares of gold out onto the dark ground. It looked reassuring, as houses always do at night, when all the lights are blazing.

She gazed up the sky. It was clear and bright with stars.

After a moment's panic when the darkness enveloped her, Dusty used her phone to light the way; still no signal.

She tried not to think of Zelda's stalker as she headed on up the path towards the top of the garden. What if it wasn't a pap that had left the note? What if Zelda hadn't been imagining things going bump in the night? There were moonshadows everywhere.

She began to wish she had brought Ed with her. But she could see that he wanted to be left alone with Flora; her lovely cousin was smitten.

Dusty's boyfriend, Alex, was not only her first boyfriend, but her first proper friend too. Someone she could trust absolutely. They had met fortuitously, just after her mother's death.

Her childhood had been quite lonely. Famous by default, Dusty's friendships had been restricted to her family and a few other children of the super-famous, who lived similar twilight lives, dodging their parents' limelight, keeping their secrets and trying to be normal, with no real idea of what normal might be. Since she had met Alex, he and his family had given her a glimpse of real domestic life and she was hooked.

Having finally got some signal, she sank down onto the same stone bench that Zelda had been sitting on earlier, as she waited for Alex to pick up.

She heard a rustle and crack of a branch trodden underfoot. Her heart started beating fast.

Alex answered, 'Hello.'

Dusty daren't make a sound.

Her mouth was dry. She held her breath.

Alex said, 'Hello, hello!' Then, thinking that Dusty had made a pocket phone call, he hung up.

Dusty heard the buzz of the dead line. There was another crunch. Someone was walking along behind the wall and they were getting closer. She shrank back into the shadows. Her heart was pounding.

She decided to make a run for it.

Springing off the bench she ran down the lawn. She would have made it, if the dew hadn't made the grass so slippery. She went down with a crash and her phone flew from her hand.

She started to scream when she felt strong hands grab her arms.

'It's OK. I'm not going to hurt you. You can stop screaming.' The voice sounded calm and kind.

Dusty screamed again but less desperately. The front door flew open and Jake and Boy ran outside.

'It's alright, everyone. It's me! Sorry I gave you a fright.' Frank let go of the screaming girl's fragile arms.

Dusty burst into tears and ran back into the house as Frank bent down and picked up her phone. He held it out to Jake.

'Sorry I frightened her. I was just having a look round to make sure there wasn't anyone suspicious about tonight. I know the police are supposed to be on duty but I haven't seen anyone. So I thought I should check the place myself.'

Boy said, 'Thanks, Frank, good idea, but a bit of a fright for Dusty. What was she doing out here anyway?'

'Phone call, I expect.' Jake took the phone from Frank. 'Thanks, sorry. Yep, not much signal in the house.'

'OK, well, all seems to be fine. You haven't seen anyone or anything?' Boy asked.

'No, all clear,' Frank replied.

'Thanks for checking.' Boy turned to see that Zelda was standing in the doorway.

He called out, 'Everything's OK, nothing to worry about.' He patted his friend on the shoulder. 'Thanks, Frank, see you tomorrow.'

'Tell the girl again, sorry I startled her.'

'Will do.'

As Boy walked past Zelda, who was still waiting tentatively on the threshold, their eyes met.

'I told you all there was someone out there.'

'But there wasn't.'

'Yes, there was.'

'Only Frank.'

'No, not only Frank.'

She was beginning to look furious again. Her low-cut dress made her bosom heave like a Mills and Boone heroine, and he had an uncontrollable urge to laugh.

'Well, Frank found Dusty out there, I suppose. But I don't think she is your stalker, do you?' Then he did laugh.

Big mistake.

Zelda thumped him hard, on the arm. 'Don't you laugh at me, you shit. I am being terrorised and none of you take it seriously.' Her voice rose when she saw Jake re-emerge from the kitchen.

Jake caught her arm gently. 'Stop assaulting our host, Zelda. He will throw us out if you go on like this.' He grinned at Boy, and made a sorry face.

Zelda had hurt her hand but she wouldn't give them the satisfaction of showing it. 'Oh, fuck off, all of you. I can look out for myself. I've got a *real* man coming down to protect me, so I don't need any of you. Useless load of wimps!' She stomped off upstairs.

'God, man, I am so sorry, I just don't know what's got into her,' Jake said.

'No one by the look of her!' Valentine had hobbled onto the scene.

'Oh, shut up, Val!' Jake suddenly felt furious, bleak and overwhelmingly powerless.

'I think what everyone needs is a nice big drink,' Max said.

Yes, a nice big drink did sound like a good idea. Particularly to Jake, who had had more than enough of bloody sobriety.

# CHAPTER FIFTEEN

When Karen arrived at the Dower House the following morning she was surprised by the mess. It was obvious that no attempt had been made to clear up anything at all. There were bottles and glasses all over the floor, ashtrays spilling over onto rugs and chairs.

What was left of the food was still where she had laid it out the night before, but annihilated. Dirty plates were scattered all over the house, and she even found some on the lawn. It looked like the morning after a rave rather than a quiet little family supper. She set to work tidying it all up.

The first person down was the boy from the accident, Valentine. He was undeniably a very handsome bloke. With his floppy blonde hair and a beautiful smile she could see that he had charm. Not the sort she admired though, and there was something else about him, something not quite right.

Her father always said that people were like horses, some of them were just born 'a wrong 'un', and that was the vibe Karen was getting from this young man.

Valentine hobbled across the kitchen. 'Oops, what happened here? Looks like a bomb's gone off! I went to bed early so it wasn't me.' He put his arms up in a 'hands off' gesture and gave her his most disarming smile.

'So you didn't have supper either then?' Karen was feeling quite grumpy.

Valentine didn't reply, but sat down, making it look a lot more difficult than it was. He pretended to be captivated by a story in the newspaper. He always ignored grumpy women.

There were fresh croissants on the kitchen table, which Karen had brought with the papers. She watched surreptitiously as he broke off a piece and popped it into his mouth. The golden crumbs stuck to his lips; he licked them slowly and said, 'Yum, yum.'

Gathering up a rubbish bag, Karen tore herself away, finding herself disconcerted by how mesmerising the crash boy was to look at.

*

Zelda smelt him before she saw him. She turned over to find Jake lying, fully clothed, on the bed next to her. His eyes were wide open and very red; was he drunk?

She propped herself up. She wasn't feeling too hot herself but Jake looked truly awful. 'What happened to you?'

'I don't know, I just ... I'm sorry, Zelda. I'll go back up to London for a while, get to some AA meetings. I think it's just too soon for me to be doing this stuff. I feel horrible.'

Zelda was suddenly completely enraged. '*You* feel horrible!

What about me? Perfect fucking timing, Jake, thanks! You can't just leave me here in this hell hole.'

'I've been lying here thinking about this for hours. You said you had someone coming down to protect you, so you'll be fine. Anyway, you can't come back to London with me. The paps would be all over you. We've only just left, be sensible.'

'Sensible! Coming from you? Christ, you are so selfish.'

'I have got to go. If I don't, I'll be right back where I started.'

'You are right back where you started. A fucking mess! I can't believe you would do this to me now.' Zelda got up and stormed into the bathroom, slamming the door behind her. The whole house shook.

*

While Zelda took her bath, she calmed down and realised that she might have overreacted a bit. She began to wonder if she should offer to help Jake to manage his drinking. They were in the country; how hard could it be? Somehow, she had totally forgotten, in all her years of experience, that 'managing' Jake's drinking had never been a success. But she needed him with her. Things had improved between them and she didn't want that to slip away. She had decided; being parted from him wasn't an option. She intended to change his mind about leaving.

By the time Zelda came downstairs everyone was gathered around the kitchen table having breakfast, and Jake was clutching a cup of coffee, trying to look sensible.

Valentine struggled to his feet and gave his mother a smacking kiss on the cheek. 'Morning, Mommy, dearest. My cab has just arrived, I'm giving Jake a lift back to London.' He tapped his plaster-cast and grinned. 'Time to get this off.' He hopped towards the door.

With those words, Zelda's hopes were dashed.

Cleo had been quietly observing the scene, and now said, 'Very nice, everyone leaving the moment we arrive!'

Jake got up. 'Sorry, Cleo, things to do, you know.' He looked at Zelda. 'I'll leave you the car, OK? Call you later.'

'How? The fucking phones don't work.'

'Will you call me when you can then?' He didn't catch her eye and he wobbled a bit as he picked up his small suitcase.

'I'll probably have been murdered before then.'

'You've still got us to protect you, darling,' said Max.

He gave his daughter a little hug. She shrugged him off.

*

Karen watched from an upstairs window as Valentine was manoeuvred safely into the cab. Jake looked in a bit of a state. She had been collecting empty bottles from all over the house, so she wasn't surprised some people looked rough, more amazed that they weren't dead from alcohol poisoning.

She would be interested to hear what Frank had heard from the Banburys about the evening. Boy often shared things with Frank. They were close friends as well as boss and employee, which was why Frank was prepared to work for Boy for such a pittance. This wasn't something that Karen disapproved of at all. They had a nice life, a cottage on the estate and enough money to get by. They knew how lucky they were.

As she looked down at the little family group below her she

couldn't help feeling they weren't so lucky. There was Dusty waving goodbye, clasping her baby sister; two lost girls.

The cab left a trail of dust as it sped off up the drive. It would take a while to settle; but the dirt that this family kicked up wherever they went might be a different matter altogether.

Karen went back to her work.

# CHAPTER SIXTEEN

It was late morning and very warm by the time Zelda set off for a run. She had decided she would rather take the risk of being murdered than getting fat. In her despair she had guzzled two croissants with lashings of butter and jam that morning. They needed to be worked off a.s.a.p.

She bumped into Cleo on her way out. 'Do you want to join me?' she asked.

'Oh, no, darling! I'm not doing so much physical training for this job. We'll only be sitting in a boat, nothing to do at all. If I get myself too fit I'll just go a bit stir crazy, and I don't want to be wound up like a coiled spring.' She managed to make it sound like a reproach.

Zelda certainly felt 'wound up like a coiled spring', particularly by her mother. 'OK, whatever you say, but I think you'll find your little boat trip is a bit more arduous than you seem to imagine. What if you have to help pull the boat across miles of ice? Or swim, if you capsize?'

Cleo looked horrified; these were clearly not things she had considered. Zelda was pleased and her tension eased a little. There was nothing quite as gratifying as 'getting to' her mother.

She set off towards the lake. No headphones today, she wanted to keep her wits about her. As she turned onto the track she pushed herself to go faster, to feel that burn. She stopped to catch her breath when she reached the wide path that opened onto the dark, breeze-rippled lake. Wild geese flapped away from her, across the water. Zelda watched them go.

Suddenly, a figure stepped out of the woods. She felt her sinews stiffen, and squinting up her eyes she desperately tried to see who it was. It started to move towards her with a long, confident stride. She wanted to turn, to run. But she was frozen, rooted to the spot. The figure raised an arm in salute.

It was only Boy. As he drew nearer, she gasped, 'Jesus, you gave me a fright.'

'Sorry, but it is my lake!'

'I know it's your bloody lake.' She was still panting from exertion and fear. 'It's your house and your mercy that we have all been thrown onto. I do know.' She stared down at the ground then, with a deep, careworn sigh, she lifted her head and looked him directly in the eye. 'I am grateful. I probably don't seem it, but all the things that have happened lately have thrown me a bit. I'm sorry.'

'I'm sorry too. We did get off on rather a bad foot; your foot in my face!' he teased.

Zelda pulled at her tracksuit bottoms self-consciously and

her cheeks went a little pink. They were both reminded of the moment that Boy had knocked her over and pulled her trousers down.

'I was just coming down to see Jake,' he said.

'He's gone back to London.'

'Oh?'

'Yes, something urgent came up,' she improvised.

'I was a bit worried about him last night.'

So he knew.

Zelda looked out at the lake, her expression one of such sadness and disappointment that Boy felt a sudden urge to comfort her. For the first time he could see another side to his old friend's relationship with his wife, recognising that Jake wasn't playing quite the supporting role Boy had always imagined. The burden of responsibility must have weighed heavily on Zelda, and now she looked fragile and very alone.

He stepped forward and reached out, just at the moment Zelda turned away.

'Don't worry about Jake. He'll be fine, he always is.' She tried to sound plucky as she prepared to continue her run, but stopped suddenly, as if she had remembered something. Glancing back over her shoulder, she said anxiously, 'You don't mind if the children and I stay on, do you? Without Jake, I mean?'

'No. No, of course not. Stay as long as you like.'

She looked relieved, said, 'Thanks', and smiled her lovely smile.

Boy was alarmed to find that his heart leapt. The idea of

having her in the Dower House was suddenly, unexpectedly pleasing. He watched Zelda as she sprinted away from him, her perfect bottom gently jiggling in its tight black tracksuit. Boy felt a pounding surge of desire for her and his imagination took lascivious flight. He trudged off up the track, feeling another stab of guilt. Frances had been away for so long, perhaps he was just desperate for a shag?

In his heart he knew that to give way and make any sort of play for Jake's wife would not be a good idea at all. The rest of his anatomy was clearly not so convinced; he vaguely considered stripping off and jumping into the lake to cool down. As cool down he must. He was an honourable man and, unlike his father, he had never touched another guy's wife. He certainly didn't intend to start now.

He resolved to put all thoughts of Zelda from his mind and avoid seeing her. How hard could it be to resist?

He strode purposefully back up to the Court and found Doone in the kitchen, shelling peas in a disgruntled fashion.

'Hey ho, Doone, what's up?'

'Nothing.'

'Peas! Yum. Well done. I didn't know we had any.'

'We don't, Frank brought them from his garden. Flora has asked the Spenders to come up for supper tonight.'

'What? Shit! Since when was Flora our social secretary?'

'She said it was an accident. She went down to see the kids and she bumped into the monster's mother.'

'Cleo? And Zelda is not a monster. She's just a woman under pressure.'

'We are all women under pressure.' She glanced up at her father. 'And when did you start defending that woman? I thought you said she was a spoilt cow?'

'Well, I have got to know her circumstances a bit better and I realise that, underneath, she is ... well, not what she seems.'

'Oh, my God, you haven't got a thing for her, have you?'

'Of course not, don't be ridiculous. I love your mother.'

'Yeah, yeah, yeah, and she loves you.' Doone stopped shelling peas and lit a cigarette. 'That's why none of us have seen or heard of her for eighteen months.'

Flora walked in. 'Hi, Dad.'

'Doone tells me you have *accidentally* asked the Spenders up here for supper. How did that happen, exactly?'

'Cleo Spender was there when I went to see Ed and Dusty. She said she hadn't seen the house for years and she looked very sad. She told me she was going back to London tomorrow, so I said, "Would you like to come up to the house this evening?", meaning for a drink, and she said, "We'd *love* to come to supper, how sweet of you to ask!" So I couldn't say, "I didn't mean supper."' Flora shrugged. 'They aren't all coming, some of them have gone back to London: broken boy and the dad.' She smiled. 'Sorry, Dad, it's only like five of them, I think?'

Boy smiled at his daughter. 'I'm sure we can rustle up something.'

'You're sure that *I* can rustle up something, you mean,' Doone said. 'Have you found your wallet yet? I need to get to the village and I am not coughing up any more to subsidise your social life.'

Was this his social life? Boy wondered. Yes, he supposed it was . . . and so much for avoiding Zelda Spender.

Now that she was out of sight he was able to put his feelings back in perspective. He was confident he would not have any problem resisting her siren charms. It had also occurred to him that there was no evidence that she was in the least bit interested in him – quite the contrary, in fact. He needn't have worried. Everything was going to be fine.

# CHAPTER SEVENTEEN

Jake took a final drag of his cigarette and let it fall into the gutter. He stamped on it and turned to face the old church hall, in Chelsea. He hesitated, suddenly feeling overwhelmed with remorse and shame over his failure to keep sober. The double doors swung open and his AA sponsor miraculously appeared. He greeted Jake warmly and gently led him across the threshold.

The atmosphere in the room was warm and welcoming. Everyone sat down and went through the introductions to the meeting.

When the time came for someone to 'take the chair', to share their experiences with the group, a young woman stood up whom Jake had never seen before. She was wearing skinny jeans, a T-shirt and no make-up. She gathered up her long chestnut hair and twisted it over one shoulder. She was mesmerizingly beautiful. He guessed she must be in her early thirties. The room went particularly quiet. She certainly had everyone's attention.

'Hi, I'm Sophie. I'm an alcoholic and an addict.'

Everyone said, 'Hi, Sophie.'

Jake watched in awe as she laid bare the destruction and trauma of her life on alcohol and drugs. Her honesty was breathtaking. She left no humiliation unexposed and many of her anecdotes were funny as well as heartbreaking. Jake found it hard to believe that such an obviously bright and beautiful young woman could have been brought so low. Yet here she was, standing before them, talking about what her past had been like but most importantly, and heartwarmingly, what her present was like, now that she was sober.

Jake realised he was gaping at her in such a captivated way that when she finished speaking and everyone said, somewhat understatedly, 'Thank you, Sophie,' his sponsor nudged him and whispered: 'Rule number one, no romantic entanglements with other members!'

Jake looked at him and smiled ruefully. 'Course not!'

'Just wanted to remind you. You look as if you've been hit by a thunderbolt. This isn't killjoying, it's simply that everyone is very emotionally exposed and vulnerable in here and if romantic attachments are formed they are dangerous to recovery.'

Jake replied, 'I get that.' And he tried not to stare as Sophie talked happily to an old lady, in a hat, at the tea table far across the room.

His sponsor continued, 'She's a lawyer.'

It occurred to Jake that the guy might be finding it hard to practise what he preached in relation to Sophie.

He couldn't help feeling that she would be the perfect poster girl for AA; if it wasn't anonymous, of course, which, luckily for Jake and many of the other very famous people in the room, it was.

# CHAPTER EIGHTEEN

Zelda had laid out an old rug on the stone bench in the garden and she was sitting quietly texting when a message came through with a ping, from her agent, Helen Baldwin. It said, 'Telephone me immediately. I have news!'

She felt her heart leap. Could this be a job? Her agent's PA answered. 'Oh, hi. I'm afraid Helen is on a conference call so she'll have to call you back.'

'When?'

'I'm not certain. She is very busy. But I'm sure she will get back to you today.'

'I don't have any phone signal where I am. So I need to speak to her now. I'll hold.'

'She will be a while. I'll get her to call you.'

'Are you deaf? I just said she can't call me! I need you to put me through to her, now!'

'Can you hold, please.'

Zelda heard the buzz as the line went dead. She couldn't believe it – that fucking girl had cut her off! She threw her phone to the ground where it bounced into a rose bush and, almost immediately, began to ring. She fell to her knees and tried to retrieve it, scratching her arms badly, drawing blood.

'Shitting hell!' She managed to reach it. 'Hello.'

The familiar fierce tone of Helen blasted down the line. 'Zelda. Hi. Sorry. My PA lost you, having trouble with your signal I hear.'

Zelda wanted to say, 'The fucking bitch cut me off'. But she decided to see how the land lay before she complained about the treatment she had suffered at the hands of Helen's imperious staff.

'Helen. How lovely to hear from you. What's up?' She held her breath.

'There's a job on offer. I think it's interesting, though it's probably not exactly what you had in mind. But it's work, good money and it might do something to salvage your cred ... that'll be up to you to some extent.'

There was a silence before Zelda said, 'So what is it?'

'Well, it's a talent show.' Helen waited.

Zelda had said she would never, ever do one of those fucking awful talent shows, as long as she lived. But now she hesitated, thinking maybe she should find out a bit more before she went ballistic. 'O ... K?'

'It's being produced by Sam Carson and his production company, Big Guns. I don't know who else is in the line-up yet. But he wants you as a judge. He has always had a thing for you, apparently.' Helen sounded sceptical, and to add insult to injury she added, 'Anyway, he likes to rescue lame ducks, so he has asked for you.'

Zelda tried to stifle her annoyance. 'What's the format?' She did hate talent shows, but Sam Carson was the king of them and if he liked her . . .

'Let me see. The format . . . yes. It's a show for anyone who used to be famous to have an opportunity to get themselves back into the limelight and . . .'

'You are kidding, right? You have to be kidding. It's a show to humiliate people who used to have some kind of fame? And they want *me* to judge that? To humiliate me! Have you gone mad?'

'Wait a minute, slow down. It's not going to be like that. Most of the people on it will have been very, very famous in the past. It's a sort of "Where are they now?" and a chance for them to shine again. It's not going to be some shabby piece of shit, Zelda. I certainly wouldn't be discussing it with them, or you, if it was,' Helen responded emphatically, trying to placate her sensitive new client.

'What's it going to be called?'

'*Fame Game.*'

Zelda thought for a minute. 'Have you talked money?'

'They are talking about very generous fees indeed.' Helen paused pointedly before she continued, 'Sam is known as a great payer and I have been told that he is very sympathetic to your situation.' Subtext: you lucky cow.

Zelda had always thought Sam Carson was a bit of an arse, but now she found she was warming to the idea of him. She knew that this might be the best job she was going to be offered for a while. Perhaps it was worth considering.

Cleo appeared from the house and started gesticulating at her to come in. She waved back in a 'leave me alone, can't you see I'm busy' sort of way.

'Well, there is no harm in letting them try to sell it to me, I suppose. Can you get them down here for a meeting? I don't want to risk coming back into town yet, so just say I'm working down here.'

Yes, make them come to her, not to seem too keen, that was always the thing. Pretend to be working in the country and unable to get away. That was how Zelda thought she'd play it.

'What shall I say you are working on?' Helen asked.

'Tell them I'm working on my autobiography,' Zelda snapped.

'You are? That's great news! I thought you said you would never do anything so tacky.'

'I didn't say that. I said it would be tacky to do one *now*. But I have changed my mind. I want the chance to put my side of the story,' she bluffed.

Helen bluffed right back at her. 'Well, I'm sure I'll be able to get you a great deal on your book.'

Zelda was silent. She knew insincere when she heard it. She had heard it a lot.

Helen continued, 'I'll get back to you when I've spoken to the guys at Big Guns. I think they are keen to get it sorted. The show is scheduled to go out very soon and there will be plenty of pre-recorded auditions to do . . . well, let's see what you feel after you've met with them.'

'Yes, let's. Thanks, Helen. Send me a text if you can't reach me.'

'Will do. Get back to writing that book!'

'Will do!'

They both hung up.

Zelda went to see what Cleo was summoning her for. She felt strangely excited, which was odd, as *Fame Game* would have been the last sort of show she would ever have dreamt of being involved in, even two months earlier. But that was long, long ago in showbiz time, and everything had changed.

At least they hadn't actually asked her to be a contestant. That really would have been humiliating. Honestly, the depths people were willing to sink to.

She could hear her mother's laughter from the kitchen; talking of depths. Well, not literally, of course, Zelda wouldn't want her mother's boat to actually sink. No, she loved her mother, just found her a tiny bit annoying sometimes . . .

'Darling, there you are! We have all been asked up to the Court for kitchen supper. Isn't that nice?'

Zelda wasn't sure; was that nice? 'Oh, really. Who asked us?'

'Granny got us all invited!' said Ed, who was bouncing a laughing Willow on his knee.

'I did not "get us invited". You do talk nonsense, Ed.' Cleo was peeved by another 'Granny' reference. If Ed went on with it she was really worried that it might stick. Then, when that baby could speak, it would be calling her 'Great-granny'. She shuddered.

Ed gave his mother a look that said, 'She did!' Zelda believed him. She made a small throat-cutting gesture behind her mother's back.

'I've just had a nice lucrative job offer,' Zelda said brightly.

'Have you, darling. How thrilling.' Cleo didn't sound thrilled.

'Can't talk about it yet, still very early days. But I think you will be pleased for me when you find out what it is. There might even be a little slot in it for you, Mother!'

'What will we be pleased about?' Max said, as he came in from the garden, carrying a trug full of white roses.

'Mum's got a job,' Ed said proudly.

'It's not confirmed yet. Still top secret,' Zelda said.

Cleo responded triumphantly, 'Well then, we won't ask you another word about it. We certainly don't want to jeopardise your chance of a lovely job with all our excitable chatter. Mum's the word!'

'Well done, darling. I knew you would be fine. How divine are these?' Max thrust the roses under Zelda's nose but she pushed them away; she'd had quite enough of roses for one day. The scratches on her arm were beginning to really sting.

Cleo watched her daughter beadily as she rubbed her arms. Zelda looked back at her mother. 'What?'

'Your arms? Darling! You haven't been – you know?'

'What? Self-harming! Oh, for fuck's sake. What's the matter with you? I scratched them when I was retrieving my phone from a bush, OK? Bloody hell!' Zelda was pink with indignation.

\*

There was talk of walking up through the park to Banbury Court for supper.

'Jake has left me his car, so I'll drive the lazy ones,' Zelda offered.

'That was kind of him. He's always so thoughtful, Jake. You are very lucky to have such a lovely husband,' Cleo stirred.

Max knew it wasn't the ideal day to be singing Jake's praises to Zelda, so he intervened. 'That's a marvellous plan; all those wearing sexy heels, in the car; all those not in sexy heels, walking. I shall, of course, be wearing very sexy heels!'

Which got a laugh from the kids.

By the time Karen had arrived to babysit, everyone was finishing their first drink of the night. The house had almost been drunk dry, but Max had cannily stashed a bottle of champagne before he'd gone to bed, when he saw how much everyone was getting through. Particularly Jake, who had been back on it in a big way.

The teenagers had set off ahead, so it was only the three of them drinking. They polished off the bottle in record time and mother and daughter tottered out to the car.

Max noted that from behind they could be the same age. They were wearing similar clothes, dark trousers and silky tops. Their high platform shoes were lengthening already unnaturally long legs. His wife and daughter had what Max considered to be huge advantages over the majority of their sex. They were both very beautiful but there was something else too, something thrilling and indefinable. Something that made him feel proud, particularly after a few hastily quaffed glasses of Bollinger.

No matter how tricky Cleo could be, she would always be the only woman he could ever love. In fact, Cleo was, literally, the only woman Max had ever loved. Otherwise, he had loved young men.

This was always something that was understood between them. Cleo had had her other interests too. Until Kate's book, these things had been kept discreetly between them. But since those revelations the reality of their somewhat flexible situation had seemed tarnished and slightly seedy.

Cleo had nominated Max to drive the car. He hopped into the driver's seat, still very agile for his age. Cleo patted him on the knee. 'Here we go, darling. I think you will adore Banbury. It is so beautiful and holds so many very happy memories for me.'

Max remembered the 'Guy' period, quite early on in their marriage. He knew Cleo was enjoying rubbing his nose in it; she was going to take a while to get over all the humiliations in the press. That girl Kate had a lot to answer for. It never occurred to Max that he might have a bit to answer for too.

'Get moving, Dad, I'm getting all creased in the back of this vile old banger!' Zelda said.

Max put the beautiful old Merc into gear and swept out of the gate.

*

Banbury Court was bathed in a golden light, lending it an extra ethereal beauty. A multitude of windows looked out over the graceful land that surrounded it, unchanged for generations.

As they drove up towards the house, Zelda wondered what a challenge such a massive restoration project would be; very expensive, that much was certain. Rewarding though. She had overheard somebody saying that it needed a couple of million spent on it, which seemed very little compared to what she'd had to shell out to transform their old home in London. She tried to not think of the house she had loved, which had been hailed as one of the most beautiful in the world. But that was all gone now, all lost by bloody Lucien Dark.

Zelda found she couldn't bear to think about their life in London, or Jake and what had happened to make him return to the mews without her. He had been a different person when he'd stopped drinking, reliable, dependable, a grown-up. Now she needed to rely on him more than ever and he had failed her. Her disappointment and fear made her feel small and vulnerable. Not something she enjoyed at all.

As she sat in the back seat of the car, with her parents in the front, she felt fifteen again and surprisingly comforted by their presence. As Max stopped the car outside the imposing front steps at the Court, Zelda put one hand on each of her parents' shoulders and squeezed.

'Thanks for being here,' she said.

Max turned to his lovely daughter and smiled. 'Thank you for asking us, darling.'

Cleo was mistrustful of her daughter's tender tone, thinking that it was probably a precursor to a request for money, so she changed the subject. 'Oh, it looks so much bigger than I remember it.'

'That's what they all say, my darling,' Max quipped, and leapt out of the car.

He opened one of the vast front doors and guided his women through, into the empty marble hall. Their footsteps echoed loudly. There didn't appear to be anyone about.

Max called out, 'Helloooo.'

Nothing.

Then the sound of scampering feet in the distance and a giggle heralded the arrival of Kitty.

Her cheerful face appeared, all sunshine and smiles, as she flung open one of the mahogany doors. 'Hi, sorry! We thought you'd come to the back. No one really uses this entrance any more. We are in the kitchen.' And she opened the door wide, to let them through.

Zelda had forgotten that she had already seen the kitchen, only a couple of nights before. She must have been quite pissed though, as she couldn't really remember it very well at all. She vaguely recalled talking to Frank? Then nothing.

She'd had no idea it was so fabulous. Just the kind of decoration she adored, in fact. She knew it was the sort of room only a woman could have designed, and found herself wondering what Frances was like. No one seemed to talk about her at all; very mysterious.

She would have been interested to know that when Boy and Frances were first married, he had been surprised to learn that his new bride was a bit of an heiress. Frances had kept it a secret but, unlike most secrets, this had turned out to be a surprisingly good one.

The first thing Frances did when she moved to the Court was to turn the decrepit old ballroom into one massive room to actually live in, installing a fabulous Smallbone kitchen and arranging various dining and seating areas, all very comfortable and relaxed, in the ultimate family room.

The immense, grand fireplace was restored and log baskets were piled high on each side of it. Those were the happy days before the logs would be the only form of heating in the house. French windows had once opened out onto a beautiful formal walled garden. Frances had replanted it with vegetables and flowers, making it useful as well as lovely.

The work on the house had progressed slowly over the years, the dining room had been restored and the main bedrooms decorated. Then the children's rooms, as each of their girls were born. It had taken fifteen years for Frances's moderate fortune to dwindle away to small, then tiny, then nothing. Resentment had taken its place.

Now Boy greeted everybody warmly, handing out drinks. He'd found a secret cache of wine in the cellar, murmuring, 'Behind an old door that I didn't even know was there! More secrets! Who'd have thought?'

Zelda was watching him as he said this and she saw a fleeting glimpse of something; what was that, sadness? As he handed her a glass, their fingers touched, their eyes met; just briefly, but long enough for them to feel the bombs falling. They both looked away.

Dusty went out to talk to Doone, as she picked some lettuce from the garden.

'Is Charlie coming over this evening?' Dusty asked.

'No, he's gone back to London.'

'Have you been going out for a long time?'

'We're not going out.'

'Oh, sorry! I thought you were together.'

'Nope.'

'Oh.'

'Why?' Doone straightened up. She was wearing denim shorts, old green wellies and a T-shirt with an American flag printed on it.

Her slim arms dangled by her side, the bright green lettuces in her hands resembling giant pompoms. But no one could look less like an American cheerleader than Doone.

'Just thought you looked good together, that's all.'

'No point! He's in a band and we all know what that means. I'm not interested in a boyfriend I have to share. Ever!' She jumped out of the vegetable bed and strode back into the house.

Dusty felt wrongfooted somehow. She was only trying to make polite conversation.

*

They had finished the pea soup and were just about to start on some delicious roast chicken when Valentine arrived unexpectedly. In celebration, he did a little dance to demonstrate that he was no longer encumbered by his plaster-cast. Then he grabbed a chair and plonked himself down next to Flora, with a grin.

Zelda sprang up and kissed her son. 'Oh, darling, you are "you" again. Hurrah!'

Ed could see that his brother was certainly *that*. He couldn't believe Valentine could have moved in so fast on Flora: the one girl he was mad about! To be fair, he hadn't told Valentine he was interested in her. But he felt his brother might have asked, before he started riding roughshod over everyone, as usual.

Doone ignored the new arrival but leant in, quite close, as she put a bowl of salad onto the table. Valentine grinned. He knew it; she did have good legs! Those shorts were very cute, a surprising choice for such a serious girl. He'd like to have thought she'd worn them just for him. But of course she couldn't have. She didn't know he was coming back down so soon. No one did. In fact he'd rather taken himself by surprise.

But London had seemed so hot and boring after he'd left the hospital. He'd rung Lily, but she was busy, though she told him she had made some appointments to look at country houses later in the week. She also said that she would still bring the limo to take him round with her, even if it wasn't strictly necessary, now that he was 'free of his encumbrance'. Somehow the word 'encumbrance' sounded deeply erotic when whispered in her French accent. 'It will be fun,' she'd said, and Valentine knew that was true.

'You must be so pleased to get that vile contraption off,' Max remarked.

'It was pretty restricting. A sort of chastity belt.' Valentine watched out of the corner of his eye, to see if he could tweak Doone's interest. Nothing.

He got Ed's attention again though. 'A chastity belt? Ha ha! Not what I heard.'

Valentine ignored him and turned to Cleo. 'Very excited about your new adventure. Aren't you scared?'

'Oh, no, darling, you know me, I'm never scared of anything.'

'Except obscurity, you're scared of that,' Zelda said with an icy smile.

\*

It was well after midnight by the time they started to get up to go. They had had a very amusing time once things had settled down, and Zelda and Boy found themselves chatting to each other with the ease of old friends. They had all finally relaxed and the Spenders began to tell hilariously self-deprecating stories about their lives, in the age-old luvvie tradition.

Everyone knew that people mostly got famous for the simple reason that they wanted to be loved and to earn that love, they entertained. To witness the Spenders launched into a full-on entertainment-fest was awe-inspiring. Doone could suddenly understand what others saw in this family, and everyone was exhausted from laughing so much.

Unwilling to leave, Cleo was insisting that Boy show her and Max around the house. So Zelda said her goodbyes. She told them she would drive Dusty and Ed home first. Then she would return for the others, since they certainly couldn't all fit into Jake's car in one go anyway. So that was the plan.

Cleo dragged Max off to the drawing room, saying she remembered exactly where it was. 'A lovely room, we had so much fun in there.' Max trailed after her, only a little disgruntled by her game. Dusty and Ed ran outside to the car. Their excited voices carried back into the house, through the dark.

Zelda and Boy suddenly found themselves alone, standing facing each other in the marble hall. 'Thanks for having us all.' Zelda smiled, avoiding Boy's eyes.

'No! Thanks for coming. It's lovely to have everyone here, brings us all back to life really. It has been so . . .' Boy stopped.

The 'to kiss, or not to kiss, goodbye?' dilemma had struck them both.

Zelda had stepped forward to peck him on the cheek but, as he turned his head infinitesimally, their lips met by mistake. Just a light brush but it felt like a blow. Zelda looked away, embarrassed but rooted to the spot. Boy put his hand behind her head and suddenly, he was pulling her towards him, kissing her gently. Within seconds gently had become passionately and Boy felt an overwhelming urge to push her down onto the cool floor and tear her clothes off.

The marble hall felt hotter than it had in its entire history.

Boy murmured, 'Stay.'

Reluctantly, Zelda stepped away from him. 'I've just got to . . .' She gestured towards the door. 'Then I'll be back.'

As she turned and walked away she could feel him staring after her, and could hardly breathe. The cool evening air hit her, like a slap in the face, as she stepped out into the night.

This wasn't a good idea. She knew that, not a good idea at all.

*

Back at the Dower House, Karen had been despatched and Dusty went off to check on Willow.

Zelda hugged Ed spontaneously, which surprised him. She

asked, 'Are you having a nice time, darling, with all your new pals?'

'Er, yeah?'

'I'm sorry things have been so horrid. But they are going to get better, I promise.'

'Everything's fine, Mum. You'd better go and get Granny before she eats Boy alive.'

Was her mother interested in Boy? That hadn't occurred to Zelda. God, how embarrassing, she thought. Bloody hell, she needed to get back up there fast, or God only knew what would be happening.

\*

Having whizzed upstairs for a super-quick, but comprehensive, face and body overhaul, Zelda was in the car and ready to begin her new adventure.

Before pulling out of the Dower House drive, she glanced in the rear-view mirror. The light from the house illuminated her perfect features and she was pleased with what she saw. She smiled, thinking some things might be over, but not everything. She had still got 'it' and some fantastic new things were just about to begin.

She felt a surge of excitement, hope and confidence.

Zelda drove fast. The car rattled over the cattle grid. A low summer mist lay on the ground and the headlights picked out the trees in ghostly silhouette. Zelda shivered; she never liked driving alone at night, particularly in the country. At least it wasn't far.

A tree stump loomed up ahead and Zelda wondered if she

had somehow wandered off the drive, as she couldn't remember having seen it before. As she drew closer it suddenly moved! Swung out in front of the car! She began to swerve to avoid it, and as the car hit the rough grass it started to bump. The tree stump turned, and Zelda suddenly saw what it was . . . a man in a long, hooded cloak. As the car raced past, narrowly missing him, Zelda looked up and saw his face. She began to scream; it was the face of a monstrous creature, gnarled and hollow-eyed. She almost lost control of the wheel but somehow got it back.

She was still screaming when she looked in her rear-view mirror, to see him raise something and turn towards the car. It was a gun. A *gun*! Zelda swerved back onto the drive. She felt the car hit something soft, then a sickening thud. She screamed again and drove on, not daring to look back. The lights of Banbury Court glittered up ahead, guiding her to safety. She was too frightened to pull up at the front of the house, in case the 'thing' had somehow flown after her. She skidded around the corner and screeched to a halt around the back. She flung herself out of the car and hurled herself at the door. It was locked, so she started banging on it, screaming, 'Help! Help!' She looked back towards the corner of the house. Could she see the figure looming out of the darkness? Just then the door opened and she fell into Boy's arms.

'Whoa there! What's happened?' Boy held her firmly.

Zelda was gasping for breath. 'He's out there! He's coming. Hide! Everyone must hide!' She was frantic. 'Lock the door, lock the door!

Boy locked the bolt. 'There you are. Safe now.' He began to lead her through to the kitchen. 'What did you see? Who's out there?'

'Call –' gulp – 'police! He's got a gun!' Zelda's voice was shrill.

Boy led her into the kitchen.

When Cleo and Max saw what a state their daughter was in, Max jumped up. 'Darling, what's happened?'

'There's a horrible thing outside. Close all the curtains, doors!' She gave another scream.

'They are closed,' Boy said kindly. 'I've just locked up everywhere, so we are quite safe. You are alright. I'm here. He's not going to come in, OK? Try to tell us what you saw. Then I'll get onto the police.'

'It was ho-horrible. Long black –' gasp – 'cape thing, gnarled face.' She was shaking. 'He had a gun.'

'Gnarled face sounds like a mask, darling. Could it have been a person trying to scare you?' Max asked gently.

'It certainly seems to have worked. Try to calm down; here, dry your eyes.' Cleo handed Zelda a handkerchief.

'He's here, outside, now and he's got a gun!' Zelda's voice was rising.

'You stay with your parents for a minute. I'll just go and have a quick look around.' Boy looked at Max. 'Get her some brandy, I think there's some in the bottom of that cupboard.'

Zelda shrieked after Boy, 'Don't go out! Can't you hear what I am saying? He's got a fucking gun!'

Boy called back, 'So have I.'

They heard a door slam and then everything went very, very quiet.

'Nobody believed –' gasp – 'me.' Zelda continued to shake. Max found the brandy and tried to get her to drink some. She took the glass and downed it in one. 'Can I have a cigarette?'

Cleo looked on. 'He is obviously trying to scare you to death. Jake said he thought it was a pap. But this sounds like a nutter.'

'Ring the police!'

Max went to the house-phone and dialled 999.

As he asked for help Zelda suddenly remembered something and started to yell at Max. 'Oh, God! The children are home alone! They are home alone! Tell the police to go straight there *now*. They have men outside. Tell them!'

Max did as he was told.

Zelda was shivering. 'Where is Boy? Oh, God, what's happening?'

'I'm here.' Boy walked in, carrying a shotgun. 'Can't see anyone. Let's get onto the police.'

'I have, they are on their way. I've sent them to the Dower House. We just realised the kids are there on their own,' Max said. He looked worried.

Boy was worried too. 'Let's all go down there now. Give me couple of secs. I'll get Frank over to hold the fort here. The girls are all asleep so he can just keep a lookout.' He held Zelda's hands. 'Will you be alright to come back down there with me? I'll take us all in the Land Rover.'

'Is it close to the house?'

'I'll bring it right up to the back door, OK?'

'OK,' Zelda sniffed.

Frank was there in an unfeasibly short time. Zelda wondered where he lived.

Boy bundled Zelda and her parents into the Land Rover and, revving the engine, he cracked off at speed down the drive. Max had tried to ring Ed and Dusty to tell them to lock all the doors and not to let anyone in. But he had failed.

'There's never any signal at that fucking house! It's so dangerous,' Zelda whimpered.

Boy drove on without a word. Zelda put her hands over her eyes as they hurtled through the park.

Boy said, 'Zelda, can you remember roughly where you saw him, so that I can tell the police where to look? There's nothing out there now, I promise. If you could just look.'

Zelda made a small gap between her fingers like a frightened child, but what she saw made her scream.

Boy jammed on the brakes. Cleo shot forward and hit the back of his seat.

'Ouch!'

The headlights picked out a bloody mess on the road. Boy kept the engine running, wondering whether to get out a take a closer look. But perhaps it was a trap? Zelda was still screaming, muffled slightly by her hands over her face.

'It's a sheep. It's alright, everybody, it's only a sheep. We'll go round it.' He couldn't believe it; the bastard had killed one of his animals.

Zelda calmed down a bit. 'I hit something after I'd gone past him. My car hit something. I've just remembered. Do you think he put it there to make me stop?' She turned her anguished eyes to Boy.

'I think you probably just ran it over.' Boy had found the sheep killer. 'I'm sure you wouldn't have been able to see it, what with the mist and everything. You were in a panic, can't be helped.' But he was a bit upset. Boy adored his sheep.

'Lucky sheep killing isn't still a hanging offence, darling.' Max patted Zelda on the shoulder.

'I've broken a fucking fingernail and I really hurt my knee when you stopped like that. Your family always drove too fast,' Cleo said petulantly.

'Oh, for God's sake! After all I've gone through tonight, really?' Zelda turned to her mother furiously.

Everyone was quiet.

As they pulled up outside the Dower House a police car swerved in after them. Its blue light flashed comfortingly, in the darkness.

The front door flew open and Boy saw a complete stranger standing on the threshold. He got out of the Land Rover and raised his gun.

Zelda called out, 'David!' and ran towards him. 'Oh, thank God you are here.' She flung her arms around him.

Boy looked on in astonishment. Who the fuck was David?

The policeman walked up behind Boy and said quietly, 'Just put the gun down, sir. We won't be needing that now, will we?'

Boy lowered the gun. 'No, Officer, it seems not.'

Cleo said, 'David, thank goodness you are here, in the nick of time too!' as she swept past the man and into the house.

Zelda turned to look at Boy. 'Boy, this is David, my head of security. He has come to guard us!' She turned back to David. 'I've just seen that horrible stalker . . .' and she led her handsome, ex-SAS security guard into the house.

Boy felt strangely redundant and not a little hurt. He turned to the police officer. 'Where the hell are your men? Sergeant Powell gave his assurance that you would be protecting this family 24/7. There have been a number of incidents and not one of your guys is in sight! Tonight Miss Spender has been completely terrified by someone in a hooded cape and mask. He raised a bloody gun at her as she drove through the park! Did any of your men see anything? Apprehend anyone?'

Boy was suddenly furious, not only with the police, but also because he felt instinctively that, in his new role as Zelda's protector, he had been usurped by some muscle-bound prick. She had fallen into the guy's arms!

'Would you like to show me where this sighting occurred, Lord Banbury, and I will have the area searched thoroughly.' The policeman looked sincere.

'I'm going to check that everything is alright here first. She saw him about halfway up the drive. There's a dead sheep around the spot, she ran it over after . . .'

'She ran over a sheep, sir? Is it possible she was so distressed by the incident that she imagined the . . . obstacle?'

The officer had heard Sergeant Powell regaling everyone at the station with stories about the 'hysterical fantasist' superstar who was staying at Lord Banbury's mother's house.

'No, that is not possible. Miss Spender has been terrorised since she arrived and it is your duty to ensure that it stops right here, right now. So please get on with finding the person responsible and get Sergeant Powell to ring me. I need to have a word.'

'I think he'll be asleep, sir.'

'Then wake him *up*!'

'Very good, sir. I'll just be off to have a look round then. Dead sheep, you said? Somewhere on the drive?'

Boy watched the police officer as he drove away, flashing his blue light, which didn't seem wise. Surely that would alert anyone who was trying to hide? Idiot! He wondered what was really going on.

He was reminded that he didn't know Zelda at all. The policeman's sceptical comment had made him feel uneasy. Could she have made all this up? When he'd been showing Cleo and Max round the Court earlier, Cleo had taken him to one side and confided, 'Let me just say one thing to you, Boy. Zelda is desperate for attention, always has been. She has to be loved by everyone, always. This fall from grace has unbalanced her, she is quite unstable so . . .'

Max had found her whispering and cut her off. 'Cleo, leave Boy alone!'

Boy was shocked by Cleo's disloyalty. But it had sowed a seed of doubt in his mind; could Zelda have pretended to be that scared? He knew she was a good actress but if this evening's performance had been faked, she'd have got the Oscar that had famously always eluded her.

So far that evening she had kissed him – he temporarily forgot that, strictly speaking, he had kissed her – and now he had witnessed her flinging herself into the arms of another man.

This had all happened since her husband had left her alone for . . . barely a moment. No wonder his pal had hit the bottle again. Jake's wife was obviously very unreliable indeed. Sexy as hell; but extremely erratic.

He went into the house. The kitchen was alive with chatter and excitement, and Max had poured more drinks. Boy noticed that the new man didn't appear to have one. But everyone else did.

Zelda waved a glass at him. 'Boy, my saviour! Have a drink.'

'No thanks. I need to get back to the girls. Just wanted to check that everyone was alright. But I can see that you are.'

His voice sounded cold. Zelda appeared confused, but said, 'Oh, OK.' She moved to follow him out into the hall. 'Thank you for looking after me, sorry I was so hopeless.' She stood close to him.

Boy turned and looked down at her lovely face, which was a mess of smudged mascara, almost clown-like. Despite himself he smiled.

She was looking him directly in the eye. What could he see? Nothing. He stepped backwards, away from her. He noticed something in her eyes then: hurt, disappointment? Or was it just that he wasn't doing what she wanted him to do? Her mother had said she wanted everyone to love her. Well, he didn't think he would, just because she wanted him to. These things weren't that simple.

He knew he needed to walk away.

Zelda, sounding panicky, blurted out, 'I'm sorry I killed your sheep!'

He looked down at her. 'It's OK, could've happened to anyone.'

He was pretty sure Zelda could destroy anyone too. But he wasn't going to let her get to *him* any more.

He opened the front door just as Cleo walked past them. ''Night, Boy. Thanks for a lovely and rather thrilling evening. You were magnificent.'

''Night,' he said and closed the door behind him.

\*

Zelda suddenly felt overwhelmingly exhausted. She returned to the kitchen where Ed was cross-examining David about his work in Syria.

'Did you kill anyone?'

Max intervened. 'That's not a question you ever ask a soldier, Ed.'

'But he's a gun for hire these days, aren't you, David?'

David's handsome face remained non-committal.

'Thank God you are here. It has been so frightening . . .'

Cleo interrupted. 'Well, we are off to bed. Early start in the morning.' She glanced slyly at her daughter. 'I've told David what I am going to be doing for the new show. He says it will

be very tough but he thinks I can do it. Didn't you, David?'
Without waiting for him to reply, she continued impatiently,
'Come on, Max.'

'Yes, yes, yes.' Max followed her out. ''Night, all.'

Ed and Dusty stood up too. Ed suddenly asked, 'Where's
Valentine?'

Zelda looked bemused.

'Is he here somewhere? I haven't seen him,' David said.

'He was with us, up at the Court. He must still be there!'
Dusty said.

Ed looked at his mother accusingly. 'Have you left him
behind?'

Zelda thought about it for a moment. 'I suppose I must have
done.'

David laughed. 'Well, he's old enough, it's not like you've
abandoned a child in a supermarket.'

Zelda didn't know what he was talking about.

Ed was furious. 'You'd better go back and get him!'

'I'm sure he'll be fine. There are plenty of rooms at Banbury
Court and anyway, he seemed to be getting on very well with
those stroppy girls.'

Which was exactly what Ed was upset about. As he stomped
off upstairs, he yelled, 'You should ring Boy and tell him that
there is a fucking fox in his hen-house!'

Zelda didn't think she'd be doing that. She knew she had
already blotted her copybook with their host quite enough for
one day; could a person really be so upset about a dead sheep?
Very odd. Anyway, whatever, she certainly didn't want to make

things worse by alerting him to Valentine's presence. She was confident that her son would be able to handle the situation perfectly well; he always could.

She was so relieved to see her loyal security guard. David's strong reassuring presence made her feel quite overwhelmed with gratitude.

'Thank you for coming to my rescue so fast, I don't know what I would have done if you hadn't been able to come. I still don't know how I will be able to pay you.'

'Not a problem, as I said when you rang. I have just earned a fortune on my last mission. I can wait until you are back in the black, which you will be in no time. It will be nice to spend some time in the peaceful countryside. I was head of your security team for four years, after all. Helping you out now is the least I can do, so don't even think about it.' He smiled encouragingly. 'Now do you want to tell me exactly what's been going on?'

David really was a very good man.

*

Valentine had overheard the commotion when Zelda burst into the Court in hysterics, and he'd decided to keep his head down. He saw it as an opportunity. He had caught a glimpse of Flora as she disappeared up the back staircase, so he followed her, whispering, 'Flora, there has been another sighting of my mother's stalker. Your dad is taking everyone back to the Dower House now, so I'm going to stay with you to protect you and your sisters.'

Flora looked apprehensive. 'Where was he?'

'Oh, somewhere down the drive.' He waved airily. 'We'll be fine. I'm here anyway so you don't need to worry.' He smiled his most winning smile. 'Show me where everyone is sleeping, but quietly, we don't want to wake them and scare the life out of them, do we?'

Flora wasn't sure, but she tiptoed along the passage and obediently showed him all their rooms. Hers was next to Doone's, which was either convenient or not, Valentine couldn't quite decide which.

He followed her into her room and closed the door softly.

'Shouldn't we leave that open, to hear if anyone is in the house?' Her eyes suddenly looked wide with fear.

Valentine sat down next to her on the bed and lit a cigarette, offering her a puff, which she accepted. He noticed that her small pale hands shook a little. He placed his hand lightly on her back. Her skin was cool, just the way he expected it to be. She was a cool girl. He watched her as she took a deep drag on the cigarette. Her dark eyes closed as she inhaled. Then two little streams of smoke poured from her perfect, studded nostrils. Valentine slowly coiled her long dark hair around his hand and pulled it, gently.

He whispered in her ear, 'You're not scared, are you?'

She laughed nervously. 'No!'

'I meant, you're not scared of me, are you?'

'Should I be?'

The door flew open.

'What the fuck are you still doing here? Or need I ask?' Doone stood on the threshold.

'This isn't how it looks,' Valentine said, and he gazed defiantly into her blazing eyes. 'There is someone dodgy outside, Zelda saw him on her way back up. So your dad's taken everyone home and I have stayed on to protect you all till he gets back.' He looked sincere. 'Flora was scared, so I was just looking after her.'

'Seriously?' Doone continued to glare. 'I think she'd be safer with your mother's stalker. Get away from her.'

Flora was embarrassed, but quite relieved to see her sister.

Kitty suddenly appeared. 'What's going on? Why are you shouting?'

'It's nothing to worry about, go back to bed.' Doone kept her eyes firmly on Valentine.

Kitty suddenly noticed him. 'Oh, OK, Well, 'night, all. Sleep tight, don't let the bedbugs bite!'

'They already have! So what shall we do now, Valentine? Now that you have *looked after* my sister – what next?'

Valentine stood up. 'Maybe we should all go downstairs and wait for your dad to return? You have totally got this all wrong.' He nudged Doone gently as he passed and went out onto the landing. Saying, very quietly, so that she could only just hear him: 'Would you rather I'd looked after you?'

Doone was incredulous and her heart was thumping with indignation. To her horror, she realised that she was wearing only a very see-through '30s nightdress. She scuttled to her room to get her dressing gown. As she glanced at herself in her bedroom mirror she felt confused. Her cheeks were slightly flushed. What was she feeling, really? Was it possible that what she felt was jealousy when she saw that ridiculously handsome, cocky bastard with her sister? No, he was just the sort of person she loathed. So why was her heart pounding? She wrapped her grandmother's old embroidered velvet gown around herself and set off downstairs.

She felt nervous. If there was a maniac roaming outside the house, perhaps they really were in danger. Of course! That was why her heart was turning somersaults, she told herself.

When Frank greeted them all in the kitchen and explained that their father had asked *him* to come over to look after the girls, Doone and Flora both knew, instantly, that Valentine had lied to them.

Doone was even more furious with him then, and with herself too, for enjoying his company so much at supper, laughing at his jokes, almost being taken in by him. She felt like a fool. The Spenders had brought nothing but trouble with them. Just as she had warned her father that they would.

The girls returned to their bedrooms. Neither spoke as they stomped upstairs.

\*

When Boy returned home, he found Frank and Valentine happily ensconced in his kitchen. Valentine explained that he had only gone off to the loo and when he'd got back everyone had left without him! They all had a laugh and Valentine drove the old Mercedes down to the Dower House. A number of romantic disasters seemed to have been accidentally averted that evening.

When Valentine got back he found his mother sitting at the kitchen table with their ex-security guard, David.

'Hey, man, that was quick, where did you spring from? SAS – yeay!'

David stood up. He was an impressive sight, tall and fit, the archetypal rugged soldier. He spoke softly. 'Your mother phoned me. So I got down here as soon as I could. I'm just off to have a look around outside, so I'll see you in the morning.'

He looked at Zelda kindly. 'Don't worry, I'll stay up. You all get some sleep now.'

Zelda and Valentine wandered out.

'Thanks so much. Such a relief that you are here,' Zelda said as she wafted upstairs.

David noticed Valentine's limp. He was reminded of the crash that had almost killed Zelda's son. He didn't think the guy looked too beaten-up though, considering. He turned out all the lights downstairs, and sat quietly in the dark. He felt at home, at peace, at last.

Only one little problem to be resolved here, and he couldn't see that it would be much of a problem at all.

David was ready for action.

# CHAPTER NINETEEN

Things were a little fraught over breakfast.

Cleo instinctively knew that a request for funds was coming any moment so she said, 'Darling, I'm so happy about your new job, whatever it is. Our car is here so we do have to leave. I'll ring later.' She air-kissed her daughter and swept out.

Max went to hug his daughter. 'Bye, darling.'

'Dad, I need to ask you something . . .' Zelda felt uncomfortable asking for money in front of everyone.

Particularly as Karen had just walked in, unaware of the tricky conversation that Zelda was attempting to instigate in Lady Banbury's kitchen. She picked up on the atmosphere and tactfully said to David, 'If you follow me I'll show you your room. It's just above the garage, I think you'll be . . .' The room fell silent.

Zelda said, 'We're fine here, David, thanks.'

David nodded respectfully. 'Call me if you need me.' And he followed Karen out.

'Anyway, Dad, I wondered if you could lend me a little to

199

tide me over? I have got a meeting about this new show soon, so should be able to . . .' She was smarting with humiliation. She felt about fourteen years old, and not in a good way.

Max was backing towards the door.

Valentine looked up. 'If you're short of cash, I can give you some, Mum. Pots of it at the moment, flowing from my agency like a river. Couldn't spend it in bloody hospital, so I can easily bung you some.'

Zelda hugged her son. Thank God for her beautiful golden boy, she thought.

Max was thinking the same thing. He called merrily, 'Well done, darlings. 'Bye!' and he was gone.

'How much do you need? I can get some cash when I'm out and about with Lily.' Valentine was pleased with himself.

'Oh, darling, thank you! I'll have a think.' She smiled gratefully at her son.

*

Jake had spent the previous day trying to think objectively about his family's future.

He and Zelda had had so many ups and downs over the years; it was hard to tell if this down was any different. He knew that their life together had always been built on dangerously shifting sands and he was beginning to worry that they could be in real trouble now.

The AA mantra of 'accepting the things you cannot change' seemed wise counsel at this point. Jake certainly accepted that he couldn't change their financial situation, he couldn't change the fact that Kate had blown the family's reputation to smithereens and he couldn't get Zelda a job.

But he could get on with writing his novel and he could stay sober. Those would be his priorities and hopefully everything else would become clear as he went along.

When he was considering the repercussions of his drinking, he kept finding himself being drawn back to thinking about Sophie, and the things that she had said. He tried to convince himself that this was what you were supposed to do with other people's life experiences in AA. But then he'd remember her hair and her smile and her honesty. He thought he could get away with admiring her honesty – but the hair and smile, not so much.

Now he was trying to concentrate on the Sunday papers when his phone rang and Zelda's name flashed on the screen. He hesitated, then picked up saying, brightly – too brightly? – 'Hey! How are things down there?'

Zelda told him about her stalker and the dead sheep. She told him how frightened she had been. She didn't mention Boy at all.

Jake was worried. 'Jesus, Zelda, why didn't you call me?'

'I didn't want to worry you, when you were trying to get yourself ...' She improvised, since in fact it hadn't even occurred to her to call him. She suddenly remembered something else. 'Anyway David is here now, so I feel less scared. The police have been useless. David can deal with the guy. He's brought a gun.'

Jake wasn't sure of the wisdom in that, but David had always been incredibly reliable as their head of security. So he said, 'Good. Try not to worry. If you're sure you're alright? I can come down if you want me to?'

'No, you need to be there. I do understand that, Jake. Sorry I have been such a nightmare. You can get on with your book and get straightened out. That will be the most help.'

'I'm the one that's a nightmare, I've been useless. Things will get better.'

'Yes, I know.' Zelda paused dramatically. 'In fact they already have!' She told him about *Fame Game*.

'That sounds terrific!' he lied; it sounded grotesque. But, if anyone knew that beggars couldn't be choosers, it was Jake.

They hung up on good terms; a team again. They both felt very relieved.

*

Valentine had decided to tackle the frosty Dusty situation. He always felt discomfited when girls were 'off' him for too long. Things had been very tricky between them for ages.

Dusty had, understandably, been shocked to discover that Valentine was her half-brother, rather than her cousin as they had always been led to believe. Although she could hardly blame him for that particular surprise, what she could, and did, blame him for was sleeping with her mother and producing a baby: Willow.

When all those devastating, shameful facts had been uncovered, the news had blown Dusty's world apart. She had barely been able to look at Valentine since then. However, she loved her baby sister more than anyone in the world, so her feelings were very mixed and confusing.

Valentine was fairly confident that she didn't suspect him of any involvement in her mother's death. But he knew it would be wise to make amends. She was a clever girl and he needed to keep her close, make sure she saw him in a better light.

So now he smiled and said to Dusty, with warmth and enthusiasm, 'C'mon, let's take Willow out for a walk and have a proper chat. We haven't done anything together for ages, have we?'

He turned and picked his baby daughter up from the floor. It was the first time he had touched her since before the accident, and he was surprised at how big she'd grown. He still couldn't quite believe that she was his. What on earth had he been thinking?

That had been the thing though, he hadn't been thinking at all in those dark days. Drugs had made him do the strangest things. That was one of the benefits of his time spent in hospital, to get drug-free. Apart from the morphine they'd kept him supplied with, he'd been as clean as a whistle. Maybe the odd little slip here and there with Lily in the past few days. But nothing like the stuff he had been into before. He felt better, more in control. He planned to keep it that way.

He certainly knew he couldn't afford another fuck-up like the Georgia debacle. He had got away with that and he knew he was lucky. In fact he was lucky to have got away with a lot of things.

Not least, he was lucky to be alive.

# CHAPTER TWENTY

Zelda's meeting had gone well with the Big Guns team. She was disappointed that Sam Carson hadn't come down to Oxfordshire to see her himself. But his people seemed very professional and showed deference and respect, which she hadn't felt from anyone in a while. It made her feel a lot better, more confident.

She had spent ages getting dressed before they arrived. Trying to find just the right thing was difficult without her stylist and ex-best friend, Shona. She still couldn't believe that betrayal, which hurt more than most. At least Shona hadn't done a 'tell all' like some people, but then again, perhaps it was only a question of time, Zelda thought bitterly.

She hadn't had to pick out her own clothes for years and the few things she had brought with her in the panic-packing, when they had escaped London in such a hurry, seemed woefully unsuitable.

In the end she decided to look very relaxed indeed. After all, she was supposed to be spending her time writing her autobiography. If she did ever write one she would certainly be outing that disloyal bitch Shona!

Yes, she would wear jeans and a crisp white shirt. The 'relaxed look' took far more effort to achieve perfectly than the 'red-carpet look'. Fortunately, she was good at doing her own hair and make-up. It was the one really useful thing that Cleo had taught her to do well.

She arranged her hair in an artful ponytail, and her make-up looked 'barely there' though it certainly was there, in abundance. With her jeans belted and high Charlotte Olympia shoes, it wasn't very country. Zelda felt good.

Her eyes were clear; she had slept well. She had finally dared to take her hard-core sleeping pills, now that she knew David was on site to protect her. She felt safe in his familiar, reassuring presence and she was determined to put the trauma of the previous evening behind her.

With a few Adderall to perk her up, and keep her appetite down, she almost felt back to normal again.

The Big Guns laid out their plans for the show and Zelda had to admit that *Fame Game* didn't sound like such a bad idea after all. The production values were going to be fantastic. The budgets were huge and some of the stars who had signed up for it already were really impressive. So Zelda was happy to play ball. By the time the meeting had finished, the Big Guns team were all completely charmed and totally hooked.

They could all see what the boss had seen in her now; Zelda Spender was beautiful, smart and really, really funny, and they had all laughed at her jokes a lot; too much? There was no such thing as 'too much' as far as Zelda was concerned.

She knew she'd had them at 'Hello'.

Her agent, Helen, was pleased with her. She stayed behind for a moment after the Big Guns had returned to their car. 'That was good, Zelda, well done. I'll get back to you with all the figures when we've agreed them, then we can get this signed.'

Then Helen gave Zelda a surprisingly strong hug. 'Can't wait to see the book, glad you are using your time-out so well.' Zelda wondered if Helen knew they were playing a game or if she actually believed Zelda was writing a book.

As the car pulled away Zelda waved. She also found herself wondering if Helen was a lesbian. She realised she didn't know that much about her new agent. She must Google her. Then she remembered she couldn't, or not easily anyway. The Internet situation really was a drag, but she would ask David about it, as he knew about communication things and was bound to be able to sort it out.

The house was quiet when she went back inside. Valentine had been whisked away by Lily, in a limo, and the kids had gone up to the Court. Zelda made herself a cup of mint tea and was sitting quietly in the drawing room when there was a masculine, 'Hello!' from the hall.

Zelda jumped up nervously and peeped around the doorframe. It was Boy, looking particularly handsome, strong and somehow rather wholesome. Zelda stepped out. 'Hi.'

Boy turned to look at her. 'Sorry, hope I didn't startle you.

Just wanted to check you were alright? No more trouble? Your, um, guy is here?'

She felt flustered, tried to look cool. 'Yup, everything seems to have settled down, thanks.' Her voice sounded clipped and harsh, not how she meant it to at all.

Her performance when they had seen each other last made her cringe. No wonder he had given her the cold shoulder. She wondered if she should apologise about the sheep again? Would that help? Or the kiss, should she apologise about that?

She fixed him with her violet eyes. 'Come on in, can I get you anything?' and she sashayed past him, leaving behind a fragrant trail of Obsession in her wake.

'No, I don't need anything, thanks. I just wondered if I might ask you to consider doing something for me?' Boy said.

Zelda was surprised. 'Um, sure. If I can.'

'It's the local fête on Saturday and the person they had organised to open it has just backed out. They asked if I knew anyone and I just thought you might like to get out ...'

Zelda wasn't sure how to the play this. The village fête! Was he serious? Going anywhere in public was really difficult and, since Kate's book, she felt it would be tantamount to suicide. Crowds could be very unpredictable.

In panic, she answered a little too sharply, 'But I'm trying to keep a low profile! Don't you think that might alert people to my being here?'

'OK. Just thought I'd ask. I don't see why anyone would work out that you were staying here though. You would just be the wife of my friend who is helping us out. But if it makes you feel uncomfortable doing something so beneath you?' He turned to go.

Zelda could see he was livid, but she felt that he hadn't considered her position at all. She realised he couldn't understand what it was like to be as famous as her, but he might try.

Before she could work out a way of explaining this to Boy and retrieving the situation, he was leaving. She wondered if she should go after him. Tell him how she felt. She felt panicky, so she just let him go, and watched as he strode off up the drive.

Why did she feel such an overwhelming desire to run after him, to hurl herself at his strong retreating back, to throw her arms around his neck, to cling to him, to kiss him? Tell him that she would open his fête, gladly?

Why didn't he turn around, glance back? If only he would, then he would notice her standing there and he would be able to see her properly. Not only the selfish, superstar her; but the real, lonely, frightened her.

But, to her dismay, he didn't turn around, he just kept on walking and Zelda watched him forlornly until he had disappeared from view.

She went back into the drawing room and slumped into one of the saggy, but surprisingly comfortable, chintz sofas. She suddenly felt a wave of panic; what was going on? She was alone in the country, fighting with and, it could be said, lusting after Jake's oldest friend. Nothing good could come of that, she knew it.

Now that relations between her and Jake had improved,

albeit infinitesimally, this wasn't the moment for any of this insanity. She wondered if the stalker thing had unbalanced her, blown her judgement? But her judgement in matters of the heart had never been good and her long marriage to Jake had been interspersed with endless separations and reunions; it might have been one of the longest marriages in show business but it was also, frequently, one of the rockiest.

When she and Jake first met, he had just begun his meteoric rise as a brilliant television scriptwriter. He was handsome and funny and Zelda had fallen madly in love with him. He had reminded her of Richard E. Grant in *Withnail and I*, one of her favourite movies, as he was hilarious and he had that same handsome shambolic look, tall and skinny with messy, dark hair; he had even worn a similar floor-length military coat. But, unfortunately, he had turned out to be more like Withnail in his drinking habits than was altogether healthy, for his career or his marriage.

Zelda and he had somehow stayed together but it had often been a struggle and although she knew that it didn't excuse her own behaviour, there was always a part of her that was searching for a grown-up man to love.

Her mind strayed back to Boy. Was he a grown-up man? she wondered. He was certainly quite impatient. He hadn't given her any time to explain about her concerns over the fête. In many ways he was the opposite of Jake, not least in his looks. Where Jake was dark, Boy was fair. His face was healthy and tanned and his eyes were a twinkly hazel, rather than red as Jake's so frequently were.

Somehow, Zelda found herself thinking about Boy's lips, not only the way they looked, but the way they had felt.

She began to feel hot, but it was a cool day. Perhaps it was a good thing that Boy had stomped off after all. Zelda told herself that she had probably avoided a fête worse than death – ta da! She was sad she couldn't share that old chestnut with Jake, as she knew he would have appreciated it.

# CHAPTER TWENTY-ONE

Valentine and Lily had seen three houses that day. They had made love in the master bedrooms of two of them, and the library of the other, almost getting caught out in the last house when the agent, who had been ordered to wait outside, had rushed in to find them because the owner had turned up.

Lily had instantly charmed the owner with her sweetest smile, saying, 'Johnny will be very 'appy to 'ave your 'ouse. C'est très beau. Thank you for letting me see it avec mon frère.'

She and Valentine fell into the car followed by the bemused agent, who said, 'I didn't realise you were brother and sister.'

They were giggling. Valentine replied, 'We're not, that would be sick!'

Which confused the agent even more.

'I think that is not the best 'ouse. Which one is the closer to Banbury Court? We will take that one. I like to be close to my brother.' Then Lily kissed Valentine almost all the way home. The agent didn't know where to look.

He knew that Johnny the Bastard was taking the house for

himself and this model-girl. She didn't seem like a very nice or reliable girlfriend to have.

Rock and roll, eh! he thought to himself. Maybe being a boring old estate agent wasn't such a bad thing. His girlfriend, Vicky Newman, was very kind and loyal. She also had the most beautiful legs in the world, better than this skinny supermodel. He suddenly felt overwhelmingly happy with his lot.

*

Another perfect summer's day began with a mass exodus from the Dower House. Lily had been asked to take Flora Banbury back up to London; apparently Johnny had invited her to a gig. Lily was a little bit peeved, so she had persuaded Valentine to come too. He didn't relish the thought of a car journey with Lily and Flora together.

Then he heard they would also be taking Dusty, who was going up to see her boyfriend, Alex. Things got even more complicated when Zelda refused to keep the baby with her, so now they would have to take Willow up to London as well. Not to be left out, Ed announced that he had to go too. The trip in the overcrowded limo was beginning to sound like the highway to hell to Valentine. In a flash of inspiration he thought of a way of extricating himself.

He persuaded Zelda to let him borrow Jake's old Mercedes again, promising to have the car back by the morning. This was the perfect solution because it meant Lily could travel with him.

Zelda didn't feel she could be churlish about lending her son the car. She had no use for it; she couldn't go anywhere after all and Valentine had just given her two thousand quid in cash. So she knew she owed him.

She waved them all off and gave a huge sigh of relief.

But after a couple of hours alone in the Dower House she began to feel lonely and bored. She needed to find something to do. She wondered what day it was?

Saturday?

There was something she could do. She pulled out her phone and bravely made that call.

## CHAPTER TWENTY-TWO

Cleo was gratified to find quite a few photographers waiting at the airport to record her departure as she set off on her epic journey.

The production company had sent their PR to make sure that everyone was in the right place at the right time. A television crew was there to ask her a few questions too and she answered: 'Not scared at all, I adore boats!' and 'Global warming is destroying all that ice, which is a disaster!' She almost sounded convinced herself. Luckily the PR ushered her along before the questions were beyond her.

Max had stayed at home, for obvious reasons. The last thing anyone needed now was to be reminded of Cleo's dissolute husband at such an important moment in her career. As Cleo had pointed out to him, not for the first time, when she'd left their house that morning.

Cleo looked fit and fashionable in a striped nautical T-shirt over smart navy gabardine trousers. She carried a large Chanel tote bag. Since her Everest success they were happy to supply her with things from their 'cruise' collection. In her large sunglasses and bright red lipstick she looked every inch the part of a superstar off on a jolly jaunt. The fact that the trip might be neither jolly nor a jaunt was something that the press and Cleo were prepared to overlook at this stage.

In fact, she had been told that she was only flying to Canada on this particular day. She would be meeting up with the production team and her crew there, before flying on to somewhere called Pond Inlet, which Cleo thought sounded rather sweet.

Cleo's ability to distort the facts of any difficult situation had always stood her in good stead.

It wasn't as if she was totally ignorant of the challenges that lay ahead. She had spent the previous couple of days in Dorset, with the RNLI, where she had done a sea survival course. She chose not to take too much notice of their worst-case scenarios; she knew she'd have a good team with her and was confident that they could get her out of any fix.

The lifeboat men had been very kind and some of them were extremely handsome too. Cleo was very bucked up by the whole experience.

The headlines were enthusiastic and supportive:

AGAINST ALL ODDS – CLEO SPENDER TAKES ON THE ICEBERGS

*Cleo Spender (75) is to set off on another intrepid adventure today, to cross the Northwest Passage in a small inflatable boat. She will be travelling through freezing, ice-strewn seas to highlight the damage that is being done to Arctic ice by global warming. This new challenge follows her spectacular success as the oldest woman to reach the summit of Everest. Undeterred by the new furore that has engulfed her family, Cleo carries on with her plans to conquer the icebergs and brings new meaning to the word indefatigable ...*

Apart from the reference to her age, Cleo was very happy with the positive press she was getting. She knew she had made the right decision with this show, as it would bring her the attention and adoration that she craved and it would give her career another boost. It would also take everyone's minds off the tiresome gossip around Kate's ghastly book. She was feeling very optimistic.

\*

Zelda heard the Land Rover before she saw it.

She hurried downstairs, wondering if her Louboutins were exactly the right choice of footwear for the occasion. Too late to worry now, she realised, she had to make do with what she had. White jeans and a floaty Chloe shirt were the best she could muster from her ever-decreasing and inappropriate wardrobe.

Boy seemed slightly nervous as he got out to open the passenger door for her. She immediately noticed Doone, sitting in the back.

'Oh, hi!' she said.

Had Boy brought her as chaperone?

Not to be outdone Zelda suddenly added, 'You don't mind if David comes too, do you? Just in case.'

Doone muttered darkly, sounding incredulous, 'In case of what?'

Zelda called out, 'David, we're off!'

This was news to him, but David was trained to expect the unexpected and so he valiantly sprinted out to the car and jumped into the back, nodding courteously to Doone and saying, 'Hi, I'm David.'

Doone grinned. 'No shit, Sherlock!'

*

The sun was shining and Zelda felt her spirits lift as they rumbled along the narrow country lanes towards the village. The hedgerows were wildly overgrown with cow parsley. Zelda trailed her hand outside the window and felt the gentle brush of the soft flowers against her skin. It was strange to be out of the confines of the Court. She felt like a person leaving hospital after a long illness, slightly disoriented but filled with wonder at all the beauty and variety out in the wider world.

When they arrived in the village, people were parking up wherever they could and walking towards the village green. Their faces were bright and smiling in the sunlight. Zelda felt a small flutter of excitement.

She was glad she had called Boy that morning and asked if he still needed her. He had sounded surprised, a little guarded perhaps, but pleased. She told him it was the least she could do after all his kindness to her and her family – which, when she actually said it, she had to concede was true.

She hadn't intended to bring David. She wanted to show Boy that she was capable of being a civilian. But Doone's presence had irritated her and, now that she could see the crowds, she was glad to have him with her.

Boy parked the Land Rover behind the cricket pavilion and

they all got out. David and Doone were chatting happily as they set off. Zelda put on her dark glasses. She had tied a wide head-scarf around her hair in the hopes that she would look slightly less obviously 'her'.

Boy smiled at her reassuringly. 'I said we'd go straight to the main stage for you to do the honours, if that's OK? Just in case you are mobbed!'

Zelda could tell that he was teasing. He obviously didn't expect anyone to take any notice of her at all. She tried to keep up with him but her shoes were even more difficult to walk in on grass; what had she been thinking?

He laughed as she tottered. 'Are you alright? Need a piggy back?'

'Oh, yes, that would make a great headline in the press tomorrow. *Zelda makes a pig of herself at village fête.*'

'Do you always see yourself and the things you do as tabloid headlines?'

'Well, they frequently are!' Zelda tried not to sound indignant. The guy really had no clue.

There were strings of white bunting waving in the breeze and the loudspeaker blared, 'Would dogs most like their owners make their way to the main ring, please. The judging will start in ten minutes.'

Zelda laughed. 'Was that a message for the dogs?'

'Probably!' Boy grinned.

Zelda was just beginning to feel the first hint of recognition from people as they passed. She heard her name, then it began to run, like a wave, through the crowd.

'It's her!' 'Look, there!' 'Zelda!' 'Shit!' 'I love her!' 'It's her!' 'What?' 'She's hot.' 'Look at her clothes!' 'Honestly!' 'You're kidding! It's never her!' 'Look there!' 'Where?' 'There!' 'Who?' 'Zelda Spender.' 'What a nerve!' 'It's her!' 'There!' 'Where?' ...

People started to follow them, and David put himself between Zelda and the crowd as it began to build. She knew they needed to keep moving fast, to get to the stage, to get out of reach. Boy offered her his arm.

She hissed, 'No! Keep your distance!'

He looked hurt. She couldn't explain now, but any contact with him would be captured on any number of phones and beamed around the world. You didn't need paps to be papped in a public place any more.

She just had to get onto that stage, then hopefully she could do what she had to do and everyone might settle down a bit. David supported her hand firmly as she stumbled up the wooden steps onto the small makeshift platform. David turned and stood firmly at the bottom of the steps. The crowd quietened.

The head of the WI got up to make an announcement. She was a fairly ample lady wearing a large, very flowery dress. She spoke clearly.

'I would like to welcome you all again to everyone's favourite day out, the village fête.' The crowd gave a fairly desultory cheer. 'And today we are very lucky to have the wonderful ...' She looked at the card in her hand and then at Zelda. 'Oh, there seems to have been a change of plan ... today the fête will be opened by ...' She obviously hadn't got a clue who Zelda was.

Someone shouted from the crowd, 'Zelda Spender.'

'Yes, yes, I know. Zelda Spender,' she bluffed and clapped her hands wildly.

There was a hush and Zelda took the microphone. 'Hello, everybody.'

Silence.

'I am very happy to be here today, in your beautiful village, which seems to me – having just arrived here, from the squalid city of London – to be everything that epitomises what is good about our country. You must be so happy to live in such a gorgeous place and I want to thank you all so much for making me feel so welcome here today.' She smiled bravely, and took off her sunglasses. 'I don't get out much to be honest, particularly after ... well, I'm sure you all know what. But, as I say, thank you for having me here, it means a lot to me.' She looked around at the crowd.

Was that a tear they could see in her eye?

She continued, 'And now, it gives me great pleasure to declare this lovely fête – *open!*' She grinned wildly.

There was a beat, which felt like an hour to Zelda, and suddenly people began to clap and slowly they started to cheer too. Zelda almost burst into real tears. Country people were just so sweet.

In truth, many of them had felt pretty antagonistic towards her when she had first mounted the stage. But a little bit of humility went a long way down the road to forgiveness, particularly if you were as famous as Zelda Spender. She had given this lot an exclusive and they knew it. They were thrilled. It was the most exciting thing to happen in their village for years.

She was hugely relieved as she approached the side of the stage, where Boy smiled at her triumphantly, and said, 'That was terrific. They loved you!'

She wondered how he somehow always managed to add a little note of sarcasm to every compliment.

He put out his hand to help her down the steps. 'Tea tent?'

She ignored his hand, but said cheerfully, 'Why not!' David helped her down.

As they walked briskly through the crowd, Boy was shocked to see that most people had their mobile phones pointed directly at Zelda, as she tottered past. It dawned on him that this was the reason she had been so hands-off, or one of the reasons anyway.

He recognised that having a sea of people looking at you through an electronic device and recording your every gesture was extremely intimidating. Somehow the old adage of 'it's rude to stare' had been collectively abandoned and it was clearly deemed 'OK to stare' if it was through your phone. He could see what courage it had taken for Zelda to venture out, and he was impressed and grateful.

In fact, Zelda had volunteered to open the fête out of a mixture of boredom and chutzpah. She wanted to show off to Boy and, if she had been totally honest with herself, she wanted to see him again.

The tea tent was full of cheerful families and there was a table with a real cloth on it, which was empty. Zelda realised why when she saw that it had a label on it, which read 'Lord Banbury'.

She said to him, 'How very feudal!'

'Indeed. Sit down, wench, and I will bring you cake.'

She was about to say that she didn't eat cake, but she suddenly thought, 'Fuck it.' Everyone else in the village obviously ate quite a lot of cake. One slice wouldn't kill her.

Zelda smiled and sat down with her back to the wall of the tent, so that she could see what was going on and, more importantly, so that the people could see her. She knew that thousands of photographs from people's iPhones would already be circulating on the Internet. But she didn't think opening a fête could do her reputation any harm; it was almost charity after all.

Doone insisted that David sit with them too. He had intended to stand guard, but everyone seemed benign in the tent and he rarely got the opportunity to eat with the boss. Zelda seemed happy to sign autographs for the endless stream of people who approached the table.

Once Boy returned, David tactfully turned the autograph hunters away by saying, 'Miss Spender is enjoying her tea. I'm sure she will sign that for you later.' He had a way of saying it that meant most people got the message.

Zelda ate more than a slice of cake. It was like heaven, she couldn't remember anything tasting so sweet and she exclaimed, 'God, this is delicious!'

'I think it's one of Karen's,' Boy said.

'Karen who?' Zelda replied vaguely.

'Karen who has been looking after the Dower House, and you, since you arrived?'

'Oh, right. Yes, yum!'

Leaving the tent to go and see what other delights the fête had to offer, Zelda spotted the rifle range. 'Oooh! Shooting! Can I have a go?'

The stall holder held out a gnarled hand. 'That'll be one pound, please.'

Zelda didn't have any money, so she turned to Boy. 'Can I?'

Boy turned to Doone. 'Lend me a quid, sweetheart.'

Doone looked incredulous. 'Seriously?'

'Don't worry, Lord Banbury,' the stall holder said cheerfully, 'as it's you, you can have a free go.'

'Absolutely not! Wouldn't dream of it, Tommy.' He put his hand out towards his daughter. She reached into her pocket and plonked the coin into his palm.

'Thanks. There you go, Tommy.'

Zelda picked up the gun and shot every single duck. A small crowd had gathered around them and they applauded. Zelda gave a little bow. She would have loved another go. But one look at Doone told her she would definitely be pushing her luck.

As they wandered happily past the other stalls a very handsome boy approached Zelda. He had no shirt on, but wore a red bandana tied round his head and a beatific smile, and was obviously very stoned. David moved in. The boy said, 'You are the most loveliest people I have ever seen. You are all glittery and beautiful. Can I come with you to your fairyland?'

'You're already in fairyland, mate,' David said as he stood between the boy and his boss.

Zelda ducked past him. The boy called out after her, 'Don't leave me, I love you!' Then he started to cry.

Boy rolled his eyes and lit a cigarette. 'Shall we go? Quit while we're ahead. What do you think?'

Doone said, 'Yep, I'm ready.'

Zelda would have liked to stay. People were being so nice to her. But she knew that Boy was right. The day was wearing on and people were beginning to look a bit beery and leery.

'Thanks for inviting me, Boy. I've really enjoyed myself,' she said as they trooped off towards the car.

They were almost there, when a woman suddenly stepped in front of Zelda. David was walking ahead talking to Doone and so he didn't notice until it was too late.

Zelda smiled and the woman said, 'I used to love you, but you are a very evil person. A disgusting bitch and a whore. You deserve everything bad that has happened to you!'

Boy stepped forward, and took Zelda by the arm. 'Just ignore her, the woman is drunk.'

Zelda wanted to run, to hide, but she couldn't with the stupid shoes on. As she bent to take them off, the woman threw herself at her, knocking her to the floor and pulling off her scarf, screaming obscenities. People were running towards them, phones pointing like weapons. Suddenly David was there and, with Boy's help, he pulled the woman off. He swiftly picked Zelda up and carried her across the field to put her into the Land Rover.

Boy jumped into the driver's seat and reversed as fast as he could, without running anyone over.

'Bloody hell. I am so sorry. Are you alright?' Boy looked white.

'I think so,' Zelda said bravely.

Doone observed carelessly, 'I think that's what they call bitch slapping.'

David was silently mortified. He had let his guard down while chatting and Zelda had been assaulted. His boss could have been seriously hurt. He knew he must never, ever let that happen again. He did not say another word to Doone, who had seemed perfectly pleasant until she had shown her true colours with that uncalled-for remark.

The atmosphere was distinctly frosty and awkward.

Zelda sounded demoralised when she asked, 'Could you drop us back at home now?'

'Yes, of course.' Boy didn't know what else to do or say.

They had been having such a lovely day but it had gone awry. He couldn't help thinking that there was a pattern: every time he was anywhere near Zelda it seemed some sort of catastrophe followed.

Perhaps it was a warning, fate intervening.

He thought, not for the first time, that it might be better for everyone, particularly Zelda, if he stayed away from her from now on.

She'd said something about a show in London. Perhaps she would soon be off his hands.

# CHAPTER TWENTY-THREE

Jake had woken early that day, at his little mews house in London. Wrapping a sarong around his waist he went down to make himself a cup of coffee. There was a package on the doormat, addressed simply: *Jake*. He opened it and found that it contained a copy of the infamous Kate's book: *Dead Rich*.

There was no note, or anything to say where, or from whom, it had come. Despite the furore surrounding its publication, Jake had still never actually read it. He had resisted that temptation. Of course he had heard about most of its contents; the entire family had been ranting about all the 'unfair, untrue, vile slurs' that it contained.

But he had instinctively known that it might contain stuff about Zelda that he wouldn't really want to know. She had mentioned some of it and apologised with an uncharacteristic humility. But he wasn't sure that she had mentioned all of it. Kate had known almost everything about her boss's life and by all accounts she had not held back in the telling.

But now he found himself home alone and the temptation

was too great. He was pretty sure that he would be strong enough to cope with whatever secrets Kate had revealed to the world and he convinced himself that he probably ought to know it all, now that they were making a fresh start.

However by the time he finished the book that afternoon it was clear that he couldn't cope after all.

He'd gone and got a bottle of whisky to help him get through the last couple of chapters.

Amongst the things he'd known nothing about was Milo.

*

Zelda had regained her composure. She poured herself a glass of water.

She and David had just returned from a late afternoon run, which David had suggested as the best way of alleviating the stresses of the day. He had apologised profusely to her for what had happened and was very relieved that she didn't fire him.

Not that Zelda could fire him; he wasn't being paid anyway.

She was thinking of going to have a bath, when she realised that she hadn't checked her phone for a while. Picking up the glass, she went out into the garden. It was an idyllic summer evening. Zelda could almost see the point of the country, when it was like this.

It had been the most perfect day, until that awful woman had spoilt it. At least she felt Boy might have a clue about what she was up against now. She looked back across the lawn, at the old house. The mellow stone was romantically robed in a tangled riot of roses, clematis and jasmine.

She could see that the Dower House was beautiful, now that she was used to it. It could do with a massive makeover inside, but it had potential. If she was actually writing a book, she reflected, she could be quite happy living somewhere like this.

Weirdly, she felt safer again. It was as if the crazy woman attacking her had reminded her that her world would always be full of lunatics of one sort or another and she had always managed to survive them so far.

At least there had been no other weird incidents here at the Dower House. She was even beginning to wonder whether she might have imagined some of the things that had happened. Perhaps it really was just a stray pap having a bit of fun with her. She had been under a lot of stress and some of the pills she took, to keep herself together, did have some unpredictable side effects.

She walked about until her phone picked up a signal and began to scroll through the messages.

There was one from Helen. It said, 'Good news! The deal is signed and sealed. Details of call dates and times to follow. Congratulations!'

Zelda jumped up and down. The fees agreed with Big Guns were phenomenal, far better than Zelda had expected, and Sam Carson had insisted that she have a stake in the show too, which meant that if it went well she could make a lot of money. He liked to keep his stars motivated apparently. Or that was what Helen told her, anyway.

In fact, as soon as Helen realised that Big Guns had called in Zelda at the last moment, to replace someone else, she knew that her client's position was strong. When she discovered that Sam had quite a thing for Zelda too, she took the opportunity to drive a very hard bargain. She wasn't the best agent in London for nothing.

Zelda texted Helen with her thanks and she asked for Sam's telephone number, so that she could thank him personally. Her knight in shining armour!

She scrolled through her other messages. There was one from Jake.

It simply said, 'I want a divorce.'

Zelda stumbled up the lawn and fell onto the stone bench. What the fuck was this? He'd been fine when they had last spoken!

She rang him. He picked up and she knew immediately that he was drunk. But not so drunk that he couldn't explain why he had sent that text.

He had read *Dead Rich*, and the bit about her affair with Milo, the family's personal trainer, had been the final straw.

Zelda was always amazed by how quickly a good day could turn bad. This one had turned spectacularly bad and Zelda had no one to turn to. Not even bloody Shona.

She felt overwhelmingly lonely and sad. Drunk or not, she was terrified that Jake might mean it this time. Could this really be the end for them, after all they had been through? She didn't know the answer and as she gazed out upon all the beauty that surrounded her, she felt bereft. She made her way back into the house.

David watched her from the window of the little flat over the garage. He had just got out of the shower with only a towel wrapped around his waist, and he looked very fit and toned. If anyone could have seen him standing there, they would have noticed fresh scars on his back. Syria had marked him, both his body and his mind.

His lovely boss looked beaten. He wondered what was going on now? This family lived their lives on such a rollercoaster, sometimes it made him feel quite sick, just watching them.

*

When Jake's extended family turned up at the Mews that afternoon, they found him wandering about, blearily clutching a glass and asking, 'Whas going on? Where are you going?'

Upon hearing they were all off to Johnny's gig, he said, 'Can I come? I haven't been to a gig for shuch a long time. I should've been in a band, you know? I love ... that music shtuff.'

'Apart from the fact that you can't play an instrument or sing a note, Dad,' said Ed, 'that would've been a great career choice for you.'

Jake swayed and Ed said, 'Dad, you are really fucking pissed.'

'I wissshhh I was!'

Ed started to lead his father towards the stairs. 'If you are coming with us you will need to have a little lie down first, OK? We're not leaving for a couple of hours. C'mon, Dad here we go ... upstairs.' Ed was used to dealing with Jake in this condition; he had been doing so all his life.

Jake's brief spell of abstinence had been good, but it wasn't what Ed was used to. Looking after his father was a more familiar role and he fell back into it easily.

While he was upstairs, Dusty found the incriminating copy of Kate's book, picked it up as if it was made of hot metal and chucked it into the rubbish bin. Then she called a babysitter to come over and look after Willow while they all went out.

The children were back in charge of the asylum.

*

Dusty and Ed were the first to see the pictures of the bitch-slapping incident on YouTube and Twitter. Ed texted his mother to check that she was alright.

After Dusty had left to meet up with her boyfriend, Alex, Ed and Flora found themselves alone in the open-plan living room of the Mews. With Jake and Willow sleeping upstairs, Ed began to clear up after his father.

Flora watched him and asked, 'Is your dad often like that?'

'He's been better lately. But there has been a lot of stuff going on between him and my mum.' He couldn't resist adding, 'The Valentine thing really knocked him back.'

'It must have been a shock for you to find he wasn't your brother?'

'He's still my half-brother.' He looked at her directly. 'You will be careful, won't you. Valentine's like really weird with girls sometimes.'

'What do you mean? I'm not interested in him!'

'Oh, I thought . . .' Ed tried to mask his relief.

'I think he's just been flirting with me to annoy Doone.' Flora was a perceptive girl. 'Anyway I don't fancy him at all. I

234

know he's your half-brother and everything but, no offence, he gives me the creeps!'

Ed laughed gleefully. 'None taken!'

Now all he had to do was fend off that old bastard Johnny and all would be well.

# CHAPTER TWENTY-FOUR

Cleo was greeted at Toronto airport by one of the production assistants on *Against All Odds*, a very good-looking boy called Hector. He reminded her a little of Rock Hudson, her old squeeze who had turned out to be no squeeze at all. There were a pleasing number of photographers to greet her and welcome her to Canada, which helped to put her in a very good mood.

She had been booked into the best hotel in Toronto – the Four Seasons. She was shown to her suite on the top floor, which was huge, modern and very comfortable, with a stunning panoramic view of the city. Cleo was delighted and chuffed that she was being looked after properly. This boded well for the trip and the show. Cleo liked things to be done right.

She intended to have a little rest before joining up with her old pal, the director of the show, Tom Maddison. They hadn't seen each other since the wrap of their last triumph, *Cleo Climbs Everest*, and she was looking forward to seeing him again. Hector informed her that Mr Maddison would be waiting for her in the bar at 7 p.m., before taking her to dinner.

When Hector got back to his downtown, slightly down-at-heel hotel, he told the rest of the production team that Cleo was 'lovely' and 'really friendly'. The cameraman had been on the Everest show, so he knew different, but he didn't disagree with Hector. Everyone would soon find out what the woman was like to work with and anyway, he certainly couldn't fault Cleo Spender on courage. She was a very plucky old broad, he had to acknowledge that.

Cleo arrived downstairs, later that evening, in a singularly good mood. She waved gaily at Tom when she finally spied him across the bar. She shimmied through the tables, aware of the frisson that she caused when people realised who was in their midst. They all fell silent; awestruck by her legendary beauty.

She greeted Tom warmly, with almost a hug.

'Good flight, I hope?' he asked. 'Thought we'd have an early supper. Ah, here comes another of our little group. I don't think you've seen each other for a while. Cleo, here's Milo.'

Cleo felt her blood run cold. What did he just say? Milo! She tried to compose herself before turning round, then she found herself looking down into the darkly inscrutable eyes of her ex-personal trainer.

It really was him: Milo! He was still as extraordinarily handsome as ever, but not quite the same as when she'd last seen him, because now, here he was sitting in front of her, in a wheelchair.

She tried to sound calm when she lied, 'Milo! How wonderful to see you again.' She bent down to air-kiss him.

'You too, Cleo. It's been a while. You look well. Fit and ready for our new challenge?' He raised a quizzical eyebrow and smiled.

Cleo was in shock. Every fibre of her being was screaming: Does he know? Does he know what had happened that day on Everest? She tried to compose herself, wondering what the hell was going on. Then she froze; what was that he'd said? Did he just say 'our' new challenge?

When Cleo had regained some control of her emotions, she turned to the director and said, icily, 'Can I have a word, Tom? Now!'

*

The conversation with Tom Maddison had not gone as Cleo expected. He had followed her out of the bar where she had impatiently demanded of the hotel manager that he find somewhere private for them to have a little chat.

They were soon installed in a chic little anteroom where Tom patiently explained that Milo had been so popular on Cleo's Everest show that the broadcaster felt he would be a brilliant addition to the team on *Against All Odds*.

'But he's in a fucking wheelchair!' Cleo exploded.

'That's what makes it even more great. Gives it a really human element.' Tom smiled reassuringly. 'You worked so brilliantly together on the last show and you know Milo well. We thought you'd be pleased to have him on board.'

Cleo wasn't sure how to play this. 'Well, I am pleased, of course I am. Just a little worried about how he will cope, in a wheelchair, in an inflatable boat, in a fucking freezing, dangerous sea! That's all.'

'He's been training and he is more than capable of coming on board with us.' Tom sounded firm.

Cleo could see she would have to be more emphatic. 'Well, I don't think it will work, not for me anyway. I'm sorry, Tom – you'll have to tell him it's off.'

'We can't do that, I'm afraid, it's all been agreed with the broadcaster.'

Cleo was unable to restrain herself. 'Well then, you will have to tell the broadcaster that you no longer have Cleo Spender for your bloody *Against All Odds* show!'

'You might want to think about that, Cleo. Milo is perfectly happy to work with you. If anyone had a grievance it would be him anyway.' He looked at her triumphantly. 'Wouldn't it?'

'Why would Milo have a grievance?' she dissembled.

Tom decided to show his hand. 'If there was a sound recording of a particular incident on Everest, what would it reveal, do you think?'

Cleo tried to look non-committal. Inside she was screaming: 'sound recording?' She was lost for words. If Tom had a recording of her 'allowing' Milo to slip off Everest, it would be catastrophic. Was that possible?

She wanted to shriek, 'He slipped off that bloody mountain – I nearly died trying to save him!' She knew that wouldn't be wise though. She bit her lip. What was it she'd said, as he slipped away from her? She tried to remember ... something about kissing and telling from hell?

But Milo had survived, and he hadn't kissed and told

anything, so Cleo was desperately trying to work out what this all meant.

She stalled. 'I have no idea. Why don't you tell me?'

Tom continued, 'Oh, I don't think I have to spell it out, do I? The less said about it the better, I'd say! Obviously, if such a recording existed, I would never allow it to be released. I have too much respect for you to put you in such an embarrassing and, let's face it, legally tricky, situation.' Tom smiled. 'We both need this show to work, don't we? So let's just get on with it.'

Cleo realised that Tom was a hell of a lot sharper than she'd thought. He'd been so gentle and kind on Everest. Now the gloves were off and it looked like she was going to have to roll with the punches.

Tom said, 'If you are good with that, let's go and have some dinner, shall we? I'm starving!'

Cleo replied, 'Yes, let's!'

But after their little chat, she really wasn't hungry at all.

*

Doone reversed the old horsebox into the stable yard at the Court and jumped down onto the concrete. She saw Frank as she walked through the kitchen garden and waved, but he didn't see her. She entered the kitchen through the French windows.

Boy was sitting at the kitchen table with a letter in his hands. He looked up and she wondered if he had been crying.

'Are you alright, Dad?' She used that unfamiliar form of address instinctively, to comfort him.

'It's a letter from your mother.'

'She can write?'

'She says she's thinking of coming home.'

'Big of her! When?'

'She doesn't say.'

'Dad, why are you upset? Isn't this good news? You've missed her, haven't you?'

'Yes, I have missed her, darling, of course I have. But when I said she was coming home, I meant back to England, not necessarily here. She hasn't made her mind up yet. But she wants to see you – she wants to see her girls.'

'Seriously? That's it? After eighteen months of "finding herself" that's all she can come up with?' Doone was livid. 'Well, she won't be seeing me! Because I fucking hate her for what she's done. So write and tell her to put that in her hipster shit and smoke it!'

'She hasn't sent a return address!' Boy smiled at his furious daughter. 'So I'm afraid I can't tell her to put anything anywhere. Much as I would like to.'

Doone crossed the room and gave Boy an uncharacteristically warm hug. 'We've got along without her till now. No reason why we can't continue, is there?' She put the kettle on the Aga. 'Maybe we shouldn't mention this to the others. They will be so disappointed when she doesn't show.'

'She might show,' he said, loyal to the end.

'Yeah, well, let's just deal with that if she does, Dad, shall we?' Sceptical to the end.

Boy smiled gratefully at his eldest daughter. He had come to depend on her to pick up all the slack, particularly where her sisters were concerned, and she'd made a good job of it.

'Where are the girls anyway?' he asked.

'I just dropped Kitty at Pony Club camp and Flora has gone to London,' She replied, which sort of illustrated his point. He'd had no idea about Pony Club camp or Flora and London. He decided not to ask. He'd had quite enough bad news for one day.

# CHAPTER TWENTY-FIVE

By the time Zelda went to bed she was distraught and what her father would describe as 'slightly the worse for wear'.

She hadn't meant to get so cranked up. Jake had been drunk after all, and he often said things he didn't mean when he was drunk. But, as she sat alone in that borrowed house, she suddenly felt as if she was living on borrowed time. She was forced to reflect on how tenuous everything in her life had turned out to be. In the past months everything she knew, and depended on, had gone: her homes, money, career, reputation, her so-called friends, and her confidence – all gone.

Now was her husband going too? Jake who, despite everything, she had always relied upon to be there for her, no matter how awful things were? Now he was pulling away from her too!

She had started drinking what remained of the vodka, just after David had checked in on her. She'd asked him if he wanted to join her in a drink. But he'd turned her down kindly, saying, 'No thanks, want to keep my wits about me and booze makes me sleepy. You wouldn't want me to fall asleep on the job, would you?'

And she'd had to admit that she wouldn't. So he was somewhere outside, protecting her. While she was wallowing in despair, quaffing vodka, inside.

It was only because there was hardly any booze left in the house that she didn't go on, and on. She wanted to drink until she had wiped out all the awful thoughts she was having. But she had run out of alcohol, so she was forced to keep on thinking.

What if they really did get divorced, where would she live? The Mews was Jake's and it was the only house they had left. How ironic that in all the years that they could have afforded to divorce they hadn't and now they couldn't afford anything at all, Jake was considering it.

She suddenly remembered she had just got a job, so she could rent a house if she had to . . . or would she just stay here? Yes, she was fine here for the time being.

She made some Marmite toast and did a bit of something she hadn't allowed herself to do for ages – comfort eating. She turned on the television; it only showed BBC1. There was nothing on that she wanted to watch.

She decided on an early night. It had been an exhausting day, an emotional rollercoaster. Perhaps things would look better in the morning. She locked her bedroom door before getting into bed and she immediately fell fast asleep, like a child.

\*

The atmosphere was electrifying. Music thumped out and lights swept across the stadium. The O2 was packed and as Johnny and the Bastards moved into the final part of their show, the crowds went berserk. There were fireworks going off all around the stadium, a giant Eiffel Tower rose slowly out of the stage covered with flashing lights and Johnny was climbing it while singing his most famous rock anthem. Everyone was jumping up and down and screaming along to the lyrics.

Flora stood gazing at her idol, in stunned amazement. She was standing in the VIP area along with Lily, Valentine and Ed.

Dusty was there too, with her boyfriend, Alex, happily singing along with their arms entwined. Jake stood, slightly unsteadily, with his extended family. He was drinking Coke, with a tiny bit of rum in it. Ed handed his bottle of water to Flora and she took a swig, smiling happily at him.

Just before the concert had begun one of the security guys had ushered them all backstage. Johnny had whispered to Flora to come to his dressing room again after the show. Her pale skin had flushed with pride and pleasure. She couldn't believe how friendly Johnny was towards her.

She watched her idol as he finished his climb with a theatrical flourish, right at the very top of the tower.

His bare chest glistened with sweat and mascara ran down his cheeks, and as he screeched the final bars of the song, the Tower suddenly started to fall . . . everybody screamed, but at the last moment it stopped and Johnny nimbly jumped the last couple of feet onto the floor. The crowd went wild.

Johnny blew a kiss in Flora's direction and left the stage

followed by his band. Ed watched aghast, knowing he would have his work cut out trying to protect her. But he was determined that he would.

Jake watched the familiar antics of his sister's old love and had to admit that the guy still had it. No wonder Georgia had been so cut up when he'd left her; they had been good together for a while. But Jake knew that guys like Johnny didn't have much romantic staying power. Georgia should have known that too, she'd been in the business long enough.

He could see that Lily seemed to have worked it out though; she was all over Valentine like a rash. Not that she would have any more luck there. Jake knew Valentine was cut from a cloth that was even more emotionally fickle. Cut from his wife's cloth, in fact.

Yes indeed, his loved ones were made of very defective stuff. The fabric of their lives was getting more torn and ragged by the day. He got a flask out of his pocket and surreptitiously added a bit more rum to his drink just as Johnny and the Bastards returned to the stage to perform the first of many encores.

It was going to be a long night.

# CHAPTER TWENTY-SIX

Zelda woke suddenly. The house was silent. No light came through the curtains so she blearily realised that it was still night. She heard something tap, tap, tapping on the window. She was wide awake now. There it was again!

She wanted to call out to David; he said he would always be able to hear her. She sat up and was beginning to get out of bed when she heard a sickening thump and a dragging noise above her head.

Was it coming from the attic? Her stomach flipped. It was moving towards the bedroom door, across the ceiling, while she was frozen, unable to move at all. She opened her mouth to scream but no sound came out. Her legs were weak, but she dragged herself into the bathroom, where the window faced out onto the front drive. If she could get it open she could call out to David from there. She desperately wrestled with the catch, with fingers like jelly. Her skin felt shrunken, contracted and tight all over her body. She had only opened the curtains a fraction but, as she finally got the catch free and began to lift the sash window, she saw something.

Something that ran across the drive, towards the house, something that she had seen before.

Not something that she had imagined either, but something real, here and after her! The sight of it finally released her voice. She screamed David's name and waited for him to call back to her.

She could hear her own voice echoing into the night. Then nothing. David didn't call and he didn't come. Everything was deathly quiet.

Zelda knew she needed to do something, but what? Her heart was pounding. She took a deep breath and began to think. If she called for David again she would be giving her position away. She didn't dare imagine what might have happened to him.

She heard a door slam downstairs. It was only a matter of time before 'it' found her. She was going to have to get out of the house. He was already in there somewhere so she would have to climb out of the window. If she could get onto the roof of the veranda she could climb down. Then what? She grabbed her phone and looked at it desperately, hoping for a miracle; but nothing! She might just be able to make it across to David's flat and wake him up. He must be sleeping.

Yes, she told herself, she could do this. She heard something – footsteps on the stairs? Suppressing a squeak, she felt a surge of adrenaline. Hitching up her nightie she was up and out of the window, frantically closing the curtains behind her so that she couldn't be seen from inside. She clambered down the wisteria-clad trellis, painfully scratching her arms and legs. She was glad she had done her own stunts in 'Festihell', as they had involved a lot of climbing. When she hit the ground she hesitated and listened carefully. Deathly quiet. The grass was cold and wet underfoot. She ran across the lawn and out onto the drive.

She daren't look back, because now she could hear the sound of her bedroom door being beaten down. She suppressed a squeal of fear.

There was just enough light from the moon for her to make out the doorway that led to David's flat. She opened it quietly and felt her way along the wall to the stairs, her shin catching painfully on something metal. She tried to be as quiet as possible. All she could hear was the sound of her rasping breaths and her raging, thumping heart. The upstairs door was ajar and when she pushed it gently it opened with a creak.

She knew at once that the room was empty. She looked around desperately but it was too dark to see anything properly. She needed to find his gun. She frantically opened drawers and rummaged under his pillow. Nothing. She peeped out of the window. To her horror, lights were being turned on all over the house. Another quick look at her phone, still no signal. She knew there was nothing for it; she was going to have to run. She felt her way back downstairs and bumped into the same obstacle, only this time she realised what it was: a bike! Could she ride out of there? It seemed like a better idea than running and she was suddenly aware that she had no shoes on.

So the bike it had to be. She wheeled it towards the door and shoved it outside. Light was flooding out of the Dower House, every window ablaze and every curtain open. She jumped into the saddle and wobbled before disappearing into the darkness.

As she peddled on up the drive she decided to head for the Court, to throw herself on Boy's mercy again. The idea of riding through the park on a bike was hideous but it was a moonlit night and now that her eyes had adjusted she found she could see quite well. She was beginning to gather speed as she rode past the gateposts when she felt hands reach out and grab her. She screamed and tried to push them away. But she couldn't break free. The bike wobbled and she fell, kicking out and screaming.

She could hear a voice. 'Zelda, it's alright; it's me! Zelda, it's David.' Light from his torch blinded her.

'David?' She continued to struggle. 'David! Where the fuck were you? He's in there! He tried to fucking kill me.' She was gasping for air.

'Oh, my God, I am so sorry! I heard you call out, but when I got into the house I couldn't find you. Your bedroom door was locked but you didn't answer when I called. I had to force it open.' He helped Zelda to her feet and bent to pick up the bike as he continued, 'Then I saw that you'd climbed out of the window. So I have been searching for you everywhere. What happened to the plan to stay where you are and call till I get there?'

'I did call! But you didn't come! So I had to get out myself.

Did you see it?' She was shaking. David wrapped his jacket around her.

'Let's go back to the house and you can tell me what you saw.'

'You must be out of your mind, I'm never going back there!' She felt her legs beginning to give way.

'I have switched on all the lights, double- and triple-checked everywhere – there's no one there now, I promise. You will be safe with me.'

'I want to go home,' Zelda cried. Then she remembered that she had no home and tears rolled silently down her cheeks.

David picked her up and carried her back along the drive. 'I'm here now, OK? No one can hurt you. Let's get a nice cup of tea and work out what's going on here. Eh?' His boss felt lighter than ever. In the past he'd sometimes had to lift her when she was drunk, but never scared legless like tonight.

He felt her body stiffen as they neared the house, and he reassured her, 'It's OK, we're alright.'

'But he's got a gun,' Zelda muttered weakly. She suddenly wondered if he did have a gun? Had she seen it? Or was it that she remembered it from before?

'I've got a gun too, remember?' David put her down in the hall and held her, while she found her feet. 'Let's get that kettle on.'

Zelda looked at him with gratitude. 'Why is he doing this, David? I am being scared to death, stalked, terrorised and the police don't care, Jake doesn't care, Boy bloody Banbury doesn't believe me.'

'Well, I believe you, I am going to get the bastard and when I do, I am going to make him *very* sorry.'

Zelda was surprised by the look in David's eyes. It was almost frightening. But that was what she needed, someone who believed her and someone who was prepared to do anything to protect her.

He placed the cup of tea in front of her and she grabbed his hand. 'Thank you for being here with me, you are the only person in the world who cares for me, do you know that?' she said, overwhelmed with gratitude and quite a lot of self-pity. She suddenly laughed bitterly and blurted out, 'Zelda Spender and her bodyguard! How very Whitney!' Which wasn't quite what she meant. Now she was worried that he might misconstrue her allusion to the plot of 'The Bodyguard'.

She felt embarrassed, so she let go of his hand.

When she looked up he was watching her closely. 'Let's just go through what happened, shall we?'

She took a sip of tea, which had sugar in it but she didn't complain. She told him about the knocking on the window and the dragging on the ceiling. Then the sight of the thing on the drive before it disappeared into the house. The footsteps on the stairs, the breaking of the door ... She wanted to weep with fear when she thought about it all again.

'Right, well, I have checked the house and it is all clear. I think we can both agree that the footsteps, the door bashing and the lights were only me, trying to get to you, because I had heard you scream! I can investigate more in the morning. If you want to get back to bed now, I can sit outside your door for the night?'

'I'll never get back to sleep again.'

'Perhaps you could just have a lie down? I'll be right there. So no need to worry.'

Zelda had never noticed before that David had a trace of a Welsh accent.

'You promise you won't disappear again?' she said.

'I didn't disappear.'

Zelda stomped upstairs and David placed himself on an upright chair, on the landing, outside her bedroom door.

'Now try to rest,' he said and quietly closed the door behind her. 'I'll fix the broken lock in the morning.'

'Thanks, David. Night,' she said, quietly certain that she would never be able to sleep ever again.

But oddly, the moment she lay down, she fell into a deep slumber, instantly.

# CHAPTER TWENTY-SEVEN

The cameraman greeted Cleo warmly. She hadn't quite remembered who he was when he'd first said hello. But she had *pretended* to remember him, and she thought she'd got away with it.

The cameraman realised immediately that she had no clue who he was. He wasn't surprised, or offended, since he was used to being invisible, it was almost something that his job demanded. He got the best footage when people forgot he was filming them. He had to admit the camera did love her though. She was an extraordinarily beautiful woman.

He had already done a bit of filming as they left the city in a small plane. They flew up to Pond Inlet, where they were to meet the rest of the team and the boat. He noticed that there was very little interaction between Cleo and Milo, which struck him as odd, as they had always been on good terms on Everest. Very good terms indeed, as they had frequently shared a tent.

He reckoned it must have been something to do with the guy being in a wheelchair. He couldn't help thinking Cleo

Spender wouldn't have much interest a man in that unfortunate position.

They checked into a tiny motel and waited for their first briefing from Bear Grylls, who was making a quick guest appearance to give the trip a spectacular send-off.

Everyone was excited, particularly Cleo, who adored Bear and was looking forward to getting some good footage of them together. She was disappointed when she discovered that Bear was not going to be able to join them in the boat. He had already done the Northwest Passage and it might have served as a warning to Cleo that he didn't want to do it again. But she was very keen. Couldn't wait to get started, in fact.

The team had been instructed to meet in the foyer at noon.

The motel was very basic, simple and, Cleo was happy to see, clean. Since the Everest expedition she was accustomed to basic and prided herself on her ability to muck in. She had been told that they were only going to be using it for the day anyway, as they were to begin their epic journey early that afternoon.

She was busy repacking her small bag when someone came to tell her that Bear had arrived. She rushed out to see him. Wearing her waterproof jumpsuit and a fur-trimmed hat, she knew she was a picture of glamour and elegance. Something that Bear kindly commented on, when they greeted each other like long-lost friends. Bear was his usual charming and engaging self, and the cameras caught his cheerful interaction with Cleo, giving the director exactly what he needed for the opening sequence of *Against All Odds*.

They all went down to inspect the RIB that would be their

home for the duration of their intrepid attempt to pass through the Northwest Passage.

Cleo couldn't quite believe her eyes when she saw it; the RIB looked about the same size as the small dinghies that ferried her from her chums' yachts to Club 55, in Saint-Tropez. It was *tiny*.

Was this seriously what they expected her to travel in? To venture through the wildest, coldest, most dangerous seas on earth? With a man in a wheelchair, a director and a couple of crew?

She thought they must have been kidding, until she heard Bear telling everyone tales of his adventure, in exactly the same-sized boat. It didn't sound like an adventure to her, it sounded like a suicide mission.

But she certainly wasn't going to make a fuss now. She didn't want Bear see her fear. She would have a word with the director later. There must be a way of making the programme without exposing themselves to the kind of dangers that Bear was suggesting.

He finished his talk with a few kind words about Cleo, saying that he knew what she was capable of and was sure that she would rise to this new challenge with great fortitude. There was a huge cheer and round of applause from the crew and a small crowd of tourists, who seemed to have appeared out of nowhere. Although Cleo wondered why anyone would be mad enough visit such an inhospitable place as a tourist.

She gave a little bow to the audience and gave Bear a smacking kiss for the camera, or at least partly for the camera, mostly for herself.

# CHAPTER TWENTY-EIGHT

Zelda felt very low after her latest trauma. She knew that she must leave the Dower House as, despite what David might say, it was too dangerous to stay. He had let her down twice now and, this time, she could have been killed. She was almost frightened to death as it was.

She pulled on an old pair of shorts and a T-shirt. She glanced at her perfect face in the mirror and decided to forgo her usual make-up, something that had been a compulsory part of her morning's routine for years. But, no one was paying her to look good now. She felt she didn't need to bother any more, when the only people who ever got to see her were David and a crazed stalker.

She couldn't imagine why anyone would be persecuting her. Any previous problems she had had with stalkers had been minor, just people who got hold of her telephone numbers or email addresses, but those were always easily dealt with.

There was one fairly tenacious guy, she suddenly

remembered, who had stood on the pavement outside her old house in London. He had stayed for a few weeks and then moved on. But he had never attempted to cross the threshold or even speak to her. It had been a bit sinister to see him waiting there like that, but he was passive and you could see his face. He wasn't lurking about at night, in a mask, with a gun!

This new stalker was a different story altogether. He had been in the house. This guy had taken it to a whole new level and Zelda was terrified.

It was infuriating that no one else had seen him and, apart from the original note, there was no other evidence that Zelda could use to convince people that he was real.

So, when she got downstairs to find David in the kitchen making a cup of coffee, she was disappointed to hear him say, 'I have been checking up on a few things. There is some wisteria growing up the side of the house, which has branches trailing across your window and would account for the tapping. Also, and you are not going to like this, sorry to say, there are rats in the attic – which would explain the dragging noises above your head.' He watched his boss carefully.

'Well, that still doesn't explain why there is a horrible, terrifying, masked man standing glaring at me, at every turn – does it?' She sounded indignant. 'Don't fucking tell me you think I'm imagining him too?'

'No, I wouldn't say that; you know what you saw. But, what I would say is this: the mind can play some pretty weird tricks when a person is under duress. There have been times when I have wondered what was real and what was not. On this last Syrian mission, I wish that every horrifying thing I saw had been a figment of my imagination. It does your head in.' David looked anguished as he gazed out of the kitchen window.

Zelda was too annoyed with him to be sympathetic. 'Well, I haven't been to Syria. Although I did meet Assad once, at a party – thought he seemed like rather a weak man actually, how wrong was I! Anyway, I am not imagining anything. I am being terrorised by a maniac and so I've got to leave. I just haven't decided where I can go yet.'

David asked, 'You're not worried that he might follow you?'

'I don't know! But what I do know is that I feel very vulnerable here. Even with you looking after me; particularly after last night.' She looked at her security guy accusingly.

'I will make sure that doesn't ever happen again. I will do the night watch inside the house. You will be quite safe with me here. I promise.'

Zelda wanted to believe him. She needed time to get herself together, to get fit, rested and ready to face the world again. Ready to begin *Fame Game*. Ready to get back into her real life.

Helen had insisted that until the show went on air, she must stay out of the limelight, which really meant, out of London. So she couldn't go back up to town yet, either to sort things out with Jake or even to stay with Max, her darling dad. She was stuck here and weirdly, now that the sun was out, everything looked different again, no longer threatening and frightening but calm, bucolic and, some might say, romantic.

Boy sprang into her mind, unbidden, and then, just as she was thinking she ought to clear her head by going for a run, there was the unexpected sound of a roaring engine outside the house, followed by a loud crunching swoosh of gravel. Zelda jumped up and peeped out of the window. As if on cue, Boy had appeared, and he was riding a very battered vintage motorbike.

Zelda went out to greet him.

He looked young and carefree in a crumpled white linen shirt and jeans, which were torn because they had worn out, rather than as any kind of fashion statement.

Boy grinned at Zelda as he stepped off the bike. 'Thought I should check in, make sure my humble tenant was managing after yesterday's trauma. Still home alone?'

David sloped out of the house and across the yard, without acknowledging Boy.

'Ah, of course; never completely home alone.' A shadow crossed Boy's face, fleetingly.

Zelda's heart turned over. Was Boy jealous of David? She couldn't quite look him in the eye when she said, 'I'm fine, thanks, yesterday was . . . well, apart from the . . .' She ran her hands through her tangled hair and changed the subject. 'Nice bike!'

'It was my dad's. It's old, but it's fast.'

'Just like him, according to my mother!' Zelda teased.

This handsome man was smiling at her and it suddenly

made her feel happy. She didn't want to spoil the moment. She decided not to mention the stalker, or anything horrible right now. As her mother would say, yesterday is gone.

'I'm just riding over the estate, looking at the sheep, in fact. Or the ones I have left!'

'I would never have hurt it on purpose, you know,' she said, while thinking, not the bloody sheep again.

'You wouldn't hurt anything on purpose, would you?' he asked quietly, watching her carefully.

She wasn't sure where this was going, but she thought she might just go along with it. Her heart was racing. 'No I wouldn't.' She looked directly into his eyes and felt the shock of their connection.

'Do you want to come with me?'

She was a bit dazed. 'Where?'

'To look at the sheep!'

'On that thing?'

'Yes, on this thing. I won't go fast.' He swung his elegant leg across the bike and restarted the engine with a loud rev.

Zelda shuddered and, stepping forward, she jumped nimbly onto the back of Boy's bike. She put her arms around his waist and leant forward as he pulled away, shouting above the noise, 'You can go as fast as you like!'

The bike throbbed beneath them as Boy tore off up the drive, then he steered off-road and they careered out across the beautiful park, weaving through the trees. He called back to her, 'Not too bumpy for you?'

She didn't know how to reply to that. It was very bumpy,

and she knew it could get a hell of a lot bumpier if she did any of the things she was imagining doing with Boy, as they raced across the exquisite landscape of his beautiful estate in Oxfordshire. So she didn't say a word, just wrapped her arms more tightly around his firm, warm torso and let the real world slip away.

*

There was a chink in the blind, letting in a tiny shaft of very bright light, which was hitting Jake directly in the face. He moved his head to get away from it, because his head really hurt.

He focused and looked around the room, a vast and very modern living room. A room Jake had never seen before in his life.

He looked down; he was fully dressed, lying on a vast grey felt sofa. He pushed himself onto his elbows and then, slowly swinging his legs to the floor, he contemplated standing up. He felt very sick as he scanned the shining glass and chrome that surrounded him. He could see that this wasn't a room you could be sick in, although it looked sterile enough to be a hospital. Jake suddenly felt he needed a hospital, with nurses and men in white coats; people who could save him, save him from himself at least. But Jake knew only too well that the only person who could save him now was himself. However, 'himself' was proving to be a spectacularly unhelpful person.

He stumbled from room to soulless room, calling out a couple of times, 'Hello, hellooo.' But nobody answered. Jake was alone in a stranger's house. How or why he was there was a mystery; how long he had been there, or who with, was also a blank.

He stumbled out into another bright summer's day, and hailed a cab.

He rested his fevered brow on the cool glass of the taxi, even though the vibrations from the engine brought bile to his throat.

'You alright, mate?' the cabbie asked. 'Tied one on a bit? Not surprised! Read about your missus, none of my business, but you're better off without that hassle. She's a lovely-looking lady, don't get me wrong, most of the lads would like to . . .' He honked his horn and shouted out of the window at a cyclist, 'If you wanna die go home and take a fuckin' pill!'

Jake did want to die and, when he got home, he certainly intended to take quite a number of pills.

*

The RIB flew across the calm, glassy sea.

They had been waved off by a small, friendly group, mid-afternoon. Cleo felt encouraged; if this was an indication of how it was going to be, this trip would be a breeze.

She had positioned herself as far away from Milo as possible. His wheelchair was strapped down near the stern of the boat, so Cleo had settled herself on a small seat across the bow. She had already realised that this was the best angle for the camera, which had been rigged up on a pole. Apparently, the cameraman was not going to be on board with them, but would travel with the support team and would only film when they were on land. Cleo had been annoyed by this news at first.

But when she was actually in the boat she realised that it would not have been at all comfortable or practical to have anyone else on board.

The crew of two, Nils and Lars, were reassuringly professional and heartwarmingly handsome, so the trip had got off to a flying start.

The noise of the engine made it difficult to make herself heard, so Cleo had to content herself with admiring the spectacular scenery, as the RIB tore northwards. She was just beginning to feel a little bored, when the waves started to build and big, steep white caps reminded them all, sickeningly, that they were moving towards some very inhospitable seas.

By the time the crew put the RIB to shore it was 10 p.m. at night, but still light – as Cleo was soon to discover, there would be very little darkness on this trip, which was disconcerting, since she knew that she looked at her best at night. The savage, harsh northern light would mean she had to pay extra attention to her make-up at all times.

The director helped her out of the boat and onto the shingle beach.

Not at all the sort of beach Cleo was used to. Bleakly grey, sharp-stoned and forbidding, it led onto a relentlessly empty landscape. A biting wind was blowing and despite their warm, insulated clothing they were all cold, tired and impatient to make camp.

The director assisted the crew as they lifted Milo from the boat. This was no mean feat and Cleo couldn't help feeling a little shiver of Schadenfreude when she saw them struggling. After all, she had questioned the wisdom of bringing a paraplegic on such an adventure. Having finally got him ashore, the crew expertly pitched tents in the lee of a small crop of rock. Cleo decided to be helpful and volunteered to collect some firewood.

'Good idea,' Tom, the director, said.

'Don't go far. Bears!' one of the crew remarked nonchalantly.

Cleo couldn't remember his name. Nils? Lars? She supposed she'd work out which was which at some point. Bears indeed! If only Bear *was* still with them. He was so much fun. Everyone said he was an inspiration to the young, but Cleo thought he was quite an inspiration to the old too.

'Be careful!' Milo called out, as she trudged off across the shingle.

She raised her hand gaily, without looking back. Milo really didn't know? Cleo could hardly believe it. She felt the panic of seeing him again, for the first time since his 'accident', beginning to subside. If he didn't know, there wasn't much of a problem.

So, here he was, back in her life, uninvited, and although he seemed perfectly agreeable, she couldn't help wondering how and indeed why he had wanted to inveigle himself onto this particular venture.

The director had said Milo was very popular with the public after their Everest show. Well, she knew that, she'd read the press! She knew that he would gather even more fans for doing this gig in his wheelchair. He might even improve the show's ratings. Which was galling but also useful, Cleo had to admit. Better ratings, better profile, better future.

Cleo decided that she might as well buckle down and play the game. The stakes were high, but they always were when you were playing to win. Cleo knew how hard it was to maintain any level of fame, particularly for any woman over thirty; and Cleo had been playing the game for a long, long time. She was good at it and she intended to stay that way.

She clambered up a rocky bank and, when she reached to top, she found that the landscape was nothing but rock and ice for as far as the eye could see; not a tree in sight. They had let her go off alone, in bear country, looking for wood in a place with no trees.

A less confident woman might have read something into that, but Cleo was not to be trifled with. As she stomped back down the slope she saw a pile of driftwood away to her right. On closer inspection it was a pile of planks, some of which even had rusty old nails sticking out of them. Cleo didn't have to be a nautical genius to know what they were. They were from a ship, a wrecked ship.

She walked proudly back to camp and let her bounty fall in a noisy clatter onto the beach, saying, 'Right, let's get some water boiled. I could murder a cup of tea!'

Tom Maddison watched with amusement, thinking, ah yes, there she is, the indomitable Cleo Spender. He had recorded her to-ing and fro-ing with his small hand-held camera.

Lars and Nils were impressed, and Lars went off to collect

more of the wreckage. He was very excited by Cleo's find, wondering which ship it was from. So many had been lost in these treacherous waters, but hardly any wreckage had ever been found.

He hoped this wasn't an omen.

# CHAPTER-TWENTY-NINE

Doone was in a very bad mood by the time she returned to Banbury Court. Her night at Charlie's house-party had not gone as she had hoped.

She'd thought that Charlie had asked her over to be with him, but as the night wore on it became increasingly obvious that he meant to share her with a terrifying model who always hung out with him called, improbably, High. Doone had been curious about her name until she realised it was a nickname, and an apt one, judging by the amount of drugs the girl took.

At first Doone had thought High was just being friendly towards her. Tactile, then way too tactile ... then suddenly Charlie was sitting between them, kissing Doone, but then he was kissing High.

Doone was a bit drunk by that stage and asked Charlie what he thought he was doing?

Charlie replied, 'Well, you and High, I hope!' and then he laughed and leant forward to kiss her again.

Despite her drunkenness Doone's reflexes were still fast

enough to pour her drink into Charlie's lap as she said, eloquently, 'Fuck you, you fuck!'

'That's what I was hoping you would do!' he said and turned to grin at High, who laughed unpleasantly. He looked blearily back at Doone. 'You seem to have spilt your drink over me. Would you like to lick it off?' Then he glanced down at his crotch with an expectant smile on his face.

This was not turning out to be anything like the romantic scene that Doone had imagined. She found herself wanting to hit him. But when she raised her arm, a large bloke she hadn't even noticed before caught it in a vice-like grip. He said, 'No hitting the artist, lady. Might be time you went home.' Then the brute had picked her up and carried her through the house, not flinching as she tried to kick him, and pushed her out onto the drive, closing the door firmly behind her.

She stumbled tearfully back to the Land Rover only to discover that she had left her coat, with the car keys in its pocket, in the house. She couldn't face going back in straight away, with a tearstained face. Too shaming.

Luckily, she never locked the car in the country, so she was able to crawl in and have a little crying lie down on the familiar worn old seats. When she woke up it was morning. She really needed to get her keys.

She passed Aaron on the drive, getting into a Lamborghini with a plain girl, and they were laughing happily. She looked vaguely familiar to Doone.

She snuck back into the house and immediately ran into Charlie.

He greeted her with a diffident, 'Hey, you, I wondered where you'd got to. Thought you were with me and then you disappeared. You weren't with Haz, were you? He's got a nasty dose! And ...'

Doone interrupted him. 'No, I was *not* with one of your disgusting friends. I had to sleep in my car because your people-thugs took my coat and hid my keys!'

'My people-thugs?' Charlie took a drag of his cigarette and eyed Doone warily. 'I didn't know I had people-thugs.'

'Well, you do and they are horrible,' she said.

The bouncer appeared out of nowhere and handed Doone her coat. She tried to put it on, to hide her dismay. The bouncer helped her into it.

'Thanks,' she mumbled.

'Can one of my people-thugs get you a cup of tea?'

High appeared on the staircase, naked. 'Charlie, I have something here for you.' She looked Doone straight in the eye. 'Hey, Doone. Always the bridesmaid, never the bride, eh?' Then she smirked and wiggled her perfect arse slowly back upstairs.

Charlie grinned at Doone, raised his eyebrows and said, 'If you've changed your mind?' and gestured upstairs.

'Nope, I think I'll pass,' she replied icily, but a part of her wanted to laugh.

Charlie shrugged and said, 'Duty calls!' Then he turned and took the stairs two at a time.

The bouncer said, 'If there's nothing else, Miss, I can see you to your car?'

'That won't be necessary.' She drew herself up to her full height. 'I'm not an idiot, I can find my own way to my bloody car.'

But she felt exactly like an idiot. How could she have been so naïve?

She had really liked being friends with Charlie. Having somewhere to go, away from Banbury Court and her family, had been great. Now she had blown it, been uncool, misread the situation and behaved like a coy virgin. She felt mortified and humiliated.

Not that she would have dreamt of getting into any of the stuff Charlie was hoping she was up for, but she could've handled it better, stayed friends with him. Kept her options open.

Now she had ruined it and all she had to go back to was her boring life at home.

\*

When she got back, her mood was not improved by the sight of Zelda Spender, sitting on the kitchen table, in tiny little shorts. Her head was thrown back, dark hair tumbling, and she was laughing with Boy. Although they were not standing close together, Doone could instantly feel that the atmosphere between them was electric.

She looked daggers at her father. 'Any more news from Mum?'

Boy ignored her, saying, 'Doone! There you are! Come and have some coffee, here, sit.' He gestured solicitously to a chair.

Although Doone really wanted to sit and chat to her dad, to feel his comforting kindness, she certainly wasn't going to with that woman there. No way. So she simply turned on her heel and left the room.

Zelda watched Boy curiously as she asked, 'Is there news from your wife?'

Boy's face was inscrutable. All the joy had been sucked out of him, out of the room too. As he lifted his eyes, she saw a fleeting glimpse of pain. 'I can't talk about it.'

So he still loved his wife? Zelda felt this realisation like a blow to her belly. Why was he flirting with her, then? What was she to him, a diversion, a consolation in his loneliness, a quick shag? Well, she didn't intend to be any of those things. She felt the hurt deeply.

She slid off the table and made for the door. 'I'd better go, thanks for the ride.' Her voice sounded hard.

Boy seemed distracted. 'I'll take you back.'

'No, I need some exercise. I'll walk.' She was still tempted to say yes, to jump back onto his bike and feel his warmth and strength, to hold him tight. But she could see that would be a mistake. She had mistaken his kindness for something else and that was quite enough disappointment for one day.

*

She half-walked and half-jogged home, but began to feel a little nervous when she reached the part of the drive that was sheltered by woods on either side. She heard the sharp crack of a snapping twig, then a rustle in the branches up ahead, and stopped in her tracks; her heart was almost thumping out of her body.

She should have put her pride to one side and allowed Boy

to drive her home. She turned to run back up the drive, just as a deer leapt out across her path and thundered away. She screamed then bent over and grasped her knees as she waited for the blood that was pounding in her ears to quieten. As she straightened up, the Land Rover pulled up beside her.

Boy called to her through the open window. 'Are you alright?'

'Just a deer.' She brushed her hair from her eyes, suppressing the tears that threatened to come.

'Ah-ha! Terrorised by the animal kingdom again!' he teased.

Zelda knew then that he would never take her seriously. He didn't think she had a stalker and therefore he must think her a sham, a headcase, a fraud. He was just a polite man, pandering to the nutty wife of his best friend. How could she have misread him so badly?

'I'm fine, please don't bother yourself about me. I've been looking after myself all my life and I intend to continue to do so without help from any bloody man!' She stomped off to find David.

Boy felt confused. Why was she angry with him when he was looking out for her? Zelda blew scarily hot and cold. He knew that his desire for her had almost got the better of him ... if Doone hadn't come back, he wasn't sure what might have happened between them.

But he had a pretty good idea, and the thought of it had stirred a deep yearning that was urgently demanding satisfaction.

He needed to pull himself together. She was his best friend's wife and no matter how attractive, she was also a lunatic. He was already married to one of those; the last thing he needed was involvement with another.

It was fortunate that Doone had interrupted them, in the nick of time, and saved him from a catastrophic error.

*

When Zelda walked back through the gates to the Dower House, her heart leapt again. Jake's car was parked outside the front door. She was relieved at the idea of seeing him. Her feelings towards Boy were powerful and confusing, and she knew she needed to get herself back together before she made an utter fool of herself.

She and Jake just needed to sort things out. Now that her career was on the up again, all he had to do was to nail his drinking and get back to his novel. Then he needed to be persuaded to forgive her. She ran her fingers through her hair, took a deep breath, and walked apprehensively into the kitchen to greet her husband.

She was disappointed when she found Valentine there instead. He was sitting at the kitchen table, chatting and laughing with Flora Banbury.

'Hey, we were wondering where you'd got to?' He stood and hugged his mother.

'Is Jake here too?'

'Uh, no. Sorry, he's gone AWOL again. Ed and Dusty have stayed up at the Mews, I told them to text when he reappears.' Valentine lit a couple of cigarettes and handed one to his mother.

Zelda took a deep drag, the smoke streaming into her lungs, momentarily soothing her battered heart. That old familiar blow of disappointment felt worse than ever today. Jake going AWOL was a very bad sign; she sensed their future ebbing away, and this time it felt worse than it ever had before.

Valentine put his arm around her and gave her a squeeze. 'I'm just going to drop Flora up to the Court, then I'll be back, OK?'

Zelda nodded and took another drag. Flora uttered a tiny, ''Bye!' as she slunk out.

Zelda couldn't know that Flora felt sorry for her, that she could see something that Zelda always tried to hide: being one of the most famous women on the planet wasn't all it was cracked up to be.

David knocked gently on the kitchen door and, walking in without waiting for an answer, found his lovely boss crying. He wondered what had been going on while he slept. He didn't need much sleep, but he did have to get some. He was only human.

But Zelda wouldn't tell him what was wrong, claiming it was nothing. It didn't look like nothing. David was worried that he was missing things.

David thought of himself as a perfectionist and this situation felt as far from perfection as it was possible to get.

*

As Valentine pulled up outside the back door to the Court, he noticed Doone's face, white against the dark window panes, watching them. So he casually leant across the car to kiss Flora on the lips. Annoyingly, she turned her head so that he just brushed her cheek, lightly.

Flora muttered, 'Get off!'

He got out and ran around the car, chivalrously holding out his hand to help her. Then he said loudly, 'That was fun!'

Doone emerged from the house looking piqued, but stunning. Valentine gave her his lingering look and said quietly, 'Hi, where did you spring from?'

She ignored him. 'Flora, why haven't you been answering your fucking phone? I had something important to talk to you about.'

'Oh, sorry, it ran out of battery,' Flora answered absently. 'Why, what's happened?'

Doone blurted, 'Mum's coming home!' She hadn't meant to say anything. But she somehow she just couldn't resist giving her sister a jolt. She didn't know why she felt so annoyed with Flora. It meant nothing to her, if she wanted to cavort about with Valentine; Doone really had no reason to stop her.

If she hadn't been so annoyed she might have noticed that her little sister was not in the least bit interested in Valentine.

Valentine watched the two girls together; he was intrigued. He could see that Doone was rattled. Was she beginning to fall for his game after all? He hoped so. The more he saw of her, the more he fancied her. Most women were a pushover for Valentine. The thought that Doone's dogged determination to resist his charm might be showing a little chink of vulnerability sent a sharp little thrill of excitement pulsating through his highly tuned body. He would keep up the pressure. The chase was well and truly on.

Flora said, 'When?'

'I don't know, but she wrote.' Doone looked contrite. 'Soon, I hope.'

She thought of Zelda laughing in their kitchen and then she thought of Valentine trying to kiss Flora. Like mother, like son, both trying to wheedle their way into the Banburys' lives. But Doone was never going to let that happen.

'Your mother was here earlier. Tell her to keep her grubby hands off our father.' She sounded livid. Flora looked astounded.

'Don't you think you are being a bit paranoid? I think you'll find they are just friends. Like Flora and I.' He smiled and put his arm around the younger girl, who shrugged him off.

Valentine leant towards Doone and said, his voice low, 'You seem to have a rather dirty mind. Not everyone is planning to fuck each other all the time you know!' He enunciated the word 'fuck' very softly, close to her face.

Doone wanted to slap him. The humiliations and frustrations of this day suddenly bubbled up and overwhelmed her. She lifted her hand, but Valentine caught her wrist adeptly and held it tight. 'No need for that! I get the picture, you don't like me!' Then he leant forward and planted a warm, gentle kiss on her lips. 'But I really like you, so what can we do about that?'

Flora had had enough of witnessing this weird scene. She ran off towards the house to try to find her father. To find out about their mother, their errant mother, who was coming home!

Doone remained rooted to the spot, her eyes glinting with indignation. Valentine stepped closer, so that the length of his body was lightly touching hers. He felt her shudder. Ah, yes, she was almost there, he would make her wait now. Wind her up. Make her want him so badly she would almost have to beg.

He stepped away from her again.

Just as he got back into the car, he looked up coolly and said, 'Glad to hear your mother is coming home. It's lonely when someone you love doesn't love you back.'

She didn't tell him that her mother wasn't coming home at all. She'd merely written to say she wanted to see her daughters. She didn't tell him that she didn't want to see her mother either, or that he was right; it was lonely when someone you loved didn't love you back.

Doone knew the truth of that; she had felt lonely for most of her life.

She turned and walked slowly into the house, waiting to hear the engine start and take Valentine away. But he didn't start the car, he wanted to see if she would turn back to look at him before he did. He wanted another sign. He watched her long slender legs carry her away but she didn't turn. He leant forward and was just about to turn the key when she suddenly glanced back over her shoulder, before being swallowed by the darkness of the house.

Ah! There it was! He started the engine, throwing the car into reverse.

He'd had a good day, and this was going to be an interesting summer; the weeks that stretched ahead were full of promise. He accelerated fast down the back drive.

He suddenly felt euphoric and glad to be alive. He had an unexpected, brief flashback to his accident and took his foot off the gas. After all, there was no hurry; he had all the time in the world. Valentine knew he was a very lucky person and that he had much to be grateful for.

Now he was going to cheer someone else up, someone who hadn't been quite so lucky lately: his mother.

He reflected on Doone's remark about Zelda having designs on Boy. He knew that was possible, likely even, since the guy was incredibly handsome and funny. Not solvent though, he had that in common with Jake. But he was sober, unlike Jake. He could see the appeal and his mother had always been a woman who needed constant reassurance about her desirability.

Her world was, or had been, full of millions of fans who loved her, worshipped her even, and he knew that she got some gratification from that. But she always needed more; they were alike in that respect, always needing, craving, demanding more. To be desired, loved and wanted was what Valentine and Zelda had in common, above anything else.

He wasn't sure that his mother was quite prepared to go to the same lengths as he was to get what she wanted, but he couldn't be sure. This Banbury episode was going to be interesting for both of them. He wondered if he should encourage her? Jake seemed to be a lost cause and Valentine's loyalty would always be to his mother, above anyone.

It might be fun to antagonise and tantalise Doone a little bit more as well.

They were in the country so, after all, there was nothing else to do.

*

He found Zelda lying, almost naked, on a rug on the lawn. She was texting and didn't see him as he approached.

He was sometimes surprised by how beautiful his mother still was. She had the body of a woman half her age and she wore a tiny bikini with a relaxed and confident air rarely achieved by younger girls.

She almost jumped out of her skin when he spoke.

'Flaunting it again, I see!'

'Jesus, Val, you frightened me!'

'Sorry, yeah, just saw David, he said you'd had another scare.'

'I did! No one believes me though.'

Valentine threw himself down next to her. 'I believe you.'He patted his mother on the bottom. 'Are you sure it's a good idea to be laying out the goods like this, with a maniac on the loose?'

Something in his teasing tone made Zelda realise that Valentine didn't really believe in her stalker either. At least he had the decency to lie about it though.

'Have you got a cig?'

Valentine lit one and gave it to her.

He lay back next to his mother and they were quiet for a moment.

'Where's that model of yours?'

'She's moving Johnny into the house they've rented. It's only a couple of miles away.'

'How convenient.'

'Yes, isn't it? Then again I hadn't reckoned on having such an attractive girl even closer to home.'

'Leave Flora alone, darling. She's too young for your games and you should have learnt by now never to shit on your own doorstep.'

'You can talk.'

Zelda wasn't quite sure what he meant. Was he referring to Milo? Or had he already sussed her interest in Boy? He was very quick, not much got past her golden boy.

'Anyway, I meant Doone,' he said.

'You can't be serious.'

'I know she's tricky, but she's a challenge. There aren't many of those around these days.'

'Tricky? She's terrifying!'

'Maybe she is just trying to warn *you* off her lovely father.'

So he knew.

Zelda said, 'Her father isn't interested in me. He thinks I'm a mad spoilt bitch.' She stubbed her cigarette out in the grass.

Valentine lent over and tickled her. 'Well, he's not a fool, you are a mad spoilt bitch.'

'Get off, Valentine!' she squealed.

A shadow fell across their bodies as they lay giggling on the ground. Valentine looked up.

David was standing over them. 'I'm going into the village. Do you need anything?' He sounded odd.

Zelda looked up at him. 'Karen dropped some stuff off earlier, so we don't. Oh, maybe a few bottles of wine?' She looked at Valentine. 'Have you got any cash on you, for David to get some booze?'

'Yep. You haven't spent what I gave you already though, have you? There's nothing to buy down here, for Christ's sake!'

'No, of course I still have it. I just don't carry cash in my bikini.'

Valentine casually pulled out a few notes and gave them to David. 'Could you get vodka too? Thanks, mate.'

David was dismissed.

# Chapter Thirty

Cleo found it difficult to sleep. The endless light of a night with hardly any darkness meant that the tent was too bright. She tried to cover her eyes, but she still felt restless and anxious.

Not least because the crew had talked everyone through the protocols of safety on the trip with particular attention to 'being vigilant about bears'. It was only then that Cleo realised they hadn't actually been joking before. Apparently there was real danger from grisly bears and, further north, from polar bears too. Which was why Cleo was wide awake when the wind started ripping at the canvas of the tents so ferociously that she wondered if they might get blown to bits. She daren't stick her head out of her tent to see how the others were doing for fear of the bears and consequently had not slept a wink by the time the wind died at 6 a.m. and she heard calls from Lars for everyone to get up and prepare 'for leave'.

They were soon skimming across the most spectacular sea on the planet. As they powered through the water there were seabirds swooping all around them and seals watched passively as the RIB flew by.

Cleo glanced across the boat at Milo, to find that he was watching her. She smiled at him coyly having decided, during her sleepless night, that the best way to deal with an unknown quantity was to get to know it better.

Milo smiled back. Which was encouraging.

Tom carefully manoeuvred himself to sit next to her at the prow. He had to speak loudly to make himself heard above the powerful engine.

'It's going to be a long day. Are you alright? You look tired.'

Cleo was frosty with him. 'I'm fine, what's the ETA?' she shouted back, pulling her sunglasses out of her pocket and putting them on. 'Tired' needed to be hidden at all times.

'Not sure. Heading along the Devon Island coastline. It will be spectacular, apparently. Nils says we'll be amazed.'

Nils was right. Nothing could have prepared them for the sights they would see that day. A spectacular wall of glaciers ran alongside them for miles, some of which collapsed as they passed, pouring heavy clouds of ice into the sea. The seabirds swooped around them and, at one point, Cleo screamed when a whale rose up very close to the boat and, as it gently submerged itself again, it covered them all with its fine plume of spray. They watched in silent awe as it gracefully rose and fell across the dark water.

Having recovered her composure Cleo called out to Milo, 'Seeing that makes it all worthwhile, doesn't it?' She was aware that she was on camera. So she gave a huge triumphant smile.

Milo answered, in his familiar husky broken English, 'We have whale of time!'

So he was doing jokes now? Cleo fake-laughed and turned back to look out for other dangers, feeling very weary suddenly and longing for dry land.

As they travelled onwards, Lars and Nils shouted for everyone to be on the alert for 'bergy' water, which was floating sea ice and very dangerous, allegedly. Cleo muttered that it didn't sound as dangerous as a bloody whale almost capsizing the boat.

But she was proved wrong as, shortly after she had spoken, the boat hit ice and almost capsized. Milo was thrown from his chair and Tom hit his head on the bar that the camera was rigged on.

It took a while to check out the boat and see if any damage had been done.

Cleo helped Nils to get Milo back into his chair. Although he couldn't move his legs, Milo's arms were still very strong. In fact, Cleo thought, if he had been sitting in a normal chair no one could ever know that he was paralysed at all. He was in great shape and all at once Cleo felt quite nostalgic. They had been very close, she and Milo. Not just as lovers; he had been steadfast in his dedication to her fitness for the Everest challenge and had tirelessly worked for her and her family for years. Too tirelessly in some cases, best not to think about *that* now though, Cleo thought, as she clambered back into her position at the prow of the RIB.

An eerie fog began to roll across the sea behind them, until they were engulfed. They had to slow right down and didn't reach the outpost until late.

By the time they arrived Cleo was delirious with hunger and exhaustion. Tom insisted that she eat something and she obediently grabbed a plate of food and retired to a small, rough sleeping hut. She was asleep before she had even managed to take her clothes off.

She dreamt of icebergs and polar bears and tiny people falling softly, like snow.

*

Cleo made her way to the showers and was soon outside, dressed, in full make-up and ready for anything. The cameraman wanted to film her watching the boat being refuelled and she obliged him with some excellent footage of light-hearted banter with the support team.

She also did a piece to camera about the whale sighting and generally waxed lyrical about the Arctic experience so far. She might have been a little overdramatic in her description of events: the whale 'almost capsized the boat' and 'we were nearly swamped by collapsing ice walls!' and 'we almost lost Milo overboard!'

But she remembered to get some stats in too, about the plight of the declining glaciers: 'All this sea ice could vanish by 2030 and the world will be changed forever.' She didn't think it sounded like such a bad thing, when, as far as she was concerned, most of the world seemed quite horrible. But she had been told that it was a bad thing, and that it was also her job to get that message across.

Cleo prided herself on her professionalism and she had a remarkable memory for facts and figures, having spent years learning endless meaningless dialogue as an actress.

So, as she sat calmly giving a lecture on global warming, in the background to her shot, Milo was wheeled down to the shore and lifted back into the boat.

She turned to look at him and then back to camera, saying, 'Yes indeed, the Arctic is a beautiful and dangerous place. A place that must be preserved at all costs, no matter how great. Each of us must play our part. Which is why I am here today, with Tom, Milo, Lars and Nils, risking our lives, to bring your attention to this most serious threat to the future of our planet and therefore,' she paused dramatically, 'to the future of mankind.'

Cut.

# CHAPTER THIRTY-ONE

Zelda was feeling a bit hung-over when she pottered down-stairs to begin another beautiful summer day. She felt mellow.

Valentine and she had had a lovely evening together, gossiping and drinking, and he had cooked for her then they had danced; had they danced? Yes, they had, she could remember some of it, dancing and singing and having fun with her son, just the tonic she needed. She wondered if he was up yet. Jake's car had gone again so it seemed he was.

She found a note on the kitchen table: *Gone to meet Lily. Love you x V.*

She heard the roar of the lawnmower outside and saw Frank behind it, shirt off, out across the grass, a very cheering sight she thought.

David appeared. 'Morning, everything alright? No frights in the night?' He had heard the music and laughter from the house and knew that Zelda was probably feeling a bit fragile.

'Everything's fine, thanks, David.' She smiled at him. 'Do you want to get some sleep? Frank's outside so I'll be alright.'

This was uncharacteristically thoughtful of Zelda. David seemed pleased.

He said, 'Yes, that would be good. Thanks, just ring this if you need me.' He gestured to a side table and then picked up an old hand-bell and gave it a vigorous ring.

It was surprisingly loud and made Zelda flinch. 'OK, OK! That's great, will do, thanks.'

When he had gone she rummaged in the kitchen cupboard for some Nurofen and disappeared back upstairs to have a bath.

As she lay amidst the bubbles she thought about Jake. She still hadn't heard from the kids in London. Was it possible that he was still AWOL? She knew that it was possible; likely even. He could often be gone for days. She had the fleeting wave of anxiety that always crossed her mind: what if something had happened to him? But she knew from experience nothing would have happened to him, apart from himself. *He* would have happened to him and he was quite enough.

She needed to start concentrating on work. Getting herself back out there would be cathartic. She knew everything else would fall into place when she was working again. There was too much thinking-time in the country. Zelda badly needed the distraction of work.

Helen had biked the call sheets to her. The first auditions for *Fame Game* were going to be filmed soon. She needed to work out a proper regime, with no more nights on the razz with her eldest son, that was for sure.

She got dressed slowly. Pulling on her tracksuit she decided to go for a bit of a run. That would sort her out, mind and body. She went downstairs and suddenly remembered that she'd given David time off for a sleep. She didn't want to risk running without having anyone with her.

Looking outside, she caught sight of Frank putting the mower away, pulling his shirt back on. She went over to talk to him. 'Thanks for the mowing. What do we owe you?' It had suddenly occurred to her that they had never paid him, or Karen for that matter.

Frank spoke without looking at her. 'Nothing. Boy looks after it.' He did up his buttons. 'The walled garden could do with some work too. But I've no time today, got to do a bit more clearing, up by the lake.'

'Oh! Are you going up there now? I really need a run. Could I come with you? I won't be in the way, just don't want to be up there on my own, you know? No one to hear me scream!'

'Sure. Can you run in those shoes though?' Frank glanced down at her feet.

Zelda realised that, inexplicably, she was wearing her marabou Louboutin slippers. 'Ha-ha. I'll just be two secs, quick change. Sorry, do you mind?'

'Nope, that's fine. I'll finish up here.'

So Boy was paying her bills and he didn't have any money. She was touched. She pulled her trainers on, left a note for David, then she was out of the house again and ready to roll.

Frank strode off up the drive and as she jogged along next

to him, she saw an opportunity to find out a bit about Boy's wife. But she wasn't quite sure how to put it.

She tried, 'They are such a lovely family, the Banburys. Is Lady Banbury away for much longer, do you know?'

'Nope.'

Zelda was none the wiser. Was that a 'nope', she's not away for much longer, or 'nope', I don't know how much longer she's away for? Or possibly 'nope', they are not a lovely family? She could tell she needed to rephrase the question.

'My husband and Boy are old friends, you know. But Jake only met Frances a few times. He said she was a bit scary.'

No response. Zelda was getting annoyed. She ran backwards in front of Frank. 'Was she a bit scary?'

Still nothing. Frank really wasn't susceptible to Zelda's charms at all. She gave up and when they reached the top of the hill by the lake she ran on ahead. 'Thanks, Frank,' she said sarcastically, really quite miffed. He watched her go and then disappeared into a thicket to retrieve his chainsaw.

Zelda ran on. She was just drawing level with an old boat-house when Boy suddenly stepped out and she almost ran into him. She squealed. He had given her a shock. She could hear the loud revving sound of the chainsaw, from across the lake.

'What are you doing out here? I thought you weren't meant to go anywhere without your protection officer.' Boy said.

Zelda heard a trace of mockery in his voice. She puffed, 'He's sleeping. Frank walked me up.'

'Still quite a few men running around after you, then?'

'Some people do believe that I might actually be in danger.'

'Well, if I was your stalker right now, you would be in danger, wouldn't you?' Boy's eyes were hard to read. 'Frank can't hear you and your guy is sleeping.'

Zelda could see the truth in what Boy was saying but she was damned if she would admit it.

She felt that jolt again as she met his eye.

'But you're not my stalker, are you, Boy? What are you to me?' She no longer felt shy, she felt reckless; her blood was up. 'What am I to you?'

She stepped boldly towards him. He paused for a moment, his face very close to hers; she could see sweat on his brow. She held her ground, her heart was pounding. 'You are nothing to me,' he murmured, but then he kissed her. Not the kiss they had shared before. This felt altogether more serious.

Zelda knew there was no going back from this one. She felt his heat and power as he pushed her backwards into the boat-house. He pressed her hard against the rough wooden wall, he had one hand in her hair and with the other he pulled down her tracksuit bottoms. She undid his belt, his skin hot in her grasping hands.

Boy felt all his frustration dissolve, as he urgently thrust himself into her. He had wanted this from the moment he had laid eyes on Zelda. Hating her was just a blind. He loved her! He wanted to make love to her forever. They were kissing deeply as they came together, so there were no cries to ring out across the lake. No sounds to give them away.

Frank had switched off the saw for a moment. He was just beginning to wonder where that nosy actress had got to, when he saw her saw emerge from the boathouse on the other side of the lake.

Followed closely by Boy, tucking in his shirt.

Well, well, her questions weren't just idle curiosity about his boss then. It certainly looked like she had got the answer to her question now.

It didn't seem like Boy expected his wife back any time soon either.

Boy held Zelda's hand. 'There you are, see what happens when you wander out and about without any bloody men! Very dangerous, I'd say.' He smiled down at her. 'I think you are going to need round-the-clock surveillance from now on. Can't have a man looking after you who sleeps on the job, now can we? I'll walk you home.'

She grinned. 'Too right you will! Do you always operate a policy of droit de seigneur over your tenants?'

'Only the really, really sexy ones.'

'Have you had a lot of those?'

'None.'

'I thought not.'

'Thanks!'

'No! That wasn't a criticism, far from it. I just thought you might not have done that for a while. You were very . . . keen!' She laughed and kissed him.

'It has been a while and, as a matter of fact, I'm still feeling pretty keen.' He put his arm around her waist and pulled her towards him. 'I think I will walk you home,' he squeezed her tight, 'then I will take you upstairs.' He pushed her away from him gently. 'Then I will slooowwly make love to you, until the walls shake.' He drew her back towards him and held her close.

'Sounds good to me!' she giggled. They stopped, kissed again and then Zelda broke away from him. 'And here I was thinking you hated me!'

'I do hate you, in a very loving way.' He pulled her along behind him. 'Come on, hurry up, home!'

'Home.' That sounded so good to Zelda. She wondered where he meant, his or hers? Then she remembered that they were both his anyway, so it didn't really matter.

*

Boy dropped Zelda back at the Dower House, where she was just going to change her clothes quickly and get back up to the Court for supper. Apparently, Doone would be there too, so Zelda thought that might be quite interesting.

She wasn't worried. She and Boy had spent such a passionate and deeply bonding afternoon in one of the bedrooms at Banbury, she knew that no amount of Doone's disapproval could destabilise what had begun between them.

Boy had led her into a vast grand room with a four-poster draped with dark red brocade, where he'd blithely told her, 'The Duke of Windsor slept here, quite often.'

Much later, Zelda said, 'I hope he enjoyed himself as much as we just did.'

'I'm sure he did, Wallis was with him!'

'Are you saying Wallis would be more fun than me?'

'No, I'm not saying that. But then again she was by all accounts pretty experienced ...' He laughed.

Zelda wanted to say, 'I'm pretty experienced.' But decided against it.

She leant in to kiss him, and said instead, 'Well, you are a royally great lover, Boy. I am your humble subject and you must do with me what you will.'

'Be careful what you wish for!' Boy pulled her towards his taught, naked body.

By the time Zelda got home that evening, she was feeling pretty pleased with herself. She was surprised to find Valentine back at home.

'Hi, darling, I thought you were seeing Lily?'

'She couldn't spend long. Johnny is down and he wanted her.' Valentine sounded peeved.

'I'm going up to the Court for supper. Doone will be there. I'm sure you can come too if you want to?'

Valentine considered his mother. 'Is that where you've just come from?'

Zelda feigned indifference. 'Yep.' She was a good actress, but not that good.

'Seriously? Already! God! I leave you alone for one minute.' Valentine laughed and went to high-five his mother. 'Respect! One down, one to go!'

'Oh, honestly, Val! Sssh, you can't say anything about this to anyone. Particularly not to Doone.'

'Or Jake?'

Zelda looked anguished. 'Oh, God, why does everything have to be so complicated?'

'It doesn't. It's just more interesting this way.' He poured them both a drink, and they clinked glasses. 'To interesting!'

'To interesting, to catastrophe, to disaster, to devastation, to ruin,' Zelda said.

'OK, calm down, it's only love; it's meant to be fun.' Valentine couldn't help wondering if what he felt for Lily was love? Because if it was, then sometimes, it certainly wasn't fun.

He was hurt to be turned away by her for that old ruin Johnny; it had happened before and made him furious. He needed to think about what he could do about it. Being subject to his or her whim was not a position Valentine liked to be in. He liked to be in charge and he needed to think of a way to get Lily all to himself.

Doone seemed like a good place to start. Give Lily a taste of her own medicine.

Zelda scampered outside to text Boy. She asked if she could bring Valentine to supper too?

He responded immediately, 'Good plan. An army required to restrain me from ravaging you on the kitchen table.'

'Shall I bring David to protect me?'

'No, he looks too strong. I don't actually plan to be restrained for long. You have been warned.'

'I'm shaking all over.'

'I might have to come and get you right now.'

'Down, Boy.'

'If that's a command, I can't wait.'

'You have to wait. It's called delayed gratification.'

'I know a lot about that!'

'Hmmmm.' Zelda chuckled and headed back towards the house.

David appeared, saying sharply, 'You're alright then. You left a note, said *gone for a run*. When you didn't come back, I went looking for you.'

'I went up to the Court,' she hesitated just a beat, 'for tea.'

'I can't protect you if I don't know where you are.'

'Sorry. Didn't think.' Zelda tried to look contrite.

But she really didn't have time for David getting arsy with her now. The trouble with staff, she thought, not for the first time, was it was often difficult to strike the right balance, to have them there when you needed them and not when you didn't. David seemed more out of sync than he used to be; for one thing he never used to question her, just calmly did her bidding. She hoped he wasn't going to start getting awkward now.

She had apologised, and she couldn't do more.

*

David emerged from his flat just as Valentine and Zelda jumped into the car and were turning around in the drive.

Zelda told her son to stop. The roof was down, and she smiled up at her security guy. 'Evening, David, I meant to say we are out tonight. Do take the night off.' She was planning to stay at the Court, but suddenly realised it might be best if David didn't know what was going on, at least not until things became clearer. 'There won't be any need to do night watch,' she added quickly. 'Valentine will be in the house with me so we'll be fine.' She smiled sweetly up at him.

He said, 'Great, thanks,' and gave a casual wave.

But he didn't mean 'great' or 'thanks'. Being told you had the night off on the actual night wasn't of much use to anyone. He strode back up to his room. There were things he needed to organise. He had a life to live too, which wasn't something that Zelda ever seemed to allow for.

But David tried not to mind too much. He understood. Zelda was special and he would always make allowances for her.

# CHAPTER THIRTY-TWO

The day began with big seas and was soon swallowed up by gloomy fog, which was not an auspicious start.

They all knew that they were heading for Resolute Bay, the furthest outpost in the Arctic, and that thereafter they would have to pass through the unforgiving ice field that was the infamous Northwest Passage.

Before they set off that morning, Lars had explained to them, and to camera, that the route had only become navigable since 2007, for the first time in history. Despite the massive disintegration of the ice, they would still have to be break through it in some places.

He reminded them that it was extremely dangerous.

Cleo thought it sounded like hell, but no one would ever know it. She jumped into the RIB with the agility of a thirty-year-old and gave a cheery wave as they pushed off to what, she was quite certain, would be a very testing day.

She felt encouraged when the sea calmed and the fog began to lift, but not for long, because it soon became clear that there was a vast wall of ice up ahead which went on and on, for as far as the eye could see. The wind off the ice was bitterly cold and they had to spend tortuously long hours pushing their way through the frozen sea.

As if playing a giant game of chess, Lars moved vast floating chunks of ice out of the way with a boat hook. They crept agonisingly slowly through the creaking mass, well aware that it could easily turn and crush their boat at any moment.

Cleo could hardly breathe, suddenly feeling very claustrophobic in the RIB. What if it was crushed? Would they have to get out and stand on the shifting ice and wait to be rescued? What had those handsome lifeboat guys said? She couldn't remember and she wasn't sure she wanted to know now either.

They were far, far away from civilisation, as far away as it was possible to be, dependent on the durability of a small inflatable boat and a boat hook, versus a world full of belligerent icebergs. She couldn't help thinking that her present predicament made the Titanic seem like a safe bet. She also noticed that Lars and Nils were looking stressed, not a good sign as they had been very calm and cheerful up until this point.

Cleo retreated deep into the blanket that Lars had draped around her, closed her eyes and waited for the worst to happen.

Eventually, Tom Maddison cried out, 'Clear water!'

Cleo opened her eyes and was very relieved to see that it was true.

The engine roared and they flew off at speed, around the

edge of the icepack and on, and on, until they reached the welcome sight of Resolute Bay.

Just a tiny cluster of buildings, but what buildings! Warmth! Feet on dry land! It looked ravishing to Cleo and the tiny hotel was quaint but seemed just perfect. She would have a little lie down and a warm-up. Then she would be ready for action again. They were all meeting for dinner in the dining room at nine.

Cleo would be made-up, dressed and ready for that cameraman in no time.

The trials of the day were behind her now and tomorrow still seemed far away. The simple pleasure of being alive made Cleo feel revitalised and invigorated. She really did thrive off challenges; she felt chuffed with herself, she hadn't shouted for 'a helicopter to get me off this fucking boat!' or any of the other screaming and swearing stuff she had felt like doing at the time. She had maintained her dignity, despite being frozen and frightened to death – almost.

She was sure everything was going to be alright from now on. After all, she was tackling global warming practically single-handed ... she drifted off into a fantasy; perhaps they would make her a Dame.

\*

By the time Cleo arrived in the restaurant, supper had already begun. She could hear raucous laughter from some way off and was a little put out that it continued, without pause, when she entered the room. She had made quite an effort getting ready and although she was only wearing jeans and a little Prada snowflake jersey, her hair, make-up and jewellery were all pretty gorgeous, so she was expecting to be noticed.

Then Tom noticed her and stood politely. 'Cleo, here you are! Join us!' And he pulled out a chair next to himself, the only empty chair in the room. On the other side was Milo, smiling warmly at her. She knew she had to sit between them, so she smiled thinly and took her place as gracefully as she could.

'Thanks for waiting!' she said, almost teasingly.

'Sorry, the owner is also the chef and when it's ready, apparently it has to be eaten immediately, or he gets a bit "Gordon",' Tom said.

'It looks – interesting.' Cleo wrinkled her nose at the mountain of stew on her plate. 'What is it?'

'Stew.'

'I can see it's stew, what kind of stew?' Cleo did think it smelt delicious and was about to tuck in when the owner appeared.

He looked rather sweaty and insisted on kissing her hand. 'Hope you like polar bear?"

'What?'

'My polar bear stew, I hope you like it.'

Cleo put down her fork and looked crestfallen.

The owner patted her on the back and said, 'Just kidding, it's beef!'

Everybody howled with laughter, except Cleo, who looked as if she might stab him in the eye with her fork. She was so hungry, she thought she'd just taste a quick mouthful. It was delicious.

Milo said, 'Good, eh?'

'Mmmmm.'

'So are you speaking with me now? It has been few days.'

'It's been *a* few days.' Cleo had forgotten how charming his broken English was.

'I don't understand. Cleo, I hear nothing from you, all this time. What is it I ever do except help you?'

Cleo turned to him then and fixed him with a glacial stare. 'I know what you were *going* to do, Milo. So don't start this. You know why I haven't spoken to you.' Attack was always the best form of defence.

Milo looked mystified. He ran his hands through his thick fair hair in confusion or possibly in despair. He shook his very handsome head.

Cleo continued, 'You didn't do it after all. I appreciate that, so let's just leave it, shall we? The past is the past.'

Tom was listening to this exchange with interest, while pretending to pay attention to a very attractive young guy from the support team.

The past was never the past as far as Tom was concerned. He really wondered what Milo knew of the events that led to his accident. He wondered if he should attempt to find out. It might be interesting.

\*

Cleo rang Max before she went to sleep that night. She suddenly had an overwhelming need to hear her husband's voice.

'Hello.'

'Max, darling, it's me.'

311

'*Hello.*'

'Max, can you hear me?'

'*Can you hear me!*' he yelled.

'Yes, I can hear you loud and clear, you don't need to shout. That's the point of the telephone.'

'Sorry, darling, just thinking of you so far away makes me *yell.*'

'You're still yelling.'

He quietened down. 'Are you alright?'

'That's why I'm ringing, to say I am.'

'Oh, thank God. I have been worried. Jamie showed me some stuff on the computer about the Northwest Passage and I've been in a bit of a panic.'

Ah, yes, Jamie: their butler, always burning to serve. 'It's fine, great fun really.' She didn't want Max to worry too much. 'The oddest thing is, they've brought Milo too.'

'What, Milo your . . .' Max sounded surprised and then sarcastic, '. . . *trainer.*'

'Well, he was your *trainer* too.'

They both realised that this line of chat wasn't leading them anywhere constructive.

'Anyway, he's here, in a wheelchair.'

'In a wheelchair? In the boat!'

'Yep.'

'Well, I don't suppose he can get up to much in that case!'

'No.' Cleo realised that was true and was annoyed to find she felt a little twinge of nostalgic disappointment.

'Whose idea was *that*?' Max was shouting again.

Cleo lowered her voice. 'The director said it was the broad-caster's.'

'Oh, well. I'm sure you will sail through it, darling. Troublesome ex-staff or not!' Max sounded sincere.

Cleo missed him then, missed their lovely house and their luxurious life. 'I don't know why I'm doing this. I think I must be mad. It's quite frightening.'

'Oh, darling, not long now and you will love it when it's done. Everyone will be so proud, I will be so proud. And think of all the filthy lucre!'

Ah, yes, Cleo thought, the money. Her money, her hard-earned money. Not the inheritance business that Max had always thrived on, but hers. There was satisfaction in that.

There was a crackle of static on the line.

'Better go. Lovely to hear you.'

'Lovely to hear you too, darling, love you.' Cleo hung up.

She did love Max, her rock, her standby, go-to guy. Her husband.

He'd been almost perfect when they were first married, one of the richest men in England and only a little bit gay in those days, or so she'd thought. Now he was the gayest man in England and only a little bit rich. Anyway, what the hell, it had worked well for both of them, for over forty years. His most recent indiscretions had only caused her embarrassment, rather than any real pain.

She felt cheered up by their little chat. He was right; she would be fine. She should just settle down and enjoy the ride. She looked out of the metal window of her bedroom, out into the endless light that was the northern night. The sea glinted and glistened out in the bay.

Cleo realised that she could just see it, the ice field, in all its frozen, cruel glory. The ice field that lay waiting for her.

# CHAPTER THIRTY-THREE

Ed found his father fast asleep on the sofa when he got back to the Mews that evening. He was still dressed in the clothes that he'd been wearing to the concert a couple of nights before.

This wasn't an unusual state for Ed to find Jake in. But it did make him sad. His father had been doing so well. Off the booze he had been a different man, responsible, reliable and still funny too. Yes, Ed thought, he really preferred his dad sober.

He bent over him. 'Dad, Dad, it's me. Wake up!'

'Whah, wha. Ed, mate.' Jake groaned as he opened his eyes. 'Aw, man, I am so fucking sorry.'

'It's not your fault, Dad.' Ed sat down next to his father and lit a cigarette to mask the gut-wrenching smell of old booze and sweat.

'Can I have one?' Jake asked. 'It *is* my fucking fault, Ed. I'm the one who got drunk. Nobody forced me.'

'You were, like, upset.'

'Not an excuse, lots of people get upset. They don't get shit-faced and wake up in a stranger's house though, do they?'

315

'Maybe not. This isn't a stranger's house. It's yours.'

Jake groaned some more. He decided not to share the mystery of his lost time with his son. 'Where's Dusty and that nice boyfriend?'

'Out.'

'Willow?'

'With them.'

'Good, I don't want her to see me like this.'

'She's just a baby, Dad, she won't mind.'

'I meant Dusty.'

'She knows you've been missing. She understands.'

'Does she? I wish I fucking did!'

'You just need to keep going to those meetings.'

'I know. I'm going to have a bath then I'll get off to one. Get this sorted once and for all. Can't go on like this. Too shaming.'

Jake shuffled off upstairs. Ed thought he suddenly looked older; the boyish good looks had been knocked into touch. Ed had to admit that his father was the perfect cautionary tale, an anti-role model for tipplers.

He glanced at his phone and found there was a text from Dusty. They were on their way home. She said she'd pick up something for supper.

They were like a real family, a real underage family; not uncommon – there were plenty of other families like theirs around. Ed had observed that many of his richest friends led lives similar, in their neglect, to the kids on the local housing estates. They just had bigger houses.

Most of his friends came from broken families, with parents

who were incapable of growing up. A lost generation, he thought, not the kids, but the parents; the very spoilt parents. Robbed of their sense of purpose by their trust funds and with love lives blighted by unrealistic expectations they were ruined by having it all.

His own family was a typical example and Ed felt sorry for them. His mother, father, brother – they were all a mess. He wished they would sort themselves out.

But he knew that there was very little he could do to help them. All he could do was look after himself, so he went to the cupboard and pulled out a bag of crisps, popped a can of Coke and turned on the telly to watch *EastEnders*.

By the time Dusty and Alex got back, Jake had left for his AA meeting.

Ed looked at his phone: it was a text from Flora. 'Stuck in London can I stay at yours?'

Ed couldn't believe his luck. He texted back, simply a 'Yup', then hastily ran upstairs to take a shower.

Later on, when Flora was there and Ed was trying to look busy and popular on his phone, he suddenly remembered to text his mum.

He wrote, 'Jake lives!'

Which was all he felt Zelda would be interested to know – if that.

By the time she picked up the text the following day, their world had been turned on its head once again.

# CHAPTER THIRTY-FOUR

'You're kidding?'

Boy tried to look casual. 'Nope.'

'And you expect me to cook for them? Again!'

'Don't see why not.'

'Because they are both ghastly and I hate them?' Doone wondered why her heart was pounding.

'Come on, Doone, really?'

'Yes, really, they are bad news. I mean she's your oldest friend's wife for a start.'

Boy looked gloomy. 'They are going through a difficult time.'

'Nice of you to step in to help, I'm sure Jake will appreciate it. What a pal.'

Boy finished laying the table and lit the old candlesticks that were laden with drips of melted wax. 'Well, they are coming to supper, so I will have to cook for them if you won't.'

'I suppose poisoning them might be a solution.' She made a long-suffering face at her father. 'OK, I'll do it. But on one condition.'

'What's that?'

'Promise me you won't let her sleep here.'

'Of course she won't be sleeping here, Doone! What kind of man do you think I am?'

'You're a man kind of man.'

'Hmph! So you'll cook?'

'I will.'

Valentine walked casually into the kitchen. 'You will what?'

Doone didn't miss a beat. 'I will stab you if you annoy me.'

'Well, you might as well stab me now, because I always seem to annoy you.'

Boy interrupted, 'Where's your mother?'

'She's gone in search of a loo.'

Boy headed for the door. 'I'll get us some wine.'

Zelda was walking towards him down the long west passage, looking ravishing in a floaty white dress. He could see the outline of her perfect body through the thin fabric. She gave him an enchanting smile as she drew near. He grabbed her and pushed her against the doorway to the cellar, and she squealed as he kissed her feverishly, before he took her hand and pulled her down the steps behind him.

He said, 'Come with me, help me with the wine.'

The nightclub smelt boozy and sweet. He grabbed her by the waist and guided her onto the dance floor but they weren't going to dance. He almost threw her onto the banquette and lifted her soft chiffon skirt. She wasn't wearing pants.

'Is this a tasting?' she asked.

He laughed against her lips, 'It is.'

Later, she pulled his hair and whispered, 'You can fuck me now!'

He didn't need to be told twice. They had to be quick, which wasn't a problem because they had both been well beyond the point of no return, long before they'd even laid eyes on each other that night.

They lay panting on the velvet cushions for a minute. Then Zelda squealed, 'Wine, wine!'

'Stop whining, it wasn't that bad, was it!'

'No time for jokes, they will know!'

'They know already.'

'Doone knows?'

'Yep.'

'Shit! Valentine too, but he's OK with it.'

'We'll talk about it later. You go on up, look ill or something. I'll bring the wine in a couple of minutes.'

'We don't have to pretend. How old do you think they are? Ten?'

'Go on, go! Or I'll have to spank you!'

'Oh, God, you haven't been reading *Fifty Shades*, have you?'

'Course not! Go!' he laughed.

So she knew that he had.

Zelda chuckled to herself as she skipped up the dusty stairs. She felt overwhelmingly happy and she hadn't even had a drink yet.

Valentine was gaily chopping onions when his mother emerged.

He raised his watery eyes. 'Alright, Mommy, dearest?'

'Fine. Hello, Doone, thanks for having us. It's great to get out of the Dower House, going a bit stir crazy down there to be honest.'

'So I've heard.' Doone handed Valentine a big bunch of basil.

'What do you want me to do with that?' he asked.

'Pulverise it.'

'Will do, then what?'

'Then come and hold this.'

Valentine did as he was told. He made himself useful, kept the flirting to a minimum and made everyone laugh a lot.

He wondered where Flora was. He knew she wasn't with Johnny. He thought it best not to ask about the sister now. Things seemed to be going along quite well with him just play-ing it straight. Which was a bit of a novelty for Valentine, because playing it straight seemed to be working a treat.

He caught Doone's eye as she was laughing and he saw her defences drop, just for a moment. But if he had got them down once he could get them down again. He hadn't enjoyed himself this much in ages. Nor had his mother by the look of her.

It was all quite a turn-up. He was pleased. The night wore on and everyone sparkled and shone in the candlelight.

Boy announced that he wanted to show Zelda the long gallery. That was what he'd said anyway. So Valentine was alone with Doone. He began clearing the table, and they chat-ted amiably as Doone washed up. He stood next to her and seemingly accidently bumped her.

'Sorry! No touching, I know.'

322

Doone looked him directly in the eye. 'What?'

'You don't want me to touch you?'

'When did I say I didn't want you to touch me?' Doone turned herself towards him slightly. Her hands were dripping bubbles.

'You might not have actually said it.' Valentine mirrored her body angle. 'But you implied it. Well, a bit more than implied it; you are quite frightening, you know.' He looked at her quizzically from beneath his long blonde fringe.

'Am I frightening you now?'

'Not so much now, no.'

He would let her come to him.

Her tempting lips were a couple of centimetres from his. He held still.

'Now?'

'Not sure.'

She kissed him.

It worked!

She kissed him gently and then with a passionate hunger that took them both by surprise.

He grabbed her by her soapy hand and pulled her upstairs. They kissed as they fell through her bedroom door and they kissed as they made love. Valentine didn't always bother much with kissing but, after this, he planned to take it up, in a big way.

Kissing Doone was something he hoped to be doing, quite a lot, for the foreseeable future.

Who knew cold could blow so hot?

By the time Zelda and Boy returned to the kitchen, Doone and Valentine were just finishing the clearing up.

'There you are! We wondered what had happened to you. About to send out a search party,' said Valentine. Who wasn't the only person in the family to think that attack was always the best form of defence.

'Fabulous dinner, thanks, Boy, and Doone, thank *you* too.' He gave her a subtle but scorching look. 'OK, Mommy, dearest, let's get a move on before we outstay our welcome.'

'Oh, do you have to go? Have another drink, some coffee, tea?' Boy looked desolate. Doone gave him a warning look.

Valentine raised his hands and started walking backwards towards the door. 'No, don't tempt us any more. We will just want to stay and stay and stay. Wanting more and more and more.' He said it softly, with rhythm. He looked across at Doone. He could see that she got the picture.

Boy led Zelda out to the back door, whereupon Valentine raced across the kitchen, jumping over a chair to kiss Doone, just once more.

'See you later,' he said.

She didn't say a word. She didn't need to. Her eyes told him she would barely be able to wait until tomorrow to see him.

He'd got her! Easy.

His heart was pounding as he raced down the drive with his mother sitting silently next to him, lost in her own romantic fug.

He'd got her, yes. But it might have occurred to him, from the way his heart was racing, that in fact she had got him.

\*

When they got back to the Dower House, David had kindly left all the lights on. In fact he was in the kitchen when they walked in.

He stood up. 'Just wanted to make sure the house was secure until you returned. Goodnight.' He left them to it.

'Thanks, David, 'night!' Zelda called after him vaguely.

Valentine poured them both a glass of brandy, which he'd found hidden in a welly in the back kitchen. Which made him speculate that old Lady Banbury might have been a bit of a lush.

'Thanks for bringing me back, darling. So annoying that prude Doone made Boy promise not to let me sleep there! I know you would have liked a bit longer to work on mission impossible.'

'Ah, mission accomplished in fact.'

'You're kidding?'

'Why would I joke about a serious thing like that?'

'Bloody hell, Valentine. How do you do it?'

'Well, how do *you* do it? No, actually, don't tell me, I really don't want to know. Ugh.' Valentine fake-shuddered.

'I don't fake-shudder like that for a start!'

Valentine put up his hand. 'Enough!' They both laughed.

'Congratulations, darling! I didn't think that would be possible.' Zelda suddenly looked serious. 'You didn't force her, did you?'

'God, no! Of course not, what do you take me for!' He lit a cigarette, took a deep drag and said, 'For Christ's sake, you know as well as I do that Kate told a lot of fucking lies in that book. Why would you think *that* wasn't one of them?' His cheek twitched.

Zelda could see that he was livid. 'Sorry, darling. I didn't mean that at all, I was just kidding.'

'Well, don't, it's not funny.'

'No it's not. What an evil little cow Kate is. Can I have a cig?'

'Sure, help yourself, I'm off to bed.' Valentine stubbed out his cigarette, and stomped out.

Who knew that hot could blow so cold.

Zelda finished her cigarette. Valentine could be so touchy sometimes. But she wasn't going to let his little strop ruin her perfect day, her perfect night, or her dreams of her perfect future.

She poured herself another glass of brandy and sat fantasising about life as the new Lady Banbury. She would earn enough to restore the estate to its former glory. She and Boy would have wonderful house-parties, full of beautiful people. They would laugh, make love and live a lovely, happy, carefree existence.

She knew *Fame Game* would get her career on track again. Then, before she knew it, she'd be back in LA and making proper money. They could buy a house in London and maybe, after a few more movies, a flat in New York, as she missed her old brownstone. But she mustn't think about that, about the things she had lost. She mustn't think about Jake or Boy's wife, who she still knew less than nothing about.

She must look to the future, her exciting new, glittering, thrilling future.

The next Lady Banbury emptied her ashtray and turned out all the lights.

She went to lock the front door and close the huge hall curtains.

She almost had a heart attack. The Face was staring at her from outside the window. It lunged towards her. She screamed and screamed and ran to the bottom of the stairs. Valentine appeared at the head of the staircase. 'Jesus, Mum, what is it?'

'He's there!' Her voice tore out of her like a saw. 'He's there, outside the window!'

Valentine skittered down the stairs and put his arm around Zelda's shoulder. He felt a bit vulnerable wearing only his pants.

'Ring the bell, ring the bell!' she shrieked.

'What bell?'

'In the kitchen.' Zelda gesticulated frantically.

Valentine glanced at the window as he went past and was relieved to see nothing there, just his reflection. He found the bell and rang it vigorously.

There was a banging on the door moments later. 'It's me, David, let me in.'

Valentine unlocked the door and was very reassured to see their security guy: cool, strong and clearly ready for action. He had a gun in his hand.

'What happened?' he asked.

Zelda was sitting on the stairs, shivering.

'She saw a face at the window,' explained Valentine.

'*The* Face, *the* Face!' Zelda shrieked between ragged breaths.

David said, 'Right, lock the door after I leave and don't let anyone in until I get back, OK?'

Valentine nodded.

Zelda looked up at David. 'If you find him will you kill him?'

'I might just do that, Zelda. I think that bastard has it coming to him. Don't you?' He rushed out into the night, without waiting for her answer. Zelda certainly did think he had it coming.

She needed a pill. She couldn't breathe.

'Val,' she said, tentatively getting to her feet, 'will you come up to my room with me? I need some pills.'

'Course. Come on. Up we go.'

Valentine noticed that his mother was tottering a bit. Brandy or fear? Or both? He wasn't sure. What had she seen in the window? Her own reflection perhaps?

He didn't dare suggest that, but he knew it was a possibility. They had drunk quite a lot up at the Court and then again, here . . .

He followed Zelda into her bathroom.

There was a dead rat in the bath.

Valentine could tell this was going to be a long night.

# CHAPTER THIRTY-FIVE

The sea ice had been swept away by the wind and the tides, so that conditions looked promising for the next leg of the *Against All Odds* expedition.

The cameraman was there to see them all off again. He was pleased he had got some very atmospheric stuff during dinner the previous night. He managed a few more takes as they loaded up and pushed off, and his work was done for the day.

He admitted to himself that he was very glad not to be in that tiny boat. Everest was tough but this looked altogether more frightening, since there were even more things to go wrong. He didn't like water much either, couldn't even swim in fact, not something that anyone had thought to ask him when they booked him as crew on this show.

He felt a cold chill as he watched them disappearing through the clearway towards the Barrow Strait.

Earlier Lars had said, on camera, that they were heading for the first really serious ocean conditions that day.

He wasn't sure that Cleo and Milo had been told that yet. He shuddered, turned, and went back to the nice warm hotel.

*

Nils was helming the RIB with consummate skill, or that's what Lars told them he was doing. He had to shout it above the roar of the engines and the tearing wind as they took some fearsomely steep waves.

It didn't look like consummate skill to Cleo, as she lay on the floor of the dingy. She clung to the camera rig and screamed every time the RIB pitched down the swollen waves. She was frozen and drenched and terrified beyond all care; her language would make a scaffolder blush.

Milo was like a latex pyramid, lashed to the floor of the RIB. He was wearing a sou'wester and a vast black waterproof cape. His face was set in a rictus grin, the effort of remaining upright was exhausting and he was beginning to swear too.

Soon, all that could be heard above the roar of the engine and the elements was every expletive ever uttered.

It became a sort of swearing competition, as they all searched for increasingly vile and arcane invective to hurl out at the Arctic sea. They had reached a dazzling climax of profanity when Cleo suddenly yelled, 'Blow!'

'Seriously? Blow?' yelled Tom.

'It's all I've got left,' Cleo yelled back.

'I bet that's not true!' Lars grinned and disappeared under another heavy wave of spray.

'Not true at all,' Milo chipped in. Cleo wasn't sure that anyone would have heard him above the din. But she had heard him and when she turned to look at him he grinned, just before another huge flume struck him hard in the face.

Eventually, the storm calmed. Lars and Nils scampered deftly around the small boat, baling it out, tying things down and generally reorganising the RIB.

Lars congratulated everyone for keeping their cool and awarded Tom the 'most filthy swearing' prize. He told them that they were heading for a small island group in uncharted waters, off King William Island.

'We should be able to anchor up there in a couple of hours. Then we can get dry and get a brew going. OK?'

It did sound good, well, the tea bit anyway; the two hours to get there sounded, and felt like, two years to Cleo. Everyone felt very bonded by the time they finally arrived. Nothing like a swearathon, in a storm, to bring people together.

The island was much less than Cleo had hoped for. Just a desolate scrap of rock, about eight yards high and a few hundred yards long, it was barely larger than the yachts Cleo usually spent her summers on. She wandered off to find somewhere to go to the loo, pleased that she was able to rough it just as well as flush it.

She got back to the boys to find them struggling to tilt the RIB up onto its side. 'To make a windbreak,' Lars explained.

They would certainly need one of those, as the wind was icy and their clothes were wet. Lars continued, 'Everyone needs to strip off wet gear and get into some dry, before we are getting hypothermia here.'

Cleo crouched behind the RIB and whipped off all her wet

gear. Teeth chattering, she was swearing again, using some of the new words she had just learnt. Once she had put warm, dry clothes on, she was happier; who knew clothes could feel this good? Forget couture, thermal was the way to go.

She saw that Milo was struggling to get his top off. She grabbed it and pulled firmly. 'I've got you. Come on, let me help with the rest.' She leant down and quickly whisked off his wet boots, then undid his jeans. This felt all too familiar. 'Tom, can you help me to lift Milo?'

Tom was stronger than he looked. They soon had Milo in dry clothes too and Nils had lit the paraffin stove. They all huddled round it, in the lee of the RIB, as Lars brewed up some tea and added a healthy slug of rum to each mug.

'An Arctic cocktail,' Cleo said. 'Yum.'

Which they all agreed it was. They went on drinking rum for quite a while, until Lars suggested that they take it in turns to get some sleep. Someone would need to stay up on bear watch.

Cleo thought they were teasing her again, until she saw Nils sit down on the rock and pull a rifle from its case.

Milo said, 'I'll take first watch if you like? I'll be sitting here anyway, with nothing to do.'

'Do you know how to handle a gun?' Nils asked.

'Sarajevo,' Milo replied.

Everyone looked at him expectantly, but he left it at that. So Nils just handed him the rifle and before long everyone but Milo was fast asleep.

Cleo woke with a start. She had been dreaming of bears again. She looked out from the tarpaulin. It was dark, so it must have been about one a.m. It was dark for such a short time each night that it seemed particularly spooky now that she was used to constant light. She heard a faint scraping noise.

'Milo,' she whispered.

'Yes.'

'Are you alright?' She crawled out of the tent.

'Yes, I was trying to have a pee. But I fell out of chair!'

'I'll wake the team.'

'No, leave them sleep, you hold chair for me, I'll lift myself back in.'

'Right.' Cleo moved quietly towards his voice.

She felt the wheelchair before she saw it. 'I've got it.'

'Hold the gun, I don't want shoot myself.'

She saw a small glint of metal. Milo was handing her a gun. That was interesting; he really couldn't know what had happened on Everest or he wouldn't be so reckless as to put a gun into her hands, would he?

Cleo took the gun and felt an overwhelming rush of relief. Apart from Tom, no one knew what she had done to Milo, including Milo himself, that much was clear at last. Tom needed her as much as she needed him, so it really was possible that everything would be OK.

Cleo felt the wheelchair rock as Milo heaved himself back into it. He gave a small groan.

Then there was another, much louder groan, more of a growl – from a few feet away. Cleo stepped back. She felt her blood run cold. There was a sudden rush of warm air, and a strong smell of beast as tons of polar bear hurled itself towards them.

A shot rang out and there was a thud. Followed by silence.

Lights began to go on and then there were voices. 'What's going on?'

'Cleo, what happened, are you OK?

'Where's Milo?'

# Chapter Thirty-Six

Zelda woke in the king's bed. Boy was gazing down at her. 'Hey, there you are. Everything's alright, you're here now. Safe.' He smiled reassuringly.

Zelda smiled back up at him. 'Thanks for letting me stay. I'm so sorry, Boy. I know everyone thinks I've gone mad. But I did see the Face and it had put a rat in my bath.'

'You don't have to keep reliving it over and over.' He stroked her hair from her eyes. 'I have spoken to Sergeant Powell and he's on his way over to the Dower House now. He and your guy will sort it out. You can stay here, everything will be fine.'

Even in Zelda's wildest fantasies she hadn't seen things moving quite this fast.

She knew that she had been a bit hysterical after the rat sighting, so Valentine didn't have much option but to get her out of the house. She couldn't help feeling that it was fairly opportunistic of him to bundle her into the car, race back up the drive to Banbury Court and then almost beat the door down until Boy appeared, dishevelled and bemused, and was forced to offer them both beds for the night. But there probably hadn't been another option. She could bet her life that Valentine wouldn't have spent a moment of time in the room he had been shown to either.

She was right, of course.

Doone had woken to hear knocking on her door. She didn't seem in the least bit surprised to find Valentine standing before her, in the middle of the night, dressed only in his pants. She just let him into her room, wordlessly. He was shivering a little from the cold night air and, to some extent, the shock from his mother's hysterical shrieking.

Doone rubbed him down to warm him up. Her coolness seemed to have evaporated, leaving a warm and loving woman. Valentine felt comfortable in her arms as they kissed softly. He had never slept with a girl like this before; he felt calm and fell into a deep and dreamless sleep.

It was the first night he had slept without dreaming of Georgia's traumatic death.

He woke the next morning feeling strangely optimistic. For the first time in a long while, he realised he felt happy.

*

The Serpentine was one of Jake's favourite places. He and Georgia had often gone there, as children, to mess around in the boats on the lake, and so it had always reminded him of her.

He sat down on a bench and pulled the pushchair up close to his knees. He found himself quietly telling Willow all about her mother. He knew she was too small to understand him, but he felt an overwhelming urge to talk about his sister, tell her baby daughter all about what she had been like, as a child. Things had come up about their tragic past in one of his meetings, and now he found himself thinking about their childhood a lot.

Willow gazed up at him as he spoke and she smiled and chuckled. Jake could see the resemblance to his sister in her sweet baby face. She was fair and blue-eyed like her mother; then again, that was like her father too. Valentine, Valentine – what a complicated mess that all was. Things had been going wrong for his family for so long, at such breakneck speed, it had been almost impossible to process everything.

He had been told that he needed to take it 'one day at a time', and maybe one thing at a time. A lot of what had gone on was too painful to think about. Zelda – had he been too quick to forgive, after everything she had done? Or had he not really forgiven her at all? Had the Milo revelation simply been his excuse for a 'final straw'?

Her behaviour had been humiliating, but he knew he still needed to address his own performance, which had been pretty horrendous too. The question was, could they find a way back? He had told her he wanted a divorce. He remembered doing that, he'd been drunk when he said it, but was that what he wanted? He'd always thought if she changed, he'd change. But maybe it was the other way around?

Willow began to whimper. Jake stood up and grabbed a few crusts off a plate from an empty table outside the café.

He threw some into the water and the ducks flapped about

wildly and gulped it down. Willow squealed. He gave her some crusts and she threw them, but they didn't go far; in fact they landed on someone's boot.

Jake looked up, and said, 'Sorry!'

'That's OK! Always grateful for a crust!' she said.

Jake recognised her instantly. He smiled and said, 'Hi.'

He wasn't sure of the protocol. Could he say he loved what she had said at the meeting? How brave she was? How nice her hair was? Maybe not.

'I've seen you at meetings, haven't I? I'm Sophie,' she said.

Jake chickened out and feigned a vagueness he certainly didn't feel. 'Oh, yeah, of course. Hi.'

Awkward!

'Is this your daughter? She's so sweet.' She bent down and smiled at Willow.

'No, she's my sister's, was my sister's. She's dead, my sister, I mean.'

'Ah, yes, you said. I was at that meeting.'

He realised he was being ridiculous. He bit the bullet and blurted it out. 'I loved what you shared with the group. It was extraordinary, very moving, so raw ...'

'Living it has been pretty moving and raw too!'

'Yes, of course, sorry! I'm new to this, not sure what you're meant to say or not say yet.'

He found himself pushing Willow along the path by the lake and Sophie was walking with him.

'I think you're meant to say whatever you feel like saying.'

Jake was pretty sure it wouldn't be a good idea to say what

he felt like saying at that particular moment. Because he felt like saying, 'Walking here with you feels like the most natural thing in the world. Please don't go. Stay and talk to me forever.'

But he didn't say that. He simply said, 'Sometimes I say too much.'

Sophie smiled kindly and said, 'Hmm!'

## Chapter Thirty-Seven

Karen was humming along to the radio as she tidied up her kitchen. She placed a couple of cups of coffee on the table, careful not to spill them on the clean red gingham cloth.

Frank sat down. 'There's been more trouble at the Dower House. Apparently, Ms Spender isn't happy.'

Karen replied, 'That woman is a ticking bomb.'

'A ticking bombshell, more like! She stayed up at the court last night.'

'You think she's a bombshell?' Karen looked peeved.

'Nah! But Boy does.'

'Seriously?'

'Fraid so.'

'Bloody hell!'

'See what I mean? This could be bad news for us, Karen. Boy's a good boss, but he's innocent where women are concerned. She would not be nice to work for.'

'You're telling me!'

'We need to have a think.'

'Should you warn Boy? Tell him what she's like?'

'That never works! Anyway, he knows what she's like and he likes it.'

'He was always a bit of a masochist. Bring back Frances!'

'Be careful what you wish for!'

'You're right, either way we are fucked.'

'I wish there was a way to get rid of her.'

'Well, she sure doesn't scare off easily.'

'No, she doesn't, does she?' Frank stood up slowly and wandered out.

*

Ed was buttering toast. The baby was sitting in her high chair, laughing as Flora encouraged her to eat some Marmite fingers. Dusty had left them in charge while she nipped to the shop.

The subject of Johnny came up.

'He's so great!' Flora said.

'He's a bit like old for you, isn't he!' Ed tried to sound OK with it.

'What do you mean?'

'You know?'

'He's not interested in that!'

'Duh!'

'He's not! He likes talking to me about his songs. I write stuff, he likes it. We talk. That's it.'

'Maybe he's just trying to lull you into a false sense of security.'

'No, he isn't. He just likes being with young people, helps him creatively. He said he's not that interested in much else these days. Maybe that's why he's cool about Lily and your brother.'

'Maybe.' Ed was a bit sceptical, but relieved too. He placed the new batch of toast on the table and sat down. 'What kind of stuff do you write?'

'Is there a guitar here?'

'Yep – somewhere.'

'If you get it, I'll play you something.'

'Yeay!'

Ed rushed upstairs. His heart was pounding. Flora Banbury was going to play him one of her songs. Just him ... and Willow, of course, but she didn't count because she was just a baby.

This must mean that she liked him.

# CHAPTER THIRTY-EIGHT

Cleo wanted to take the polar bear back to England and get it stuffed.

'Not really practical in this boat, Cleo, but let's shoot some film of you with it, shall we?' Tom suggested, unable to quite believe his luck.

He only wished he'd been awake to film it as it was happening. Although that might not have worked; Cleo had said it was so dark, she didn't even know what she had shot at first, 'The bear or Milo!'

Tom wasn't sure whether to laugh or not when she'd told him that. She really was one hell of a woman, Cleo Spender!

'Luckily, I spent a lot of time shooting when I was younger. My pal Guy Banbury had a wonderful estate in Scotland. We used to stalk stag there in the '70s. Such fun!' she said, to camera.

Cleo leant against the massive mound of white fur that was her grisly trophy. She raised one elegant leg and rested it on the bear's foreleg, the gun hanging loosely at her side.

When Tom had finished filming Cleo in various poses he

turned his attention to Milo, who said, 'Cleo saved my life. Quite simple she saved my life.' He looked as if he might weep. His eyes sparkled with emotion, and Tom zoomed in.

'I will never forget what she is done to me.'

Cut.

\*

The Daimler arrived at 6 a.m. to whisk Zelda to London. Today was the day she was to begin filming the first round of auditions for *Fame Game*.

She had been up since 4 a.m. getting ready. There would be hair and make-up artists and stylists waiting for her when she arrived. But she still wanted to look her best for her new beginning.

Big Guns had got her a new stylist after she explained that Shona was no longer working for her. She had a chat with the lady, who sounded great. She was getting her a couple of rails of clothes, from all her favourite designers, so that she would have plenty to choose from. Zelda was excited.

When she arrived at the studio there was a riotous rabble of press at the gate, and the familiar flashing and banging as she passed in her car gave her a sudden thrill. It was like coming home.

She stepped out of the car and security surrounded her. The journalists went wild. She could hear them shouting. But there was so much noise she couldn't hear exactly what they were saying.

Which was lucky, as a lot of it was pretty abusive and unkind.

She was amazed to see Sam Carson, with his distinctive white cropped hair, coming out to greet her. He kissed her and made a big show of taking her arm and showing her off to the crowd.

She was touched. She didn't know the man but he really was putting himself out for her, and she felt lucky. He led her into the television studio.

'Follow me. I'll show you where you are.' He turned and smiled at her, showing his very white teeth. 'Really happy you agreed to do this, Zelda. I hope it will work well for both of us.'

She smiled back. 'Thanks, Sam. I'm really excited and very appreciative too. You have really stepped up for me. I shan't forget it.'

'Oh, I won't let you!' He grinned and opened a door for her. 'This is yours.'

It was a vast dressing room, full of rails and rails of designer clothes, long make-up mirrors, sofas and a huge flat screen TV. There was a massive gold star on the door, bearing the name ZELDA SPENDER. There were a lot of people loitering about, who were all wearing black.

'This is your team. Team, this is Zelda Spender.' He watched as his team stepped forward and introduced themselves to her. Some seemed a little nervous.

'I'd better get on, see you in the studio at noon.' He turned to leave.

Zelda wanted to hug him, but thought better of it. The atmosphere changed the moment he closed the door. So it was him that made them nervous.

The stylist suggested they try a few outfits before anything else. By the time Zelda went down to the studio to meet her fellow judges and see some of the contestants she was very happy indeed. The clothes were sublime, the stylist brilliant and the make-up artist made her look about eighteen.

She was back in the groove and it felt so, so good. She felt like she had been away forever.

*

The format of *Fame Game* didn't appear to be significantly different from any other talent show.

What soon became obvious to everyone, though, was that the stakes were considerably higher. The contestants weren't simply people who wept and said, 'This means the world to me,' or 'I've always wanted this more than anything' or 'I just want a better life.' The *Fame Game* contestants were people who had already had it all and they'd had a better life . . . then somehow, one way or another, they had lost it.

Zelda was amazed by the eminence of the stars who had signed up for the show. Many of them had once been huge.

The producers had made short documentaries about each contestant, which the judges watched on their monitors as they were broadcast. What was different was that, unlike the normal format of 'this is me and my family at home with my gran', the clips showed the contestants' dazzlingly successful past, not only film of them performing but also showing their houses, cars, marriages, album sales figures and so on.

Then they switched to an interview with the artist explaining where they were now and how it had all gone wrong. It was sobering viewing.

The first contestant on their screens was the lead singer of a '90s band. When the show aired, everyone would be sure to scream at their TVs, 'It's Ian! I *loved* him ...' and then they would watch with horror as the tale of his career and its decline was rolled out before them: fame, fortune and all the madness and excess that went with it, then the break-ups, dud albums, divorce, tax problems, dodgy management and in fifteen years Ian had gone from hero to zero.

The other contestants were variations on the theme.

What immediately became clear to the producers of the show was just how poignant the stories were, and how vulnerable their artists were too. The contestants in regular shows always said they wanted to win the competition because they didn't want to go back to their ordinary jobs.

This was in glaring contrast to the contestants on *Fame Game* because, when their careers had died and money ran out, they couldn't get a regular job at all. 'How many ex-superstars have served people in their supermarket, garage or pub? None?' the show's sultry voice-over asked. 'How many lawyers, accountants, butchers or bakers do you know who were once famous performing artists? You said it – none!'

So it became clear that winning *Fame Game* was life or death to all of the contestants. Quite literally in one case, a young woman who'd had two platinum albums in the early noughties. Then she had married a con man, who left her when he discovered that she had a serious degenerative illness which could only be treated at great expense in the US. He'd taken all her money with him when he went. She had sunk into such depression and helplessness that she was unable to record anything. This was her chance to get her career back and get healthy too.

There was an American rock star in trouble with the IRS, whose comeback tour had flopped and who was now in dire straits. There wasn't much demand at the job centre for a man who infamously tore bats' heads off, with his teeth.

He looked very chuffed when Zelda told him that she had been mad about him since she was three years old! Which got a laugh. She soon had the audience eating out of her hand.

As the VT rolled out the stories, Zelda became increasingly aware of how fortunate she was to be sitting on *this* side of the desk. After the last contestant had performed for them she turned to Sam Carson and mouthed, 'Thank you.'

From the look in his eyes she knew he understood exactly what she was saying. She owed him, big time. She was pretty sure he would be collecting at some point. She wondered what it would cost her? There was always a price to be paid, she knew that. She had been in the business a long time and whatever it was it wouldn't hold a candle to the desperate humiliation she had seen before her tonight.

The studio audience were going wild. Sam was on his feet applauding the acts, and she and the other judges got to their feet.

Everyone knew that this was going to be Sam's biggest show yet.

*

Doone found Kitty alone in the study watching *Fame Game*.

'Hi there. Is it embarrassing?'

'It's lovely!' said Kitty.

'Really?' Doone sank down onto the sofa next to her little sister.

The cameras were close in on Zelda, who was being kind and funny to Ian.

'She's so pretty and nice, isn't she?' Kitty was starstruck.

'Kit, you know what she's like, you've seen her here, a lot!'

'I know, but she's like a different lady on this show.'

'She's an actress!' Doone said.

'Yes, but she's lovely, isn't she?'

'If you say so, kiddo.'

'Is she going to be our new mummy?'

'Of course not! What makes you think that?'

'Daddy likes her.'

'Daddy's mad and a bit lonely,' Doone said, thinking she was pretty mad and lonely herself. She hadn't noticed that Boy had just materialised in the room and was standing right behind them.

He said quietly, 'Doone darling. I think you and I need to have a little chat.'

As they left Kitty called out, excitedly, 'Daddy, will you ask her to get me Sam Carson's autograph?'

Her father called back to her. 'You can ask her yourself, she'll be here tomorrow.'

*

Karen brought the papers to the Dower House after the first *Fame Game* had aired. The reviews were fantastic, for the show and for Zelda. It seemed as if her recent past had been totally forgotten.

351

Overnight she became:

*Our most glamorous and hilarious star.*

*Zelda at her bright and beautiful best playing 'judge' on* Fame Game.

Fame Game *ratings break all the records for Sam Carson's brilliant new show, with Zelda Spender reinventing the term 'judge' and making it into a show of her own. Caustic, funny and dazzlingly bright, she makes a tired format new again.*

Her agent, Helen Baldwin, was inundated with requests for interviews. But she advised Zelda to keep her head down for a little longer. Let the excitement build. There were still concerns that interviewers would stray from the subject of *Fame Game* and try to get into older, trickier, stories.

Zelda knew there was truth in that and she was perfectly happy with Helen's advice. It meant she could continue to hide away in the country, with Boy. Which was where she wanted to be, more than anywhere.

It was beginning to look as if she really might be able to have her cake and eat it after all.

# Chapter Thirty-Nine

Valentine had spent the afternoon with Lily in London. They had been booked for a photographic shoot together and it was a blast. They both got a bit carried away. The photographer was no stranger to pharmaceuticals and they were all as high as kites by the time the shoot was over.

They hadn't spent any time together for days, as Valentine had been so preoccupied with Doone, he'd almost forgotten about Lily. Now here she was again and leading him astray so easily. How could he have forgotten about her – she was the most thrilling girl in the world. He had already fucked her in the tiny bathroom of the studio. Much to the amusement and embarrassment of the photographer's team, who could hear exactly what was going on, until someone decided to turn the music on full blast.

They partied all night, first at the studio, then some of them went on to a club. Then it was back to the house that Lily shared with Johnny. He was at their new gaffe in the country apparently, working on songs for the next album.

Valentine woke to find a number of models in bed with him, not only Lily but also beautiful Elsa and ... what was her name? Very famous? Nope, he couldn't remember, anyway 'her' and Claus, the most famous men's underwear model in the world. It had obviously been quite a night. Valentine's recollections were hazy. He looked over at Lily; she was watching him carefully. She gave a sly smile and gestured to him to get up and dressed. They did, quietly and quickly trying, but failing, to find their own clothes amongst the tangled mess on the floor. They soon gave up and grabbed the first things that came to hand and tiptoed out of the room.

Lily whispered, 'I am going down to Oxfordshire. Come too?'

'Hell, yes!'

They ran downstairs and out onto the drive where one of Johnny's drivers was waiting for them. He opened the door and they fell into the car, giggling.

'I'm starving. Can we stop somewhere?' Valentine asked.

'Certainly, sir, just tell me where.'

'Mcdonald's!' He looked at Lily for her approval.

'You are a disgusting boy!'

'I thought that was what you liked about me?'

They kissed.

Valentine suddenly felt a small, unfamiliar pang of remorse. Or perhaps it was just hunger? He couldn't be sure.

*

When Valentine woke, the car was pulling up outside Lily and Johnny's house in the country.

'Oh, we're here. I thought we were going via mine?' He blinked at Lily.

'Sorry, I am sleeping too, so we are here now. Come inside, say hi to Johnny. Then you should go, he is annoyed with me for seeing you too much. We have to cool it.' She shrugged and stepped out of the car.

She told him this *now*? Valentine was gutted, furious. He followed her in.

She called out, 'Johnny!' pronouncing it charmingly, with a soft J.

Johnny appeared out of the dark panelled gloom of the hall. 'Oh, hi. What's up?'

'I just arrive. I gave Valentine lift.'

'Yeah, I see that.' Johnny looked peeved.

'I need sleep.' Lily wandered past him, kissing his cheek softly. 'See you later.'

She disappeared upstairs without even a 'goodbye' for Valentine. She really was very French.

Johnny gestured to Valentine to follow him down to the kitchen. Said he needed to have 'a word'.

The 'word' soon took rather a surprising and alarming turn, because rather than being about Lily, it seemed that Johnny wanted to talk about his old squeeze, Georgia. He wanted to talk about her baby Willow; about the fact that Willow was Valentine's daughter – he knew.

More than anything, it was soon quite clear that he wanted

to talk to Valentine about the events surrounding Georgia's death. Most particularly who might have supplied or, he said darkly, administered the drugs that killed her.

Valentine remained cool. 'Lucien supplied her. He always did, you of all people should know that, Johnny.'

Johnny looked him straight in the eye. 'Convenient for you, though? With Georgia dead, you thought no one would ever discover your dirty little secret? Surprised no one in the family has sussed you since they found out Willow is yours. S'pose they all got sidetracked by your own paternity shock-horror show.'

Valentine felt an icy tentacle of fear wrap itself around his heart.

Johnny leant across the table and said, very close to Valentine's face, 'You don't fool me with your fuckin' golden boy act, I can see you, mate, and I don't like what I see.'

Valentine blinked and went from cool to cold. He looked into Johnny's eyes and he could see that he knew. He knew that Valentine had killed Georgia.

Valentine froze.

Johnny straightened up. His skinny frame, clad in all its Goth darkness and skull jewellery, suddenly looked fearsome.

'You can see yourself out. Don't come over here or try to see Lily again. Do you get my drift?' All trace of the genial, cheeky 'Johnny' persona had disappeared. Without waiting for an answer he turned, picked up a fishing rod that was leaning against the kitchen wall, and disappeared out of the back door.

Valentine sat at the table for a while, in shock. How the fuck did Johnny know? He got up and had a swig from a vodka bottle that was open on the draining board. Nobody knew and nobody must ever know. Had Johnny just guessed? Was that possible that until this day, this moment, this conversation, he had only suspected?

But now, he had looked into Valentine's eyes and he had seen, confirmed there, the terrible thing that he had done.

Valentine began to shake. He had another shot of vodka and slunk out after him.

\*

The river shimmered in the bright summer sun and flowed coolly around Johnny's waders. He cast his line with a confident flick across the water. A swan drifted past. There were a few midges nipping at the pale skin on his exposed chest, which he slapped away with one hand.

He heard a fluttering of birds rising out of the grass on the bank behind him and the gentle flop of a fish jumping upstream. The current was strong against his legs; too strong, he wondered? He began to step back, into gentler waters, when he felt something push him hard, just behind his knees.

His legs buckled and he toppled forwards with a gasp. He felt the river fill his waders and the current flipped him and began to pull him downstream. He let go of his rod and his arms flailed wildly in the swirling waters.

He began to gather speed. Water was surging up his nose, into his mouth. He tried to shout but the river stifled his cries. As he surfaced with one final gasp he thought he caught a glimpse of golden hair; an angel? … He reached out towards it desperately, mouthing a soundless 'Help me!'

But the angel turned away, and Johnny was dragged down into the cruel, cold, darkness of the river bed.

In the bitter waters his pale fingers shrank and his flashing diamond rings became loose, then one by one they tumbled onto the stones beneath him and were lost.

*

Doone was belting along the country lane towards Banbury Court when she saw Valentine walking up ahead. Her heart leapt.

She drew alongside him and slowed down.

'I thought you were still in London.'

He smiled and kissed her through the window. 'Had to get back, couldn't keep away. Missed your kisses too much.'

'Yuk, don't be cheesy, it doesn't suit you. Why are you walking? You should have rung, I'd have picked you up from the station.'

'Phone's dead! Anyway a walk won't do me any harm. Blow away the cobwebs.' He looked at her from under his decidedly dishevelled fringe.

'Quite a night, was it?' She sounded a bit frosty.

'Can I get in?' He hopped around the front of the Land Rover and jumped into the passenger seat, before she had time to say no, just in case she intended to. Which she didn't.

'It was really hard work. That photographer is the slowest in history. It took all fucking night. I'm exhausted, do I look horrible?' He ran his hands through his hair.

'Yes, you do.'

'How horrible?'

'Disgusting.'

'Seriously?' He grinned at her. 'Then you'd better drop me off at the Dower House, hadn't you?'

'What else would I do?'

By the time she had swung though the main gates and driven along the drive to the Dower House, Doone had somehow agreed to cook supper for Valentine later that evening, up at the Court.

He slammed the car door and nipped round to the driver's window.

'Thanks for rescuing me.' He leant in to kiss her. She pulled away.

'I don't think anyone could rescue you really, could they? You are too far gone!' She was only half-teasing and, as Valentine watched her accelerate away from him, he knew that she was right. He was much too far gone.

He walked back towards the house and, as he crossed the threshold, he looked down at his feet.

He wondered if Doone had noticed that his shoes were wet. They were his favourite Tom Fords, and he wasn't sure that they were really designed to get wet.

He thought he might have to throw them away. Which was bloody annoying.

\*

Zelda had spent most of the afternoon sitting in the walled garden making phone calls. There were so many things to organise, now that *Fame Game* was in full swing.

It had taken off like a rocket and she knew that it was only a question of time before the press would track her down. Then the idyll would be shattered. Decisions would have to be made. She needed to have a proper talk with Jake.

Ed had kept her posted about Jake's progress. He said his dad was getting to meetings and was even back to writing again. But Jake hadn't rung her himself, nor she him, for more obvious reasons.

She and Boy were in love. He had told her that he wanted her to stay with him at Banbury Court forever. Which was a lovely idea, what she had been dreaming of, in fact. A sort of fairytale that might have a happy ending, she hoped.

Zelda had begun to appreciate the obstacles in their path when she became aware of how much money she would need to earn to support this new lifestyle. Particularly now that all of Boy's children were home again, back from London and the camp thingy. When added to all her dependents, that made for a lot of hungry mouths to feed, minds to educate, stuff in general.

The lovely, romantic house needed a fortune spent on it just to keep it ticking over. Apparently it guzzled money, or it had guzzled all Boy's money anyway, as he was broke.

Which wasn't an insurmountable problem. Zelda was used to a broke man. This brought her to thoughts of the other obstacles that inconveniently littered the path to true love: the fact that she was married, and despite appearances to the contrary, so was Boy.

Her phone rang; it was her agent's office. She picked up. 'Hi.'

'It's Helen. Good news, Zelda. You have been confirmed for the sequel to *Dark Nights*. Contract's on its way. Good money. Very excited. Well done.'

So maybe money wasn't going to be such a problem after all. But time might be; she would need to spend a massive amount of her time away from Boy and Banbury Court, working.

When she had finished talking to Helen she made a few more calls. She would need another PA at this rate.

The thought of it made her sick after her experience with Kate, whose book seemed to have drifted out of the media's collective consciousness for the moment. Zelda knew better than to think that the stories it contained would be forgotten. She knew that this was just a brief honeymoon period for her: her redemption.

They would build her up, up, up and then would take the greatest pleasure in bringing her down again. When her relationship with Boy was made public would probably be the most obvious time and place for all that to kick off. So, there were still plenty of reasons for them to keep their love under wraps; the more she thought about it the more she knew they should tread carefully.

Perhaps she didn't need to have that chat with Jake quite yet.

Only Valentine knew and he wasn't going to tell. Of course, Doone knew too but she didn't seem like the sort of girl who would go to the press. Zelda didn't really know what sort of girl Doone was, but she was willing to try to find out. She knew that she would have to get along with Boy's girls, if they were to have any kind of future together. He adored his daughters; that was clear. So she must adore them too. Lucky she was a good actress, because children really weren't her thing at all.

She felt a little pang of guilt about Willow. She hadn't given that baby a moment's thought. She must get a nanny sorted out. Dusty would be back at school soon and so she needed to get some backup in place. More expenses, more stuff to organise. She lay back on the lawn, exhausted at the thought of all her responsibilities.

Her mother suddenly sprang into her mind. She wondered how she was getting on. She speed dialled her dad.

Jamie answered. 'Sir Max Spender's residence.'

'Jamie, it's Zelda. Is Max there?' She thought her father's butler was ridiculously old-fashioned and he was only about twenty-eight.

'Hold the line, please.'

'Hello.'

'Max, Dad, it's me.'

'Hello, my darling. Lovely to hear you. Well done on the show, hear it's going terrifically well.'

'It is, thanks, and more jobs coming in, so should be solvent again soon.' She knew that was something her father would like to hear.

'Marvellous! Hurrah!'

'How's Mum getting on?'

'She rang the other night. It's going well, I think. She said it's bloody cold and frightening. Nearly sunk by a whale.'

'It would take more than a whale to sink Cleo.'

'I hope you're right.'

'Anyway, just checking in. I'll nip in and see you when I'm next up.'

'That would be lovely. Love to see you. How's Jake?'

'He's getting along fine. Writing, sober – he's in London with the kids. Haven't you seen him?'

'Yes, I have. I just wondered if you had.' Her father sounded serious, which was very unusual. Max was never serious.

'No, I haven't actually *seen* him. Just heard news from Ed. I'm letting him get on with it. It's complicated.'

'But you're alright?' Max sounded concerned.

'I'm fine, you know me. Knock me down and I just get right back up again.' She didn't want to worry him by mentioning her stalker's recent antics.

'You know you can always come back and stay here if you need to.'

'Yes, I know, Dad, thanks. But I'm fine, really I am. Everything is going great.'

'If you're sure, darling. Love you.'

'You too.'

She wondered why she felt so sad after she hung up.

*

Zelda had just made herself a cup of mint tea when Valentine stepped up behind her and said, 'Boo!' and so she spilt it every-where.

'Jesus! You gave me a fright. What are you thinking? I didn't even know you were here, for fuck's sake!'

'Oops, sorry, I forgot. I got back earlier. Late night, just been catching up on some kip before tonight.'

'What are you doing tonight?'

'Supper at the Court.'

'Me too!' She smiled at her wayward son. 'You can drive me.'

'How was London?' She meant, how was Jake?

'Fine.' Valentine lit a cigarette. 'You know, work.'

Zelda was glad Valentine was working. Although he was about to go into his final year at Oxford he was willing to work hard between studying and he was earning a small fortune. He was resourceful like her. She was proud of him; he was a wonderful boy, a wonderful man.

She gave him a hug. 'I love you, darling.'

He hugged her back. 'Ditto.'

David walked into the kitchen. 'Will you need me to drive you up to the Court this evening?'

Zelda let go of Valentine and picked up what was left of her tea. 'No, you're off duty, thanks, David. Valentine is going to take me.'

'I've got some things to do so if you don't mind I might take twenty-four hours off.'

'No probs. You'll be around tomorrow, won't you, Val?'

'Sure will.'

'I need you to drive me up to London at some point, David. I've got so many things that I *have* to do.' She looked martyred.

'No problem. I'll be back tomorrow, early evening. Text if you need me. See you then,' David said.

Zelda looked grateful and gave him a beautiful smile. 'Thank you. Where would I be without you?'

He smiled back and gave her a salute, then he was gone.

'Mother's loyal army!' Valentine said.

'Hardly an army; one man! Most of the other troops turned out to be extremely disloyal: Kate, Shona, Lucien!'

'Yeah, see what you mean!' Valentine took a drag on his cigarette. 'But you've got me on your side too, you know. Me and David and . . .' He pretended to think.

Zelda punched him on the arm.

'Let's have a drink to celebrate!' he suggested.

'What are we celebrating?'

'I don't know, there must be something.' He took a bottle of champagne from the fridge. 'To your two-man army!'

# CHAPTER FORTY

The final leg of the *Against All Odds* expedition had begun. Cleo was looking forward to it, now that the end was in sight.

Or she was until they hit the worst storm of their journey. It began with dark rain and as the sea began to swell even Lars and Nils became nervous. They darted about the small boat, lashing everything and everyone to anything they could find. The waves got bigger and bigger and icy winds tore through them.

Cleo suddenly had a flashback to her RNLI course and remembered something about the sort of seas you were most likely to capsize in. She sensed that they were in the middle of just such a sea. She knew too that there was no chance of a rescue if things were to go wrong.

They said these seas were unforgiving; why was this all coming back to her now?

She desperately sought out the men's faces through the spray. Tom's was rigid with cold and fear. Milo looked at her and she saw courage in his eyes. His steadfast gaze held her for a moment and she felt safer somehow. Which was ridiculous of course. He would be the last person to be able to help if things went really wrong.

Multiple waves broke over the console. Nils was thrown to the floor as he tried to protect it with another tarpaulin and he cried out in pain. There was nothing more to be done. They sat silently waiting for the end that they knew must surely come. The storm raged and crashed and seethed around them for what seemed like forever.

Just when they felt they couldn't take any more, the sea finally began to quieten, and the wind died as suddenly as it has begun. They motored slowly on to Pearce Point, in silence, too exhausted and shocked by their shared experience to speak.

Cleo could never have believed that she would be so delighted to see a small group of Nissan huts on a grey rainy shore. But to her they looked like Capri in spring, and she wanted to shout with relief.

Crowded into the mess hall later on that night, Nils told Cleo that he had thought they wouldn't make it through. He told her she had been very brave, at which she hugged him and almost wept.

The cameraman was there to capture this wonderful moment and Cleo was glad she had made an effort to look her best, despite the trauma of the day. She was in the arms of a handsome man, being filmed. It didn't get much better than that as far as Cleo was concerned. She was a very happy woman and so glad to be alive.

Later, everyone was singing happily. Someone had produced a guitar. Cleo hadn't played for a long time. But she had done a couple of musicals and someone remembered and asked her to give them a song. So she did, and was met with wild, raucous applause. So the evening did get even better after all.

Cleo went and sat next to Milo and he told her about his new baby, and his beautiful wife Lana. He looked Cleo in the eye. 'I have missed your family. I loved you all so much.'

Cleo said, 'Milo, you loved us *all* far too much. I mean, my daughter, my husband, me! Really, you must admit you went too far.'

'I was carried away with love.' He looked quite drunk and forlorn.

'Well, it's all behind us now, Milo. You have your lovely family and I have mine. So we can put it all away?'

'I will never speak of it again.'

'We will make this show the best we possibly can, then we'll go on to great new careers, both of us will, I just know it.' Cleo suddenly felt uncharacteristically generous about Milo's career.

Tom appeared at her shoulder. 'Just wanted to say well done to both of you. Terrifying day. Handled valiantly. This will be huge. Bloody brilliant.'

'You too, Tom. It was scary, wasn't it?' Cleo gazed into the distance. She had a vision of herself with the Queen, and the Queen was awarding her a damehood.

'Glad you came now?' Tom asked with a little glint in his eye.

'Sometimes you just know what's right, Tom. When to do the right thing, don't you think?' She fixed him with a determined stare.

'Yes I do, Cleo. Doing the right thing is what I do best. I shall spend a little extra time in the editing suite when I get back. Just to make sure we iron out any little glitches that might be tricky in future.'

So they understood each other. They all clinked glasses and drank up.

Everything was, against all odds, going to be marvellous.

# CHAPTER FORTY-ONE

The kitchen at Banbury Court was alive with noise and laughter. The radio was blaring and Doone was impersonating Kitty's riding instructor. Kitty kept interrupting.

Then a squabble broke out.

'She didn't say you had a good seat!' said Doone.

'She did!'

'She said you had big feet!'

'She didn't!' Kitty looked furious.

Doone laughed. 'OK, she said you had a good seat, now will you finish laying the table? Get glasses, we need two more.'

A voice from the doorway said, 'Make that three more, I'm home!' And Frances walked into the kitchen.

Kitty screamed and threw herself at her mother.

'Mama, mama!' Kitty held onto her neck.

Doone froze. 'We weren't expecting you.'

'No, I thought I'd surprise you!'

'Really? After all this time, not a word of warning?'

'Nice to see you too, Dooney. I didn't know I had to *warn* my own family!'

She smiled her winsome smile. Her hair was longer, and thicker than Doone remembered. She looked glowingly healthy, tanned and wiry. Her wrists were bound with hundreds of friendship bracelets and she had rings on her toes. Doone thought she looked exactly like her gap-year pals, only a lot more wrinkly.

She felt an overwhelming desire to slap her mother's face.

Flora had followed Frances into the room and appeared to be smilingly pleased with herself. Doone immediately realised that Flora was *with* Frances; they must have arrived together.

Was this Flora's idea, then, this surprise family reunion?

She wondered if Boy knew yet. Where was he? Should she find him? Warn him?

Too late, he walked into the kitchen, at that very moment. Followed by Valentine and Zelda.

Frances had her back to the door, so she didn't see him enter. She didn't see his face when he first saw her. Which was lucky, because his face fell a mile. He went from an excited, proud, smiling man to a wreck, in two seconds.

He exchanged an anguished look with Doone, rallied and said, 'Frances, there you are! We wondered where you'd got to.'

Which was all he could think of to say to a woman who had deserted her entire family and remained incommunicado for eighteen months. He had to make a joke of it – otherwise he would have had to kill her.

Frances turned, and said, 'Hello, Boy.' Then she threw her arms around him.

Which was when she noticed that two of the most famous people in England were standing behind her husband, in her kitchen, and looking at her with barely concealed animosity.

She let go of Boy and put out her hand towards Zelda. 'Hi, you might not remember me, I'm Boy's wife, nice to see you after all these years. Is Jake here?' But as soon as she touched Zelda's hand something told her that Jake wasn't with her.

Frances had very finely tuned instincts; she liked to think they had been honed by her time spent learning from the amazing awareness seminars of Si Singh, in Udaipur.

One thing was for certain, her instincts were shouting, 'Cuckoo, cuckoo in the nest!' She was amazed by how much could rush through her brain in such a short space of time.

If she had been able to see the thoughts running through Boy, Zelda and Valentine's brains in those same few nanoseconds, she might have been quite shocked.

There was a deathly, embarrassed silence.

Kitty broke it. 'Mama, come and see my room. We changed it, come and see!' She grabbed her mother's hand and to everyone's huge relief she dragged Frances away.

'Jesus Christ!' Boy looked at Zelda. 'I am so sorry.'

Zelda smiled at him bleakly. She was totally lost for words.

Valentine walked across to Doone and kissed her. 'Awkward or what?'

Flora looked surprised. Since when did Valentine kiss Doone on the mouth?

Doone said, 'I think you might have to go. It's going to be too difficult.'

Boy interrupted, 'No, it will be more awkward if they go. How would we explain it?'

Zelda's heart sank. 'Well, you could tell her the truth.'

She saw terror in Boy's eyes then and she felt his terror seep into her.

'I think we need to just carry on. You are just friends, here for supper, nothing wrong with that.' Boy looked fraught.

Zelda was livid. 'There is quite a lot wrong with that, actually.'

Flora was watching her father like a hawk. What had been going on while she was away? Everything felt all wrong. This was meant to be a wonderful family reunion.

There was a silence. Valentine's phone rang. 'Saved by the bell!' He answered it with a flourish. 'Hi.'

Silence.

They watched him as he listened.

He put his hand to his forehead. 'I'm coming over. Be strong, Lily. I'm on my way. *Je t'aime.*' He hung up. The colour had drained from his face. 'There's been an accident. It's Johnny. He was fishing.' He looked at his mother. 'He's drowned. I have to go to her. Will you come with me?'

'Yes, of course. Let's go.'

Flora burst into tears.

Frances reappeared as they were leaving. 'What's going on?'

'Johnny's dead!' Flora wailed.

'Who's Johnny?'

Doone swept past her mother, 'You wouldn't know, would you. Because *you* haven't been here.' Her face was close to her mother's. She was furious, with Frances, with her father, with Zelda, but most of all she was furious with Valentine.

He had said to Lily, '*Je t'aime.*' And although she knew he'd said it to comfort her, he'd also said it as if he meant it and, in that moment, she knew that it was true.

She looked across at her anguished father's face. He was stricken too. She had warned him. Told him they shouldn't have allowed that family anywhere near them. Now look what had happened.

Broken hearts all over the room.

Kitty was crying now, in sympathy for Flora. They clung together and left the kitchen.

Frances had chosen one hell of a night to return home. She instinctively knew that she needed to start picking up the pieces, find out what was wrong and try to bring comfort to her unhappy family. She had been away for far too long. She wasn't expecting anything to have changed much since she left. But she could feel that everything had changed dramatically. She looked across at her handsome, familiar husband, Boy.

He wore an expression of such sadness and disappointment her instinct was to fling her arms around him, to hold him. She momentarily forgot why she had left him, why she thought she wanted to divorce him, why she'd thought she didn't love him any more.

Then she remembered that final fight, in the nightclub, when she'd broken a bottle over his head, and the blood had gone everywhere. She remembered the look of shock and anguish on his face. He had been devastated by that final terrible, stupid fight over money, and then she was gone, running away like a delinquent schoolgirl.

Boy slumped heavily into a chair and poured himself a drink. Doone crossed the room quietly and hugged her father. She kissed the top of his head and a tear fell into his beautiful hair.

'We'll be alright, Dad.' And she really hoped that it was true.

Frances watched her husband and daughter together and felt very much like a stranger in her own home. She had behaved like a child, she could see that now, and she hadn't been there for her children. She had a lot of making up to do. She wasn't sure where to start.

\*

By the time Zelda and Valentine reached Johnny's house, the press were there already, and although they were being held back by police at the gate, they still managed to get pictures of Valentine and Zelda: *Rushing to the side of Lily to comfort her in her darkest hour*, as the papers would put it the following day.

Lily looked tiny, crumpled in an enormous chair in the drawing room. Her eyes were red and puffy.

Valentine went and held her hand. 'What happened?' But she couldn't answer him, she just opened her arms to be held and he hugged her tightly.

Sergeant Powell walked into the room. 'Ah, Ms Spender, here you are! I am sorry for your family's loss.'

'Well, he wasn't quite our family, you know. But a very good friend, a very dear friend.'

Peter Powell couldn't help wondering if he would ever meet Zelda Spender when she wasn't in the middle of a crisis. These people!

She said, 'Can you tell us what happened?'

'It seems he was fishing and he must have stumbled. Waders filled with water, strong currents. He'd have been swept away, drowned instantly. A very common accident, I'm afraid, very common. People think fishing is a sedate sport but it's not. It's very dangerous indeed.'

'Oh, poor Johnny!'

'I wonder if you could ask your son if I might have a word. Whenever he's ready. In the next room?'

'Yes, of course, Inspector.' Zelda smiled through her tears. 'Thank you so much.'

Valentine took a deep breath and followed the policeman.

He calmly answered Sergeant Powell's questions. 'Yes, I was here. Not sure what time. Lily went up for a sleep and I had a quick cup of tea with Johnny. Then I walked home.'

'You were the last person to see him alive, as far as we know.'

'Oh, right?'

'Did he mention to you that he was going fishing?'

'No, actually, he said he was going back into his studio to write.'

'Is that so?'

'Yep.' Valentine looked sad. 'He was a very good friend of

my family's. I'm sure you know he lived with my aunt for a number of years. We all loved him very much.'

These theatrical types talked about love a lot, a bit too much, Peter Powell thought. They bandied it about, but it seemed to him to be a fairly loose term. He felt they would say 'I loved him' in the same way as normal people would say 'I knew him'.

So they all loved Johnny the Bastard. Fine. He just wasn't sure why they felt the need to share that information with him. He hadn't asked: 'Did you love the deceased?' Had he? Of course not; because it wasn't *relevant*. He was just trying to get to grips with what had happened to the degenerate old rocker. He wouldn't be at all surprised if they found plenty of alcohol and other substances in the guy's bloodstream.

When they'd fished him out of the river, one of the young PCs had observed, 'He looks just the same dead as alive – freaky!'

Peter Powell remembered looking up from his newspaper a few days previously and saying to his wife, 'Have you seen these pictures of Johnny the Bastard? He looks half-dead!' Which made him feel a bit peculiar, now that he came to think about it.

He thought it likely that the guy had stumbled to his death, whilst under the influence. He wondered if they should start breathalysing blokes in waders? It might save a few lives … his mind wandered.

Valentine spoke politely. 'Is that all, Officer? I'd like to go and look after my mother and our friend, if that's alright.'

'Yes, yes, lad. Off you go.'

Valentine couldn't believe it. The guy had barely questioned him at all. No wonder his mother's stalker hadn't been caught by the local plod. He didn't think it would be a good moment to complain about that now, though.

He went back into the drawing room and poured some large drinks, for his mother, for Lily and himself.

Sergeant Powell stuck his head round the door. 'We're just off. We'll be in touch in the morning. Ring the number I gave you if you have any questions, Miss Lachasse.' Then he disappeared.

Valentine had never heard anyone use Lily's surname. She was always just Lily.

She looked at him over the rim of her glass. 'I should not have slept. I should have gone with 'im. He was always so clumsy.' She started to cry again.

A young policeman entered the room, walked straight up to Lily and said, 'Can I have your autograph, Lily?' He pushed his notebook towards her.

She took it meekly and signed. He left, looking pleased with himself. Valentine considered going after him and kicking his head in, but realised that might not be wise. They were all used to insensitive autograph hunters, but that guy was something else.

He turned to his grieving girlfriend and continued as if they hadn't been interrupted. 'There wasn't anything you could've done. He had a wonderful life. You made him very happy. He was a lucky man.' Valentine gave her hand a squeeze and looked across at his mother. 'Shall we take Lily home with us?'

'No, I cannot go. I must sleep in our bed. The staff is here. You go,' she said. 'I want to be alone.'

Valentine leant forward and kissed her on the forehead. 'If you're sure? We'll speak in the morning. Eh?'

As Zelda and Valentine swept out of the drive a few paps, on motorbikes, peeled off after them.

Valentine had to drive around, very, very fast for ages to lose them. In the end the most resilient proved impossible to shake off so Valentine was forced to drive the guy off the road. He flew into a ditch and as Valentine glanced in his wing mirror he saw the pap stumble out again. No harm done.

They drove back to the Dower House in silence and went quietly to bed.

There was a lot of re-evaluation to be done, by both of them.

Zelda fell fast asleep the moment her head hit the pillow.

*

She was woken by Boy, standing over her bed, whispering softly, 'Zelda!' He was clutching a cup of coffee.

She sat up a bit and said, 'Hi. Is that for me?'

'Yes, sorry to wake you.'

'What time is it?'

'About ten.'

'Oh, God. I must get up.'

'I need to talk to you. I'll leave you to get dressed.'

She reached for his hand. 'You can talk to me here.'

'No, I can't. I won't be able to say what I need to say to you if I have to see you lying naked in bed. It just won't be possible. So you need to get dressed.'

'I don't like where this is going.' Zelda searched his face. His eyes looked pained and desperately sad. She wanted to hug him so much. She reached out her arms to him and saw him hesitate. 'I just want to hug you,' she lied.

Then, to her relief, he weakened and was in her arms, in her bed.

She had negotiated a stay of execution.

*

By the time he left Zelda's bedroom later that morning, Boy had begun to change his mind about everything again. He needed to tell Frances what had been going on and he needed to tell her that he wanted a divorce.

He turned to say goodbye to Zelda on the doorstep. She was wrapped in a sarong and looked particularly beautiful. He knew he was doing the right thing. He kissed her goodbye, a long lingering promise of a kiss. But Zelda pulled away from him suddenly. 'Did you hear that?'

He blurted out, 'Jesus! Not the stalker again?'

She was instantly indignant. 'No! That clicking sound, a photographer! It came from over there.' Zelda pointed to some shrubs on the corner of the drive.

'I'll go and look.' He wandered over to the bushes and peered in. But there was no one there. He started to walk back towards Zelda, when suddenly there was a flurry behind him. He turned to see a man running off up the road and disappearing around the bend.

'Go after him,' Zelda fumed.

So he ran. But the guy was long gone. This meant that they

were found out. Everyone would know now: Jake, Frances, his girls. He had an overwhelming sense of dread.

Why did he feel like this, when this was what he wanted, wasn't it? Zelda was perfect for him. He felt such desire for her whenever she was near. But sometimes, after they had made love, he saw other things in her that he didn't like so much; things that frankly scared him.

Well, there was no going back now. He would have to tell Frances. Then, no doubt she would bugger off again, the girls would be bereft and it would be all *his* fault.

Zelda looked at him strangely. 'You do know that was a photographer, don't you?'

'Of course.'

'It means we are busted.'

'I know.'

'Try not to look so thrilled about it!' she said sarcastically.

'It will affect a lot of people, Zelda. It might be alright for us, but it won't be alright for our children, or Jake or Frances.'

'It *might* be alright for us? You're not sure, are you?' She was devastated.

'No, I am sure. I just think the price everyone else will have to pay is too high.'

'Well, that's very empathetic of you, or should I say pathetic!' She was getting quite worked up. 'I shouldn't have to remind you that your wife doesn't care. My husband has already asked for a divorce. All our children are practically grown-up except ...'

He realised she couldn't remember his children's names. 'Except for ... Kitty?'

'Kitty!'

'and ...'

'and ...'

'and Flora!'

'Yup, them.'

'Oh God, Zelda. We really need to think about this.'

'There's no time. That picture will be everywhere by this afternoon.'

'Don't you know anyone who could stop it for you?'

She looked at him aghast.

She did know someone. In fact she knew someone who would want it stopped anyway. Sam Carson. Sam wouldn't be happy about this at all. His star was supposed to be rehabilitated, not reverting to type.

Zelda felt a little tremor of panic run amok through her chaotic mind. She really needed to get that picture stopped.

She looked into her lover's eyes and said, 'OK, I can probably do that. I will do it because you want me to. But I don't want anyone to get hurt either, I'm not a monster, Boy. I'm just a woman who wants to be with you. But if you need to time to decide whether you want to be with me, then you can have it. I'm going back to London today. I'll stay with my dad. That picture won't appear. You can let me know when you have decided.'

Boy looked annoyingly relieved. 'Thank you.' He stepped forward to kiss her.

'Jesus! Are you mad! No kissing!'

'No, of course not. Sorry.' He went and got onto his old motorbike. The engine spluttered into life. Zelda watched him until he disappeared around the bend, then she went to get her phone.

She rang Sam, who didn't sound pleased. But she knew he would sort it.

Then she rang David and asked if he could come and get her. She needed help getting all their stuff back to London. He answered on her first ring.

He assured her that he'd be there soon; he'd bring his old 4x4. She could always depend on him.

At least, leaving the Dower House, she wouldn't have to worry about that loony in the mask terrorising her any more.

She rang her father to tell him she was coming home.

# CHAPTER FORTY-TWO

Cleo was thrilled when she heard that they were only fifty miles from Tuk and the end of their journey. The weather conditions were perfect, apparently. She felt very excited; it was a job well done.

They set off through beautiful calm, clear seas. They were all very up, laughing and joking as they sped through the most remote and breathtakingly beautiful place on earth. Seabirds called and hundreds of seals watched them, popping their heads up to blink in surprise at the RIB as it flew past.

Cleo realised that they hadn't seen another polar bear, and she felt a bit disappointed about that.

'Why haven't we seen any more polar bears, Lars?' she yelled.

'They hided when they heard you were coming with your gun!' he yelled back.

'Oh, ha ha.' Cleo was thrilled. She could tell that Lars and Nils would be regaling everyone they met with that tale, for years to come. She was gutted that she'd had to leave her trophy behind, though. It would have looked fabulous at the house in Gstaad.

Oh, well. You can't have everything, she thought sadly. But Cleo did have almost everything. So she could probably struggle on without a stuffed bear. Everyone would know she had done it anyway. It would be in the show. That was the important thing.

When they roared triumphantly into Tuk there was a small group waiting to greet them. The support team was ready and waiting to pack up the boat and there were some news teams too.

Cleo was delighted, jumping nimbly out of the RIB and onto the shingle, smiling triumphantly for the cameras. 'Thank you, thank you.'

Then she suddenly remembered something. She dashed back down the beach to help get Milo out of the boat.

She beckoned to the cameras to come closer. 'You all know Milo, don't you? It is such an amazing achievement for him to have completed this very gruelling challenge. But I would just like to say that, without him, and all the things he has taught me, I would never have climbed Everest. I would not be here with you today at the end of this feat of endurance without Milo's training and support. He may be in a wheelchair now. But I think we should all watch this space. Because none of us have heard the last of Milo.' Everybody clapped. Cleo knew that sometimes it paid to be magnanimous.

Tom Maddison looked on with interest. Cleo really was a very surprising woman.

He needed to get everyone organised, as the plane would be picking them up the following morning, and they still had a bit of filming to do. The sponsors were going to be very happy indeed.

# CHAPTER FORTY-THREE

Valentine pottered down to the kitchen and made himself some breakfast. Karen had just delivered the papers, which were all full of Johnny's death. So he wouldn't be reading them today.

He buttered some toast and spread it liberally with Marmite. Then he wandered outside to greet the day.

His mother came down from the garden clutching her phone. 'I'm going back to London. Do you want to come with me?'

'Where are you going to stay?'

'Good question! I'm going to Dad's. You can come too?'

'Not sure what I'm doing yet, might come up later.'

'Well, our time is up here. So David is on his way back to help get our stuff out.'

'Did I miss something? While I was sleeping?'

'Quite a bit actually.'

Valentine munched the last piece of toast. 'God, that was good, do you want some?'

'No, but I need coffee. Come on, I'll fill you in,' she said.

He didn't need to know all of it, but some of it only he could understand.

He gave her a hug when she'd finished explaining that, amongst other things, she thought Boy had got cold feet.

'Got to be honest, never really saw you as a country-life country wife. He's a lovely guy, don't get me wrong, but expensive to run and you've got one of those already, a cheaper one and one that knows you well. Understands you.'

'One who has asked me for a divorce.'

'Was he sober?'

'No.'

'Doesn't count.'

'What happened to in vino veritas?'

'It's bollocks.'

'Oh, I don't know any more, Val. I feel very sad.'

'Look, a lot of shit has happened. You are doing brilliantly. Career back on the go and everything; reasons to be cheerful galore!' He smiled and handed her a cigarette. 'We just need to get you back to London, back to fucking normal.'

He needed to speak to Lily, see what she wanted to do. Then he might nip up to Banbury Court, explain to Doone that he had to be back in London to support Zelda.

He didn't like the idea of saying goodbye to Doone, though. It made him feel depressed just thinking about it. Maybe Zelda's mood was rubbing off on him. He went to have a shower, to get dressed and pack. He would take Jake's car back up to London later on. He suddenly remembered he'd promised that he would do that, days ago!

Jake hadn't pestered him about it. He was good like that, easy-going and always generous about sharing his stuff, which was lucky really, because he'd had to share Zelda, quite a lot, over the years.

\*

Banbury Court seemed deserted when Valentine strode into the kitchen, later on that morning.

Frances stepped in from the walled garden and stretched out a muddy hand. 'Hi, we didn't really meet properly. I'm Frances. Sorry about your friend.'

'Thanks. I wondered if Doone was around?'

'She's here somewhere, but she's avoiding me. I'm getting the silent treatment.'

'Isn't that what you gave them?'

'Touché. Yes, I suppose it was. I don't know how the time slipped away so fast. I'm hoping to make amends. With everyone.' She looked at him pointedly.

'Good luck with that.'

Doone walked in, turned on her heel and walked straight back out, without a word.

Valentine went after her.

He caught up with her as she crossed the marble hall, put his hand on her arm gently, and said, 'Doone, stop!'

'Leave me alone!'

'What have I done?'

She turned her steady gaze onto him. Her eyes were like flint. She didn't say anything.

Valentine was unnerved. He'd imagined breaking the news

to her gently that he had to go back up to London. But she was obviously livid with him. He wondered if she was upset about Lily, the fact that she was free now, free of Johnny? Or was there something else?

He needed to know what was going on. What she knew or thought she knew . . . So he said, 'Tell me, please, what have I done to upset you so much?'

'You know.'

'I don't, seriously, tell me.'

'Think about it.'

'I can't, I'm really bad at this kind of thing. You have to tell me. Are you breaking up with me?'

'Yes.'

'And you won't tell me why?'

'I'm going to let you work it out.'

He felt his heart pounding with fear and frustration. Why the fuck did she have to be so enigmatic? People usually broke up with him over jealousy about other girls. Was this about Lily . . . or worse?

Had she noticed his wet shoes? That was the question, had she worked out what he'd done? She wasn't going to tell him now, that much was clear. He felt sick. Perhaps he should try to kiss her.

He stepped towards her; she didn't move. He kissed her, she let him but she didn't kiss him back. He was really panicking now.

'Please don't do this. I love you, Doone.'

'That's another lie.'

This wasn't going anywhere good. He ran his hand through his hair and gave her the benefit of his most anguished look, then he decided to get the hell out of there. He turned on his heel and walked away, his feet echoing across the marble hall. It was a lonely sound.

As he closed the door behind him, Doone said quietly, 'Shit!'

Then she went looking for Boy, who had spent most of the morning hiding from Frances in his study.

\*

Boy poured his daughter a drink. The Spenders had packed up and gone and now they were both feeling shell-shocked.

Boy handed Doone a glass. 'Are you alright?'

'Think so.'

'Seems like a crazy dream.'

'Nightmare. I did warn you.'

'Should've warned yourself.'

'Hmm. I know.' She bravely smiled up at her father; his warrior girl.

He sat down next to her on the worn-out old chesterfield sofa. A pile of books fell to the floor but neither of them moved to pick them up. They sat in silence for a while.

'Your mother.'

'Your wife.'

'She wants to come back, for good. What do you think?

'I don't know. I'm off to Uni again soon. You'll be the one that has to live with her.'

'I'm used to having you in charge. Not sure if I can cope with her again.'

'Only you can decide that.'

'She's inherited another vast amount of money. A spinster aunt died.'

'You're kidding!'

'Nope. She says the main reason she left was because she felt so resentful about money and now she has lots again, she thinks we'll be OK.'

'That simple, eh?'

'She seems to think so. Kitty and Flora are pleased to see her.'

'They are forgiving girls.'

'It is natural to love your mother.'

'Hmm. It's natural to love your wife.'

'I think I've got a bit mixed up over the Zelda thing.'

'Not the only one.'

'Maybe I just need time.'

'Maybe we both do.' She reached across, took her father's hand and gave it a squeeze. 'In the meantime, she can put her money where her mouth is and get the fucking roof fixed. My room is getting bloody damp.'

'Good plan. The Land Rover is about to give up the ghost too.' He grinned wickedly at his daughter. 'She may be able to buy our love.'

'It won't be cheap.'

'Love never is.'

They laughed grimly.

Doone stood up. 'I think I'll take Oscar for a walk. Clear my head. Mum's in the kitchen.'

Boy finished his drink in one gulp. 'Right. I'll go and see her then.' He stood up, took a deep breath and walked out into the hall.

To keep an estate like Banbury Court together was a very expensive business. Boy loved it more than life itself and so he had always been prepared to do whatever it took. His eldest daughter understood that.

So did his wife.

*

Jamie helped David to unload the car outside the Spenders' house in London. Zelda rushed on ahead, to find her father.

Max was in the garden. She waved gaily when she saw him. 'Max!'

'Darling girl! You are here.' He ran towards her, still agile for a man of almost eighty. He gave her a huge hug and a kiss.

'The garden looks lovely,' she said, suddenly feeling over-whelmed with nostalgia for its familiar beauty. She raised her eyes to the converted church at the other end of the garden, her old home.

'The administrators haven't found a buyer for it yet, you know. Market's dead,' Max said.

'So they didn't need to kick us out quite so fucking fast after all!'

'I'm sorry. It must bring back a lot of sad memories. Shall we go inside?' He took her arm and led her into his lovely house and got her a huge drink.

'What news of Mum?'

'They should be flying back to Toronto tomorrow. It's done. They made it. She was on the news.'

'I didn't see it. Haven't been watching much telly. I always seem to miss her triumphs.' She felt a bit guilty. 'There's been so much going on.'

'I know, darling. It'll be on again later. Were you alright down there? What happened about that stalker, did they catch him?'

'No, they bloody didn't. But, you know what? I finally realised it was probably just someone trying to scare me off. I began to wise up the last time I saw it. It never made any attempt to hurt me and God knows there was plenty of opportunity. I just think it was someone wanting me to leave Banbury Court.' She sighed. 'I've left now, so that's it. Over.'

'I can't imagine why anyone would ever want to get rid of you; very odd. You are a brave woman, just like your darling mother. I am so proud of you both.'

He crossed his elegant drawing room and topped up her drink. 'When are you going to see Jake?' he asked.

'Oh, I don't think he wants to see me.'

'Nonsense! He loves you.'

'I'm not sure about love any more, Daddy, I'm very bad at it.'

'Oh, no. You are good at it. Look at how long you and Jake have been together; through thick and thin. Never underestimate the strength of that bond. Look at your mother and me!'

Zelda grinned. 'Exactly, I rest my case.'

Her father laughed. 'Come on, you must be hungry. Jamie has been cooking all morning in anticipation of your arrival.'

'Ah, yes. Wonderful Jamie, where would you be without him?'

'Indeed!' Max held out his arm and Zelda linked hers through it and squeezed.

It felt good to be home.

# CHAPTER FORTY-FOUR

Zelda had a day of non-stop beauty treatments booked in, back to back. She was preparing for her biggest day of filming on *Fame Game* and she wanted to look her best. She had forty-eight hours to get into perfect shape and she was planning to really go for it.

She asked David if he would mind driving her up to Harley Street the following morning. She knew that the word would soon be out that she was back in town, no matter what lengths she went to, to keep her head down. The press would be onto her again. She told him she would need him to drive her, and for security, at least until *Fame Game* was finished. She could even start paying him, at last!

He seemed pleased.

She knew that she ought to make time to go over to the Mews, to see Jake and the rest of her family too. The idea of it filled her with anxiety.

She found herself wondering how they were all managing.

She felt a twinge of guilt that she had left Dusty in sole charge of Willow, with only a bit of help from Ed. She knew that she was not a good example of a responsible adult, and she had got far too caught up in her own life. She felt ashamed of herself.

She rang Jake when the last therapist left at seven. He picked up straight away.

'Hi,' he said.

'I'm back.'

'I heard.'

'Sorry I haven't rung before.'

'It's OK. I've been busy too.' Pause. '*Fame Game* is good. Well done.'

'Thanks.'

Pause.

'How are you getting on?' 'I wondered if . . .' They both spoke at once.

Zelda said, 'Would you like to meet up?'

'Of course, I was just going to say the same thing.' He said it politely, like a stranger.

Zelda suddenly felt very nervous. 'What about tomorrow, in the afternoon some time?'

'You tell me when, I'll make sure I'm here.'

Where else would he be, she wondered.

'Would three be OK? Will the kids be there? I feel bad, I've hardly seen them.'

'I'll see what they're up to and get them to be home for tea.'

'Lovely.'

'See you then.'

'Yup.' Zelda hung up. That was so weird. She felt sick.

*

The 4x4 waited on a double yellow line outside a building in Harley Street. It had blacked-out windows. Zelda dashed from the building and jumped into the back seat, wearing a head-scarf and dark glasses.

'Made it! Not a pap in sight,' she said, but a part of her was a tiny bit disappointed.

David smiled over his shoulder, and handed her a Starbucks. 'I got you this. Your favourite.'

Zelda took it. 'Aw, thanks, David.' She was trying to stay away from dairy, but, with the old familiar cup in her hand and the delicious smell, she just couldn't resist it. She took a little sip. 'Yum.'

David smiled. He was pleased with himself.

*

The broadcaster rang to speak to Max before the lunchtime news went on air. Jamie took the call. He arrived in the garden looking anxious and handed the phone to Max without a word.

'Who is it?'

'It's about Lady Spender.'

Max took the phone. 'Hello, hello.'

He was silent. 'Well, do they know where? How long have they been looking?' He was very pale. Jamie pulled over a garden chair and Max sat down. 'You'll let me know?'

He gave the phone back to Jamie and said, 'Her plane has gone off radar. They think it must have come down. They are out looking for it now.' He leant forward and put his head in his hands. After a few moments Jamie helped him up and into the house.

'Would you like me to ring Zelda?' he offered.

'No, no, I'll do it. Thanks, Jamie. She will be alright, won't she? She's always alright.'

'Of course she will. She's climbed Everest! She'll be found and fine in no time, I'm sure.' Jamie tried to look convinced, even though he knew her plane must have ditched in the most inhospitable, inaccessible place on the planet. He'd recently done quite a lot of online research about the Arctic. It sounded like hell on earth.

Max tried Zelda, no reply. Her phone seemed to be switched off.

'Don't worry, I'll keep trying her for you,' Jamie said kindly.

Max switched on the news and waited.

\*

When Dusty returned to the Mews with Willow, Jake was in his little study, writing. She knocked on his door. She looked very pale and wan, and had been wearing black since Johnny's tragic death.

She had taken it hard. In many ways he was probably the closest thing to a father figure she had had. She had been very fond of him. Johnny and Georgia had been together for some of the most formative years of Dusty's childhood. Her real father only dropped in and out of her life occasionally.

'Can I come in?'

'Course. Just doing a bit of editing. Come here, sit down.'

Jake cleared a space for her, amidst his chaotic filing system, on an armchair.

She didn't sit down. 'I have just had a weird call from Johnny's lawyers. They said I have to come into their office with my guardian. That's you.'

'Uh huh.'

'They said that Willow and I are the main beneficiaries of Johnny's will.'

Jake was astounded. 'Well, that's because he loved you both very much. That's very thoughtful of him, darling.'

'I said you'd ring them.' She handed him a scrunched-up piece of paper.

'Yes, of course. Will do.'

Jake began to take on board the significance of this news, what it would mean for Dusty and Willow. If what she was telling him was true, then she and her baby sister were going to be very rich indeed. He knew that this was very good, but also slightly bad news.

As their guardian, he would be responsible for making sure the money didn't destroy them before they were old enough to handle it. He needed to get onto the lawyers a.s.a.p. and find out what this would all involve, for himself as well as the girls. Money had never really been his thing.

He held out his arms and Dusty fell into them.

'Poor Johnny,' she sighed.

'I know. It's all very sad. I'm so sorry, Dusty.' He hugged her tightly. His poor little niece had suffered enough loss for a lifetime.

They looked up to see Willow crawling towards them. She grabbed the arm of the sofa, pulled herself up, and took a few tentative steps towards them.

She said, 'Dudu!'

They both shrieked, 'She's walking!' and Willow fell back down, onto her bottom. She looked surprised and then clapped her tiny hands.

Jake felt a surge of optimism. Perhaps everybody would be standing on their own two feet again, some time soon.

*

Ed burst into the Mews. 'Have you heard?'

Dusty looked up. 'What?'

Jake was just sprinting downstairs.

'Granny's plane has disappeared!' He was breathing fast and looked very pale.

'Jesus! Where?'

'On their way home!'

'Do you know if it was the little one or the big one?' Jake asked. He went white.

'No! Switch on the news. Give me your iPad.' Ed was panicking. Dusty handed over her computer. He looked it up. 'It's the little plane.'

Jake turned on the TV. There was nothing about it. He tried Sky. The tickertape flicked past on the bottom of the screen. It said: *Cleo Spender's light aircraft missing in the Arctic.*

Jake rang Max, but he had no more news. He sounded very wobbly. Jake tried to make reassuring noises. He rang Zelda, but her phone was off. He looked at his watch. She was due to arrive to see him shortly, anyway.

He'd had a bath and washed his hair in anticipation of her arrival. Clean jeans, laundered shirt. All seemed pointless now though; she would be walking into another full-blown crisis, rather than a conciliatory chat. Poor Cleo, Jake thought, this was not good. Max said the production company was keeping him apprised of all the developments.

Apparently, Milo was on board the missing plane too. Jake felt a stab of remorse. He had been so angry about Zelda's dalliance with Milo; it was what had set him off on his latest binge and now the guy had probably died in a plane crash. Jesus!

He made cups of tea for everyone, with lots of sugar. He tried Zelda's phone again. Nothing.

They waited.

Ed got a text from Flora. 'Sorry about your granny, hope she's OK.'

They waited.

Max arrived. 'I couldn't bear it at home alone. Jamie will ring if they ring there. They've got my mobile number too.'

Jake got Max a drink and asked, 'Have you spoken to Zelda yet?'

'She never listens to the news.'

'Do you know where she went? She was meant to be here half an hour ago.'

Max was distracted. 'What? No, she didn't say.'

They waited.

By six they were going a bit stir crazy. 'At least it's daylight almost all night over there,' Ed said, scrutinising the iPad. 'They can keep searching for them all night.' He tapped some more. 'They are behind us time-wise.' Which he knew was neither here nor there, but he felt he must keep supplying his grandfather with useful information.

Photographers had begun to gather outside.

Max's phone rang. They all jumped. He fumbled with it. 'Hello?' He listened. 'Yes, I see. Thank you for letting us know.' He hung up and took a breath. 'They have picked up a signal from the plane's navigation system. No radio contact, though.' Max put his head in his hands. He knew 'no radio contact' really meant 'no sign of life'.

# CHAPTER FORTY-FIVE

Zelda woke in darkness. Her head was killing her. She tried to move. She couldn't feel her hands. Were they tied? She could smell cardboard. Where was she? She was sitting up; was she in a box? She was in a box! She felt a tidal wave of panic wash over her. She wriggled and scrabbled about desperately. There was a tiny chink of light near the top of the box. She tried to look out of it, but all she could see was a bit of ceiling.

She listened to see if she could hear anyone. Everything was deathly quiet.

She said, 'Hello. Is there anybody there?'

Had she been taken hostage? God forbid someone would want a fucking ransom!

What had she read about hostage situations? Not much. She had played one in a film once, what did she have to do then? She tried to remember. Make them see you as a person. Well, this one must know she was a fucking 'person' already.

A shadow passed over the light chink. There was somebody there.

'Hi, could you let me out please?' She wondered if her captors spoke English.

Silence.

Then a horrible growling voice answered, 'Not yet.'

Zelda scrabbled about with fear and was almost sick.

She thought she might die of fright. She recognised that voice. Where from? Where from? It was from that fucking hostage movie! It was! It was a voice distorter; something that was used by kidnappers, terrorists or maniacs!

But why would anyone kidnap her? She wasn't worth anything. Everyone knew that, thanks to Lucien, she had no fucking money. Even the bloody Taliban would know that.

Why else would someone kidnap her if not for money . . . her mind raced.

There wasn't another reason.

Unless they wanted to . . . to . . . kill her.

She suddenly remembered her recent conversation with her father, blithely telling him that her stalker was just someone trying to scare her away from Banbury Court. She'd also told him that he hadn't attempted or intended to hurt her. But now here she was, at some maniac's mercy. It couldn't be a coincidence.

A ploy from her movie came back to her. 'I need to go to the bathroom!' It was an American movie.

'Wait,' it growled and wheezed.

She daren't look out through the chink of light again. If she saw *the* Face she knew she would die of fright.

She needed to know what it wanted. 'What do you want?' she asked meekly.

'You will know what I want, soon enough,' it growled.

Zelda felt sweat begin to trickle down her back. She tried to loosen the ties on her wrists. She wondered where David was. She remembered his face as he had turned around and smiled at her in the car. Oh, God, they couldn't have killed David, could they? After all he had been through, to get killed by some random nut job, while trying to protect her.

She heard a door close and a lock turn. Had her captor gone out?

'Hello, hello.' No reply.

She desperately tried to push at the walls of the box, but they were too thick. She tried to gnaw at the chink with her teeth, but her nose got in the way. She thrashed about in furious frustration and felt a paralysing wave of claustrophobia crash over her.

She took deep yoga breaths until she had calmed down.

She listened for other sounds. Perhaps there was something that could give her an idea of where she was. She could hear water dripping, but nothing else. She wondered what time it was. Would anyone have noticed she was missing?

Jake? She was meant to be meeting him, what would he think when she didn't show?

He'd think she'd flunked it and he'd just get on with his life. The way he'd been getting on with his life while she was at Banbury Court.

And the children, she was going to see them too. What would they think when she failed to turn up? She realised they wouldn't think anything either.

She had been no use to them at all. Not even since Johnny died, which must have been awful for Dusty. She was too caught up in her own fantasy life to spare a thought for any of them, so why would they spare a thought for her now? She began to weep softly.

After a long session of self-recrimination she decided she needed to pull herself together. Nobody would notice she was gone, not for days anyway. Jake would think she had just pissed off somewhere and so would her father. She knew she would have to help herself.

What could her tormentor have meant when he said he would show her what he wanted? She shook. What would he show her, 'soon enough'? She whimpered with terror.

She knew she must appear to remain meek and hope that he intended to take her out of the box to tell her what he wanted. She suppressed another squeal of fear. When she was out of this tiny space, she would see how the land lay and make a proper plan. The thought of it made her want to hide forever.

She suddenly remembered she was meant to be filming *Fame Game* soon. She wished she knew what time it was, what day it was even. At least *they* would notice if she didn't show up; or would they just think that she was flaky too? She could hardly bear to imagine Sam Carson's wrath. If she fucked up *Fame Game*, as well as her family life, then the kidnapper might just as well kill her. Her life would be over for sure then anyway.

She began to feel really sorry for herself.

Hours went by, that felt like years. She shouted for a while but no one came, not even her kidnapper.

She wriggled about until, surprisingly, she fell asleep.

*

Jake was beginning to get very anxious; still no word from Zelda. He was worried that she might have misunderstood the rather stilted conversation they'd had when they arranged to meet. But he hadn't wanted to go into things with her over the phone. He had learnt a thing or two about what to say and when to say it.

Not least from Sophie, who had been very kind when he blurted out that he loved her, over a cup of coffee, after yet another AA meeting.

She had gently explained to him something that he vaguely remembered his sponsor mentioning at some point. It was simply this: in the vulnerable, emotional state of recovery people were very susceptible to latching onto others whom they suddenly felt they could empathise with, and who could empathise with them. This sometimes felt like love.

He'd said, 'But what if it is!' He sounded like a child, even to himself.

She was very kind and told him he was a lovely man and that she was touched that he liked her, but that they could only ever be friends. She also told him that she thought the most important thing, for a happy life, was to have a really honest relationship with your close family. She gently suggested that he might be wise to concentrate on that for the time being. She pointed out that there were a lot of people in his family that needed, and deserved, a great deal of love and attention. He had thought she meant the children.

But, he began to realise, she had also meant Zelda; she was in need of some love and attention too.

Sophie was a wise woman; it had taken him a day or two to work out what he now acknowledged, that everything she'd said was true.

It was time to grow up.

When they met again, he'd told her he was happy they were friends. He also said that he still thought she had loveliest hair he had ever seen.

She'd given him a hug, which had just felt really nice.

*

Valentine answered a call from Lily as he was walking home. Her voice sounded small and sad. 'Are you OK? Have you news of your grandmuzzer?'

'Not yet, I'm just heading to the Mews to find out what's happening. Do you want to come over later?' He really wanted to see her.

'I go to France now. Johnny has left me the house there and I must go before 'is funeral.'

'I'll come with you?'

'*Non*, you have to be with your family.'

'I will come to the funeral with you though.'

'You will need to be with your family then too. I am happy Johnny left everything else to them.'

'What do you mean? To who?'

'To Dusty and Willow.'

'He did?' Valentine's mind was whirring.

'You did not know this?'

'No, I didn't. Wow!'

'He always say he loved them like they were 'is own children.'

Valentine couldn't help thinking it was lucky Johnny didn't have any real children in that case, because he saw remarkably little of Dusty and Willow after he split from Georgia.

He had certainly made up for that now though.

'He was a great man,' he said.

Lily sniffed. 'I have to go. 'Bye, Valentine.'

Valentine had to sit down on a bench and have a quiet ciggie to calm down. This was momentous news; apart from anything else, it meant that his baby daughter, Willow, was an heiress! This was going to be game-changing.

Valentine had not anticipated this at all, and felt quite breathless. Bloody hell! He had an uncontrollable desire to laugh. But this wasn't a day for laughter. The emotional twists and turns made him quite dizzy.

This will business could be very, very good for him, or very, very bad.

Only time would tell which.

# CHAPTER FORTY-SIX

Zelda dreamt that she was judging *Fame Game*, the crowds were applauding and laughing, when suddenly, all the lights went out.

When they flickered on again she was alone in the studio, and all the crowds and the other judges were gone. A spotlight followed a figure as it strode onto the stage. It was wearing a cloak and when it turned into the light she saw the Face.

She was frozen in her chair, unable to move her legs or to make a sound. There was an eerie drumbeat throbbing through the auditorium, louder than her heart, which felt as if it was about to explode.

The Face took a bat out of his cloak, which fluttered pathetically before he crammed its head into his mouth and bit down, viciously. She could see his jagged teeth and blood spurting everywhere. She felt it hit her face, warm and metallic on her lips. She looked down and her white dress was running with blood. She looked up and the Face was right in front of her with its mouth opening, wider and wider, until it covered her head. It smelt of death. She felt the teeth close around her neck.

*

When Valentine finally showed up at the Mews, everyone was gathered around the television. They were all glued to the screen, which had the same information running on a loop: *Cleo Spender's light aircraft missing in the Arctic.*

They were all watching, willing it to change to *Cleo Spender – found,* but it just kept coming round again: *Cleo Spender's light aircraft missing in the Arctic.*

Valentine hugged Max. 'I'm so sorry.'

Ed told him about the distress signal. 'That'll be her. It will.'

'Did they say how long till they can get to it?' Valentine asked.

They all tried not to think of the cold, the fearsome sea, the crash itself. Even though the plane's signal had been picked up it didn't mean anyone was alive. They all knew that, but nobody said so.

Max was stricken. 'They said they'd call again.'

Valentine looked around at his family. 'Where's Mum?'

'We're not sure, she was meant to be here hours ago.' Jake sounded disappointed. 'She's not answering our calls.'

'I'll see if I can track her down,' Valentine said. He went outside to make a call.

*

Max was given the news, just before dawn.

A small plane had been sighted and identified as Cleo's. Search and rescue helicopters had been dispatched to the site. Bad weather was coming in but they would be attempting to reach the wreckage within the hour.

Max wept as he woke everyone in the Mews to tell them. Jake wasn't asleep anyway; he was really worried about Zelda now, everything felt wrong.

Valentine burst into the house. He shouted upstairs, 'Jake! Come down. We have to go . . . now!'

\*

Zelda heard a loud banging noise followed by the sound of splintering wood. She was disorientated. Was she being rescued? There was an almighty crash.

She began to yell, 'I'm here, I'm here!'

A knife pierced the box close to her face and she screamed.

Hands reached in to pull her out. Her legs had gone to sleep. She couldn't stand.

She looked up into David's face. He had a cut over one eye. He said, 'It's OK, I'm here now. You're alright. Let me get these off.'

He cut through the ties that bound her wrists.

She could barely speak. 'David. Thank God!'

'It's OK. We have to go now, hurry! Lean on me.' He put his strong arms around her and lifted her. 'Come on, we're getting out of here.'

He dragged her through the dark building and out into

blinding dawn light, lifting her into the 4x4. Then he jumped into the driver's seat and sped off.

Zelda felt a surge of relief. She was free! She managed to speak. 'Oh, David, thank God! What happened?'

'The bastard had me when I got out to open your door. I was knocked out and tied up too. It took a while to work myself free and get to you. I am so sorry.'

'He's real.'

'He was.'

'Who is he?'

'You don't want to know.'

'Have you called the police?'

'No.' He glanced across at her.

'We have to get him arrested or he'll come after me again!' Her voice rose in panic.

'He won't be coming after you again.'

'What do you mean?'

'He's dead.'

'You killed him?' Zelda couldn't help feeling a wave of relief.

'I had to. He came at me. Couldn't risk what he might do to you, if I didn't stop him.'

Zelda tried to work out what this all meant. It occurred to her that David might be in trouble. 'You killed him in self-defence and in my defence. If you tell the police that, they'll understand.'

'I need to get us away, keep you out of danger, that's my priority.' His face was impassive. Glancing in his rear-view mirror, his eyes narrowed and he began to accelerate.

'But David . . .'

He snapped at her, 'Be quiet, Zelda. I will handle this. You asked me to protect you, that's what I'm doing. Where is your husband – eh? Or your son? Useless bastards! No, you need me to keep you safe.'

She was feeling very confused and increasingly alarmed; he was talking gibberish and driving so fast. She wondered if the knock on the head had made him go a bit bonkers. Perhaps it was just panic, but he was being uncharacteristically rude and frightening.

He had rescued her, she was very relieved and grateful, but now that she was out of danger she wasn't sure what his problem was. The police had to understand what had happened. What else could David have in mind? He couldn't be hoping to pretend it hadn't happened, that he hadn't killed anyone, could he? She quickly glanced at him, noticing his face was set hard and he was driving even faster.

Her feet were tangled in something on the floor and she looked down at a pile of dark fabric. She wriggled her feet and the fabric moved, revealing a corner of something. She recognised it instantly. The Face! The Face was on the floor of David's car! She turned away from him in a silent scream, covering her mouth desperately, to prevent the sound of her naked fear from tearing out of her.

In a petrifying, blinding flash she knew that it was *him*. David had been terrorising her! She also knew that she couldn't let him know what she had seen.

The adrenaline rushing through her system condensed her

senses to the single, vital task of self-preservation. Every fibre of her being was concentrated in this moment.

Somehow she needed to reassert her authority.

She tried for normality but only managed to squeak, 'What time is it? I need to get to the studio by eight.'

He ignored her. A police siren began to wail. Why would David do this to her?

He turned right sharply and the car skidded. He said calmly, 'Put your seat belt on. I don't want you to get hurt.'

She lost control of her emotions then, and she screamed, 'Fucking hell, David. Stop the car!'

He continued to ignore her and was totally focused on outrunning the police car. She could hear two sirens now.

'Stop! This isn't going to look good for you. You must stop this.' She was pleading with him. She grabbed his arm.

Whatever his crazed plan was, he was going to kill them both in a car crash, if she didn't think of some way to slow him down.

*

The speedometer hit ninety. They tore on, through the deserted streets.

Zelda saw a rubbish lorry pull out ahead of them and everything went into slow motion: the flashing lights from the police cars, the sirens, the screeching breaks. Everything was noise and light.

David braked and swerved and somehow the 4x4 stabilised and Zelda opened her eyes to see that they were inside a multi-storey car park. The tyres squealed as David accelerated and the car climbed higher and higher. They reached the top floor and she suddenly saw the sky. For a moment Zelda felt a surge of hope that, now they had nowhere else to go, David would finally be forced to stop.

But, to her horror, he put his foot down harder and drove the car at full speed towards the barrier; towards the void.

David turned to her and said, 'I only wanted you to love me!'

*

Jake ran to the gap where the car had torn through the fence and disappeared over the edge. He was screaming Zelda's name. Valentine was hard on his heels. The car lay smouldering, ten floors beneath them. Smoke streamed from the bonnet. Police cars were converging on it.

Jake threw back his head and screamed, 'Noooo!'

The sound of an ambulance howled back at him, from the abyss of the street below. He fell to his knees and leant his head on the broken, twisted metal and wept. He called her name, 'Zelda!'

'Ouch, fucking hell!'

It was Zelda's voice!

He stood up and spun round. His face was ashen.

She was lying on the concrete, behind a pillar, where she had rolled and bounced as she'd flung herself out of the car. Valentine was already there, crouching by his mother's side.

Jake ran to her. 'Oh, my God! Is she alright?'

Zelda's eyes flickered. She opened them and looked at her husband.

'Am I in heaven?' she asked.

Jake said, 'No! Thank God you're still here, on earth, with me! Hold on, darling, the ambulance is nearly here. Can you hear it?'

'I can.' She looked at him sideways without moving her head. 'Sorry I'm late.'

'Oh, God! I thought he had driven you off the edge.' Jake looked shell-shocked.

'Take more than that loony to drive *me* over the edge!' She smiled bravely.

Valentine laughed, 'You say that now!'

Jake gripped her hand. 'Is anything hurting?'

'Everything.'

A photographer appeared out of nowhere and began taking pictures. Two policemen grabbed him and pushed him away.

An ambulance man felt for Zelda's pulse. 'Alright, love. We're going to get you to hospital, OK? Just have to check you over first.'

'Watch where you put your hands!' she said.

Jake smiled. If she was joking she was probably going to be OK.

He put his arm around Valentine's shoulders. 'Well done, my son, well done.'

\*

Jake held Zelda's hand all the way to the hospital. She was so relieved to see his handsome face as he reassuringly smiled down at her. She felt the past few days and weeks slip away, like some nightmare fading into nothingness. She would forget about Boy and Banbury Court and everything else that had happened there. Jake need never know about it and they could begin to rebuild their lives properly.

When she looked into Jake's eyes she could see love there. How could she have doubted it, there would always be an unbreakable bond between them. Max was so right.

She couldn't wait to throw her arms around her husband's neck and kiss him.

'Ambulance man! I feel fine really. Can I go home now?' She kept her eyes on Jake's.

'Just have to let the doctors check you over first, love. Make sure you're shipshape,' the ambulance man replied cheerfully.

He couldn't quite believe he'd got Zelda Spender in his ambulance, but he was determined not to let it show that he knew who she was. There were moments when people needed privacy, and he knew that one of those moments was when you were in the back of an ambulance.

'You look shipshape to me!' Jake grinned.

Zelda smiled back up at him, weakly. Perhaps now wouldn't be a good moment to mention the last thing that David had said to her: 'I only wanted you to love me!'

What had he meant? Men were a mystery and it seemed David was even more so than most. She tried not to think about him, alive or dead. It was all too scary and sad. Her eyes filled with tears.

Jake didn't think this was the moment to tell Zelda that her mother's plane had gone missing.

He would wait until the hospital gave her the all-clear. Then he would break it to her gently.

*

Valentine got back to the Mews and had to struggle through a crowd of surging photographers and rubber-neckers. The throng was very noisy and expanding fast. Fortunately, the police had arrived to start pushing them back.

When he finally managed to get into the house he found that Jake had already called home to let everyone know that Zelda was safe. So Valentine regaled them with every detail of the car chase. It proved a very effective distraction, while they waited for news of Cleo. No one could quite believe that David could have done such a dreadful thing.

But Valentine could. He had been quietly observing David's behaviour around his mother, as it became increasingly odd. Just little things, at first, things no one else would notice. But Valentine knew a lot about obsession. What it could drive a person to do.

So he understood what had happened. He might need to explain it to his mother, though. Valentine couldn't help thinking there were easier ways to make a woman love you than trying to scare her into your arms. But David had obviously lost the plot.

Sergeant Powell, on the other hand, clearly had not. He wasn't quite the hopeless provincial plod Valentine had thought. In fact, he had turned out to be very sharp indeed and if he was able to solve this crime then who knew what else he was capable of?

When Valentine called him to tell him that Zelda was missing, he was surprised to discover that Sergeant Powell had been even more suspicious about David than he was, and was already a few steps ahead of him.

So the euphoria Valentine felt knowing that his mother was alive and safe was tinged with anxiety too. He had underestimated Sergeant Powell. The question was, had Sergeant Powell underestimated Valentine?

*

Sergeant Powell anticipated that there would be press conferences and interviews relating to the case of Zelda Spender and her stalker, now deceased. His wife would be chuffed, seeing him on the telly. She loved all that fame nonsense, but it was nice to be able to make her happy.

They would be asking how he had solved the crime and saved Ms Spender's life. It was simple really. Sergeant Powell adored technology; he believed it was the most useful weapon in his armoury in the fight against crime, since the invention of the truncheon, anyway. He was certainly against all the namby-pamby right to privacy laws everyone was always going on about. Nobody had the right to privacy if they were committing a crime, not as far as he was concerned.

He would explain that he had been observing David's comings and goings on the CCTV at the Dower House, with interest. He had recently had his surveillance department look back through old CCTV footage of the village and surrounding area. They had come up with sightings of David's 4x4 from around the time of the Spenders' arrival at Banbury Court. So he knew that it was logistically possible that David had been responsible for all the stalking incidents. But, he needed proof. When he heard that the family was leaving, he decided to have a tracking device attached to the suspect's vehicle, to enable him to keep an eye on his movements, once he had left his jurisdiction, just in case anything untoward happened.

When the son rang to tell him that his mother was missing he was able to pinpoint the whereabouts of the 4x4 with ease. He was confident by then that wherever the security guy's car was, Zelda Spender wouldn't be far away.

If an ordinary police patrol car hadn't gone by and spooked the suspect just before Sergeant Powell was able to apprehend him, it would have been a faultless operation, and the stalker would still be alive to fully explain his motives. In the sergeant's experience 'crazy' didn't always need a motive though.

He was proud of his achievement in solving this case. Oxfordshire was a beautiful county, but its inhabitants were not as benign as the scenery. Sergeant Powell was looking forward to getting to the bottom of some of the other unsolved crimes, which had been piling up in his in tray.

He had thought that the Johnny the Bastard drowning was accidental. But it had been reported to him that the guy always wore his diamond rings, night and day, and as there were none on his body when he was found, that case would require further investigation.

He felt confident; he was on a roll.

\*

Jake broke the news to Zelda about Cleo when they were in the cab on the way home. She couldn't believe it at first. It was too much to take in. Jake held her hand tightly as they sped through the London streets.

The cabbie dropped them off at the top of the mews. There was a Sky TV truck blocking the entrance.

As they walked down towards their little house, they heard an almighty roar go up from the crowd, followed by wild applause.

Jake shielded Zelda and pushed her through the unruly throng, with the help of some police officers. With so many cameras around, Zelda was pleased she'd had the foresight to borrow some make-up from one of the nurses. There was a surgical dressing on her slightly injured forehead, which looked more dramatic than it was.

Max was standing on the doorstep with microphones pushed into his face from every angle.

Jake and Zelda could just hear his voice ringing out above the crowd. 'As I say, it has been confirmed, they've found my wife! On an ice floe, very cold, but she's alive!' His voice wavered and the crowd roared and applauded wildly.

Max composed himself. 'They are being flown to Toronto, where they'll be taken to hospital for check-ups, frostbite and so on, then she should be allowed home again in a couple of days.' He suddenly spied Jake and Zelda making their way through the crowd.

'Darling, there you are!' He held his arms high in the air. 'Could everyone be very kind and let my daughter through, please?'

The crowd gave way minutely, just for a moment, and Zelda and Jake were popped through, like champagne corks.

Zelda fell into her father's arms and the crowd went mad. The press couldn't believe their luck. News of Zelda's ordeal was just beginning to filter through to them.

A journalist shouted out, 'Max, you've lost and found both your wife and daughter all in one day. How do you feel?'

Max jumped in the air and hugged Zelda again. 'I feel like the luckiest man in the world.'

The crowd cheered.

Another voice rang out. 'Miss Spender, your fans will be very happy to see you back in one piece. Will you be well enough to continue working on *Fame Game*?'

'Of course! It's my job and I love it. It's what I do; what my mother does too. As you can tell, we are both prepared to lay down our lives for you!' She smiled her most enchantingly plucky smile and reached for Jake and Max, hugging them close. The photographers went berserk and the crowd cheered. She hesitated, and continued triumphantly, 'Fame is a very dangerous game, but today, I'm happy to say, I think we won!'

She lifted Jake's and Max's hands in hers and shook them in a victorious salute.

Then they turned and went inside.

So, that was her public life restored to its former glory. Now all Zelda needed to do was rescue her private life too.

She looked up at Jake and smiled. He smiled back.

Maybe everything would be alright after all?

But, as Valentine would agree, you never quite knew what would happen next, when you lived in the rarefied atmosphere of Britain's favourite family.

# ACKNOWLEDGEMENTS

I am so grateful to everyone who has helped, supported and encouraged me to write *Fame Game*, the sequel to my first novel, *Dead Rich*. I couldn't have done any of it without my fantastic, heroic, legendary agent, Ed Victor.

Huge thanks, too, to Maxine Hitchcock for her kindness, enthusiasm and tact and to Susan Opie, whose wisdom, humour and tenacity have made the editing process such a pleasure. The wonderful support of Garry Blackman, Susan Boyd and Matthew Bates is something I shall always be eternally grateful for.

Also thanks to Ian Chapman, Hannah Corbett, James Horobin, Carla Josephson and the brilliant team at Simon & Schuster. Maggie Phillips, Linda Van, Rebecca Jones, Edina Imrik, Hitesh Shah, Charlie Campbell, and Jennine Carpenter have all been absolutely fantastic. I also have the marvellous and intrepid Bear Grylls to thank for the Northwest Passage inspiration.

Last, but by no means least, thanks to my family, Theo and Coco for their terrific encouragement and support, Emerald for her wise, kind editorial advice and all my friends for being so endlessly fabulous, funny and inspiring.

Oh, and thanks to my mother – for making me tone down the swearing . . . a tiny bit!

**Louise Fennell**

# Dead Rich

The Spenders are Britain's Favourite Family – they are glamorous, rich and very, very famous: everything that their celebrity obsessed culture requires them to be. Their charisma and looks ensure that they are constantly praised and hounded by the press. The public adores them. They live what appears to be a charmed and enviable existence.

But in the claustrophobic confines of their exquisite houses, there is a darker reality. Isolated and hemmed in by the paparazzi and their crazed fans, they are trapped in their fame. Constantly surrounded by an army of long-suffering employees: stylists, PAs, personal trainers, drivers, security teams, hair and make-up artists, managers, agents, publicists – they are never alone but always lonely – with nothing else to do but 'drink and fight and screw', they breakfast on prescription drugs, lunch on vodka and dine on anything illegal they can get their hands on.

Their privileged, high profile lifestyle is shattered when tragedy strikes – tearing apart the fragile fabric of their existence, and sending them spinning out of control . . .

**Paperback ISBN 978-1-47112-851-6**
**Ebook ISBN 978-1-47111-047-4**

**Jackie Collins**

# The Power Trip

A Russian billionaire and his state of the art yacht. His beautiful and sexy supermodel girlfriend. And five dynamic, powerful and famous couples invited on the yacht's maiden voyage.

A senator and his lovely but unhappy wife. A very attractive movie star and his needy ex-waitress girlfriend. A famous black footballer and his interior designer wife. A male Latin singing sensation and his older English boyfriend. And a maverick writer with his Asian journalist female friend.

Could this be the trip of a lifetime? Or a trip from hell?

Whatever happens on the high seas doesn't necessarily stay there . . .

*The Power Trip* – take it if you dare.

**Paperback ISBN 978-1-84983-142-0**
**Ebook ISBN 978-1-84737-981-8**

### Jane Costello

# All the Single Ladies

**Samantha Brooks' boyfriend has made a mistake. One his friends, family, and Sam herself know he'll live to regret.**

Jamie has announced he's leaving, out of the blue. Jamie is loving, intelligent and, while he isn't perfect, he's perfect for her – in every way except one: he's a free spirit. And after six years in one place, doing a job he despises, he is compelled to do something that will tear apart his relationship with Sam: book a one-way flight to South America.

But Sam isn't giving up without a fight. With Jamie still totally in love with her, and torn about whether to stay or go, she has five months to persuade him to do the right thing. So with the help of her friends Ellie and Jen, she hatches a plan to make him realise what he's giving up. A plan that involves dirty tricks, plotting, and a single aim: to win him back.

But by the time the tortured Jamie finally wakes up to what he's lost, a gorgeous new pretender has entered Sam's life. Which begs the question . . . does she still want him back?

'Close the doors, open a bottle of wine, get out the chocs and enjoy this wonderfully witty read. Jane Costello at her best' Milly Johnson

**Paperback ISBN 978-0-85720-553-7**
**Ebook ISBN 978-0-85720-554-4**

**Milly Johnson**

# A Winter Flame

*The final part of the brilliant seasonal quartet . . .*

**'Tis the season to be jolly . . . But can Eve find happiness through the frost . . . ?**

Eve has never liked Christmas, not since her beloved fiancé was killed in action in Afghanistan on Christmas Day. So when her adored elderly aunt dies, the last thing she is expecting is to be left a theme park in her will. A theme park with a Christmas theme . . .

And that's not the only catch. Her aunt's will stipulates that Eve must run the park with a mysterious partner, the exotically named Jacques Glace. Who is this Jacques, and why did Aunt Evelyn name him in her will?

But Eve isn't going to back down from a challenge. She's determined to make a success of Winterworld, no matter what. Can she overcome her dislike of Christmas, and can Jacques melt her frozen heart at last . . . ?

**Paperback ISBN 978-0-85720-898-9**
**Ebook ISBN 978-0-85720-899-6**

# BOOKS AND THE CITY

*Home of the sassiest fiction in town!*

## If you enjoyed this book, you'll love...

| | | | |
|---|---|---|---|
| Bad Angels | Rebecca Chance | £6.99 | 978-1-47110-166-3 |
| A Winter Flame | Milly Johnson | £7.99 | 978-0-85720-898-9 |
| Thoughtless | S.C. Stephens | £6.99 | 978-1-47112-607-9 |
| Stay Close to Me | Helen Warner | £6.99 | 978-1-84983-295-3 |
| The First Last Kiss | Ali Harris | £6.99 | 978-0-85720-293-2 |
| Dead Rich | Louise Fennell | £7.99 | 978-1-47112-851-6 |
| Walking Disaster | Jamie McGuire | £7.99 | 978-1-47111-514-1 |
| Slammed | Colleen Hoover | £7.99 | 978-1-47112-567-6 |
| The Power Trip | Jackie Collins | £7.99 | 978-1-84983-142-0 |

For exclusive author interviews, features and competitions log onto

**www.booksandthecity.co.uk**

**Credit and debit cards**
Telephone Simon & Schuster Cash Sales at
Bookpost on 01624 677237

**Cheque**
Send a cheque payable to Bookpost Ltd to
PO Box 29, Douglas Isle of Man IM99 1BQ

Email: bookshop@enterprise.net
Website: www.bookpost.co.uk

Free post and packing within the UK.

Overseas customers please add £2
per paperback.

Please allow 14 days for delivery.

Prices and availability are subject
to change without notice.